MOSAIC

ALSO BY SARAH FINE

The Reliquary Series

Reliquary
Splinter

Servants of Fate

Marked
Claimed
Fated

Guards of the Shadowlands

Sanctum
Fractured
Chaos
Captive: A Guard's Tale from Malachi's Perspective
Vigilante: A Guard's Tale from Ana's Perspective
Stories from the Shadowlands

Of Metal and Wishes
Of Dreams and Rust
Of Shadows and Obsession: A Short Story Prequel to Of Metal and Wishes

The Impostor Queen
Scan (with Walter Jury)
Burn (with Walter Jury)

MOSAIC

THE RELIQUARY SERIES BOOK III

SARAH FINE

This is a work of fiction. Names, characters, organizations, places, events, and incidents are either products of the author's imagination or are used fictitiously.

Published by 47North, Seattle

www.apub.com

ISBN-13: 9781503939561
ISBN-10: 1503939561

Cover design by Jason Blackburn
Based on series concept by Faceout Studio

Printed in the United States of America

For Lam, who carried me across the finish line

CHAPTER ONE

Need is a funny thing. Sometimes it's just a hum in the background. Sometimes it grows like ivy, patient but relentless, sliding tiny tendrils into your mortar and crumbling your walls. Sometimes it rises hard and fast, breathtaking in its urgency.

Sometimes it's all three combined, and that's when it becomes truly terrifying. That's when you realize there's no way to stop or go back, because whatever you were before, the need is a part of you now. It has shifted your very foundation.

Losing something that necessary might not destroy you. You might be strong enough or stubborn enough to endure.

But you will never be the same.

"Dammit," I whispered. "It's never the same." I glared at the timer on my phone, frozen at six minutes, thirty-eight seconds: fifty-eight seconds longer than last time. I shoved it back into my purse. A gust of frigid wind lifted my curls as I stood there scowling, lacy snowflakes dancing around my body and fluttering their cold kisses across my cheeks. I shivered and shifted my weight, my feet aching. I trained my eyes up the street, the black bricks shining wet under the streetlamps, to the club I'd just left. I could still hear the insistent thumping of bass.

I hoped Asa had had better luck.

Wincing as my heel caught in a crack in the bricks, I started to make my way up the street, easily tuning out the conversations around me. When we'd first arrived in Prague, my brain had strained for understanding like it did every time we hit a new place. But after a few days I got used to it, and the foreign words washed over me, much like the wonder I'd first felt about traveling. Now, only eight months later, I was mostly focused on the job.

And I needed to be. Tomorrow night would be big. Our plans were in place. Well, Asa's plans were in place. As usual, I was a few steps behind.

When I reached one of the orange mailboxes that hung on selected buildings around the city, I pulled the postcard out of my coat pocket. E-mail would have been more efficient, but Asa was kind of paranoid about it, and my parents probably liked seeing my actual handwriting, knowing their daughter was alive and well and having a grand time traveling the world as a public relations liaison.

Hey, Mom and Dad! Prague is so cozy and quaint this time of year. I've been working a lot and haven't gotten to see much of the town, but I hear the Christmas markets are amazing! I've been within a few blocks and I swear the smells are to DIE for. I'll snap some pics to show you when I visit. Sorry I won't be home for Christmas this year. Next year, I promise. I hope you both are doing well and that Dad isn't eating too many Christmas cookies. He needs to watch his cholesterol!

Love,
Mattie

I sighed and slipped it into the mailbox. I hated lying to them, but what was I supposed to say?

Hey, Mom and Dad! Asa and I are here in Prague to steal a hot relic stuffed to the gills with Ekstazo magic. Asa has the buyer lined up and says we're going to make a cool million off of it because apparently it's überpotent, but that's only if we can manage to smuggle it out. It's currently in the custody of some scary mobsters who work for this boss named Volodya, who may or may not have once owned Asa's mom, but we don't really talk about that because the whole topic makes Asa super grumpy. Just add it to the list of emotionally sticky things that we do not discuss. Assuming I make it out of this heist with mind and body intact, I'll write again soon.

Love,
Helga Nordford (or whoever the hell I am this week)

So, yeah. I flagged a cab and headed for the rented flat where we'd been camped out for the last several days, offering a sad smile to the glittering storefronts bedecked with ribbons and candles and lights. This would be the first Christmas I'd spend away from home. Instead of waking to the smell of baking bread and pie, I would be on a plane headed to London, to a buyer awaiting the magic I'd have tucked inside my chest. Instead of opening presents, Asa would help me open my vault. Instead of giving gifts, I'd be offering up illicit magic for cash. And then we'd be off before someone could pin us down. Only Asa knew where. But he'd said going home now wasn't an option. It might be dangerous, and not just for us. There was no way I was going to put my family in the crosshairs of an assassin.

So here I was. Life had changed a lot since the spring. One thing hadn't changed, though. I slipped my hand into my pocket and held the tiny parcel I was saving for the right moment, one I wasn't sure would actually happen. My heart beat a little faster as my fingers slid over the ribbon-wrapped paper. The gift was small but felt huge, like everything did when it came to Asa. And with every day that passed, the stakes were higher—for my heart, at least.

As I climbed the narrow staircase to our flat, I held my breath. What would he say when I told him about the timing of the security shift change? Would he postpone the plan? Would he be spiky or sweet?

Would I crave him any less today than I did yesterday?

Would I be even one step closer to understanding where this *thing* between us was going?

The flat greeted me with silence and darkness. I unwound the scarf from around my neck and hung it on the coatrack, then flicked on the lights and walked down the hall to peek into his room. Nothing but a bed, table, lamp, chair, his duffel, and two toolboxes.

He was supposed to be home. "I hate when you do this," I whispered.

More accurately, I hated worrying about him.

I went back to the living area and settled in to pace around the tiny Christmas tree Asa had brought home the day after we arrived. My gaze flicked to the clock every few seconds. I counted each step, pushing the gnawing fear away. Asa was fine; he was always fine; he was never not fine.

A few minutes later I headed for the kitchen. I would make dinner. I would—

He'd left a note taped to the blender.

> *Corner of Opletalova and Ruzova. Wear your comfy shoes.*

I groaned. "At least you gave me a heads-up about the footgear." I put my coat back on, slipped my feet into the sneakers Asa had gotten me in Barcelona, and headed back out the door. Would we be meeting our conduit there, or was Asa doing some sort of side deal? Why did he have to be so darn mysterious? Hoping I wouldn't end up fleeing for my life, but now fully prepared to do so if necessary, I tromped toward the intersection as snow spiraled through slants of warm light. The sidewalks were busy even at this hour, people laughing and chattering, the spirit of the season evident in their red cheeks and huge smiles. I felt a pang in my chest as one couple walked by, holding hands as they crossed into Wenceslas Square. It was the location of one of the Christmas markets I'd written my mom about, the one I didn't have time to explore.

The sight of Asa under a streetlamp made my stomach tighten. His long, lean body practically vibrated with tension as his eyes swept from corner to corner, ever vigilant. He had a paper sack clutched in one hand, his gloved grip hard—was there a relic in there? Something he'd stolen? Despite the cold, he wasn't wearing a hat, and his dark hair glinted with melting snowflakes. His crooked profile made me sigh. *It's never going to get any easier, is it?* I thought to myself.

That was the moment he spotted me. His body sagged a little, maybe relief, maybe annoyance, and he strode over to me. "I've been freezing my ass off out here."

I scowled. "We have phones, you know. There's this process called texting—"

"You were supposed to be home by ten."

"You were, too!"

He let out an exasperated breath and then looked me over. "You okay?"

"Fine."

"You don't sound fine. You sound hangry."

"Haven't eaten yet," I grumbled. *Too busy worrying about* you.

He grinned, sharp and triumphant. "Well then, the first thing we're gonna do is feed that little monster inside you." He grabbed my hand, and I let him tow me along the sidewalk beneath trees sparkling with lights, fighting the urge to lean closer and smell his familiar scent, one that conjured equally both danger and safety.

"Where are we going?"

He waved his paper sack toward the square.

"The Christmas market?"

"You wanted to go."

"I never said that."

He bumped my shoulder. "You didn't have to, Mattie."

I bit my lip as we crossed the street and entered the square, which was filled with red-roofed booths like tiny cottages, all decorated with holly and strung with buttery-yellow lights. A towering Christmas tree stood in the center, luminous and gorgeous. Parents walked by with their bundled-up kiddies on their shoulders. Asa made a goofy face at one solemn yet adorable little girl, and she rewarded him with a wide smile that made me laugh. Asa squeezed my hand.

Why did he have to act like this? Why had he brought me here? What did it mean?

I'm not stupid. It's just . . . Asa was so complicated. And if I didn't know exactly what he wanted from me, I couldn't protect myself if he decided to turn tail and run. So I guarded my heart with iron bars.

Some of them had become kinda loose, though.

Asa kept me close as we wove our way along the crowded paths. The smell of roasting nuts made my mouth water, and the sights . . . something out of a fantasy. Booths full of carved ornaments, little paddocks full of sheep and ponies, musicians playing carols on every corner, with strings of lights wound around every railing, every tree, every window, all sparkling and glowing. I grinned as we reached a booth displaying hats for sale, and on impulse I grabbed a striped one with a pom-pom on top and earflaps ending in tassels. Asa probably could have dodged me if he wanted, but he let me cram it over his head and then stood there, one eyebrow arched, as the hat's long tassels swayed beneath his chin. "Not exactly my style."

"I think you look adorable." And damn if it wasn't true.

He snorted and pulled the hat off his head, placing it back on the pile. "Not exactly my goal."

"What is your goal, then?"

"At the moment? Sausage." He chuckled when he saw my stunned expression. "For *you*, Mattie." He steered me toward the kiosk, and I nearly fainted at the rich scent of sizzling meat and hot grease. Within minutes, Asa had acquired sausage, bread, nuts, a pastry, and coffee, and he guided me over to a little bench and sat me down. "Eat."

I took in the feast spread across my lap. "Aren't you hungry?"

He gave me a little smile. "I ate the salad you left for me in the fridge. And the bag of nuts you tucked in my coat pocket. Also, the carrot sticks you put into my pack."

"Thought you might need a snack," I mumbled, looking away as I tugged off my gloves and set to work on the sausage. It hadn't taken long at all for us to settle into this rhythm, this place where I took care of him, where he took care of me. It had been too easy. I kept telling myself that this was how a team functioned. It wasn't personal—it was our business. "How did the reconnaissance go?"

He sat down next to me, and I held my paper plate a little tighter to keep from running my hand over his dark waves to smooth them down. "Our conduit's all lined up. And I was there when the dealer's team delivered the relic to the club. Volodya's reliquary will probably arrive from Moscow by tomorrow night at the latest. We're racing the clock on this one. We can't hesitate."

"Do we know what kind of Ekstazo magic it is yet?"

He shook his head. "Couldn't dig up anything on what he's gonna use it for, and they have it really well packaged. I won't know for sure until I've got ahold of it. But there's no doubt it's worth a lot. The dealer has brought in some heavy hitters to guard the damn thing and switched out the security staff you were supposed to spot."

"So the dudes I've been watching and timing all week—"

"Gone."

"Great. But if the dealer brought his own guards in, won't you be able to feel them coming?"

"They're not naturals—they're mercenaries, and they've been in this game longer than the two we dealt with in Atlanta. They may know me by sight. I'll send their pics to your phone so you know who to look out for at the club. I've recruited a few more helpers to act as our decoys."

"Great. There goes our commission."

"Listen to you, all cutthroat." He smirked. "There'll be plenty left for us."

"Like in Sydney?"

His head hung back as he groaned. "Are you ever gonna forgive me for that?"

I held back the smile that said I already had, dammit. "I literally had to sell the clothes off my back to pay for our escape, and that included one very sweet pair of Gucci sandals that I miss to this day."

"You definitely couldn't run in those."

"But they made my legs look awesome."

"No argument there."

"So, what are we doing here?" I asked as my cheeks grew warm. "Are we meeting someone?" I poked the paper sack in his lap and whispered, "Did you steal that?"

"Stop hurting my feelings." He reached inside and pulled out a small, wrapped present, complete with a cheerful red bow.

I blinked down at it. "For me?"

"I had a feeling this might be a tough time of year for you. I figured you'd need some cheering up."

"That's why you brought home that tree."

"Yep." He set the gift on my upturned palm. "Merry Christmas."

I looked down at the box. "I wasn't even sure you celebrated Christmas."

He gazed out at the festive square. "It doesn't exactly conjure fond family memories."

"I know," I murmured.

"But watching you smile as you looked at all these lights, at those little kids with their families . . ." His voice faded and he looked away. "That was good," he said quietly.

I touched his arm as my throat grew tight. Being in this amazing place made me miss my family even more, but somehow it also made me really glad I was here, in this moment, with this man. No matter that I was neck-deep in his lethally magical world—I didn't want to be anywhere else. "Asa . . ."

He elbowed me in the side and tossed me a carefree smile. "Open your gift."

I did, prying off the foil paper to reveal a delicate gold chain, from which hung a small vial. I lifted it to the light. "Is that sand?"

"From Kohler—"

"Kohler-Andrae State Park?" I asked in a shaky voice. "How did you get this?" It was my favorite beach, just south of Sheboygan, with windswept dunes and the lake that changed colors like a mood ring. "Did Ben . . ."

His smile grew tense as his brother's shadow crept over us. "I wanted you to have a piece of your home."

And he must have asked Ben, which I knew must have cost them both. But Asa had reached out. For *me*. My eyes burned, and I blinked quickly before a tear escaped. "Dammit, Asa," I whispered. So much for keeping things totally professional. I lifted my hair and let him fasten the clasp at the nape of my neck, shivering at the cool brush of his fingertips. Then I jammed my hand in my pocket, pulled out my own little wrapped box, and shoved it into his lap.

He looked down at it but didn't move to open it. "You got me a present."

"It's not booby-trapped, I swear," I said, then sniffled.

He opened it slowly and carefully, like he didn't quite believe me. By the time he lifted the lid off the tiny box, my heart rate was in the stratosphere. "Gracie," he murmured as he laid the black-and-white photo, encased in glass, on his palm.

"It's for your key ring. Speaking of having a piece of home." I summoned the courage to look at his face, only to find him staring back at me.

"I get that. But you know what?" He leaned a little closer, and his gaze dropped to my mouth.

"What?" Oh my God, was he going to kiss me? Was I going to let it happen?

"Lately, it feels like—" He flinched and whipped around on the bench, staring at a spot across the square. "Shit." He grabbed my hand and pulled me to my feet, sending my roasted nuts bouncing across the stone walkway. "We've got a stalker." He yanked me forward, winding his way between booths.

"Who is it?"

"No idea, but we need to get some distance."

"A Strikon."

"No, a sensor." His grip on my hand tightened. "Like me."

That meant they wouldn't need to see us to be able to follow us. If they were powerful enough, they'd simply track the vibe of Asa's magic. "Any idea how sensitive?"

"Very," he said in a hard voice as he leaped into the street. I shrieked as a yellow taxi came to a screeching halt barely a foot away from him. "Come on."

I looked behind me at the glow of what we were leaving behind. "Do you know who it is?" Sometimes a natural's magic was so distinctive that Asa could tell.

"No." His brow furrowed. "I've felt it before, I think. A few times. But I don't know who it is." He wrenched the door of the cab open and bundled me inside, then barked an address at the driver—but not the one for our rented flat. "This relic is hotter than I thought, and we may not be the only ones making a play for it. We can't go back to the apartment."

"What about our stuff?"

"I'll get one of my contacts to pick it all up and have it at the airport for us." He fished out his burner phone and began texting.

"Oh, *now* texting is your thing."

He snorted. "Shut the fuck up."

"Are we going ahead or pulling out?" I asked, my voice betraying my fear.

"I never pull out, baby. It would ruin the best part." He waggled his eyebrows without looking up from the screen of his phone.

He was trying to stem my anxiety, but tonight it wasn't working. With trembling fingers, I swiped a drop of sweat off his jaw.

He caught my hand and squeezed it. "We're gonna be fine." He let out a long breath from between pursed lips. "I can't feel them anymore. We've lost the tail."

"For now." My hand slipped to the hollow of my throat and clutched the vial of sand as our cab raced along the narrow street, the bright lights a blur. Home. I used to have such a rock-solid sense of it. And now it felt like an illusion, the danger circling all around me. Asa was the rock now, anchoring me in more ways than I wanted to admit. I mutely scooted closer to him as he texted his contacts, the light from his phone painting his skin a pale green in the darkness of the cab. He gave me a sidelong glance and turned slightly, opening his body toward mine. Offering himself.

We depended on each other. We were business partners; that was all. My fingers curled into the shoulder of his coat.

"It's gonna be us, Mattie. It's always gonna be us. I'm gonna make sure."

"I know. You always do." I stared past him, out into the night. Thanks to Asa, we were always a step ahead of all our enemies, seen and unseen.

But no matter how many times we escaped, no matter how long we stayed free, I couldn't shake my dread of what would happen if they ever caught up.

CHAPTER TWO

At nine the next evening, as darkness fell over the city, we prepared to go our separate ways. Asa needed to make sure his contacts were in place, and I had to get myself in position.

"Just do what you rehearsed," he said to me. He was wearing his usual cargo pants—pockets rattling and clanking and sloshing. His leather gloves scraped my skin as he pried my fingers loose from his hand. "I'll be at the meetup right on time. I promise."

I nodded, my mouth dry. I'd had the worst nightmares after we'd holed up in a shabby little hotel at the edge of the city, and I still hadn't been able to shake the sense of foreboding that had settled on me last night. "Are you sure it's safe?"

He tilted his head. "Safe? Are you serious?" I rolled my eyes, and he nudged my chin up. "You know I've got it set up so you're not in any danger, right?"

"I'm not scared for myself, you idiot," I snapped, glaring at the stone facade of the building behind him. Anything to avoid meeting his eyes.

"You worried about me, Mattie?" His tone was pure tease, and it made me want to kick him in the shins.

I twisted away from him. "Just be where you said you'll be, when you said you'll be, and I'll be happy. I can't wait for this job to be over."

"You'll be celebrating Christmas in London, baby."

"As long as I'm not there alone," I murmured as I walked away. With each step, I pulled my determination up around me like a pair of big-girl panties. I tucked myself into a little café and loaded up on caffeine while staring at pictures of the two mercenary dudes I was supposed to spot in the club. One had a doughy, pitted face and the other a shiny bald head. Both had cold, dead looks in their eyes.

"Crap. The timing." I had completely forgotten to tell him I wasn't sure how long the shift change would take. Asa had said we had to be in and out fast. I had no more than six minutes from the time I signaled the guard change to the time I had to be waiting for him outside. I pulled out my phone and shot him a quick text, hoping he would see it before the job got under way.

Anxiety sluicing through my veins, I marched out of the café and headed for the club. Tonight I would get it completely right. Asa was depending on me. I slid my coat off my shoulders, my muscles stiffening against the cold as I revealed my black dress with a sexy keyhole neckline. The dress clung to the curves that I'd regained over months of delighting in whatever local foods I could get my mouth on—brie in Paris, cannoli in Rome, fish-and-chips in Sydney, french fries at every stop. Now I had my cleavage back, and the slope of my hips drew appreciative glances, including from Asa. I rarely caught him looking, but when I did . . . I shivered and focused on my mission, smiling up at the tall bouncer.

"Back again?" His English was perfect, his accent that sexy eastern European lilt.

"I know what I like."

"Meeting friends inside?"

"Wouldn't you like to know?"

His gaze slid up my legs. "Do they look anything like you?"

"I'm one of a kind."

He laughed and pushed the door open for me. "I love Americans."

Check. Or Czech, as it were. The bouncer was one of Asa's contacts, and he'd just said the magic words. Things were rolling, and that was the signal that Asa was already inside. I walked up the crowded hallway and into the cavernous club, peering at the distant DJ booth up on the stage. On either side of the sprawling dance floor were two tiers of booths and tables bounded by glass walls. The club was packed on this Saturday night, the music deafening and pounding inside of me.

Squinting, I looked up at a little alcove just behind and above the DJ booth, where one of the new guards was standing. He was blocking the hallway that led to where the relic was hidden. If they kept to the schedule, any minute the other guard would come and relieve him. Now I just had to delay the new dude and let Asa's contact take care of the guy up top. That would give Asa the few minutes he needed to swipe the relic and get out clean.

Sure enough, as I gyrated through the crowd, a bald guy in a gray suit slipped into the alcove, his cold eyes on the gorgeous blonde in his arms—she was Asa's contact. She sank to her knees, and Baldie leaned back, his eyes closed. Well, that was one way to distract him. I hoped he had some staying power. I had a slightly different approach planned, thanks to my partner in crime.

My gaze remained on the stairway that led up to the alcove where Baldie was being entertained while I inched my way over to the base of the stairs. I started to sweat. Where was the replacement guard? Had I missed him? If I had, would Asa see him in time? There were so many things that could go wrong.

"Excuse me," said a deep voice, close to my ear. I started and looked up to see the mercenary with the doughy face looking annoyed—I was blocking his way.

I grinned up at him. "You're a little overdressed for the party," I said, eyeing his slightly rumpled suit. "Can you dance in that?" I asked as my hand crept toward the hidden pocket just inside the hem of my dress.

He smirked. "You think I'm here to dance?" He put one foot on the bottom step.

"You should be!" I ran my palm down my hip and slipped the tiny bottle free. Asa always knew what I needed. After listening to me describe the atmosphere of this club, he'd armed me with something he said would be absolutely perfect. "Come and dance with me."

The mercenary's gaze dropped to my boobs. "Maybe later." I hadn't moved, so he took my shoulders and began to move me out of the way. And that was when I squirted him dead in the face with the contents of my bottle.

"What the—" He released me and I staggered back, then got my footing and began dancing, blending into the crowd. The mercenary wiped his hand down his face, his look of irritation transforming into a grimace of pain. His pale skin turned chalky, then he doubled over and barfed all over the floor. Other clubbers leaped away from the splatter but kept dancing—it wasn't so unusual for someone to overdo it. I'd seen the same thing happen in this very club on three separate occasions.

Wincing as another fountain of puke burst from the mercenary's mouth, I looked up toward the alcove to see the shadow of the other dude still in place. I pulled my phone out of the neckline of my dress and shot Asa a text. *Ready to rock?*

I waited for a minute, expecting to see his response. *Ready to roll.* That's what it was supposed to say. My phone buzzed. I focused on the screen.

Run

I read it just as a hard hand closed around my arm. The green-faced mercenary glared down at me. "You little bitch!"

I gouged my spiked heel into his shin and tore myself away, but collided with a couple of girls carrying glowing blue drinks. Glass shattered. My phone flew from my hand and clattered to the floor—where it was promptly stomped on by an overenthusiastic guest with slicked-back hair and sweat stains in his pits.

"No," I gasped, lunging for it just as it was kicked beneath the feet of another tangle of dancers. Its screen went dark. "Oh, crap." I glanced over my shoulder to see the mercenary, who had paused in his attack to spew all over the floor again, raise his head and bellow something up the stairs to his distracted partner. Then he snarled at me and dipped his hand inside his jacket.

Running seemed like a darn good idea.

I plunged into the writhing crowd, hoping the guy would have the sense not to shoot.

No such luck.

Even with the music pounding, the shots jolted the people around me. "Gun!" someone shouted as the crowd pressed back against walls and columns. With the strobe lights stroking the stampeding mob with pink and blue light, I had a clear view of the second mercenary bounding down the steps, his pants hanging open and his gun out. My heart in my throat, I turned toward the exit, only to find it blocked by a crush of bodies all trying to escape. And I was at the back, a small but convenient target as the sick guy, who could barely stand, pointed his thug partner in my direction.

Just as the mercenary raised his weapon, though, I was yanked to the side. Our bouncer contact pulled me toward a narrow hallway with brutal force and sweaty palms. "You can get out through the fire exit at the end of the hall," he said. "For God's sake, get out." He disappeared through a doorway marked "Employees Only" as a few squealing women shoved past me. Another gunshot made me dive after them. I was too terrified to look behind me—there was nowhere to dodge or hide anyway, just a long corridor leading to a lit sign that read "Východ."

I prayed that meant "exit." But as long as it put a metal door between me and my pursuers, I really didn't care. The girls in front of me hit the door with such force that it flew open, and I was through in an instant. The frigid air was filled with the sound of sirens. Like the others, I ran toward the street. I had no idea how many minutes had passed, but I decided to go to our prearranged meetup spot, which was one block up from the club, anyway. I hoped Asa would be waiting.

Assuming he'd gotten out safely.

A sense of dread welled up in me, making me shudder. And when I reached the street and turned toward our rendezvous point, I realized I had another problem—three police cars had arrived on the scene, and the road was packed with terrified clubbers. Some of the cops were cordoning off the area and pushing people back, not letting them pass on the sidewalks, while others ran inside the building.

It had been a crazily fast response. Had it been even a minute since the first shot was fired? Reeling and disoriented, I looked around, knowing I needed to reroute. Even if he had gotten out, Asa couldn't exactly hang out on a street corner, out in the open. And yet, I knew he wouldn't leave me behind—which meant he would risk himself to get me.

I leaned against a streetlamp, realizing that I'd lost my coat somewhere inside. "Oh God," I said in a choked voice, avoiding the curious gazes of a few passersby. I wrapped my arms around myself. Asa would have no way of knowing I'd lost my phone. What if he'd texted me another place to meet?

"Oh God. Oh God." I jumped into action and sprinted down the block, away from the chaos, then hooked a sharp right, planning to skirt around the crowd and come at the intersection from a different direction. But just as I reached the corner, a slender young man with a swoop of brown hair appeared and blocked my way.

"Hello there," he said in a distinctly Russian accent. He fondled his ornate silver belt buckle, and his eyes settled on my chest. "Something tells me you're the girl I'm looking for."

"Nope," I said. And then I ran. No looking back, just an outright sprint in the opposite direction. I could hear the thumps of his footsteps behind me and the huff of his breath, enough to know he was right on my tail and would tackle me at any second.

But then a motorcycle turned the corner and roared halfway down the block, approaching fast. My Russian pursuer let out a sharp grunt, and I turned to see him collapse onto the pavement, unconscious. Asa came to a screeching halt right in front of me, helmet on, holding his baton, which he promptly collapsed and shoved into his coat before tossing the spare helmet at me. It hit my chest, and I caught it by sheer reflex as I gaped at him.

"Come on," Asa roared. "Get those little legs moving!"

I crammed the helmet onto my head and threw myself onto the bike behind him. "How the heck did you find me?" I was so relieved to see him that I giggled, high-pitched and near hysterical.

But as soon as I wrapped my arms around him, my laughter died. Something was wrong.

His entire body was drenched with sweat and trembling. Not with weakness, but with tension. It felt as if he were about to explode. But I held on tight as he took off again, shooting us down the block away from the club. "Are you okay?" I shouted.

"The helmets are wired," he said, the sound completely clear, his voice as shaky as his body. "You just busted my fucking eardrums."

"Sorry," I whispered.

"Just don't fall off." He tilted the bike and executed a sharp right turn that made my stomach swoop.

"Are we being chased?"

"See for yourself."

I glanced at the mirror on the handlebars and saw two black cars less than a block away. "Who is it?"

"Volodya's people. They arrived just as I was swiping the relic. God, you have to stop touching me that way."

I flinched. "What?"

"Fuck," he whispered. "Never mind." His hips shifted between my thighs and he leaned forward, but I had no choice but to lean with him if I wanted to stay on the bike. He moaned.

"Am I hurting you?"

"No," he said in a tight voice. "Just . . . don't move. Keep your hands where they are."

Fear trickled icily into my belly. Something had happened, and I had no idea how to help. All I could do was hold on as we raced through the streets, bumping up on sidewalks, taking hairpin turns, changing direction, and finally streaking along a highway across the river. We'd left the two black cars in the dust miles ago, but Asa didn't seem to be taking any chances. Finally, he whipped the bike into an alley and came to an abrupt stop, jumped off, and sprinted along, clearly expecting me to follow. I did, as quickly as I could, my ankles wobbling and my heart pounding. Finally he stopped. I leaned against a wall and panted as he reached behind a large trash bin and came out holding a duffel bag. He knelt and pulled a small object from an inner pocket of his coat, grumbling to himself in desperate tones. After a moment he simply dropped the thing into the bag and ripped the zipper closed, his hands seemingly too unsteady to manage anything else.

"You're scaring me," I said quietly.

"Let's go." He shot to his feet and grabbed my hand, then cursed and dropped it. "Let's go."

Utterly confused, I followed him down the street. The brick streets and classic architecture said we were somewhere in the old city. Asa strode quickly up to a facade lined with flags. Beneath a glass awning a sign read "Hotel."

And *what* a hotel. As we entered, the marble floors gleamed beneath massive chandeliers. To our left lay an extremely fancy-looking restaurant, complete with tuxedoed waitstaff. Asa spoke briefly with the front desk attendant and then stalked over to the elevator.

We didn't talk as we rode up to our floor. He had me at my door in less than two minutes and shoved a keycard into my hand. "This one's yours. I'm down the hall and around the corner. 405." He was still vibrating like a live wire, and he kept his body turned halfway away from me, his duffel clutched to his front.

As soon as I took the key, he started to walk away, but I grabbed his arm. "What is *wrong* with you?"

He yanked his arm out of my grip, avoiding my gaze. "The conduit'll be here in a few hours. I'll be back then. I have to get out of here."

Then it dawned on me. "Is it the relic that's hurting you? You didn't package it at the club." Or in the alley, I realized. That's what he'd been trying to do.

"Didn't have time at the club." His fists were clenched; his teeth gritted. "I had to get out fast before they caught both of us. And then I had to find you."

"I'm sorry. That mercenary guy—"

"We'll talk later." He was backtracking stiffly. His fingers were clenching and unclenching over the strap of his bag, sweat sliding in drops down his cheekbones.

"Give that relic to me," I pleaded. "Give it to me right now. You shouldn't have it in your room."

It was Ekstazo magic, and he was more vulnerable to it than anyone.

But as soon as my hands slid along the strap over his chest, his hands closed over my wrists. He crushed me against the wall and buried his face in my neck. I gasped as I felt his tongue, then his teeth. "Asa!"

With a fierce, frantic tug, he ripped the duffel up and over his head and dropped it, but he didn't let me go. Instead, his trembling hands slid down to my hips and wrenched my skirt up to the tops of my thighs. His fingers dug into my backside as he lifted me onto my tiptoes. I whimpered as I felt the hard insistence of his erection between my legs.

"Oh fuck. Mattie." He groaned, and then his mouth was on mine, his kiss ravenous.

Now I knew what kind of Ekstazo magic we'd just stolen. And Asa was in its grip.

My body was a stream of mixed signals as he thrust himself against me, only a few layers of fabric between us. A thousand postponed yeses, a million denied fantasies, countless whispers of *finally. Finally.* My fingers itched to unbuckle his belt, to reach inside, to close my hand around him. I was slick with the mere idea of it, with the scent of him, with craving built up over months of lying awake at night, knowing he was just on the other side of the wall.

But alongside all that desire crowded a billion screaming nos. This wasn't right. Not for him, not for me. Not this way.

It was too important. My whole heart was at stake, and I knew it.

I turned my face away and pried his hands from my hips, digging my fingernails into his skin and hoping the pain would help clear his head. "Asa, stop. Cut it out."

"Can't stand it anymore," he growled against my throat. His hand twisted free and was on my leg in an instant, skimming up between my thighs. I caught him just as his fingers brushed the center of me, sending a devastating shiver of want straight through my body. "God, Mattie. Why do you always smell so fucking good?" His fingers encircled my wrist and pinned it over my head again.

"Asa. I don't want this."

"Right, professional," he murmured, nuzzling my ear. "Always so goddamn professional." The fingertips of his other hand slid under the deep neckline of my dress, over the swell of my breast, my hard nipple.

"Asa, stop! *Please!*"

As my voice broke, he stumbled away from me, his back hitting the wall. "Fuck," he snapped, running his hands through his hair, his eyes wild, his arousal tight and prominent against his zipper. *"Goddammit."* He whirled around and punched the wall. I cried out, and a framed picture of a castle rattled. But when I surged forward to try to stop him from doing it again, he bucked me off. "Don't fucking touch me!"

His voice was so full of rage and horror that I leaped back. His knuckles were bleeding as he staggered away from me. He waved an uncoordinated hand toward the duffel. "Get that fucking thing into your room, package it right, and put it in the safe. Now."

"Okay," I said, shaking. I sank to my knees next to the bag.

Asa let out a ragged breath as he braced his palms on his thighs. "Dead-bolt your door. Do *not* let me in until I've got the conduit with me and we're ready to upload. You understand?"

I didn't want him to leave. I had no idea what he was going to do, but at the same time, I knew he couldn't be with me. It might break us forever. "Yes," I said softly.

His face twisted into a grimace, then he turned and jogged up the hall and around the corner. A door slammed.

Tears stinging my eyes, I grabbed the duffel that contained our stolen relic and slipped into my room, thankful that no guests had poked their heads out to witness our craziness. I tucked the relic, which was nothing more than a carved soapstone rabbit, into one of the special lead-lined pouches Asa carried to package his relics, and then into the safe. And then I collapsed onto the bed in a puddle of confusion and want and terror and sadness, and prayed for a conduit who couldn't possibly arrive quickly enough.

CHAPTER THREE

I lasted all of two hours, and then I couldn't take it anymore. Asa wasn't responding to my texts or calls, and the phone in his room seemed to be on do not disturb. I was worried sick about him. He'd once told me how scared he was about being addicted to Ekstazo juice, how easy it would be to get hooked again, how vulnerable it made him to Knedas magic. *It's how they catch us and keep us,* he'd told me, referring to the mob bosses who would do just about anything to have a magic sensor in their stable.

I walked slowly down the hall, steeling myself against what I might find. Surely the lust that had overtaken him would have worn off by now. I turned the corner just as the door to his room opened.

But it wasn't Asa who stepped out.

A guy about my age with wavy brown hair and a half-unbuttoned shirt backed into the hallway, grinning lazily. "—do this again, maybe," he was saying. "We're here until Tuesday."

I stopped breathing.

The guy held out his hand, and he tugged a woman into the hallway with him, her curly blond hair disheveled, her strappy shoes dangling from her fingers. "Thanks for the experience," she said over her shoulder, then reached back into the room and stroked her hand downward, all flirt. But then she gasped as another hand grabbed hers and pushed it back against her own body.

For a moment, his bare arm and shoulder were visible, long enough for me to know it was his room, his body, his bandaged knuckles.

I let out a choked whimper and clumsily ducked out of sight. I leaned against the wall and heard a man say, "God, that was fucking hot," just before the pair sauntered around the corner.

The woman tossed me a glance as they passed and giggled, then slapped the guy on the butt. He flinched and squeezed her. "Stop that. I'm going to be sore for a while," he mumbled in a teasing voice as they disappeared into the elevator.

My breath wheezed as my throat constricted. "No," I said in a strained whisper. My hand trailed along the wall, along doors, as I trudged back to my room, entered, and threw the dead bolt. "It's none of your business," I said aloud. "Just business. Just business." I covered my face with my hands. "You have *no* right to be feeling this way." A sob garbled my words.

Feeling sweaty and miserable and dirty, I tore off my clothes and stepped into the shower, where I let the hot water run down my body, let it redden my freckled skin and sting my cheeks.

From the moment I'd announced that we were going to keep things professional, he'd respected the line. Sure, he joked about it. He was flirtatious in an effortlessly dirty way that made me laugh. But when it came to the boundaries, he hadn't pushed, not even once. I still looked away whenever he had his shirt off, because *damn*. But he didn't parade in front of me, either. We never shared a room or a bed. He gave me plenty of privacy, and I offered the same. I never asked where he disappeared to when we weren't together. I never poked through his stuff. I never held his clothes to my face and inhaled before tucking them in the laundry . . . okay, only a couple of times on that last one.

But at the same time, he knew all my quirks and habits, and I knew his. We had a rhythm like nothing I'd ever shared with Ben, perhaps because there was more tension between us than I'd ever felt with anyone *ever*, and so each little gesture vibrated along the lines that connected us, thrumming through me, sensitizing me to every look and every touch.

Before, in the hall, I had pushed him away because it was the only right thing to do. And he had gone off and had a little orgy with two strangers because . . . well, I guess he'd needed it. He'd needed to put his hands on another person's skin. He'd needed to feel himself inside another person's body. *Two* bodies, apparently.

I covered my mouth and squeezed my eyes shut, breathing hard through my nose. He was free to do whatever he wanted. I had no claim on him. He hadn't done it to hurt me. He hadn't done anything wrong.

It shouldn't feel as if he'd just punched me right in the heart.

And there was no way I was going to be silly and stupid and small-town about this. I scrubbed my skin and washed my hair, then dried off and got dressed. Our conduit would arrive sometime soon, and we'd upload the magic into my body before catching our flight to London, free from the worry that the magic could be detected or traced until we downloaded it into a relic for the buyer Asa had found. I'd have a significant chunk of change to deposit, to add to my already surprisingly healthy nest egg. We'd go on like before, and I would put this behind me.

I would put my ridiculous fantasies behind me, too. If it hadn't been obvious before, what I'd just seen made it so clear that Asa's tastes didn't exactly run toward the conventional. If I'd ever dared hope I could figure out what would satisfy him, or that I could be enough, that illusion had been shattered.

I should be grateful.

The banging on my door jarred me out of my churning thoughts, and I scooted over and peeked through the peephole to see Asa, looking freshly showered. "Mattie! Get out here." He was staring at the peephole. "I'm fine. Under control. It's safe."

I sighed and opened the door. "Where's the conduit?"

He regarded me for a moment, studying my face. "Just got a text from him. We're being hunted, and there are naturals in the old city. We've arranged another meetup. We need to get this thing uploaded pronto."

"Okay." I went to the safe and pulled out the packaged relic while Asa backtracked into the hallway to wait. "Are you going to be okay?"

"I know how to take care of me," he said curtly.

"Yeah, I guess you do," I muttered as I shouldered the duffel.

"What?"

"Nothing."

He stared at me for a second, then turned and headed for the stairs. We always took the stairs when we were afraid of being ambushed. I balled my free hand in my skirt as we descended, telling myself to get a grip and focus on getting through the night.

We reached the street and caught a cab. Asa gave the driver the address, and we were off. I kept my eyes focused out the window. Asa poked me in the arm. "Hey. If this is about earlier—"

"It's not."

"I was totally out of line, and I—"

"It's fine. Wasn't your fault."

"Okay," he said, drawing out the word with skepticism. "You *are* gonna have to prepare yourself for this magic, though. We should talk about what happens after. Because this relic—"

"I've handled originals, Asa. I think I can handle this."

"Didn't say you couldn't. I'm just worried that—"

"I'm not *you*, okay?" I clamped my lips shut, hating the trembling in my voice.

"Yeah," he said quietly. "Well aware."

We rode in silence the rest of the way, and it was a long ride. We finally reached a maze of warehouses rimmed by grimy roads with no sidewalks. I could see a rail depot behind the warehouses with a stretch of dingy, depressing commercial buildings on the other side of the tracks, gray brown under dim streetlamps. "This is where we're meeting the guy?" I asked as we entered the warren of buildings and the driver pulled to the side. Asa paid him and we got out. "Seems pretty convenient for an ambush—no witnesses."

"Not exactly," said Asa, whose face glittered under a streetlight, sweat beading across his forehead. He pointed up ahead to a warehouse with a few cars parked out front.

"I'm unimpressed."

"Look." He pointed to the rail depot just as a train pulled in and disgorged a small crowd of people. They were all wearing black, with spiky hair and buckles shining on their boots. They jogged across the tracks as the train pulled away, and clustered at the front door of the warehouse a moment later, entering one by one.

"Oh, great. A club. A goth club." I looked down at my skirt and flats.

"I know the owner. She's doing me a favor."

Oh, I bet she was. "Awesome," I said drily.

I followed him into the building. The bouncer at the door nodded at him and pointed down a hall to a flight of stairs. "Erik's up there already."

Asa slipped the guy a few hundred euros and strode up the hall, me in his wake. We had done this so many times before. Asa was a chameleon—he was whatever I needed him to be during a transaction. He was my handler, my dom, my charming jokester, my quietly considerate companion, whatever he decided I needed to get through a magical exchange and walk out intact.

But now the line of his shoulders was stiff and unyielding as he marched up the stairs. I didn't know whether he was focused on resisting the magic in the relic I was carrying in the duffel or whether he had picked up on my resentful vibes. I didn't have the time to ask him, either, because as soon as we hit the top of the stairs, Asa strode into the arms of a woman with killer curves and long, straight blond hair. She rubbed his shoulders and then drew back and took his face in her hands. Then she slapped him.

"You were going to leave my city without even coming to visit!" she said in accented English.

Asa rubbed his cheek. "Nice to see you again, too, Renata." He jerked his thumb back at me. "That's Mattie. She's the reliquary."

Renata cocked her hip and looked me over. She was wearing thigh-high boots, fishnets, a dazzlingly short skirt, and a corset. Her eyes were heavily lined, her over-the-top lashes thick and curving. I must have looked like a Sunday-school teacher to her. She let out an unimpressed grunt and pointed to a room down the hall. "Erik is ready. When you're done, you'll deliver my payment. We'll make sure to keep all the beasts at bay. You felt my relic coming in. And I could feel you, too." She pulled a pendant out of her neckline and held it up.

Asa nodded. "I'll recharge it for you soon as I'm done here."

"Good boy." She winked at him and headed down the steps.

"You're going to give her some of your magic?" I asked as I trailed him down the hall.

"Wow, nothing gets by you."

"I just didn't know you did that kind of thing," I said, trying to keep the hurt and irritation out of my tone. "You never have before."

"I do what's necessary to get us out alive."

He stalked into the room Renata had pointed to. I saw two soft chairs, side by side. In one of them sat a guy wearing vinyl pants and no shirt. His chest was hairless, his skin tanned and oiled. Sandalwood, by the smell of it. Asa stopped short a few steps inside the room. His chuckle was dry as dust. "Hey, Erik. Looking slick."

Erik smiled as he leaned around Asa to look at me. "Ready to go. And *hello* there."

"Hey," I said curtly. I walked over to the other squashy chair and plopped down, then handed Asa the duffel. "Let's get this done." I offered Erik my hand.

Transactions were almost easy for me now, and I'd come a long way from needing to be horizontal for every one. I asked Asa to secure me only for heavy Strikon magic or intense-emotion Sensilo magic, but for the rest I was able to remain aware and in control at this point.

Still, Asa looked concerned by my nonchalance. "Mattie, you might want to think about—"

"Let's. Do. This," I snapped, staring him down. Asa muttered under his breath and shook his head, then pulled a pair of gloves out of his thigh pocket and slipped them on. He looked down at the duffel as if it were a cornered wolverine.

Erik turned to me. "Asa said this is really good shit. I told him if it's half as good as he promises, I'll give him a ten percent discount."

"That doesn't seem like a sound business decision," I said.

Erik snorted. "You're no fun. But I bet you will be."

Before I could respond, Asa came up holding the soapstone rabbit in its lead wrapper, the top of the pouch peeled open. "I need you to do this now," he said in a tight voice.

I forced myself not to look at his pants. I didn't want to know if he was hard.

Erik stuck his hand out. "You don't have to tell me twice, mister."

Asa's jaw clenched. His eyes met mine for a moment, and I glared mulishly back. Then he tilted the pouch, and the rabbit slid onto Erik's palm.

Have you ever wanted something so badly that you knew you would die if you didn't have it? I'm talking about anything. Water. Food. Oxygen. Sexual desire is like that, too. One of our primal appetites. Instinctual. Necessary. As the magic rocketed through Erik and into me, that hit me, bone deep. It was like a stiff wind, knocking my head back, parting my lips. Then the warmth swelled up along my arm and into my chest, hardening my nipples and tensing all my muscles with need. It flooded me, and my body moved on its own, undulating, seeking relief it couldn't find. The hunger swirled into the center of me, twisting me so tight that I cried out, arching, begging for a touch that wasn't there.

And then, just as suddenly, the magic flowed into my vault, and the door closed. I sank down in the chair, panting, my ears and lips buzzing. I heard the low murmur of male voices, and my eyes blinked open. I stared into Asa's honey-brown gaze.

All I could think was . . . *want.*

Asa arched an eyebrow. "How we doing?" He looked amused but sounded a little breathless, like he'd just run up and down the stairs a few times.

I tensed to keep from moaning. "Good to go," I murmured.

"God, you look like it," said a voice from next to me. I turned to see Erik, his erection hard against the thin vinyl of his pants. I let out a shaky breath. My trembling hand reached out and stroked along his forearm, and the feel of his slick skin set fire to the glowing cinders inside me. His fingers curled around mine, and he tugged me up and out of the chair. My chest was pressed to his bare skin an instant later.

"Mattie," Asa said, right in my ear.

Erik's hands ran down my back and clasped my backside as I looked up at my business partner. As soon as I saw his face, another wave of desire washed over me. Erik was kneading my rear while his arousal poked at my belly, but suddenly all I wanted to do was have the taste of Asa in my mouth, his hands on my skin.

"I'm not going to get in your way here if this is what you really want," Asa said in a firm voice, ignoring Erik as the conduit slid his hand under my shirt. "But I don't think it is."

"Shut the fuck up, dude," Erik said, pulling the cup of my bra down and pinching my nipple.

I bit my lip as my eyes fell closed.

"Look at me," Asa snapped.

My eyes popped open at the authoritative edge in his voice. Sir's voice was speaking, and the sound awakened an entirely new level of craving.

"Say the word, and I'm leaving," Asa said. "You can fuck Erik until neither of you can walk."

"Sounds like a plan. I'll halve my fee if you get the fuck out right now," Erik said, his voice muffled as he sucked on my neck.

Asa kept his eyes on me, his voice level. "But if you ask, I'll get you out of here before you do something that you'll regret."

I held his gaze. "Like screw a couple of strangers in my hotel room?" I said, smoothing my hand across Erik's chest.

For a moment, Asa looked like he'd been kicked in the balls. But then he let out that dark, dry chuckle I knew so well. "*Aaand* suddenly everything makes sense." He grabbed my wrist and yanked me away from Erik. "Let's go."

"Hey, asshole," Erik barked. "I didn't hear her complaining."

Asa held my wrist in a crushing grip. "You want to fuck him to get some kind of sad little payback, feel free. You want to fuck him because you're horny as hell, then I've got rubbers in my bag." He wrenched me close. "But be sure that's what you want, Mattie. Be dead sure. Because you hate when magic controls you, and right now you're its puppet. If you do this, you'll hate yourself after."

"How about I just hate you now?" I whispered, my pain cooling my desire.

"Whatever you want. But make sure you're doing it for the right reasons."

I blinked at him, then tore my gaze away as Erik started to pull on my other hand. Sorrow and frustration and want crashed over me all at once. "Erik, I shouldn't," I said miserably.

Asa looped his arm around my waist and guided me toward the door. "Sorry, Erik. You heard the lady."

"Fuck you, Asa," Erik said. "You can pay my full commission, and I'm adding a five percent blue-balls fee. I'll be down on the dance floor whenever you want to do the transfer for Renata." He pushed past us and loped down the stairs.

Asa clamped his hand on my shoulder and steered me into the hallway after the conduit. The feel of his skin was intoxicating, so much hotter than Erik's, so much more potent, awakening the need again.

I squirmed beneath his grasp as we descended the steps, and the smell of sweat and sex and perfume and skin, so much skin, filled my nose, my lungs. My panties were slick, and the music thumped in my chest. The vibrations crept along my bones, landing right in the center of me. I reached the bottom of the stairs and paused, feeling Asa close behind me.

I reached back and grabbed his hips, pure reflex. For the barest second, I felt him hard against my back, and I moaned. But then his hands were over mine, pulling them from his body. Needing to feel his heat, I pushed my hips back. "Stop it," he said from between clenched teeth.

"You wanted it earlier."

Asa held my hands tight, but the pain only notched up my arousal, making me shiver. "Yeah, when I was out of my fucking mind with the magic, just like you are now." He abruptly pushed me away from him.

I whirled around. "And without it, you don't want me?"

He ran his hands over his face and through his hair, leaving it sticking up in clumps on his head. "This is not the time for that conversation. We need to get you out of here, but I have to make a little donation to Renata's piggy bank first."

"Fine. I'll dance while you do your business."

"Right. And then I'll probably find you in a bathroom gang bang with some zit-faced wannabe goth boys. If you hit that floor you're gonna start something you won't want to finish, honey."

"Jealous?"

"What the actual fuck, Mattie," he shouted. "You're not thinking straight."

I ran my hand up my body, over my breasts. He was breathing hard, only six feet away, and it was way too far. I was pissed that I needed him so badly, pissed that it wasn't mutual.

Then the main club door opened and a group of guys walked in, maybe college age, shoving each other. They smelled strongly of booze and cigarettes and male sweat. I took a deep breath as they came up the hall toward us. A few of them had bold gazes, stroking right over me, slipping up my skirt and down my shirt, and I smiled, wondering if they could see in my eyes how badly I needed someone between my legs. As they passed, I caressed the arm of a tall black-haired guy with a spiderweb tattooed on his forearm. He stopped so quickly that his buddy walked right into him. "Hey," he said to me as his friend staggered backward. The others guffawed.

"Hey." I slid my hand up his chest, which was still cold from the winter air outside.

"Hey," said Asa, taking my upper arm and dragging me back toward the stairs.

"Hey!" I tried to pull free but Asa held me tight, and the guys moved on up the hallway, forgetting me in an instant. I slapped Asa's chest as he wrenched me under the stairs, into a little alcove where the shadows were deep. He pinned my wrists against the wall. "What the hell are you doing?" I said, angrily turning my face away from his.

"My job," he said roughly.

"I don't want to be your job!" But my body arched toward his as he ran his hand down my side and grasped my hip. My mind was a storm of conflict, but my body was desperate. Starving for release. The burning truth seared its way into my consciousness—there was no one else I wanted, not really.

"Right now you don't get to decide." Asa grasped my chin and firmly turned my face back to his. "Right now you're going to do exactly what I say, or there will be consequences. Got it?"

"Let me go."

"Not a fucking chance."

"I hate you."

He smiled. "Sometimes I hate you, too, baby. Now hold on to this." He guided my hands to a water pipe that ran along the wall over my head. As soon as I grasped it, I heard a click. I looked up and realized he'd handcuffed one of my wrists to the pipe.

"What are you doing?" I asked, shrill and breathless. *Okay,* and really turned on.

"Honestly?" He leaned down, letting his lips trail down the side of my face and along my throat. "Something I've been wanting to do ever since that night in the camper."

He sank to his knees in front of me, and then his hands slid up under my skirt, his fingers finding the strip of my underwear that traversed my hip. With a jerk, he ripped them at the seam, and the scrap of fabric slid down my other leg. "You've only got one choice now. You make yourself come, or I'm going to do it for you."

CHAPTER FOUR

I moaned. "Asa!"

"I'm not fucking around, Mattie. Choose." His fingers dug into my thigh.

I rattled the cuff above my head, defiant tears starting in my eyes, even as my body throbbed for him. It knew what it wanted. I knew what *I* wanted.

Asa stared up at me, his eyes black in the darkness. His thumb stroked down my inner thigh, and I whimpered. "Give in to it. No shame. You're safe with me and you know it."

"Safe?" I laughed bitterly. Did he have any idea how dangerous he was to my heart?

"Mattie." His voice was full of warning.

"No," I whispered.

He pushed my skirt up, and I felt his hot breath on my skin. My legs parted, and his tongue followed the path of his thumb. I moaned again, the sensation exquisite and overwhelming and so much less than I needed.

"Just say it, baby. You know I've got you. I've always got you." He gently bit my soft flesh.

"Oh God." A tear streaked from my eye as I turned my face up to the ceiling, not wanting him to see. He was going to break me. He had no idea what it meant. And I couldn't detach and focus on the sensation, because it was *him*.

"Let me do this for you. I know you need it."

"And you?" I whispered, holding my breath.

"Dying of thirst." Then he pulled my hips forward and drew his tongue along the most sensitive part of me, and it was all over. I gasped at the hot invasion of his mouth, the rasp of his stubble against my inner thighs, the need coiling like a snake ready to strike, winding so tight that my heart could barely beat. He firmly lifted one of my legs and draped it over his shoulder, giving himself complete access. His fingers were bruising on my ass, but the pain only increased my frenzy. There was no hesitation in his grip, in the caress of his tongue, the flex of his jaw. He was in charge, in control. He owned me.

My free hand released the pipe above my head and curled into his dark hair, desperate to have him closer, to feel him deeper, but he grabbed my wrist and pinned it to the wall. Then he slid two fingers inside me, sending me up on my tiptoes with an overwhelming intensity that nearly made me come on the spot.

I didn't consider that I was in a crowded club, barely out of view of the people walking by less than twenty feet away. I didn't focus on the fact that I was cuffed to a water pipe, pinned against the wall, my legs spread while Asa left no part of me unexplored or untended. I didn't care about the noise I was making, the pleas bursting from my mouth. All that mattered was the mounting pressure, the peak I had to climb.

I came so hard, my body clenching, that I was hurled right over the edge of that mountain and into open air. I screamed with the ecstasy, unable to contain it.

I screamed Asa's *name*.

He was holding me so tightly that even though I was standing on one leg, my wrists restrained, I knew I wouldn't lose my footing. He wouldn't allow it. The flicks of his tongue didn't stop as I spiraled down, and each touch sent shocks of pleasure zinging up through my belly and down my legs.

Finally, my muscles went slack, and the stars behind my eyes winked out. Asa gently lowered my leg to the ground and let go of my wrist. He rose to his feet in front of me. "I told you to hold on to that pipe," he said quietly, glancing at my free hand.

Drunk with pleasure and the sight of his shadowed face, I focused on his lips, wet with my desire. "Punish me, then," I whispered.

With a rough sound in his throat, Asa pressed himself against me, his mouth finding mine. My tongue thrust against his, seeking my own taste. His fingers coiled around the back of my neck. I could feel him now, hard and ready against my abdomen. My fingers dropped to his belt, then stroked over the rigid column of his cock.

He caught my wrist and tore his mouth from mine. "No."

"Why not?"

He leaned back enough to look into my eyes. "Because I'm not gonna be your throwaway fuck."

Throwaway? "But you just—"

"I just took care of you. End of story."

Confusion and anger clamped around my heart. "Right. Your job."

His jaw clenched. "Professional as always."

"But you weren't willing to let me do the same thing for you?"

"I don't recall you offering. In fact, I recall you begging me to stop."

My cheeks went hot. "So I'm to blame for the fact that you ended up having a threesome in your room, because I didn't drop to my knees and blow you in the hallway of a five-star hotel?"

He shoved back from the wall. "We're done talking about this."

"Whatever; it's none of my business. And if you're mad at me for not sucking you off, then—"

"What the fuck, Mattie. That's not—"

"—why are you turning me down now?"

"Are you fucking serious?" he snapped. "We've been together night and day for the last eight months, and you don't know the answer to that?"

"You're the one who's got the rubbers in his bag and the horny couple in his room. I didn't think casual sex was an issue for you."

"First off, you don't know what the hell you're talking about, and second, *nothing* with you is casual," he shouted, slamming his palms against the wall on either side of me, making me flinch. "You can get on with whatever stupid little game you want to play, Mattie," he continued, his voice dropping low. "Go ahead and twist yourself up over things you don't understand. Make me your bad guy if it lets you run from the things that scare you without feeling shitty. But I'm not gonna play the hangdog here. I'm done playing, period." The flat, cold edge in his voice drew my eyes to his. "Because I can't do this anymore."

He reached into his pocket and pulled out a small key, which he used to unlock the handcuffs. My arm fell limp to my side as Asa swiped his sleeve across his mouth, picked up his duffel, and headed for the main hallway. I pulled my torn panties off my heel and left them crumpled in a corner before staggering after him.

I'd lost count of the number of times I'd fantasized about a relationship with Asa. As we worked together as a team, traveled together, ran for our lives together, shared a bathroom and a kitchen, shopped in farmers' markets, dealt with each other's headaches and chest colds, it became about so much more than our sexual attraction, though that was ever present and distracting. But I'd never forgotten one very important piece of knowledge: Asa hated cages. He'd kill or die before allowing himself to be kept in one.

I could still recall the look on Keenan's face when Asa had whispered that truth into the darkness of a grimy Bangkok alley. *It was just another cage.* Like so many things, his past with Keenan was something Asa didn't like to talk about. I knew only that they had once been close, that Asa had nearly become a Headsman himself at one point, that he'd run without leaving so much as a note—and that he'd broken Keenan's heart. The pain in Keenan's blue eyes had made that abundantly clear, as had the hope in his voice when Asa fooled him into thinking he was going to leave that alley with him and not me.

The last thing I wanted to be to Asa was a cage.

Was Asa about to break free? He'd said that he was done. I was terrified to ask what he'd meant for fear the answer would destroy me.

We flew out of Prague at four in the morning on a charter jet headed for London. The buyer for our relic was the boss of the UK, apparently, a woman named Elizabeth Botwright. Asa had just told me we were going to meet with one of her agents first, a guy named Myron Forester.

It was Christmas Eve. We'd caught a few hours of sleep during the day and were leaving a fairly desolate hotel bar after a near-silent dinner. "Do you know him?" I asked.

"I know of him. Botwright likes to surround herself with mind-fuckers. It's why I made you wear the inserts." Asa had made sure I had wire bristles affixed in the toes of my shoes before we went down to dinner.

"Where are we meeting Myron?"

"Harrods. They close at nine. Lots of people around."

"You don't trust him."

"I don't trust anyone. I just want him to give us the details and the plan. After what happened with Erik, I want to vet the conduit ahead of time."

I bowed my head as my face flushed. "What's Botwright going to do with this thing?"

"Don't really care, as long as she does it far away from me," he muttered. "Sooner we off-load it, the better." He pulled his collar up against the cold.

I did the same, feeling the tiny vial of sand dangling between my breasts, beneath my clothes, where I'd tucked it away. I'd wanted to wear it without Asa seeing, given how off things were between us.

"But you can't feel this Ekstazo magic inside me. Can you?" I couldn't. Now that I had recovered from the initial effects of it coursing through my body, it was like it wasn't there at all.

He looked at me out of the corner of his eye. "No. I'd have to be touching you."

"Listen, last night, after you . . ." I cleared my throat and spoke slowly, trying to keep my voice steady. "You said you couldn't do this anymore. Um . . ." I pressed my lips together as the tremor became obvious. "What did you mean?"

He was quiet for a few strides, and then he sighed.

"When we get this done, I think I'm gonna head out on my own for a while."

I stopped dead in the street. "What?"

He walked a few more steps and paused, still facing toward the lights of Harrods a few blocks up. "It couldn't last forever. And it's not working for me anymore."

I folded my arms over the sharp pain in my chest. "I . . . Okay, I'm sorry. I'm sorry for the way I acted. I'm sorry for—"

He turned around. "That was just the last straw, Mattie. I was headed that way already."

"Headed that way? B-b-but . . . you gave me a present," I said, my voice breaking. "You made it seem like everything was good. You . . ." A tear streaked down my face, and Asa's eyes closed. "*Please.* Tell me what I can do."

"It's not that simple," he said gently.

"But we're good together. You've said it yourself."

He gave me a rueful smile. "We're the best, baby. But I can't stand it. I need some distance."

"I'm sorry for what I said last night, okay?" I blurted out, loud enough that a passing couple gave us a look. "I was such a jerk about what happened, and you were free to do whatever you wanted! You always have been!"

"I know." He closed the distance between us. "But that's the thing. You've changed what I want. You've changed everything."

I blinked up at him. "What do you mean?"

"I told you that you could take as long as you wanted to figure this out. I thought it would get easier. I've never been more wrong about anything."

"You mean, you and me?" I whispered.

"I know you feel something for me." His gaze was steady on mine. "But I also know I'm not exactly the man of your dreams."

He was right. But my dreams were far less interesting than he was. "What do you want from me, Asa? I don't think I'm being deliberately stupid when I say I have no idea."

He gave me a wary look. "You trust me with your body. Your safety. Your sanity. Your life."

"You know I do."

"But you won't trust me with your heart."

I took a step back. "You want me to?"

He chuckled. "The things I want from you . . ." He shook his head. "But I won't play, Mattie. Not with you. I blew past that exit months ago."

"My heart is a responsibility, Asa. After Ben . . . you can't blame me for being careful."

"No, I can't. But you can't blame me for being honest. You asked what I wanted. And I just told you."

"I don't know if I can offer that," I said. "I know you have some needs—"

"I didn't fuck that couple in Prague." He rolled his eyes. "I was going to, okay? I was dead set on it." He let out a frustrated noise and ran his hands through his hair. "I was so on fire that I could barely think. I picked her because she reminded me the tiniest bit of you, and her boyfriend . . . well." He glanced at me as if trying to gauge my reaction. "Once we got into the room, though, suddenly all the ways she *wasn't* you were right there in my face, and the guy was hot, but it was all wrong. I needed something, though, so they fucked while I watched. While I told them what to do. I got off and so did they, and then they left." His jaw was rigid as he lifted his gaze to my face. "I'm not apologizing for it."

"I didn't ask you to," I said quietly. It was far kinkier than anything I'd ever experienced, but it felt strangely better to know he hadn't let them touch his body, that he hadn't been inside either of them. I let out a shaky breath. "But you scare me, Asa. You always have."

"I get it." He looked away from me, his eyes wide but unfocused. "I didn't honestly expect you to feel anything different when shit got real."

Giving this thing between us a chance might break my heart. But letting him leave, knowing I hadn't taken a chance at all, was *definitely* going to break my heart. I swallowed the lump in my throat. "But you did once say I was brave as hell."

His head swung around fast, surprise etched on his face. I reached out, my fingers closing around the sleeve of his coat. "If you want to leave—if that's what's best for you—I won't try to stop you. So I'll only say this once." I looked up at his angles and planes, the face I had come to adore.

The man I had come to love.

"I've tried to keep my distance, Asa, but not because I've been burying my head in the sand about how I felt. I'm just keenly aware of how much you could hurt me. More every day. What if I can't . . . I don't know what you want. I don't know if I'm enough. We've been all over the world, but like you always said, I'm just this girl from a small town. And I still don't know how to make you happy."

"Why don't you ask me, Mattie?" He looked down at my fingers clutched over his sleeve. "It's not something you have to figure out by yourself. That kind of defeats the point."

"The point?"

He stroked his thumb across my cheek. "Of being *together*."

My other hand rose to his chest as he slid his arm around my waist. "It feels complicated."

"Because it is. So I guess you have to decide whether it's worth it. Whether I'm worth it."

"You've already decided?"

The corner of his mouth quirked up. "You have no idea what you are to me, do you?"

"You could tell me."

His phone chimed. "Maybe I will. After our meeting with Myron." He pulled me close. "Then you're gonna do the same. And after that we're going to decide what to do, together. Deal?"

I touched his cheek. He had shaved, and his skin was smooth and chilled beneath my fingertips. "Deal."

He bowed his head as I stood on my tiptoes, and our kiss was careful, like we held something incredibly fragile between us. We both pulled away at the same time. "Ready to rock?" he asked.

"Ready to roll." I bit my lip to hold in my grin as he took my hand. I hoped Myron Forester was a timely fellow, and that this meeting was short. Because all I wanted to do was go back to the hotel and start figuring things out. Together.

CHAPTER FIVE

"Harrods on Christmas Eve doesn't feel all that festive when you're planning to meet up with a criminal," I mused as we approached the massive building glistening with lights.

Asa snorted. "You know you're technically a criminal, too, right?"

"But I'm a nice criminal."

"I could think of a few people who might disagree with you." His smile was sly. "But I wouldn't have it any other way."

"Probably because you're the one who corrupted me in the first place."

He laughed. "Uh-uh. Own it. You're the one who chased *me* and begged to come along."

I squeezed his hand. "Only because you tempted me."

His grin was as bright as any of the displays as we crossed the street and approached the department store. It was five to nine, almost closing time, and more people were coming out than going in. Asa always chose crowded places for his meets because if there were naturals, he could sense them easily. He also preferred places where we could melt into the crowd or raise a ruckus and cause enough distraction to slow down pursuers. We walked into the store and past the perfume counter, right up to a man who was examining a display of cashmere scarves.

"Myron," Asa said.

The man looked up, still sliding camel-colored fabric between his long fingers. He looked about Asa's age, with thick brown hair, a short, neatly trimmed beard, and deep-green eyes. "Mr. Ward, I presume?" His accent was pure Brit. "And . . ." He arched an eyebrow as he looked me over.

"This is Mattie. My reliquary."

"*Your* reliquary."

That was when I realized I was still holding Asa's hand. I let go and offered my hand to Myron. "Nice to meet you."

He gave me a little smile and took my hand, just as I remembered the dude was a Knedas. I curled my toes hard against the bristles in my shoe. "Charmed," he said quietly.

Then he turned to offer his hand to Asa, but Asa simply stood there. "No, thanks."

Instead of looking offended, Myron chuckled. "Understood. We're on the same side, though. Madam wants this magic safely off-loaded and packaged. She wants you to be comfortable with the terms."

Asa looked around. "Where's the conduit?"

"I wanted to meet you first. She is waiting in luxury home goods upstairs."

I eyed the lady behind the perfume counter, who was putting away samples. "Aren't they closing soon?"

"Ah, yes. But we'll be out before they lock up, and while we're here, they won't take notice of us."

I ground my toes even harder against the bristles, relishing the pain. He'd basically just told us he was manipulating the employees with his magic. I glanced up at Asa, who was starting to sweat. "Let's roll, then," he said in a tight voice. "We have plans tonight."

Myron gestured toward the escalator just as the lights in one of the sections of the store went dim. I glanced at the clock on the wall—it was nine. "I must tell you, Asa, I've been looking forward to meeting you. My employer is also very interested in your skills. She has authorized me to offer you an arrangement."

"I'm freelance only," Asa said. "So don't bother."

Myron shrugged. "I will convey the message. She will be . . . disappointed."

"Let her take a hit off the magic Mattie's carrying, and I promise she'll feel better."

The Knedas laughed, his smile all straight white teeth. "Well, she has other plans for it, but now I'm intrigued."

We reached the top of the escalator and turned toward the home goods department, but we hadn't made it two steps when Asa grabbed my hand and pulled me back. "What the fuck."

Myron turned, his brow furrowed. "What is it?"

"Naturals," Asa said, his teeth gritting, his voice low, his gaze darting first to the linens section, then to the luggage displays, and finally to the appliance area. "What the fuck are you playing at?"

Myron's eyes went wide. "What?" he whispered. "Nothing!" He looked around, his hand straying beneath his coat, probably reaching for a weapon.

"They aren't yours?" I asked.

Myron backtracked toward the escalators. "Absolutely not. Let's go."

Asa cursed and bundled me toward the down escalator, but then dragged me back. "More down there. You don't have backup tonight?" he snapped at Myron.

"No, we wanted to keep the meet from triggering the interest of rival agents," Myron replied as he jumped on the escalator to the third level.

"Looks like you failed."

"Is it Volodya's people?" I asked, my voice squeaky with fear.

"Probably."

"I know this place well, though," said Myron, breathing hard. "There's a way out. You just keep telling me what you sense."

We ran up the escalator. Asa muttered a constant stream of curses as we followed Myron past darkened restaurants and cheerful holiday displays. The Knedas pointed toward an employees-only hallway. "Feel anything this way?"

"No. All clear," Asa said, glancing behind him. "We're getting some distance."

"Maybe they didn't spot us," I asked. Asa didn't respond, but he gave me a worried look. I squeezed his hand.

"We can get out this way—there's a special staircase," Myron said as he reached a door marked "Helipad."

Asa paused as Myron opened the door and went through. "You're sure?"

"Feel free to head down the way you came," said Myron as he jogged up the steps. "But I know when I'm outnumbered, and I plan to celebrate Christmas with cold champagne and a hot woman who I will *not* keep waiting."

We followed Myron up the steps and burst into the cold night air. "It's this way," Myron called as he sprinted across the concrete toward another door marked "VIP."

Asa wrenched me to a stop just as five men and women stepped through the VIP door. We spun around to see another five come through the door we'd just exited. I let out a scared whimper as the two groups surrounded us, a few of them wearing Harrods name tags on their lapels.

Asa drew his baton and extended it, then reached in his pocket and pulled out a squirt gun, which he handed to me. "Sensilo," he whispered.

I clutched it in my shaking hand. Myron drew a Taser. "None of you wants to hurt us," he said loudly and slowly. "You'll let us go."

"Nice try," said a man with a deep, raspy voice. "But we know who you are. We're only here for these two, though." He gestured at me and Asa.

Myron and Asa exchanged looks, and the two men squared their shoulders. "Bring it on, then," Asa said. Though sweat was pouring off him, he didn't sound the slightest bit nervous, and it reminded me of how he'd calmly taken down that gun-toting mercenary in Atlanta, and then felled Jack, the conduit who wanted to arrest him, a few minutes later. The memory calmed my fear as the agents came closer. None of them had pulled a gun or Taser, which seemed like a good sign.

As one fished two pairs of handcuffs from his jacket pocket, Asa struck. He pushed a button at the end of his baton and swung it, even though he was still ten feet away from the oncoming agents. Oily liquid arced from the length of the weapon and splattered our assailants. Several of them screamed and fell backward, clawing at their eyes. Asa whirled and did it again to the agents who were blocking the door we'd just come through, downing all but two.

"Run," Asa shouted to me as he slammed the baton into one agent's legs. "Myron, get her away from here!"

Myron aimed his Taser and hit the remaining agent, and the woman went stiff and fell forward. Then he yanked the barbs from her chest and murmured something in her ear before sprinting toward me. Asa was locked in battle with an agent who had also drawn a baton, a guy who wouldn't go down even though his face was ashen with pain from the Strikon juice Asa had splashed on everyone. Myron's hand closed around my arm just as I watched one of the fallen agents rise to her feet and draw what looked like a small rifle from inside her long coat.

"Asa, she's got a gun!" I screamed. I ran forward, raising my own little squirt pistol, only to be yanked backward by Myron. The tiny weapon clattered to the concrete as he hauled me away while Asa struggled with the guy with the baton.

I watched, helpless, as the female agent pulled the trigger. Asa flinched and staggered. I shrieked with fear as Myron threw his arm around my middle and dragged me backward, my heels skimming the ground, tearing the shoes from my feet. Instead of falling, Asa merely braced his palms on his knees while the man he'd been fighting with stepped back. And as Asa hung his head, I could see the small dart that had embedded itself in his shoulder.

"Mattie," he said in a ragged voice, taking a few faltering steps toward me.

"Let me go," I screamed at Myron as the female agent took aim at Asa once more.

"I can get you out," the Knedas said.

"No! We're not leaving him."

Asa straightened just as the dart gun sounded off with three more sharp clicks. He flinched again, and the baton dropped from his limp hand. As Myron kicked a half-blinded agent away from us and wrenched the door to the stairwell open, Asa raised his head and his eyes found mine. He gave me this dopey, sweet smile as he sank to his knees, and the two agents closed in. I fought against Myron with everything I had, clawing at him as my ears filled with an insistent thumping. A bright light and swirling wind drew my gaze to a helicopter that was dropping steadily from the sky as the two agents dragged Asa, unresisting, out of the way.

"We have to go, Mattie! He wanted you to get out!" Myron pulled me through the doorway and let it slam behind us. "There's nothing you can do right now. There is *nothing* you can do! Stop fighting me!"

He was right. There was nothing I could do. Mutely, tears running down my face, I let Myron pull me down the stairs and back into the store, then down the two escalators and out the front. My bare feet slapped against the smooth floors, and my heart skittered and tapped with a new, broken rhythm. We burst back into the cold and stopped on the sidewalk as the helicopter roared over our heads and soared into the night. "Asa!" I screamed.

"I'm so sorry, Mattie. I'm so sorry," Myron said between breaths, his arm still around me even though his grip had loosened. "I'm so very sorry."

"Who were they?" I demanded, pulling away from his touch as I realized he had used his magic on me to get me down the stairs.

"I don't know." He leaned against a store window, his lean silhouette framed by flashing Christmas lights. "But we'll find out."

"How could you let this happen?" My voice cracked over my rage and fear, even as my body buzzed with numb disbelief. A few minutes ago, we'd been fine. We'd been together. And now, in the space of a few moments, Asa had been taken. He was *gone*.

"How could you let this happen?" I roared, stumbling forward and slamming my palms into Myron's chest before staggering back. My legs gave out, and I plopped to the sidewalk in an awkward sprawl, drawing concerned looks from a few pedestrians, who crossed the street to avoid us. Sobs rolled out of me as I braced my palms on the cold ground.

"We should really get off the street," Myron said quietly. "This isn't safe. Just because they have him doesn't mean they won't come for you. Especially because you're carrying—"

"I know." I had no idea what to do. I was so used to Asa being my backup, my safety net. And he. Was. Gone. "I know," I whispered.

"Mattie, let me get you to safety. It's clearly what Asa wanted. He sacrificed himself so you could—"

"Shut up," I said, tears streaking down my cheeks. "You stopped me from helping him."

"He told me to get you out!"

"Of *course* he did," I shouted hoarsely. "That didn't mean you had to listen! He's not a stupid Knedas like you are. He's just . . . he's just . . ." I bowed my head as my chest heaved with sorrow.

"Can you walk?" Myron asked gently. When I didn't answer, he slid his arms beneath mine and lifted me from the ground.

I wrenched myself away from him and bounced off another festively lit window. "Keep your hands off me," I snarled. "And while you're at it, keep your stupid magic vibes off me, too."

He let out an impatient sigh. "This way. We'll take the tube. You can't go back to your hotel. I'm sure it's being watched."

I glared at him, even as indecision bled through me. "And where exactly do you want to take me?"

"My employer has several guesthouses for visiting dealers, conduits, and reliquaries. Security is good. I'm taking you to one in Kensington."

"What if I want to leave?"

"Once the magic is off-loaded, I'm sure you'll be free to go."

What choice did I have? I had no doubt Myron could physically overpower me, and I needed my energy to figure out what I was going to do—and how I was going to get Asa back. "Fine. Lead the way." I clamped my eyes shut for a moment as fear for Asa crashed over me. He'd looked so helpless, on his knees, clearly hit with either Ekstazo magic or some kind of tranquilizer, enough to make him vulnerable. Whoever had taken him hadn't wanted to hurt him—they'd wanted to *have* him.

I pressed the back of my hand over my mouth against a wave of nausea as I followed Myron up the sidewalk. He'd replaced the cartridge on his Taser before tucking it back in his jacket. He kept his hand on it, though, as he scanned the street. We passed a few groups of revelers and last-minute shoppers, but stores were closing and the streets were emptying out. I barely noticed signs or landmarks as we walked—I was caught in my own head, still reeling. Every minute that passed was another minute they could take Asa away from himself, steal everything he'd worked so hard to be.

We headed into the Knightsbridge tube station as Myron made a few phone calls to let his colleagues know what had happened. He told them he had the magic, which was what the people on the other end seemed to care most about. Myron sounded weary and terse as he answered their rapid-fire questions, and then hung up and stuffed the phone back in his pocket. "They'll be waiting for you at the safe house," he said as he swiped a blue card twice through the slot, allowing us both to pass through to the platform.

"Yay," I muttered. "When are we going to do the transaction?"

"The arrangements are being made."

"Wait," I said slowly. "We were going to meet the conduit tonight. Where was she?"

"I am trying to figure that out," said Myron. "It could be she was in on it, or it could be they nabbed her and pumped her for information. We'll find her, if she can be found."

Another swoop of nausea made me shudder. "I need to know who took Asa."

"I swear I'll do my best, Mattie. I feel responsible."

"Because you are," I grumbled as two men and a woman staggered onto the platform, giggling and smelling heavily of booze. One of them, a slim guy wearing a snug trench coat over faded jeans, had his head down, his dark hair hanging over his brow. The other two, a man with a wide, soft mouth, and a young woman with her hair pinned up into a funky swirl on top of her head, held him between them.

Myron and I stepped to the side as they wove their way toward us and stopped, standing close to us even though there was no one else on the platform. Myron slipped his hand inside his jacket.

"Eh," said the man with the soft mouth, which had taken on a decidedly sharp curve. "Pull that out and you won't live through the next few minutes." He had a barely-there accent that I couldn't place.

I glanced down at his waist—his jacket had gaped to reveal a large knife strapped against his torso. "Let me guess. You want our wallets."

The man between them raised his head, and I gasped. It was the guy I'd seen in Prague, the one who had chased me up the street. "No, Mattie," he said, his Russian accent thick. "We want you."

Myron's hand jerked toward his Taser, but the Russian's friends both drew weapons—hers was a gun. He sighed and raised his hands in the air. "Botwright will come after you. This is her territory."

"Let her," said the Russian. "Volodya would love to punish her for stealing his property. Now leave."

Myron's eyes narrowed as a train came whooshing into the station, and the agents concealed their weapons. "I can't just let her go."

"You can if you don't want me to shoot you," said the woman, tracing her eyes up his body. "And you don't look like you have a death wish. Tell your boss we let you live to deliver the message. She won't punish you."

Myron muttered something about how she didn't know Botwright.

"Myron," I said, looking back and forth between the Russian and the Brit. "Please."

Myron put up his hands again as the doors opened, and the Russian grabbed my arm and jerked me aboard. "This isn't over," Myron said in a loud voice.

"Myron," I shouted before the Russian clamped his hand over my mouth. As the doors closed, I began to struggle, but then he leaned down and spoke quietly in my ear as the train jerked into motion, carrying us into a dark tunnel. I could feel his belt buckle digging into my back. His breath smelled of vodka.

"You should really save your energy. You have a long journey ahead of you."

His words had no effect, so I could tell he wasn't Knedas. But still hope spiked inside me. Were these the people who had taken Asa? I relaxed and nodded, and the Russian took his hand from my mouth.

"My name is Pavel," he said.

I looked back to see him smiling at me. "And you work for Volodya."

"He is very angry that you and Asa Ward stole his relic." He winced. "*Very* angry," he muttered as the other two hunched their shoulders and cringed like dogs afraid of being kicked.

Dread nearly pulled me to the floor. Still, my thoughts weren't on the danger to me. "Where did you guys take Asa?"

Pavel tilted his head, sheer calculation glinting in his eyes. "The same place we're taking you. Your cooperation could ensure his safety, or at least his survival."

My heart sped. "Okay. Then where are we going?"

"To Russia, of course." Pavel's lip curled as he looked me up and down. "I hope you can take the cold."

CHAPTER SIX

Once we got off the tube, Pavel and his friends bundled me into a car that headed straight for a private landing strip, where a plane was waiting. Looking feral and nervous, maybe afraid yet another boss's crew would try to poach their prize, the trio surrounded me as we marched across the tarmac and climbed aboard. Pavel was on his phone half the time, speaking stridently to whoever was on the other end of the line. But after listening to all of them talk for a few hours, I realized maybe that was just the way Russian sounded. Aggressive and rough, like a punch in the jaw.

I buckled into my seat and focused on breathing.

Volodya had caught us, just like he'd collared Asa's mother all those years ago, forcing her to help him hunt down relics all over the world. Arkady, Volodya's Knedas assassin who'd wreaked havoc in rural Virginia and nearly caused Ben to murder me, had told me as much. He'd made it sound romantic, as if Volodya had loved her, but I wondered if she'd been a prisoner all along. Looking around at the three agents who'd just captured me, I was guessing Volodya wasn't in the running for boss of the year, either—they seemed on edge at the mere thought of him. And Theresa had run from Volodya twice, after all. The first time, she'd fled back to the United States, where she'd married a childhood friend—Don Ward—and had the two boys. But then she'd left the day after Asa's fourth birthday, abandoning him to his father's brutal anger and turning up in Thailand with one of the original four relics.

I knew Asa's rage toward his mom covered a crushing heartbreak. We'd barely talked about it, but he'd said enough—she'd left him behind, knowing what he was, knowing what he would face. And what I couldn't figure out was why. Had she gotten bored in the confines of her hometown and taken off for greener pastures? Had she actually missed her old life?

Or had she been cornered? Had she run to escape a threat? If that were true, why had she voluntarily returned to Volodya's side? Whatever the reason, she'd escaped again fifteen years later. Disappeared into thin air. Arkady had told me she was probably dead.

Which meant Volodya was without a magic sensor. Until now.

Pavel and his friends slept in shifts, always leaving someone awake to watch me. Not that I was about to try anything at twenty thousand feet, especially when my cooperation might be the key to saving Asa's life. I stared out the window as the sky slowly brightened, as we soared east toward more danger and uncertainty than I'd ever faced before. I should have taken the time to sleep, but I was too lost in thoughts of what should have been. Asa and me together. I would have admitted how I'd fallen for him. I would have told him how much it scared me. I would have asked him what he wanted. I would have offered him anything, as long as he stayed. After months of circling, I was ready to risk my heart, and crazily, it had actually seemed like Asa might have been willing to do the same. Or that maybe he already had.

Instead, Volodya had taken him from me. I couldn't get that dopey smile of his out of my head. Asa had never looked like that before, spaced out and vulnerable. It made my eyes burn.

By the time we landed—at an airport that looked more like a military base, all gray and grim, the runway streaked with blowing snow—my body was numb with exhaustion, and my thoughts were fluttering and spinning like the icy flakes outside the window. The others were awake, grabbing their bags and stretching. They were on their home turf, but looked only slightly more relaxed.

"Where to now?" I asked.

"The boss is expecting you."

"When can I see Asa?"

Pavel grunted. "Volodya decides. We would not ever presume."

The woman, whose name was Elena, tossed me a coat that she'd pulled from one of the overhead compartments. "Cold," she said, jerking her head toward the window.

I slid my arms into the sleeves, grateful to have a shield against the frigid air as Pavel pushed open the door and lowered the stairs. A bitter, icy wind hit me like a slap, instantly turning the backs of my hands red and probably my nose and cheeks, too. I tugged up my hood and jogged after Pavel as he made for a waiting car, a boxy black vehicle with rugged tires. It was roomy inside, with two bench seats facing each other in the back. Elena and Pavel sat across from me while the other dude, whose name was Grigory, got in front with the driver.

Huddled in my too-big coat, I pressed my face to the window as we sped off the tarmac and onto a two-lane highway. "Scared?" asked Pavel.

Heck, yes. "Should I be?"

"I would be if I'd stolen from Volodya. And this relic?" He whistled and shook his head.

"It's not like it was his. You guys stole it from Garza." She was the boss of Spain, and Asa had told me her people would be on the hunt for it.

Pavel shook his head. "It belongs to whoever is strong enough to keep it. And Volodya has need of it."

"To do what?"

Grigory turned around. "This should be obvious."

His condescending sneer set me off. "Viagra isn't quite enough for Volodya these days?"

Grigory's eyes went round, and his voice trembled with outrage as he said, "You insult Volodya's manhood?"

"You told me to guess."

"Volodya is a great man," said Elena, her voice like a lash. "A great businessman as well."

"So his business is . . . oh. Ew," I said as I realized what kind of business the magic inside me could power.

"His brothels are the most exclusive in Moscow. One thing the men of this city will pour their money into," said Pavel, pushing his swath of dark hair off his forehead. "And this magic will help him crush his rivals."

My stomach swooped as I remembered how I'd felt in the moments after the magic had entered me—a hunger that could be sated only one way. I closed my eyes as I remembered how Asa had taken control. The way his stubble had scraped my inner thighs, the heat of his mouth, the force of his fingers as he wrenched me closer.

"Do you feel this magic inside you?" Pavel asked.

I opened my eyes to find him watching me with interest. "No." I rubbed my chest. "Not once it's in the vault."

"It won't be there much longer. Volodya will pull it out of you."

A chill zipped down my back that had nothing to do with the weather. Would it feel the same way it had going in? Would I be affected the same way? "I'm not letting it go until I know Asa is safe. Until I've seen him."

Pavel's eyes narrowed. "You will give Volodya this magic, Mattie. If you don't, he will punish you."

"He is very good at punishing," said Grigory from the front. His shoulders were tense, drawn up nearly to his ears.

I crossed my arms over my chest. As long as I had the magic inside me, I was valuable. I had some leverage. I just had to be strong enough to hold on to it.

Pavel leaned forward, his eyes intense on mine. "I'm going to be your conduit, you know."

I pressed back into my seat, recalling how I'd manhandled Erik in the moments after the transaction. Pavel must have seen the shadow of fear in my eyes, because he laughed. "I can't wait," he said, then jabbered in Russian to his two friends, who guffawed, the sound harsh and jarring.

We were passing signs of civilization now, heading toward the shadow of a large city within the swirling snow. Moscow. Up ahead was a bridge over a river that snaked like a white ribbon over the flat terrain. High-rise apartment buildings lined the bank on both sides. It seemed to be early in the morning, the sun barely peeking over the horizon. When I asked, Elena told me it was just after eight, and though it was still dim, the roads were pretty crowded, trucks rumbling by and motorcycles zipping past, including one weaving through traffic right next to us. We were in a sea of dingy sedans, all headed for the gray metropolis.

"Nobody celebrates Christmas here?"

Pavel rolled his eyes. "Today is not a public holiday."

Not that I was feeling very festive, but for some reason, that knowledge made me miss being home so much. I was without Asa, without my family, without any kind of safety net.

I was on my own. I sat up a little straighter in my seat. Asa was depending on me.

The driver, a guy with massive shoulders whose dark eyes periodically met mine in the rearview mirror, cursed and swerved as the motorcycle that had been weaving between cars suddenly slowed and veered toward us. Its rider, bundled in thick pants, a coat, and a black helmet, glanced over at us and made what appeared to be an okay sign.

In return, our driver shouted something and slammed his hand against the window.

Pavel turned around and shoved the guy in the shoulder, looking amused.

"Why is he so mad?" I asked. "The biker was just telling him things were okay."

"That is not what it means here," he said, making an okay sign himself. "He was calling Dmitri an asshole." He pointed at the circle made by his thumb and forefinger.

"Oh," I said. As we neared the river, the rider steered the bike directly in front of us, forcing Dmitri to slam on the brakes.

Pavel frowned and squinted through the windshield at the biker, speaking rapidly in Russian to Grigory. Grigory shook his head. Then he turned to me. "You recognize him?"

"What? No." I peered at the rider as well. "Why?"

"Dmitri just told me the guy's been following us for miles."

The enemy of my enemy *might* be my friend . . . except my enemy had captured Asa, and I might have the key to saving him, or at least locating him and seeing if he was all right. "And you have no idea who he is?"

"Could be anyone," Elena muttered, craning her neck to watch the motorcycle just ahead of us. The driver kept looking over his shoulder at us. "Volodya has many enemies." She lifted her chin and gave me a defiant look. "Though none brave enough to challenge him face-to-face." She reached into her jacket and drew her handgun. "Maybe I have the honor of taking care of this one for him."

Pavel barked at her in Russian and pushed her arm down as a blue-and-white police car bustled by, its high-pitched siren wailing. She grumbled something back as the police car edged by other slow-moving cars crossing the bridge. Traffic was almost at a standstill—we were creeping along now, and Dmitri was keeping us within inches of the motorcycle's back wheel like he was trying to intimidate the driver. Then traffic stopped suddenly, and he bumped right into the guy.

With a resounding boom the motorcycle exploded, shattering our windshield and sending flames shooting into the front seat. I screamed and threw my hands in front of my face as Pavel and Elena both lunged away from the heat, landing on either side of me. Dmitri cranked the wheel, and the engine roared. Elena shrieked with fear. We shot forward—and burst right through the guardrail on the side of the bridge.

For a moment, everything was suspended in air, the shattered glass, my curly hair around my face, a few snowflakes that had somehow crept in despite the flames. My world pitched and spun, and I caught the briefest glimpse of dirty snow before we slammed through the ice covering the river. My seat belt caught me painfully across the chest, and my arms dangled as the car rolled onto its roof and began to fill with black water. All around us, slabs of ice bounced and scraped against the car. Pavel shouted something to the others, but there was no answer. He yanked on my seat belt, but it wouldn't come undone. He slammed his feet against the door, but it wouldn't open. His expression was desperate, twisted with terror as river water flooded the roof.

Hanging from my seat belt, all I could do was bow my head and try to stay above the freezing water gushing in all around me. But then it was soaking my hair, filling my ears, splashing into my nose. I wailed, panic stealing all my words, and took a huge breath just before the water covered my face. Immersed in the black and the cold, I clamped my eyes shut and clawed at my seat belt latch. My skull buzzed from the lack of oxygen, and my chest burned.

My lungs were straining. I had a minute at most. I would never be able to save Asa, because I couldn't even save myself. I was too weak to do anything but drown—and pray for help I knew would never come.

Except it did. Hands grabbed my shoulders, and I felt the seat belt give. I was pulled, gasping, up and out of the water, then I landed on a hard surface. Blinking with shock and cold and complete confusion, I looked up to see my own chalky, pale face reflected in the motorcyclist's visor. Then I glanced down at my own body. I was completely dry.

We were back on the bridge. No . . . we had never left it. The car was pulled over to the side of the road, one wheel up on the curb, with Dmitri, Grigory, Pavel, and Elena still inside. None of the windows were shattered. There were no signs of a fire. But Dmitri and Grigory were both slumped over and twitching, Elena appeared unconscious or dead, and Pavel was hammering on the window with pure horror twisting his face. In reality he was staring right into the startled faces of passing drivers, but now I realized all he saw was black water and his own impending doom, just like I had.

"A glamour," I whispered as the motorcyclist hauled me up and dragged me toward the motorcycle—which was not damaged at all. "The tire was a relic?"

"Move your feet," the motorcyclist snapped, which was when I realized he was a she. "It'll wear off as soon as we drive away, but we'll draw too much attention if we stay." She pointed to her bike. "Get on. Now."

I was too stunned to disobey. I wrapped my arms around her lean waist as people around us who had pulled over continued to gape at the occupants of the black sedan. A few Good Samaritans were knocking on the windows, trying to open the locked doors. At least one guy was barking urgently into a cell phone. My rescuer—or kidnapper—revved the engine, and we barreled forward. She wove through the tightly packed traffic, ignoring the shouts and honks of the drivers around her, finally mounting the curb to race along the sidewalk, causing pedestrians to jump out of her way. We flew along at dizzying speed until she hooked a sharp left off the highway and raced along a narrow road. Up ahead loomed a cathedral, gold domes and spires piercing the sky. As we approached a courtyard, with a nonplussed priest looking on, the cyclist veered into it and roared into a small shack. She hit a button on her handlebar, and the door closed behind us. Then she yanked a string that lit a bare lightbulb above our heads.

"Get off," she said sharply.

I tried but stumbled, and she caught me as she dismounted.

She pulled her helmet off, and my stomach dropped. Her face was shining with sweat, and her eyes . . .

"Theresa," I whispered.

Her honey-brown eyes narrowed, and she reached abruptly through the opening in my coat, pulling out the thin chain and the vial of sand from beneath my shirt. "I don't know who the hell you are," she said, then let the vial drop, where it dangled between my breasts. "But unless you want to drown again, for real this time, you'd better tell me why you're wearing my son's magic around your neck."

CHAPTER SEVEN

I looked down at the sand vial. "Magic?"

"That thing is dripping with it."

I held it up to the light. "*Asa's* magic?" I squeezed the vial in my palm, fighting tears. He'd said he wanted me to have a piece of my home.

"Who is he to you?" Her long dark-brown hair, shot through with gray, was pulled back in a ponytail, with a few sweaty tendrils framing her narrow face. "Did you take it from him?"

"He gave it to me," I said hoarsely.

She looked me up and down. "And you're a reliquary."

My hand rose to my chest. "How did you—"

"You just rode for several miles pressed up against my back. I can feel it inside you." She rolled her shoulders and winced. "That's powerful stuff. No wonder Volodya wants it." A shudder vibrated through her. "And oh, the damage he will do when he has it."

I leaned back against the wall, still stunned by the whirlwind of the last half hour. "Can we rewind for a minute? You're supposed to be dead."

"I am dead."

"Okay." I closed my eyes and took a slow breath. "What is your corpse doing riding around Moscow on a relic-laden motorcycle, then?"

She grunted. It might have been a laugh. Hard to tell. "Not planning on staying. I'd heard Asa had stolen Volodya's property. This is a dangerous game. One no one should play." She swiped her sleeve across her face. "Believe me—even when you win, you lose. I couldn't just sit back and do nothing."

My fingers clenched tightly around the vial of sand—and Asa's sensing magic. "You couldn't just sit back," I said slowly. "Like you sat back for Asa's entire childhood?"

"Don't talk about what you don't understand."

Anger wrenched me out of my confusion. "It would be convenient if I would shut up, wouldn't it? But I've spent months with Asa. I think I know him better than just about anyone." I leaned forward so suddenly that Theresa stiffened. "You scarred him, lady. It's a miracle he survived and became the man he is. But he carries all that pain with him, all the time. It's a wound that can never heal, not really. And it's your fault."

Her eyes were shining, maybe with sorrow, maybe with hatred. "I did what I had to do, and I don't need some little girl explaining my son to me."

"Your *son*. I wonder what Asa would say if he heard you call him that."

The slap came so fast that I didn't realize what had happened until my head snapped to the side and heat radiated across my cheek. When I looked up, her face was close to mine, glistening under the harsh light of the bulb. "You don't have children, do you?" she said in a low voice.

I glared at her.

"I didn't think so. Talk to me when you do. Tell me what it's like to love them more than your own life. Tell me what you would do if you knew something truly evil was coming for them." She laid her palm on the wall next to my head. "And then tell me how it would feel to know that the only thing you can do to save them . . . is to leave them. To walk back into the jaws of the monster." The corner of her eye twitched. "To let him eat you alive."

She shoved off the wall and turned back to her bike. "Arkady and Lishka were on my trail. It was only a matter of time before they found me. Do you know of these two?"

She looked over her shoulder, and I nodded. "Lishka's dead, but I met Arkady this past spring."

Her lip curled. "He's a total piece of shit."

"No argument there."

Her face fell. "Do you know the joy he would have taken in torturing my family, just to punish me?"

I sagged a little. "I could make a pretty good guess." Arkady had taken exquisite pleasure in causing other people to hurt themselves, even to kill themselves. "So you ran because you wanted to protect them?"

"As soon as I got word from an old contact that they were sniffing around, I knew my time had run out. And I also knew I had to go back with something big enough to make up for being gone. To keep them from questioning where I'd been and who I'd been with."

"So you stole the original Sensilo relic from Montri." Arkady had said she had popped up in Thailand.

"I'd sensed it on a collecting trip I'd taken with Volodya years earlier. I knew he wanted it." Her mouth grew tight. "I thought he might set me free if I gave it to him."

Realization struck. "You wanted to go back to your family."

Her eyes met mine as she turned to face me. "I had to try. And obviously I failed. Even with that, I had hoped the relic would keep Volodya satisfied for a little while, that it would sate his desire for . . ." She swallowed. "I was wrong."

"But you did get free eventually. You asked my grandpa to help you."

"You're Howard Carver's—"

"Granddaughter."

"Explains why you have to be so close for me to sense what's inside. He was a good man, and a great reliquary."

"He died as a result of that magic, you know," I said, my throat getting tight.

She looked away. "Volodya was never going to let me go, and if he had caught me again, he'd have welcomed me back only to torture me. I had to hide. I had to convince him I was dead. If I had gone back to Illinois, if I had reached out to anyone . . ."

"I get that. But look at you now. You're here in Moscow! There was not one time in the last fifteen years that you could have reached out to your sons?" Knowing Asa, he might have pushed her away, but that didn't mean it wouldn't have touched him. "You're saying you sacrificed your life with them to save them from Arkady and the rest of Volodya's thugs. But Asa grew up with no one having his back, no one to fight for him."

It was why Gracie meant so much to him. It was also, I suspected, why he'd opened himself up to me in the little ways he had. I'd shown that I was willing to fight for him, too. And I was fighting for him now. "If you had just let him know why you left," I said to her, "he would have known he mattered to you. Instead, he grew up believing he mattered to *no one*."

Theresa waved me off. "It's in the past."

"Seriously? You've been free for all these years and you didn't reach out to him because it was *in the past*?"

"I never said I didn't reach out to him."

"Don't give me that crap. Asa would have told me if you had. He was stunned a few months ago when he found out you'd once been with Volodya. He has no idea you're still alive."

"I never said I made contact. But I know enough to understand he's doing just fine."

"Volodya has him," I snapped.

She tilted her head. "What?"

"His people ambushed us in London. They downed Asa with Ekstazo. Or maybe tranquilizers—I don't know. But they loaded him onto a helicopter and took off. They grabbed me only an hour later. They said that if I give Volodya this magic, it might save Asa."

Theresa watched me, looking troubled. "Do you know where Volodya is keeping him?"

"I didn't get a chance to find out. They were taking me to meet with Volodya when you . . . did whatever you did."

"I had no idea this had happened. I just came back from Prague—"

"Wait. You were the sensor in the square that night."

"He felt me?" she asked quietly.

"He said the magic was familiar." I sighed. "He couldn't quite place it, though."

She bowed her head. "He didn't recognize me."

"He hasn't seen you since he was four."

She ran her hand over the top of her helmet, examining her reflection in its shiny black surface. "And if he's anything like his father, he never forgets when someone's hurt him."

From what I knew of Asa and Ben's dad, that was definitely true. "So basically, you were afraid he'd reject you, and so you let him believe—*for his whole life*—that you rejected him. You might have made some selfless decisions, but you seem to think it entitles you to a heck of a lot of selfishness. Or maybe you're just a coward."

For a minute, it looked like she wanted to slap me again, and I braced myself to fight back. But then she plopped down on her motorcycle, looking defeated. "If Volodya has him, his *whole life* is over. He will never be whole again." Never had I heard anyone sound quite so haunted. But then she straightened. "We have to get him out of there."

"We?"

She nodded. "But you will have to do whatever I say. No questions."

That sounded familiar. "I guess being a bossypants runs in the family."

"I know the inside of Volodya's stronghold like the back of my hand," she said. "I know him. I know many of his people, even if they don't know me. And I know his powers. I know how he thinks. You will never succeed unless you let me guide you."

"Depends on what you expect me to do. I don't exactly trust you yet."

"You have no choice."

I rolled my eyes. "I have some skills of my own."

"And you truly expect to simply appear before Volodya and demand that he release a man who has stolen the key to financing his entire empire? A man who has skills he can use? A man who is—" She clamped her lips closed and shook her head. "The moment you make your presence known, Volodya will have you laid on a table, and he will pull this magic right out of you. And the more you suffer, the more pleasure it will give him."

"I'm a vault. He can't just take the magic from me. And I can take pain."

Her eyes met mine. "He won't need to cause you physical pain if Arkady is by his side."

"I think Arkady might be out of commission. Asa kind of ran over him."

Theresa snorted. "Serves him right. But even if Arkady is not here in Russia, he left plenty of his magic behind for his master to use. And use it he does. Use it he *will*."

My stomach roiled as I thought about being under the influence of Arkady's magic again. Unless I was in agony, there was no way I could withstand it. "I'll give this magic to him voluntarily. *After* he takes me to Asa."

Theresa's laugh was as dry and dark as her son's. "Aren't you adorable. You will have no leverage once you are in Volodya's web. He will see how desperate you are. He'll know you will do anything." She lifted up her helmet and aimed it at me so my pale face was visible in its surface. "Do you see yourself? Your feelings for my son bleed from you, and I'm not even an emotion sensor. But Volodya is. As soon as you enter his lair, he'll know your weakness. And he'll exploit it without mercy."

"What do you want me to do, then?" I asked, looking away from the fear I saw reflected in my eyes.

"You will go to him without the magic," she replied. "You will tell him it is in a safe place, but that it will be destroyed if he does not meet your demands."

"That does sound kind of clever. But Arkady said that Volodya can easily tell if someone is lying to him."

Theresa smiled. "First, you won't be lying." She arched one eyebrow. "And second, I'm going to teach you how to hide your feelings from Volodya."

It turned out eye color, magical ability, and bossiness weren't the only qualities that Asa and Theresa had in common. Paranoia and craftiness were also part of the package.

As soon as I accepted her offer of help, she opened a small trapdoor in the floor and climbed down a set of rebar rungs set into a narrow concrete tunnel. "Come on," she called. "Get moving. And pull the door closed above you!"

I twisted my hair into a knot to try to tame it, then followed her into the hole. As I slowly descended, I glanced down to see a lit space below me, where Theresa stood, fidgeting. When I reached her, she said, "The priests know the evil that is Volodya. They hide me whenever I return here. No one in this city has better information, either."

She strode along a dimly lit tunnel. I shivered as I tromped after her, my exhaustion starting to fray me at the edges. The only thing holding me together was the knowledge that every step I took brought me closer to getting Asa back.

After several minutes, we entered a small room lined with wooden shelves on three walls. The fourth was marked by a ladder leading to another vertical tunnel back to the surface. The shelves were packed with all sorts of jars and small vials of clear liquid or white powder, all of which I assumed was magic in different forms. Also on the shelves lay several knives, a few coils of rope, a stack of folded clothes, a pile of wigs, a row of metal cubes about three inches on a side, an open box of gaudy jewelry and another of makeup, and a chipped mirror.

Theresa marched up to the shelves, pulled out a pair of leather gloves from the pocket of her padded motorcycle jacket, and slid them on. When she brought the gloves out, I realized the inside of her coat was lined with a gray metallic material like the kind Asa used to package his relics. "Is that lead?" I asked.

She nodded as she flexed her fingers. "Makes it almost impossible for anyone with a sensing relic to detect me unless I'm literally on top of them."

I glanced at her pants. They were thick, probably lined with the same material. "Isn't it heavy?" Together, the jacket and pants had to weigh nearly fifty pounds, and though she was a few inches taller than I was, she was trim.

"I'm used to it," she said roughly. A drop of sweat fell from her chin and landed with a soft tap on her sleeve. She went to work, pocketing a few of the small vials, four of the cubes, and one of the knives. Then she pulled on a plastic swimming cap and donned a short wig of spiky blond hair.

"You really think that's going to keep someone from recognizing you?"

She shook her head. "*This* will keep people from recognizing me." She held up one of the cubes in her gloved hand.

"Another glamour?"

She grinned, clutched the cube firmly, and then transformed into a hunchbacked old man. I gasped and pinched my arm, but the image didn't waver. "The great thing about this one," the old man said in Theresa's voice, "is that people won't see *you* at all, as long as you stay within six feet of me." The dude put the cube in his ratty old cardigan pocket and promptly turned back into Theresa.

"What's with the wig, then?" I asked.

"For the few who can see through glamours. I'm just some dude in a motorcycle suit." She put on a pair of mirrored aviator glasses. "It would give me at least a few extra seconds if I'm made."

"Fair enough," I muttered, wondering what would happen to me in that situation. "Where are we going?"

"To a place Volodya will never look. This way." And with that, she climbed up the ladder.

I eyed the shelves of magic, briefly considering pocketing something before remembering that Theresa would sense immediately that I had it. Grumbling, I followed her upward, my limbs aching. I emerged behind a large shrub next to a sleek little red car. Theresa was already behind the wheel, her fingers drumming on the dash. As soon as I hopped in, she started it up and was off, hunched low, jaw tight. We passed through tree-lined neighborhoods with large, stately houses, then got on a highway headed away from the city center. Theresa drove quickly, weaving in and out of the traffic like a pro until she turned off into a decidedly low-rent area, where stark multistory buildings loomed along the streets. The people on the sidewalks eyed her with wary curiosity as Theresa pulled into a spot along the street and set one of the cubes on the dash.

"Let me guess—people just see an old junker," I said as we got out.

"You're smarter than you look."

I gritted my teeth. "You're so kind."

She marched toward one of the grim buildings. "Remember—stay close."

Because apparently I was invisible if I did. And as we walked through the doors of the building and into a depressing lobby with a flickering fluorescent and garbage piled in the corners, I could see that she was right. The few folks we passed looked right through me.

Theresa slipped her hand into her pocket as we hiked up several flights of stairs, passing scruffy-looking residents on the way, most of whom smelled of stale cigarette smoke, old sweat, and booze. When we reached the floor she wanted, she peeked through the door and scanned the hallway, then motioned for me to follow. Once I was through, she pulled out yet another cube.

"What does that one make people see?"

"It doesn't." She reached a door and knocked, then set the cube next to the threshold. "It senses."

"But you can already sense any natural nearby, can't you?"

"It doesn't sense magic. It senses intentions."

I was staring down at the cube when the door opened to reveal a busty middle-aged woman in a stained housecoat, with a scarf wrapped around her head, which was covered in tiny curlers. Her penciled-on ebony eyebrows rose to the middle of her forehead when she saw the bewigged Theresa standing before her, and her brown-eyed gaze darted to me immediately after. She began to jabber at Theresa in Russian, waving her arms and backing into her apartment.

Theresa peeled off her glasses and strode confidently into the room. She pulled one of the vials full of white powder from her pocket and dangled it from her fingers, shaking it gently. The woman's demeanor changed instantly. Her tense expression relaxed into a wide grin that revealed her yellow teeth, and she beckoned us past a sloppy bedroom and into another room the size of a closet, in which there were two chairs.

"Ludmilla's a conduit," said Theresa. "She used to whore for Volodya, who also used her for a lot of his transactions. But she developed a little addiction and got desperate. He caught her stealing and tossed her out."

I glanced at the vial of powder between Theresa's gloved fingers. "But I thought conduits were only affected by magic during a transaction?"

She gave me a hard look. "It's not magic. It's heroin."

"We're handing out deadly drugs to junkies?"

"We're doing whatever we have to. Take a seat."

Ludmilla was staring greedily at the vial, practically salivating. I couldn't help but think Asa would be disgusted by this. But it wasn't like I was about to walk away and leave him to his fate.

I sat next to Ludmilla. Theresa produced a fourth cube, one identical to the three she'd pulled out before. "And what's that one?"

"The relic, of course. It's strong enough to hold what you've got in there."

I shifted on my seat, once again feeling the terrible ache of missing Asa, so much so that tears pricked my eyes. Here I was: squalid Russian housing project, drug-addicted conduit, and his bewigged mother, who was turning out to be one of the hardest people I'd ever met. I stared at my lap as Theresa handed the cube to Ludmilla and gave her instructions in what sounded like perfect Russian. My clammy palms slid along my thighs. I tried to coach myself—this time would be different, and I wouldn't react to this magic like I had before. It's not like there were any guys around anyway. This would be fine.

Theresa looked down at me. "Do your thing whenever you're ready." She leaned against the wall and folded her arms.

It was so *not Asa* that my heart squeezed. He always knew what I needed. He always cared enough to give it to me. I let out a shaky breath. And now I would do what he needed. I reached out and took Ludmilla's moist hand.

Then I let the magic go. The desire flooded my body, making my chest heave and my nipples harden. Ludmilla's hand tightened in mine and she moaned. Asa's face hovered in my mind, the shadowed sight of him looking up at me as he knelt before me, my leg draped over his shoulder, his mouth hot against my tender skin. My head fell back as the fantasy grabbed hold, as it awakened every inch of my exhausted body.

A sharp poke in the arm brought me to the surface. I raised my head and looked around. Ludmilla was gone. Theresa stood in the doorway. Her honey-brown eyes were cold. "Do whatever you need to do. You have five minutes."

I swallowed, my cheeks burning. "I—"

She held up her hand. "You were just moaning his name. I don't need you to tell me any more than that."

"Oh," I said, my voice cracking.

"Five minutes," she repeated, slightly more gently. Then her tone turned flinty again. "But when you're through, you will walk out of this room and harden the hell up. You understand me?"

"Wait a second. Just because I was affected by the magic—"

"That's not what I'm talking about. You're all weepy and whiny and pathetic and wounded, and that's the last thing my son needs." Her nostrils flared, and she leaned forward. "He needs you to be hard. He needs you to be merciless. He needs you focused, strong, clever, and as tightly closed off as that vault you carry inside you. Do you *understand* me?"

"Yeah," I whispered, hastily swiping at a tear on my cheek.

"Good." She looked down at her watch. "Five minutes." The door slammed, leaving me alone in the tiny room, inhaling the scent of Ludmilla—cloying perfume mixed with the funk of boiled potatoes. I leaned my head back against the wall and closed my eyes, once more aware of the throbbing low in my belly. Asa's face rose in my mind again, and his body, hard and ready. This fantasy wasn't a memory, but a wish. His hands closed around my wrists and pinned them to the bed, and I felt his weight on me, his heat inside me. He gave me his razor-edged smile, one that made my entire self cry out for him.

My fingers sank between my legs as I felt him start to move.

CHAPTER EIGHT

I sat at the wooden table, staring at the metal cube in the center. My head was caught in a vise of pain, and my mouth was a desert. I had been awake for well over twenty-four hours. We were in yet another hiding spot of Theresa's, this one a drab apartment about twenty miles outside the city.

"I need to sleep," I said, rubbing at my eyes.

"Then this is the perfect time to work. If you can do this when you're completely thrashed, you'll be able to do it anytime. And that's exactly what you need."

"Shouldn't we start easy and work our way up?"

"Do you think Asa has time for that?"

I rested my face in my hands. She was relentless. "Go ahead, then."

"Think of him."

His crooked face, his wicked grin rose up, and my chest throbbed.

I heard the crack as the pain raced up my arm, delivered by the thin whip that she'd been carrying coiled around her wrist. When I whimpered, she leaned into my line of sight. "Stop being pathetic."

"I didn't say anything!"

She pointed at the cube in the middle of the table. "Emotion sensing. And not nearly as sensitive as Volodya."

"You didn't even tell me what to do," I said, my voice rising.

"I wanted to see if you had even the slightest ability to manage this on your own." I'd clearly failed. "Now. Why do you want to save Asa?"

Before I had the chance to open my mouth to answer, she'd cracked me across the forearm again. Two red welts stood out sharp on my freckled skin. "Cut it out!"

"No, Mattie. *You* cut it out. Volodya is a man who has no respect for life, no respect for love, no respect for anything except strength. And you're weak." She snapped the whip across my arm again.

"Ow!" I drew my arm against my chest.

She laughed, all bitterness. "Why do you want to trade this magic for Asa's freedom?"

"Because he won't survive if he's in a cage."

Crack! "Try again."

"Because I want him back!" *I need him.*

Crack! This time the whip landed across my shoulder blades, the pain barely muted even though I was clothed. I cried out and arched my back, as if that would protect me. "Stop it!"

"Apparently you need some motivation other than Asa's safety."

"What the *hell*, lady?"

Her sweat-sheened face was right in front of mine. "He's gone now. He can't help you."

"As if I needed that reminder."

She whipped me again, this time across my ribs, and I screamed. "Weak," she snarled. "You're sniveling with your desperation to get him back. If Volodya senses that, you will not walk away alive."

"Stop telling me what I'm doing wrong, and tell me what to do," I shouted.

"Stop loving him," she yelled. She jabbed her finger at my chest. "Take whatever feelings you have for him and stomp them into nothing. Forget his face. Forget the sound of his voice. Remember only that you have a mission to complete."

I hunched forward. "I can try. But . . ." My feelings for Asa had deep roots. They were wrapped around my heart like ivy. Tearing them loose would make me bleed. "It doesn't really work like that for me. I'm not a 'shut it down' kind of person."

My head jerked up at a motion in my periphery—Theresa had drawn back to whip me again. Fury driving me, I lunged forward and grabbed the cube on the table, then held it pressed tight to my chest. I wasn't completely sure how to harness the power inside relics, but I'd had some hands-on experience with the original Sensilo relic. Before Theresa could stop me, I focused on her, bolting up from my seat as my chair crashed to the floor behind me. "When Asa was small, he had nightmares," I snapped. "He was feeling magic around him, but he didn't know what it was. You know what he told me he needed from you?"

"We're not talking about me—"

"He wanted you to tell him it was okay," I said, protectiveness welling up as I remembered his pain, how alone he'd felt. "That was all that little boy wanted. For his mom to tell him it was okay."

Theresa's sorrow and regret swelled against me, pushing like a hand against my breastbone. Theresa grimaced and folded her arms over her chest. I gave her a tight smile. "Not so easy when it comes to love, is it?"

"Not when you're not ready for it," she admitted, then sniffled and looked away. "I *couldn't* tell him it was okay. I wouldn't lie to him." Her intense sadness fluttered against my body through the relic, allowing me to sense it but not absorb it.

"He knows that, Theresa. It's never been okay for him." I was surprised at how calm I sounded.

She tilted her head. "What's happening inside you right now?"

I looked down at my own hands, clutching the emotion-sensing relic as her grief subsided. "I don't know. I guess I just . . . I want to shield him. Protect him. He'd do the same for me if he were here."

She held out her hand and wiggled her gloved fingers impatiently. After a moment of hesitation, I placed the cube on her palm. Her eyes met mine. "That's something we can work with," she said softly. Her fingers closed hard around the cube. "Now—do it again."

I jolted awake to a sound so wretched that it made me tremble. My chest heaving, I slid out of the musty bed but kept the thin blanket wrapped around me.

In the room down the hall, there was a muffled thump. "I'll do it," Theresa wailed. "I'll do it. I'll do it. Just please don't—" She screamed.

My heart hammering, I grabbed the only thing in the room that could be used as a weapon—a broom that had been left propped in the corner. With it clutched in my shaking hands, I peeked into the hallway. No lights were on, but there was enough light coming through the windows from the streetlamps that I could see.

"I'll do anything you want," she said, sobbing. "Anything you want. You know I love you. You *feel* it."

I crept down the hallway, listening for another person's voice but hearing only hers. When I reached her room, I poked my head around the corner. She was on her bed, writhing. She was all alone, and completely asleep.

"I'm sorry," she said in a broken voice. "I'll never do it again. But don't make me wear it. Please."

"Theresa?" I asked quietly.

She arched, and her face tilted toward the window. Her expression was so full of agony that I rushed forward. "Theresa! Wake up." I dropped the broom and shook her shoulder.

She wrenched away from me with another cry, and her foot jabbed me square in the chest. I stumbled backward until I hit the wall. I regained my balance to find Asa's mother crouching on her rumpled bed, panting and sweating like she'd just run a marathon, her brown eyes glittering with horror.

"You were having a nightmare," I said, my hands up to defend myself in case she attacked me.

She regarded me for several long seconds, and then fell forward onto her hands and knees, her head hanging. "Did I hurt you?"

"No. I'm fine. Are you okay?"

She shook her head. "I told you. If Volodya has you, you will never be whole again." She lowered her face to the sheets, gathering them around her head while her body heaved with silent sobs.

Hesitantly, I edged toward her. "You were dreaming about him?" Morbid curiosity trailed through my thoughts as I sat down on the end of her bed. "About how he hurt you."

"Every night," she mumbled, her shoulders shaking. "And every night he did the opposite, too." She drew her arms out from the sheets, and for the first time I saw the scars around her forearms and wrists, rows of silvery circles.

My stomach turned. "Arkady told me Volodya loved you." He'd made it sound as if the man had been broken when Theresa had left him. "I don't understand—"

She raised her head, the lines around her mouth and eyes deep. "This is how Volodya loves," she whispered, holding up her arms to give me a closer look. "He loves exquisitely, and completely, until he owns every drop of pleasure, every ounce of pain. He twists and kisses and hurts and heals until there is nothing you can hide. Until he breaks you."

I pointed to her scars. "And he gave you those?"

"These are from the cuffs. His own invention. Agony and ecstasy, sometimes both at once." She ran her fingertips over the scars. "He made me wear them. He even had a little remote that allowed him to trigger the release of magic into my system. So he always knew what I would be feeling, even when I wasn't with him, even after I learned to hide my emotions from him. It took me years to figure out how to unlock them. Taking them off nearly killed me, but I couldn't be a prisoner any longer."

"How did you survive it?" Because whatever Theresa had gone through, she'd managed to function as a sensor in a boss's lair for nearly two decades.

Her eyes met mine. "I told you—I didn't," she said in a flat voice. "He ate my heart and soul. This shell is all that's left." And then she pushed off the bed and trudged past me. A moment later the bathroom door closed. I went back to my room, nerves jangling, knowing sleep was out of my reach. In the morning, I was going to seek an audience with Volodya himself. I was going to offer him a deal—the relic for Asa.

And I was going to pray that Asa would still have his soul when I found him.

"Do it again," Theresa said, leaning over the table. The emotion-sensing cube was on her palm. "I don't want to feel the tiniest twinge from you."

I took a deep breath, focusing. I'd had this feeling so many times. Fierce and hard and heavy. It was the steel in my muscles when I needed to fight for Asa, like the night Daeng had shot him in Thailand. It was the power in my blood when I needed to sacrifice for him, like the time I'd faced Reza and taken the full measure of his pain magic, just to give Asa time to do what he needed to do. Now the bars around my heart held my love safe inside instead of refusing to let it out.

Good thing you're brave as hell and stronger than anyone I've ever met, Asa had said to me. He'd believed it. He'd trusted me.

"The attack on the bridge was orchestrated by Botwright's agents," I began. "She has the magic, but she doesn't have the brothel network that Volodya has, so she is open to a trade. Botwright wants Asa's services and is willing to give up the relic to get them. If Volodya won't give up Asa, she keeps the relic he wants."

Theresa looked down at the relic and nodded. "Hopefully it will be enough. I have heard from the priests that Volodya is desperate for capital, and the magic in that Ekstazo relic is worth a great deal of money." She sighed. "But so is my son."

I bowed my head as the terror and fear inside me beat against my shield of determination. "He's not going to trade Asa for that relic. He could use Asa to steal it back, or others that are just as valuable." I said it slowly, focused on keeping my own energy level on doing what was necessary.

Theresa set the relic on the table. "No, he probably won't. But at the very least, to string you along, he will let you see him. He will want to sense whether it cracks you, and you must make very sure it doesn't. Because then you will never get Asa back."

I swallowed. "Honestly, I don't know . . ."

"Stay hard," Theresa said, her voice as biting as her whip. "Remember that you are the wall between Asa and everything that hurts him. You must not crumble."

I closed my eyes. "I *won't*."

"Mattie, if we know where Volodya is keeping him, who is guarding him, and what condition he's in, then we can make a plan to get him out. All the better if we can lure the pair of them out of the stronghold. This is only the beginning."

"What's keeping Volodya from killing me?" I asked. "I won't have magic inside me. I have nothing he wants."

"If you're there acting as an agent from another boss, Volodya won't touch you. Not right then, at least, when you're in his official headquarters."

"But I'm *not* acting as an agent of another boss."

She smiled. "Yes, you are. I have many contacts, though none of them know who I really am. Last night after you went to bed, I reached out, and I got a message through. Botwright was thrilled to hear that her magic is still in the wind, and eager to have it back, but she was willing to deal. Because she is *most* eager to stick it to Volodya. She is waiting to hear of the outcome of this meeting, but in the meantime has dispatched an agent to come retrieve the magic."

"Myron?"

"Yes, I think that's the name I was given."

My hope grew. "He did say that she was interested in hiring Asa."

Theresa nodded. "See? You can go in there knowing you have the strength of the London boss behind you."

"All right. Let's get this done." I stood up and reached for my coat. Theresa had lent me some of her clothes, just a pair of khaki pants and a plain shirt, which were a little long through the sleeves and legs but otherwise fit okay. I pushed down the excitement and fear that were gnawing on my calm. If all went well, I'd be seeing Asa soon.

Theresa and I set out, her in her lead suit, wearing her old-man glamour, while I slipped along invisibly in her wake. She took me as far as she was willing to go, and I didn't argue when she peeled off. No *good-bye*, no *good luck*, no *thank you for trying to save my son*. I could almost see the smoke trail she left behind.

I didn't take it personally. After witnessing her nightmares the night before, after taking a good look at those scars, I couldn't stomach the thought of Volodya getting hold of her again. I still wasn't sure I actually liked the woman, but it was so obvious that whatever he'd done to her in the past, the memories had never let her go. I couldn't blame her for needing to stay distant and safe, physically at least.

I walked along the street toward the city center, keeping my hand in my pocket, wrapped around the sensing relic that was projecting my intention to meet with Volodya outward for his agents to pick up. The boss's lair was located in Moscow City, the supposed financial center of the city. But Theresa had told me it was a disaster of planning and unjustified hope, a cluster of dark, half-empty skyscrapers.

Volodya had nestled himself deep in the bowels of this urban monster in 2001, around the time the first building was officially completed, and had made it his. His lair sat on the opposite bank of the Moscow River—the same one I'd thought I'd plunged into thanks to Theresa's glamour—connected to the rest of Moscow City via a pedestrian bridge that Volodya controlled.

To get there, I tromped along a wide avenue. I couldn't read the street signs, so I was following landmarks Theresa had given me, waiting for my escort to arrive.

And arrive they did, slipping quietly out of a corner café to walk on either side of me. Just two young men, smoking cigarettes and talking back and forth over my head before one of them said, in thickly accented English, "And what makes you think the Volodya will meet with you?"

"I have something he wants very badly," I said calmly. Theresa was going to hold the magic until after I'd met with the boss, just in case Myron was in a double-crossing mood. If, by some miracle, Volodya was willing to let Asa go, we were just going to hand it over to Volodya quickly and disappear before Myron arrived. Because Botwright didn't actually know who'd contacted her—Theresa's offer had run through numerous intermediaries, both human and technological—she was unlikely to come directly after us.

"And what do you have that he wants?" inquired the guy on my other side.

"The magic that was stolen from him on the bridge."

I glanced over to see the first young man pull his phone from his pocket. It really was that easy. A few minutes later, after a muttered, anxious-sounding conversation with whoever was on the other end of the line, he turned to me and said, "He will see you." He looked down at me with a mixture of puzzlement and what might have been awe.

The escorts walked beside me for the next few blocks, until we reached a square containing a massive statue of a sword-wielding man on horseback. And just beyond him lay a wide brick sidewalk leading directly to a tall, round-walled building with a blue mirrored facade. Tower 2000. Volodya's lair. One of the escorts put out his hand. "The relic you carry. Hand it over."

I pulled it out of my pocket—just a plastic subway card—and gave it to him.

The other guy held out a cell phone, running it up and down a few inches away from my body. "She has nothing else."

They opened the doors to let me into the building.

I lifted my chin and strode inside, then followed one of my escorts onto an elevator while the other headed back outside. Instead of pushing a button for one of the top floors, the guy pushed one for a lower floor—apparently the building had several underground levels. *Figures,* I thought. *Monsters live underground.*

The doors slid open to reveal what appeared to be a cement bunker. "You'll go through there," one of my escorts said, pointing to a reinforced steel door.

I glanced to either side of me, surprised. The wide lobby was furnished only with metal tables and chairs and a few threadbare couches. Water stains spotted the ceiling, and paint peeled from the walls. There were a half-dozen people in the room, black clad and sharp eyed, some of them playing cards at one of the tables. I guessed they were probably Volodya's security team, but they were young, and all of them gave off the same on-edge vibe that Pavel, Elena, and Grigory had when they picked me up. They clearly weren't surprised by my arrival. None of them moved.

My toes curled into the wire bristles I had insisted Theresa help me fit into my boots. She used other methods to resist Knedas magic, but when I told her this was how Asa did it, she smiled approvingly and found what I needed. Now I was almost wincing from the pain.

One of the cardplayers, a blond woman, must have been able to sense my discomfort—or my intention to fight any Knedas magic that came my way. "We will not try to influence you," she called. "We only act on Volodya's orders."

When we reached the metal door, I looked over my shoulder at the escort who had brought me this far. "Are you coming?"

He shook his head. "He only sees people alone."

"But aren't you supposed to protect him?"

He looked baffled. "From you? Do you *know* the Volodya?"

I tried not to cringe. "I just figured he'd have bodyguards or advisers or something."

"Our master makes his own decisions. We only carry them out." He gave me a brittle smile. "Because if we do not, it is bad." He exchanged nervous glances with the blonde at the table, and their expressions served only to crank the fear inside me a little tighter. I focused on that and not the feelings I was trying to shield as my young escort's phone buzzed.

He flinched but then straightened, clearly trying to look authoritative. "The Volodya is ready for you."

I swallowed hard as the steel door opened, hoping *I* was ready for *him*.

CHAPTER NINE

I walked on plush carpet into a dimly lit room. It was cavernous and yet startling in its silence. And as the door clanked shut behind me, the quiet became close. Suffocating.

My heartbeat was loud in my ears as I took a few more steps into the space, blinking as I tried to adjust to the darkness. The only source of light was a small artificial fireplace set into the far wall, fake flames undulating orange and yellow and red. Along the walls there were a few spindly-legged wooden side tables, upon which sat some carved animal figurines and other random objects, including a broken clay pot and a stack of dog-eared books. A pair of crossed swords, lethal blades thick and curved, was the only wall decoration. But my gaze skated over all of that, seeking the true danger.

Then a tiny flame flared to life in a corner of the room, in a dark nook blocked from the scant light of the fireplace. It went out quickly, leaving only the fleeting amber glow from the tip of a cigarette. Behind it lurked a dense shadow in the almost-total darkness, a lean silhouette behind swirls of smoke.

"Welcome," said the shadow.

"Thank you for seeing me," I said, forcing myself to take a few measured steps closer. I squinted into the darkness, trying to make out his features. But as he took another drag on his cigarette, all I could make out of Volodya were long fingers and the gray glint of his eyes.

"You are afraid." His voice was completely calm. Accented and rough. Seductive, even. Which only made it scarier.

"Of course I am," I admitted. "I'm unarmed, I'm in a boss's heavily guarded headquarters, and I don't want to die. I'm not stupid." Theresa had told me that nothing on earth could keep Volodya from sensing some of my emotions, so I might as well own up to them immediately.

"But it is worth it for you to be here. You are determined."

"Obviously."

He scoffed, sounding vaguely amused. "And you are prepared."

"Because I respect you."

"Charming," he said.

I took a big step forward but was still maybe fifteen feet from him. The distance and shadows were playing with me. All I could picture was a giant spider watching me from its web. I needed to see Volodya's face, to know I was dealing with a person and not a monster. So I held out my hand, thinking he would emerge from the darkness to shake it. "Nice to meet you," I offered.

"Oh, you don't want to do that, little girl."

My hand dropped to my side, and I wiped my clammy palm on my pants. "I'm here to make a deal."

For a moment, he simply regarded me while he took another long drag. Then he abruptly mashed out the cigarette and shot to his feet. "You dare to steal something from me," he shouted, so loud it made me jump. "And now you demand I pay for it?"

He was still hidden in the shadows, but I could see the way he moved, smooth and coiled, looking like he was about to strike.

"N-not me—Botwright!" Fighting the temptation to run back to the door and beg to be let out, I told him the story of what had happened on the bridge, reminding myself that since Theresa was the one who had contacted the English boss, she was sort of acting on Botwright's behalf anyway. I wasn't lying. "She wasn't willing to let you show up and steal it away from her territory without showing you she could do it, too. But she wants to negotiate."

His laugh was hard-edged but somehow rueful. "Conniving vixen that she is." He slowly sank back into the chair he'd been sitting in, and my heart started to beat again.

"Look, I'm just the middlewoman here. I'm just stating her terms."

"Poor little reliquary. You would like me to believe that, wouldn't you?"

"I'm not asking for pity," I said calmly.

"Perhaps because you have heard I never offer it."

Frustration pulsed inside me. "Look, I know you're probably savoring my fear and all that, but maybe we could multitask? I'm here to discuss business."

Volodya chuckled, a dry rustle in the darkness. "You intrigue me."

"I'm flattered."

"No you're not."

Great. More cat-and-mouse games.

"Oh, that's delicious. Contempt and anger and terror entwined. So potent." He shifted in his chair. "You know, I hear you are a very powerful reliquary." He gestured at my body, long fingers slipping in and out of the shadows. "And it would appear deception is in your DNA. Most people would never suspect such a soft exterior concealed a core of iron. But I . . . I can feel it."

I didn't know whether he was sensing my reliquary ability or my determination to protect the man I loved—but I seized on it. "That's what I'm told. It's a vault."

"And conceals many secrets, not all of them magical. How delicious it would be to uncover them all."

I put out my hand, as if that were going to stop him. "That's not really why we're here today, right? Besides, mystery has got to be kind of fun, especially for a man who is impossible to fool."

"Now *you* flatter *me*. And how I wish that were true." For a moment, he bowed his head, seeming to shrink before my eyes. Then he threw his shoulders back, a predator once again. "But as you say, mystery can be pleasurable. Let us discuss your purpose here. Sit down." He pointed toward a pair of club chairs near one of the side tables but didn't rise to take one.

Not wanting to offend him—and feeling glad that he wasn't moving any closer—I sat down, remaining on the edge of my seat.

He lit another cigarette, and for a moment I caught a glimpse of hollow cheeks and a long nose before he sank into darkness again. "Now," he said, exhaling a puff of smoke. "You are carrying magic that belongs to me. I want it back."

"And I'd like to give it to you. But I'm not carrying it anymore."

He went very still. "This is the truth."

"One of Botwright's agents helped me off-load it after she kidnapped me on the bridge. She has it. But she's open to a trade."

"Assuming I don't simply track this agent down and bleed her to death while I savor her pain, what would she like in return?"

The protective shield over my love turned steely. "Asa Ward."

Ash slipped from the tip of Volodya's cigarette and landed on his pant leg, but he didn't move to brush it off. "The thief," he said quietly.

"Botwright knows you took him in London. She was about to engage his services on a retrieval mission, and although the price is steep, she's willing to give you your magic back if you release him."

"She was going to engage Mr. Ward's services?" He chuckled, bitter and sharp. "This sounds unlikely to me, from what I have heard of him. Which is not much, I admit, though his name has come to my attention on a few occasions over the last several years."

His voice had turned hard. Cruel. I wondered if he knew that Asa was the one who'd run over Arkady in Virginia. Had Volodya decided to get revenge for that as well?

"I guess he's made a name for himself," I said quickly. "I've worked with him a few times, obviously. He's good, but this magic you're seeking—I've worked with it, too. It's *amazing*."

"Ah, what do you Americans call this? The sales *pitch*," he said.

"Again, I'm just the messenger."

"You think it is a good trade. The thief for my magic."

"I think it's a great deal for you. Your brothel business could crush any competitors. You'd have customers lining up outside, begging you to take their money. I've carried that magic." I gave him a knowing smile. "I know what it can do."

"Do you now?" he murmured. After several beats of agonizing silence, he continued. "Very well, then. You may tell Botwright that I accept her offer."

"Really?" I sounded too relieved and clamped my lips shut.

Volodya slowly rose from his chair, but he didn't step into the light. "You bring me this magic. Tonight. And I will give you what you want."

I thought back to what Theresa had said about trying to get Asa on neutral ground. "Um . . . no offense, but I think Botwright—and I—would feel more comfortable if we did our exchange in a place that *isn't* your heavily guarded stronghold. It's just fair, you know?"

I tried not to fidget as the silence stretched. How badly did he want his stolen magic? Suddenly I was glad I didn't have it inside me, glad he had no reason to tie me down and take it by force. If it hadn't been for Theresa, that's probably what would have happened next. But instead—

"Very well. Tell Botwright that I will personally deliver Mr. Ward to my suite at the Savoy. You will bring my magic, and I will let Mr. Ward leave with you."

"Can I see him now, before I leave to get the magic?" I asked. "She wants to know he's . . . whole."

Volodya waved me toward the door, pale smoke billowing from the shadows as he exhaled. "The thief is completely intact. But unfortunately, he is not here in the city. My people took him straight to a safe house in Yaroslavl. I can have him returned to Moscow tonight. I have no doubt he will be relieved to know *someone* finds him of some value." His words simultaneously raised my hope and sent a chill down my spine, as did the way he was watching my reaction to them.

"Um, okay. What time?"

"Let's say eleven. I have one condition, however."

"Which is?"

"*You* deliver the magic. And you do so alone."

There was something suggestive in his tone that made my stomach clench. But I was so eager to keep him happy—and to take a step closer to freeing Asa—that I pushed past it. "I can do that."

Now that he'd agreed to leave this creepy hidey-hole of his, even if he had no intention of letting me leave with Asa, Theresa and I could make a plan. We had the element of surprise. I would have Asa back *tonight*. My happiness was beating against the shield like a battering ram, drowning out my more protective thoughts. I needed to get out of there. My steps quickened as I headed to the door.

"See you tonight, dear," he called after me. "I am eager to have my magic back. Just as eager as *you* are to have Mr. Ward."

I paused just as I reached the metal door. "Botwright, you mean. Botwright is eager to have him."

His chuckle was like a cold fingertip drawn down my spine. "As you say. Tell the staff at the Savoy that you have a meeting with me. They will know what to do."

"Mention your name. Got it." Then I turned and burst through the metal door without a backward glance, fighting to hide the grin that was trying to force its way onto my face. I exited the hallway to find one of the escorts waiting, his phone to his ear.

"Da," he said before ending the call and looking at me. "You are free to go."

He took me up the elevator and held the front door of Tower 2000 open for me. I stepped into the frigid midmorning air, my heart exploding with joy.

I wasn't stupid. I knew so many things could go wrong. But hope had me in its teeth, and so did love.

With any luck, in about twelve hours, Asa and I would be together again.

CHAPTER TEN

I screamed as the flames billowed around me, licking blistering streaks along my arms and stomach, as the searing air invaded my lungs. I couldn't conquer the terror.

It disappeared in an instant, and I sagged in my chair. "That's pretty powerful," I said between panting breaths. "I couldn't shake it even though I knew it was fake."

Theresa nodded. "It will stop anyone in his tracks and give you at least a few minutes to run. Volodya's power in the city is not what it once was, but there are still many who work for him. He might be alone in the hotel room, but he will not be alone at the Savoy. Remember that."

"Couldn't forget it if I wanted to," I muttered. With only an hour until our meeting, things had gotten real. Asa was counting on me to be tough. And dangerous. I needed serious help with that last one.

With sweat beading on her forehead, Theresa picked up the powder compact with gloved hands. "Just open it up and *boom*. If you're the last one to touch it, you control it. It won't affect you." She grinned. "And the best thing about it is that it's camouflaged in conduit juice, so—"

"Wait wait wait. Conduit *juice*?"

"Ludmilla's."

I wrinkled my nose. "Ludmilla's *what*?"

"Do you really want to know?"

After thinking about it for a second, I shook my head. "But I'll take some gloves."

"Good call."

"What's conduit juice supposed to do, though? Conduits don't have magic."

"Right, and their bodies conduct it rapidly. But their cells don't absorb it. That's why it doesn't affect them. So if you cover a relic in their juice . . ."

"It conceals the magic?"

"Exactly. No one except a very skilled sensor is going to detect the power inside, even someone holding a magic-sensing relic—unless you open it. So keep it closed tightly until you want the room to go up in flames." She set the compact on the table.

"Asa never told me that," I said. "I didn't know you could use conduit, um, fluids to cover magic."

"He may not know. I only discovered it by accident."

I wasn't sure I wanted to know what that accident was. "And we all know you're not in the habit of sharing your knowledge."

She gave me a sour look. "Just remember that if you're running with Asa, he'll think he's on fire, too. You'll have to help him."

I stood up. "Always." I pulled the gloves on and picked up the compact, then slipped it into the pocket of my coat. I glanced at Theresa's watch. "I guess I'd better get going."

She let out a long breath. "I'll be waiting at the Solntsevo flat. From there I can get us out of the city. Out of the country by morning." She pulled a metal box off the shelf and handed it to me. "Please don't open that until you're up there."

It was the Ekstazo sex relic that had started all this, and even though it was encased in lead, it was still making Theresa tremble. "You got it." I tucked the box into the shoulder bag she'd given me and walked over to the ladder that led to the surface.

"Mattie, wait. There's something . . ." When I turned, she opened her mouth to say something more, then closed it. "Never mind. It's not important right now. Just—good luck."

"Thanks." I made my way up the ladder, my heart drumming its determination. I reached the top and emerged behind the thick screen of shrubbery, my only light coming from the stark moon directly above me. After closing the thick wooden door to the ladder below, I opened the box and pulled out the cube containing the potent Ekstazo sexual magic. Technically, in this form, I could use this magic on anyone I wanted . . . but after thinking about what it had done to Asa, I knew it probably wasn't the best idea unless I had a darn good escape route. I put the unpackaged relic back in my bag.

I walked up the street, the gold dome of the Orthodox church on one side, a vast park near the river on the other, and reached Red Square within a few minutes. It astounded me that Theresa had managed to hide in plain sight. But as I thought about her craftiness, her secrets, I suppose I shouldn't have been surprised. She'd become allies with priests who rejected magic, who wouldn't betray her to Volodya. She'd engaged the people Volodya had tossed aside, who he had used and broken and discarded.

Despite the late hour, there were still people out and about as I walked past Lenin's mausoleum and headed for yet another large cathedral at the edge of the square. I paid attention, acutely aware that I was carrying an extremely valuable piece of magic. But no one gave me a second look. I turned right when I reached the end of the square and followed a narrow pedestrian road past designer boutiques and restaurants. Really, Moscow was a beautiful city—I would have enjoyed hanging out here under better circumstances. Finally, I reached a busy intersection and marched up the block.

Just as I made the final turn for the Savoy, a taxi slowed and rolled along next to me. The window slid down, and the driver, a young man with a short, dark beard, leaned out. "Can I take you somewhere?" he asked, his accent barely there.

"No, thanks," I said, walking a little faster.

"I'll give you a discount," he said. "Anywhere you want to go."

I shook my head and increased my pace again, peering up ahead. Theresa had said the Savoy was right up there . . .

"Come on, lady. My fare is good—"

"Dude, no," I said. "I'm—" I gasped as I felt something hard press against my ribs.

"You're going to get in the car," said a voice from behind me. American. Familiar. "And you're going to do it right now."

I looked over my shoulder—right into the eyes of a man who had tried to kill me the last time we'd met. "Keenan."

He smiled. "Hi, Mattie. In the car. I'd hate to shoot you."

"No you wouldn't," I said, my voice unsteady with fear. My hand crept to my pocket that held the compact, but his fingers closed over my wrist, bruising.

"I won't hurt you unless you give me reason to." He glanced around us and edged even closer to me. "Now get in the car, sweetheart. Don't make this harder than it needs to be."

I did as he said, ducking into the backseat of the taxi. He slid in after me and shut the door, then holstered the gun he'd had pressed to my back. "Drive," he said to the guy behind the wheel.

"What do you want?" I asked as we rolled past the Savoy. My fists clenched. I had fifteen minutes before my scheduled meeting. Asa might be in the building right now.

"One of my sources told me Volodya would be out of his box tonight and that there was a powerful relic in play." He shifted in his seat and glanced at my bag. "And now I know they were telling the truth."

I scooted against the window. "You're not a magic sensor."

He pulled a pen out of his breast pocket. "But this is."

I clutched the bag against my chest, realizing that he hadn't taken the compact from me, which meant he couldn't sense the magic in it. "So you want to take custody of this Ekstazo relic."

"If it keeps Volodya from exploiting and oppressing hundreds of women, then the answer is yes. That's my job. And it doesn't hurt that he's desperate for the cash. Denying him that moneymaker will make him even more vulnerable."

"Vulnerable."

"His empire is crumbling. Rats are jumping ship, left and right."

I thought back to Volodya's dank spider hole, his edgy, tense young agents. Nothing like Frank Brindle's Las Vegas stronghold, that was for sure. "You think you can take him down?"

"Tonight, if all goes well."

"But I can't give this relic to you." My thoughts spun—there had to be a way out of this.

He arched an eyebrow. "How are you going to stop me?"

"Well, I can't. I know that. But I need your help. Maybe we can help each other."

He sat back, looking intrigued. "You want to deal with me?"

"Volodya has Asa," I said quietly. "He kidnapped him in London and brought him here to punish him for stealing this magic in the first place." I patted the bag. "I'm going to trade this for his freedom."

Keenan's brow furrowed. "Asa? He's here?"

"Yeah. And I know he—I know you—" I bit my lip as his blue-eyed gaze turned dark. "I thought you might be willing to help get him back."

"He strangled me with a pair of suspenders."

"I know. But he didn't kill you. And he could have."

Keenan looked away quickly, aiming his gaze out the window. "I should have known better anyway," he muttered.

I couldn't disagree, but I knew better than to say that out loud. "You still care about him."

He let out a strained chuckle. "It's that obvious?"

"I care about him, too," I said gently.

"I know." He rubbed his chest, and I once again remembered he was an emotion sensor like Volodya. "You have my sympathy, Mattie." His voice had turned bitter. "Because nothing with Asa ever ends well."

Which was my worst fear, but one I wouldn't allow to stop me now. "I agreed to give this relic to Volodya in exchange for Asa's freedom. If you want to deal with Asa directly, you can. But help me get him back first."

"I had no intelligence that Asa was even in this part of the world. Last I heard he was in Barcelona."

That had been three weeks ago. Now I knew how close the Headsmen had gotten to us then. "We were. But then we stole the relic and went to London. That's where he was taken. Volodya said he hadn't brought him back to Moscow, though, which might be why you weren't aware of it."

He nodded, then spoke to the driver. "We need to shake our network a little harder. I don't like to miss stuff like this. And head back to the Savoy."

My heart leaped. "You're going to help me?"

He turned back to me, a sly smile on his face. "That all depends, Mattie."

"On?"

"How much you're going to help *me*."

I skittered into the lobby of the Savoy only a few minutes late. Walking between two massive statues of some half-naked dudes holding the ceiling up, I approached the check-in desk. "I'm here to meet the boss," I said quietly.

The young woman immediately nodded, picked up her phone, and made a call. After a few moments of rapid-fire Russian, she hung up. "This way," she said.

I followed her down a hallway past the elevators to the guest rooms, to a smaller elevator with its own alcove. She summoned it, and when I stepped inside, she used a key to unlock a panel, on which she pushed number three before closing it up again. "It will bring you back to the lobby when you are finished," she told me.

I stepped aboard, working on slowing my breath. Keenan had promised me backup. He'd said he already had agents in position within the hotel because he'd known Volodya would be here with the magic tonight. Apparently he had a double agent inside, someone who had risked her life to get him the information. He could have simply taken the relic and probably disappeared me or whatever they'd done to Arkady, but instead he'd agreed to let me use it to trade for Asa. The catch: I had to help him take down Volodya once I had.

Now, in addition to the compact, I carried a tiny pen, similar to Keenan's sensing relic. This one didn't have magic, though. One click and it was just a pen. Two clicks, though, would dispense a hefty dose of liquid Rohypnol.

Keenan wanted me to freaking roofie the guy so he wouldn't sense anyone coming for him and so he wouldn't call for help as the Headsmen strode in to carry him away for interrogation. I didn't think bosses were usually treated that way, but it seemed like Keenan had some kind of beef with Volodya, maybe because of what Arkady had done to the Headsmen in Virginia. They were probably still recovering from the slaughter of so many of their agents.

Having never drugged someone before, I was dubious about this plan, particularly because the last time I'd been in Volodya's presence, I hadn't gotten within fifteen feet of the guy. I hadn't even gotten a good look at his face—it was possible he could walk right past me without me realizing it was him . . . though I recalled his lean silhouette, the snake-like way he had moved. It had been enough to tell me that although Volodya must have been in his fifties or early sixties, he was far from being a feeble old man. There was no way I could overpower him physically, so I would have to find a way to get close enough to this terrifying man to use speed and sneakiness. I was ready to take that risk, though. Heck, I would have agreed to dress up in a toga and do the cha-cha with Volodya if that was what it took to get Asa back.

The elevator door slid open to the third floor, and I stepped into a corridor warmly lit with flickering wall sconces. A door at one end of the hallway indicated a stairwell, and a door at the other end was open, revealing a darkened room. Knowing Volodya might sense anything amiss, I focused on Asa and what he might need once I got him back. Would he be addicted to Ekstazo again? Would he have to wean himself off? No matter what shape he was in, I would be at his side every step of the way. The protective shield slid into place over my heart, ready for battle. Determined and calm.

I held on tightly to the bag containing the relic as I reached the doorway to what turned out to be a spacious suite lit only by a single candle on the windowsill. "Hello?" I peered at the darkest corners of the space, expecting to see the glowing embers of a cigarette. I could certainly smell the smoke.

"You are late," Volodya said, his voice drifting to me from what I assumed was the bedroom, its door half-closed, the chamber also lit with candles, judging from the flickering patterns along the doorframe.

"Taxi driver took a wrong turn."

"Hmm."

I glanced around, looking for some sign that Asa might be here. "I have the relic you want," I said. "I'm holding up my end of the deal."

He was silent for a few moments. "This is the truth."

"Yeah. So . . . where's Asa?"

"He will be here soon." His fingers curled around the door. "And you are nervous. Why?"

"Haven't we already discussed this? You're kind of scary." I clutched the roofie pen. "And it doesn't help that I haven't even met you face-to-face."

"Because I am the monster in the dark," he said quietly. "There is nothing more frightening than the unknown, is there?"

"And you enjoy having that effect," I guessed.

He chuckled. "Indeed. But there is more than fear inside you." The door swung open and he emerged, moving like a predator in the shadows toward a lamp next to a wooden desk. "You and I will get to know each other better before we continue."

"Not much to know," I said, my body starting to ping with uncertainty—there was something about his stride that was eerily familiar. I took a step backward, toward the hallway, as if that were a safer place to be. "But I will tell you that . . ." My voice trailed off as he switched on the light and lifted his head.

He had been wrong. There *was* something more frightening than the unknown.

His face was angular, with sharp cheekbones and a strong jaw. Add to that his gray eyes, and he looked for all the world like a wolf in human form. My heart, so shielded under the thick covering of my determination to protect Asa, sped into a frantic rhythm as I took in his appearance, the shape of his eyes, his nose, his mouth . . .

"I am not what you expected," he said slowly, his eyes narrowing.

"I . . ." It came out as nothing more than a helpless whisper. My mind reeled, desperate to conceal a new, devastating truth.

I was looking into the eyes of the most dangerous man in Russia. I knew full well he was cruel and that he held my life—and Asa's life—in his hands.

And I was also sure he was Asa's father.

CHAPTER ELEVEN

"You're younger than I expected," I said, exhaling a shaky breath.

He inhaled, his nostrils flaring, and then smiled. "And now you're lying."

"Okay, fine. You look familiar, and obviously it startled me." What had Asa said? He was born in August, only eight months after his mother had showed up at a New Year's party in her hometown. Only eight months after she renewed her acquaintance with Don Ward, who she married less than two months later. *Shotgun wedding,* he'd told me. *I was born early.*

I'd once seen a picture of Don Ward, a proud father posing with Ben, who had just propelled the football team to a winning season. The man was stocky and thickly built, like Ben. His face was broad, not angular like Asa's. The two brothers had the same eyes, and both were relatively tall, but the similarity ended there, really, both outside and in.

Had Don known Asa wasn't his son?

Had Asa ever suspected?

Was this why Theresa had run away in the first place?

Volodya's eyes were riveted on me, and I could almost feel his power slipping across my skin. "Familiar." It was drawn out, like he was savoring it as it left his mouth.

I offered a weak smile. "Hasn't that ever happened to you? You meet someone, and you could swear you've seen them before—even though you never have?"

He came closer, moving with a lanky grace that made me ache. "I suppose. But you look more like you've just seen a ghost, dear."

"I think I just have." Theresa had some *serious* explaining to do. Did she think I wouldn't see it? Did she have any idea that I had long since memorized Asa's face, or how many times I had dreamed about it, so close to mine?

I looked Volodya over. Did *he* know? He certainly didn't act like he had any idea. Would he be kinder to Asa if he knew?

Volodya's gaunt face was a mask of fascination. "Oh my. This is exquisite."

"When can I see Asa?"

"As soon as my agents arrive with him. Shortly before you arrived they informed me they were just outside the city. Would you like a drink?"

Normally, I would have turned him down, but instead I smiled—despite the new confusion raging inside me. "Just a small one, maybe."

He grinned and got to his feet, striding over to the bar. "You are very jittery tonight. What could be on your mind?"

"I think you know the answer to that," I said as I joined him, my hand over the roofie pen in my pocket. This was going to be tricky. And maybe I shouldn't do it at all—not before I had Asa. Not when I didn't know if he was safe. What would Volodya's agents do to Asa once they found out their boss had been captured?

"What's wrong?" Volodya asked, turning to me with a bottle of what looked like vodka in his hand. "You are troubled."

I shrugged. "I'm wanting to make this exchange, that's all."

He poured the clear liquid into two tall, thin shot glasses, the openings of which were depressingly narrow. Not only did I have to use the pen without him noticing, but my aim had to be perfect.

And quick. He pushed one glass toward me and had his at his lips before I could blink. He tossed it back and set the glass down sharply on the counter. "Drink. Then I want to see my relic."

I lifted the glass and took a sip, then put it back onto the bar. "Not until I see Asa. That was the deal."

He sighed impatiently. "You are more stubborn than is convenient."

I stared up at him, a new fear starting to seep up through the cracks in my shield. "Call him."

"What?"

"Call him. If he's really on his way, whoever's bringing him has a phone, right? So call them. I want to hear his voice."

He ran the backs of his fingers along his jaw. "And if I don't?"

"Then I'm out of here."

As I took a step back, Volodya's arm snaked around my waist, and he hauled me against him. The Ekstazo relic was pinned between us.

"Mattie. Do you mind if I call you Mattie?"

I'd never given him my name. "Um. No."

"Mattie, I want you to understand your . . . situation. Everyone in this hotel works for me. I have eyes and ears all over the city. And I want my relic. Do you really think I'm going to let you leave with what is mine?"

I swallowed the lump of realization and grief that had formed in my throat. "You don't have Asa, do you?"

He smiled, razor sharp and lethally familiar. "Perhaps. Perhaps not. Either way, you will give me the relic."

I began to struggle against him. "Let me go."

"Oh," he said, closing his eyes. "Your horror . . . it's like a sip of exquisite poison."

"I'll give you poison," I snarled, grabbing the pen from my pocket and lifting it.

Hey, I couldn't get it into his drink. So I squirted it straight up his nose.

He shoved me away from him, snorting and sniffling and coughing. I hit the ground in a sprawl. "Poison?" he snapped, his fingers flexing.

"It won't kill you," I said, scooting backward. "I just wanted you to let go."

"Liar," he roared, pulling his buzzing phone from his pocket. He pressed it to his ear, and his eyes went wide. After several curt questions, he stopped midsentence, looking at the silent phone as if it had betrayed him. He turned the same look on me a second later. "Headsmen have swarmed the lobby." He paused, staring at me. "And you are helping them!"

I scooted backward as he staggered toward me. "You don't know what you've done," he said, starting to slur. "You can't let them . . ."

"You're a liar," I said, dodging out of the way and jumping to my feet. "You never planned to give Asa back."

"Because I never . . . took . . . Asa. When you said you wanted him . . . I made some calls. I know . . . who has him."

I froze. "You do?"

He nodded, swaying in place. "I . . . do. But I will only . . . tell you. If you . . . get me . . . out."

"You lied to me once already and—"

"Don't waste this chance," he said slowly, obviously having to think about each word. "Asa Ward is a prisoner."

"Tell me who has him," I shouted as I heard a door slam down the hall. "Tell me or I'm giving you up!"

"It's . . ." His eyes rolled in his head. "I can . . . help you."

He was so out of it that I could barely understand him. Caught in a web of indecision, my fingers curled around the compact as footsteps thundered down the hall toward us.

Who did I want to double-cross? The Headsmen or the boss? Who did I want indebted to me?

Keenan hadn't had the slightest idea where Asa was.

But Volodya might. And on top of that, whether he knew it or not . . . he was Asa's father.

I pulled the compact from my pocket just as the door to the suite splintered and swung open to reveal three Headsmen, with Keenan in the lead. He took one look at the unsteady Volodya and smiled.

Hoping I wasn't making the biggest mistake of my life, I unleashed the fire.

CHAPTER TWELVE

I noticed that the Headsmen were wearing silver wrist cuffs meant to protect them from Knedas magic, but Theresa's relic overpowered their defenses instantly. All three of them screamed and threw their hands over their faces, even as Keenan shouted, "It's not real!"

He stumbled forward, swiping frantically, his face a grimace of horror and pain. I could practically see the flames creeping along his sleeves and singeing his hair. "Mattie!" he roared.

"I'm sorry! I have to get Asa!" I pulled Volodya's arm around my shoulders and helped him sidestep the flailing Headsmen. He leaned on me, allowing me to pull him into the hallway and steer him toward the private elevator. I knew there might be Headsmen in the lobby, but I also knew that there was no freaking way I could safely get Volodya down the stairs.

"Basement," Volodya mumbled as I reached out to press the button for the first floor. "Basement."

Keenan was bellowing my name as the elevator doors slid shut. They opened to a long hallway leading to laundry rooms and kitchens. A few of the hotel staff came running up to us and helped me get

Volodya down the corridor. Another ran ahead, and when we emerged from an employee exit down the block from the main hotel doors, a taxi was waiting. With the assistance of a stocky cook in a stained apron, I stuffed Volodya into the backseat. Then I hopped in after him and barked out the address for Theresa's Solntsevo apartment.

"But I take you to the tower," said the driver.

"No! It's not safe there. Please."

The driver looked back at Volodya and frowned, but then nodded. I relaxed a little.

I had nowhere else to go, really. And given the fact that the Russian boss was drooling on my shoulder, I figured it might be okay. He snored softly as the driver wended his way across the city and I stared out the back window, praying we weren't being tailed.

Also praying that Theresa wouldn't kill both of us the moment we arrived.

I had the driver help me get Volodya into the vestibule of the run-down apartment building and then sent him packing.

Technically speaking, I'd just kidnapped the boss of Russia, thanks to the smoke screen provided by the raiding Headsmen.

I pressed the button for Theresa's apartment. The intercom rang and clicked over. I looked up into the camera mounted above the number pad. "Theresa, it's me. But . . . I have a guest. And it's not the one you were expecting." I pushed Volodya's chin up so his face was visible to the camera. "He's been drugged."

There was a long pause, and then the door buzzed. I managed to get Volodya through it, but then nearly dropped him as his legs gave out and his head lolled. Theresa came running down the hall, her face white. "What the hell happened?" she snarled as she got on Volodya's other side and helped me drag the unconscious man down the hall.

I told her the choice I had made, and how I had used her Knedas fire glamour. "It's very unusual for the Headsmen to target a boss directly," she said with a huff. "But then again, few are as arrogant or dangerous as this man." She was sweating from having him up against her, and maybe from the storm of emotions that must have been swirling inside her.

"I'm so sorry I brought him here," I said as she opened her door and helped me get him inside the flat. "I thought it would be better than heading back into the belly of the beast."

"What's he been drugged with?" she asked as we laid him on the couch, where he sprawled, his eyes and mouth half-open.

"Rohypnol. He's not going to remember any of this."

"Good," she murmured, her eyes on his face. "If he finds out I'm alive, he'll never stop hunting me." She slowly sat on the edge of the couch, her eyes shining with tears. "I should kill him. I should."

I touched her arm. "He said he had found out who kidnapped Asa."

"And you believed him?"

"I'm not saying I trust him at all—especially since he pretended to have Asa this whole time—but I think there's a possibility he does know. I had to make the call. But I'm going to have to ask you not to murder the dude until we find out if he's still lying." I shrugged. "If he is, I might *help* you kill him. Or at least dispose of the body. I just have to know one thing first."

"Which is?"

"Why didn't you tell me?" I asked quietly.

"Tell you . . . ?"

"This man is his *father*, Theresa. Do either of them have *any* idea?"

"Don is Asa's father," she barked.

"I don't need a sensing relic to know you're lying." I pointed down at Volodya, limp and helpless on the threadbare couch. "One look at him was all it took. Did you actually think I wouldn't see it?"

She squeezed her eyes shut. "I haven't actually laid eyes on my son since he was a child," she whispered. "I've only sensed him." She sniffled and wiped her nose on her sleeve. "Do they look that much alike?"

"It's not just how they look. It's how they move. How they stand. How they smile. It's eerie, Theresa. It's hard to believe either one of them wouldn't realize it if they were in the same room."

Her eyes went wide. "Volodya cannot find out. Neither can Asa."

"But maybe it would give Volodya more motivation to help us!"

"He *cannot* know," she said, her voice tinged with panic. "He can never know."

"It's why you ran from him the first time, isn't it?"

She looked down at her belly, covering it with her hands. "I felt him," she breathed. "Before I knew for sure that I was pregnant, I felt my son's power. It was this . . ." She let out a small, tear-stained laugh. "Little sparkling *thing*. I knew it wasn't coming from me. I knew I wasn't alone anymore. And I knew he would never survive if I didn't get him away from Volodya, from his empire of magic, from his exquisite cruelty. It was destroying *me*. How could my baby endure it?"

"So you ran back to your hometown and found a guy who couldn't say no to you," I guessed.

"Don was a good man."

"No, Theresa. He wasn't."

She turned away. "He was better than the alternative. I needed to give Asa the best chance I could. And Don was it. He owned a house. He had a steady job, and he worked hard. And he didn't know about magic."

"Did he know that Asa wasn't his?"

She sighed. "Asa was small when he was born. So small. I think the magic in me had already taken a toll on him. He got used to it after he was born, I think, and my magic became background noise for him, but in the womb, being surrounded by it day and night . . ." She shook her head. "It's a miracle he survived. Not even the doctors questioned that he was premature."

"And Don didn't doubt for a minute?"

She looked over her shoulder and gave me a sad smile. "One of my favorite things about him."

"Well, Don might not have asked questions, but Volodya asks *a lot* of them."

"But he has no idea Asa is my son, that we are connected in even the remotest way, save our abilities. No one has the slightest idea, except for you. Volodya might see a resemblance, but he won't have a context to connect the dots."

I gaped at her. "Theresa. Asa has your eyes exactly." A striking honey brown, little gold threads, mesmerizing. "It's how I recognized *you*."

"They won't figure it out," she shouted, clenching her fists and coming toward me. "If you can't keep the secret, I swear I'll douse you in Knedas juice and make you forget you ever knew my son."

She was shaking all over. Every few seconds, her eyes darted down to the man on the couch, her face radiating fear and sorrow. Once again, I was reminded of her anguished cries in the night, her pleas for mercy. Running from Volodya to save Asa had taken courage and determination. Running from Asa to save him again had to have broken her heart. Not to mention years in captivity with those magic-infused cuffs on her wrists. And now the man who had done all of it to her was only a few feet away, and all her secrets were on the verge of being revealed.

But that didn't mean I was bowing to her threat. "I'm not your enemy, Theresa. All I care about is getting Asa back safe. And when I do, you can deal with your son. But if you try to pull any of that crap on me, not only will I do my best to fight you, but I guarantee Asa will, too."

I walked over to the small bag of stuff I'd packed before leaving Theresa's hideout. She'd left it on the small kitchen table. I dug through it and pulled out the necklace Asa had given me for Christmas. My piece of Asa, of home.

Theresa's lip curled. "He probably only gave you that so he could track you."

"That might be true." I fastened the chain around my neck and felt the warm tingle of the vial against my skin. "I've lost count of the number of times he's saved me. But I've saved him, too. I've taken care of him, made sure he ate well, made sure he was warm." I chuckled. "I've hiked halfway across Tokyo and haggled with a grumpy old grocer who couldn't speak a word of English, just to get the ingredients I needed to make Asa some herbal cough medicine when he had a cold." My eyes met hers. "I can't say for sure what I mean to him. He never got the chance to tell me. But if his actions are even the slightest indication . . . He loves me, Theresa."

As the words came out of my mouth, I knew they were true. Yeah, I was always after him, trying to make sure he stayed healthy, but he was always trying to make sure I was *happy*. He always gave me the window seat. Always managed to find the best french fries, no matter what country we were in—even though he wouldn't touch the things. He was always buying me new shoes. He made me coffee in the mornings. He gave me exactly what I needed, sometimes before I knew I needed it. I just wished I'd realized what it meant earlier. "And I love him, too. I would never keep a secret like this from him. He deserves to know."

"He'll never forgive me."

"You're wrong about him." He might not have forgiven Ben completely for what had happened between them, but he'd more than shown that he could get past it when it counted. Admiration for him swelled inside me. Once I got him back, I would let him see it. I would make him feel it. "Just help me get him back safe, and we'll sort it all out."

The fear lingered in her gaze. Then she glanced down at Volodya again, lifted her head, and nodded. "I'll help you. But I can't stay here with *him*."

"What about Botwright's people? When is Myron arriving? That could complicate things."

"Hmm?" She was hovering next to Volodya's body, looking caught between fight and flight. "Oh, I don't think that'll be an issue."

"Because?"

"Because I never contacted Botwright."

I stared at her. "You lied to me."

"To keep you safe in Volodya's presence."

"But I'm still just a pawn to you. Why should I believe you're actually helping now?"

"Would knowing the truth have made it better?" She didn't sound the slightest bit apologetic. She stared at Volodya. "Especially now. It's this piece of shit who cannot be trusted. He's proven it once again."

"And yet here we are. Look—I don't need any more nasty surprises. I've had enough of them for one day." Stiffly, I turned and walked down the hall, knowing there wasn't any place to escape to, but needing to be away from *her*. I stalked into the nearest room. After a few minutes I realized I probably shouldn't have left Theresa alone with Volodya. He might be our key to getting Asa back, and for all I knew, she might smother him as he slept, caught in some flashback of what he'd done to her in the past.

I crept to the door and peeked into the hall. Theresa was standing right where I'd left her. Her gaze was still riveted on Volodya, and her whole body was shaking. Tears streaked down her face. Her fists were clenched—around what appeared to be a steak knife.

My heart stopped. But just as I started to launch myself into the hallway to stop her from slaughtering him, the blade fell from her grasp. She sank down on her knees, laid her head on his chest, and began to sob. Her fingers rose to caress his face. Volodya stirred as if he could sense it, but didn't surface from his stupor. "You bastard," she said, her voice breaking.

She clung to him like that, her fingertips tracing his features, her head on his chest, her sobs echoing in the near-empty flat, while I stood transfixed, an intruder into what felt like the most private of moments—and the most strange.

One moment she was about to kill him, and the next she was holding him like she regretted every moment they'd been apart.

I slowly approached. Theresa didn't seem to notice as I confiscated the knife and then quietly went through the kitchen drawers, removing anything sharp. I started to pad back down the hallway, then paused and looked back at two powerful, broken people, wondering at how they both seemed drawn to the person who could destroy them. And then I realized these were Asa's parents. Both of them, together in this room. These two people had created Asa Ward, in all his fascinating, gifted, resilient complexity.

Hopefully they were my means of saving him.

Turning away, I went into the dirty bathroom and rinsed away some of the fear and strain of the last few hours. I wished I could shed the sorrow that easily.

Asa was still out there, someone's prisoner. This whole time, I'd been pursuing a false lead while whoever took him had more time to hurt him. I knew I was racing the clock. I had to rescue him before he lost too much of himself or before he escaped in the most devastating and permanent way.

I flinched at the memory of Asa raising two fingers to his temple and mimicking blowing his brains out as he speculated about how Wendell, Frank Brindle's former sensor, had died. *Bet you everything I own,* Asa had said.

"Not on my watch, buddy," I muttered as I dried off and got dressed again.

When I reentered the cramped space that served as a sitting room and a kitchen, Theresa was at the sink, wringing out a wet rag. Her face was blotchy and her hands were shaking, but her expression was hard as she turned to me. "I have to leave."

"I know."

"You can stay with him until he's back on his feet. No one will bother you. There is food in the kitchen."

"Where will you go?"

She shook her head. "It's best if you don't know."

"Right." I glanced over at Volodya, who was sleeping peacefully, his hand on his chest, where Theresa's head had been only a few minutes earlier. I wondered which of them had laid it there. "Any advice on what to do next?"

"Plenty—later. I'm still going to help you. I just have to . . . It's . . ." She turned back to the sink. "Too much right now," she whispered. "If I were to stay, I might kill him." Her nostrils flared. "I want to kill him."

"Just tell me how to reach you."

She nodded toward a piece of paper and a pencil on the kitchen table. "I've written it down. Destroy that paper once you've memorized it."

I walked over to see an e-mail address and password scrawled on the paper. "What do I do with this?"

"Just log in, write a message to me but don't send it to anyone, and it will save to the 'Drafts' folder. I'll be checking it regularly. But after a week, it'll go dark. At that point, take the last two letters of the password and tack them onto the beginning of the e-mail address. Then chop off the two letters from the end of the username, and that's the new address you can reach me at. The password will be the two letters you cut off, transposed, stuck at the beginning of the old password."

I picked up the pencil and drew a little visual for myself to remember everything she'd just said, then pocketed the paper. "I'll get rid of it when I can."

She walked over to Volodya and began to wipe his brow and his cheeks with the sopping wet rag. Then she ran it over his shirt, soaking it. "He'll smell me if I don't," she said. "I know he will." She paused, then wiped his lips. "He'll taste me."

What the . . . had she been *kissing* him?

This was too weird.

"Theresa . . . I thought you were terrified of him."

"I am," she said softly.

"You *just* said you might kill him if you stay."

"'Might' sounds so wishy-washy." Hatred glinted within the sheen of tears in her eyes.

"Because he hurt you."

She looked down at the scars that ringed her forearms. "He did. So often. So much."

"And I thought you would hate me for bringing him here."

Her gaze met mine. "I do." She sighed. "Haven't you ever loved something or someone who wasn't good for you, Mattie?"

I laughed. "Oh man. Don't even get me started on your youngest son."

Her eyebrows shot up.

"Did I not mention that? I was engaged to Ben for a while. That's actually how Asa and I met."

"Ben . . ." She swallowed hard. "How is he?"

"He's a veterinarian. He got himself in some trouble with magic, but he's clean now. And I think he's going to turn out just fine." I hoped so. I hadn't actually spoken to him since breaking off our engagement.

"But he wasn't good for you?"

"He was for a while. But then he did some things . . . Theresa, you don't need to hear about this."

"And Asa? He's good for you?"

"Honestly, I don't know. In some ways he's more dangerous than Ben."

She gave me a sad little smile. "His father was the worst thing to ever happen to me. But maybe also the best."

"Are you serious? You told me he ate your heart and soul."

"And so he did. But before that . . . he taught me that I *had* those things."

"That almost sounds crueler."

"It was." She stood up. "He's accepted that I'm dead. If he hadn't, he might have realized I was involved in all of this, just by reading your emotions in response to his questions."

"I'm such a mess now that I doubt he'll pick up anything other than that."

She walked back to her bedroom and came out carrying a backpack. "Be careful. Keep in contact."

"Okay."

She stood there for a moment, just looking at me. And then she walked over and gave me a hard, brisk hug. But before I had a chance to recover from my surprise and reciprocate, she was out the door, pulling it shut behind her.

I had just finished tearing up the paper containing Theresa's e-mail and password and flushing it down the toilet when I heard Volodya stir in the other room. Relief crashed over me—it had been hours, and he hadn't so much as twitched. Now it was midmorning, and I had been getting antsy.

I emerged to find him sitting up slowly, groaning and rubbing his hands over his face. He squinted as he looked around, taking in the unfamiliar surroundings.

And then I felt a chill run down my back as he licked his lips and touched them, his brow furrowing. His head jerked up when he caught me in his periphery. "What happened?"

"We got ambushed by Headsmen."

His long fingers closed tightly around the arm of the couch. "Keenan," he growled. "He'll never get what he wants from me."

"He almost *did*. But I helped you escape from them and brought you here."

"And where is here?"

"Solntsevo."

His eyebrows shot up. "The Solntsevskaya Bratva would not be happy to find me here. They would take it as a sign of aggression."

"Then maybe we should make a plan. Do you remember what you promised me last night before you passed out? About Asa?"

He looked down at his hands, resting on his thighs. "It's all very foggy . . . though I do remember you attacking me with a pen."

"You totally asked for it. You lied about having Asa."

"No, I simply didn't correct your misapprehension."

I rolled my eyes. "'He's at the safe house in Yaroslavl,'" I said, mocking his accent. "'I can have him here by tonight.'"

"I did look into his whereabouts," he said.

"Exactly. And you told me that if I helped you escape the Headsmen, you would not only tell me where he is and who has him, but you would help me get him back."

"Oh . . . I definitely don't remember all that." He chuckled. "Your frustration is so sharp."

"Good. Maybe I can stab you with it."

"You are very aggressive for such an unassuming creature."

"You have no idea. Look—I risked my own life to get you out of the Savoy last night. And Keenan is gunning for you. Because of what I did, he's gunning for me now, too. So you can play dumb and refuse to help me, but I want you to know how pathetic I think that is. You're supposed to be this powerful magic boss, and you're refusing to honor a bargain you made to save your own stupid life."

Volodya was watching me with a sort of bemused lack of focus, like he was paying more attention to the rise and fall of my feelings than to my words. With each passing second, his smile grew wider. "If I wasn't sure before, I am very sure now," he said.

I scowled at him. "Of what?"

"This is personal for you, little girl. You're in love with the thief."

I folded my arms over my chest. "That changes nothing."

He tilted his head and pursed his lips. "Oh, but it does. The truth will be much more painful for you."

My stomach dropped. "Which is?"

"Asa Ward is now in the custody of Frank Brindle. He—"

I leaned on the couch to keep from falling. "I know who he is," I said in a strained voice. And I knew it was personal for Brindle, too, though in a totally different way than it was for me. "Is Asa hurt?"

Volodya stood up and swayed a little before regaining his balance. "Brindle is probably doing whatever is necessary."

"Necessary?"

"Yes. To break him."

CHAPTER THIRTEEN

My mouth went dry. "But Asa is valuable."

"His skills are valuable. His magic is valuable. His soul? Disposable."

It was as bad as I had feared in my worst moments. "So Brindle has him. How are we going to get him back?"

Volodya gave me a cold smile. "We do exactly what you tried to do to me."

"Steal something of his, you mean. And offer it back in trade."

He flexed his fingers. "Well, it's not his yet. But I know he wants it."

I narrowed my eyes. "Is that because you want it, too?"

He grinned, and again it was such a familiar look that it nearly knocked the breath out of me. "We all want it." He held up a hand to silence my next question. "First we must leave this place. Keenan and his Headsmen are persistent. And my people will be hunting for me. Safer for both of us if I contact them." He pulled his phone out and fiddled with it for a second, then made a call. He ended the conversation a minute later and said, "Our transportation will arrive shortly."

"How do they know where you are?"

"I turned on a tracker that only they have."

"You said *our* transportation. Where are we going?"

"Back to my headquarters. From there we will gather our resources and plan."

I bit the inside of my cheek. This guy had fooled me before, taking advantage of my blind desperation, enjoying my distress. I knew full well he might do it again.

Volodya nodded as if I'd spoken all my thoughts aloud. "Now you must decide how far you will go to get Mr. Ward back." He gestured toward the door and then walked to it, but paused with his hand on the knob. "I won't tell you to trust me, because you shouldn't. But right now, our interests are aligned. If you help me acquire my prize, I will let you use it to hook Mr. Brindle."

I had no choice but to go along with him. Heading to the door, I grabbed the bag with the Ekstazo relic. But when I peeked inside, it was gone.

"I sense you've been wrong-footed."

I sighed. "No. I got exactly what I should have expected."

"Something has been taken from you."

"So what else is new?"

He frowned, comprehending. "My relic."

"Headsmen must have gotten it."

His lip twitched up into a snarl. *"Lie."*

My heart lurched as his face began to turn a mottled pink. "Fine. Someone else took it. But it was just part of the deal, part of saving your life."

For a few long seconds, he seemed to ponder that, staring at me like he could see the anxiety pouring off me, its color and texture and shape. And then his long fingers shot out and closed around my throat. He had me pressed up against the wall a second later. "Mr. Ward is not the only one you protect. Nor is he your only ally." The corner of his eye was twitching. "You will tell me your true purpose, or I will pull it out of you!"

"Please," I rasped, his fingers tight around my neck.

"I can feel all of it," he whispered, his mouth close to my ear, raising goose bumps. "Your torment, your pain, your fear and confusion. And your *lies.*" His grip tightened, and I saw stars. "You think you've been hiding these things, but you cannot hide from me. *No one* can hide from me."

I kicked feebly at his shins and slapped at his chest, and to my shock, he let me go, tears streaking down his cheeks. He staggered back from me, his eyes wild. "No one can hide from me," he roared. "No one!"

I sank halfway to the floor, gasping for air, as Volodya sniffed at his own skin and scraped at his arms and face.

"What did you do to me?" he shouted. "What is this drug that you put inside me?"

I had a feeling what was happening had less to do with the Rohypnol and more to do with the lingering scent and taste of Theresa, so faint that it didn't quite feel real, and the weird vibes about her that he was picking up from me. "Nothing that won't wear off by the end of today," I said.

"I should kill you," he said.

"I saved your life."

"You cost me my relic, and you drugged me. You drugged the Volodya!" shouted the Russian boss before descending into a rant in his native tongue. I pressed myself against the wall and tried to stay very still, afraid that one sudden move would bring him my way again. Volodya seemed lost in his own head, raging as he paced around the couch and picked up the throw blanket and held it to his face. All the while, tears dripped from his chin, and his teeth were bared.

Asa's dad was full-on insane.

The ring of Volodya's phone cut through his snarled Russian soliloquy, and it had a sudden, dramatic effect: he straightened and brought the phone to his ear. As he spoke, his tone was smooth. He hung up after a few seconds and turned his back on me. I held my breath, relieved I had hidden all the sharps in the apartment under the mattress in the guest bedroom. His shoulders rose and fell, and then he raised his head and faced me.

"Our car is here. Let's go." He walked to the door and opened it, pausing only when he noticed I hadn't moved. "Come. You are safe for the moment."

I let out a shrill burst of hysterical laughter. "That's comforting."

"It is the best I can offer you. For as long as our interests are aligned."

I cautiously followed him into the hall and trudged toward the exit, rubbing my aching throat. "So," I offered tentatively, "what is this prize that we're going to keep from Brindle?"

"An item that has only just become available. And only those of us who are best-informed know of its power." Volodya was strolling calmly down the corridor, as if his psychotic episode in the flat had never happened. "Brindle is a collector, like myself. I have no doubt he is aware of this turn of events."

"Is it an original relic that's surfaced?"

His gray eyes flared with intrigue. "You know of these relics."

I let out a bitter laugh. "Yeah. Little bit." I'd carried two of them inside my body, and it had nearly killed me.

"Each is a great prize unto itself. But the collection . . . ah, that is the mystery."

"Where each one is, you mean?" I happened to know that the Headsmen had two of the four—the Ekstazo relic, which Keenan had said they'd nabbed years earlier, and the Strikon, which Asa had given Jack Okafor III in exchange for his help in saving my life. The Sensilo . . . that one Asa had given to Tao, who had planned to give it to Zhong, the boss of the Midwest, in exchange for his freedom. As for the Knedas, I hadn't heard a thing about it.

"No, not where they are. How they work. Understanding the secret of the original relics is a treasure just as valuable as the relics themselves." We exited the building, and Volodya walked quickly to a sleek black sedan that was already at the curb, three men in black suits and sunglasses waiting next to it. On the corner, a gang of skinny, tattooed youths stared us down, and I was actually relieved to duck into the relative safety of the car.

"But the originals work like any other relic. Just much more powerful. Right?" I asked.

He shook his head. "I mean how they work *together*."

My brow furrowed as Moscow streaked past.

"All of the magic used to reside in one person—the Sorcerer. Somehow, it was separated into its various parts and distributed to the winds of time. And if it was separated, surely it can be . . . united. Reconstituted. Imagine such power." From the ecstatic look on Volodya's face, I knew he was doing exactly that.

"If the dude was so powerful, how was anybody able to kill him?" Keenan had told me he was executed by the Romans. "Seems like he should have been able to protect himself."

Volodya turned to me. "Another mystery lost to the years. But I suspect it will become clear if we can acquire the prize."

"Okay. Now you need to be more specific."

He bowed his head over his phone, his thumbs tapping rapidly, and then he turned the screen to face me. I leaned forward to read a headline: "Rediscovered Rarities of Rome on Display for First Time in a Century." I read the first few lines of the article and raised my head. "This is at the Metropolitan Museum of Art in New York City."

He nodded. "Our prize is there. I am certain of it."

"So is it a relic?"

He shook his head and returned his attention to his phone. "It is this." He showed me the screen again. There was a photo of a mosaic panel depicting a disturbing scene—a man tied spread-eagled to a giant *X* made of wood, with dark-robed figures plunging swords into his chest, his leg, his belly, and his skull. "I believe this to be him. The Sorcerer himself."

My stomach turned as I looked at the man's eyes, wide and completely black. "Okay . . . but, how do you know? I'm no history expert, but it seems like the Romans had a rep for feeding people to lions and crucifying them and stuff. It wasn't unusual for them. Couldn't this be *any* of their unlucky victims?"

"Perhaps. But see those runes, around the edge and at the top?"

I squinted at the writing. Surrounding the death scene were runes just like the ones I had seen all over Frank Brindle's casino and in the lair of Sukrit Montri, the boss of Thailand. "What do they say?"

He sat up straighter, his excitement palpable. "That is the question. That is a language that died following the Sorcerer's death, as the naturals who flocked to him were scattered. Although we know it is the key to the naturals' heritage and perhaps to our future, we have not before had the means to translate it, though I have searched the world over. But *this*"—he tapped the top of his phone—"this could be the key to translating the *Essentialis Magia*. The lessons of Akakios and the first naturals."

Keenan had called it the bible for naturals, a mythical book full of secrets. *Pages have been found,* he'd said. He hadn't mentioned it needed translating. "But can't you just use the picture here? Why do you actually need the panel itself?"

"Because it is what is inside that matters, not just what we see. Records attached to this particular artifact indicate several layers of pigment were applied many years apart. There are images and writing hidden beneath. So not only is it a crucial piece of our history, but with the proper equipment, it could very well be the key that unlocks all the secrets."

"How do you know all this?"

Volodya looked shocked. "It's as if you think I'm an ordinary man."

I scooted a little closer to the window and touched the tender spots on my neck. "No worries there."

He continued. "I must be the one to possess this panel. I have acquired portions of the original tome, the only pages known to remain."

I wondered if that was why Keenan had been so eager to nab him. "So you're going after the key. And Frank wants it, too." Now it made sense—the man had decorated his entire casino with those runes. The entire place memorialized them. They were everywhere you looked. And yet it turned out that no one knew what they said. "Does he have pieces of the *Essentialis Magia*, too?"

"Mr. Brindle has managed to collect reproductions. Possibly the largest compilation in the world."

Maybe Keenan had some of them, too? "It sounds like a lot of people will want this thing."

"We discovered that the panel and the rest of the collection were in the archives of the museum only a few months ago, when the curator announced the plan to put them on display. This is the first time they will be available for viewing by the public, starting on New Year's Day. But on New Year's Eve, there will be a gala to raise money for the museum, and an opportunity for patrons to have a look at the rarities in a private show."

"And we're going."

"It turns out that I need a good reliquary on my team. And I've decided to give you the opportunity. If all goes well, we'll have the prize in hand by the new year, and I will help you make the trade."

I shook my head. "You would never actually trade this precious panel for Asa."

He waved my concern away. "If you end up with him in the end, does it matter how you get there?" He smirked as he watched me. "There is nothing you wouldn't do." He leaned forward. "It's the only reason I'm still alive."

For a split second, I considered telling him Asa was his son. I wanted him to have a taste of my desperation, of my longing, of my determination. I wanted to knock the calculating look right off his face. But then his brow furrowed and his nostrils flared, and I remembered exactly who I was dealing with.

Volodya murmured something in Russian but didn't translate for me. The sedan pulled into a parking garage, and when we got out, we were ushered through a tunnel to an elevator that carried us down to Volodya's lair.

"I have assembled the group that will accompany you to America," he said as he ushered me into his inner sanctum.

"Oh, great," I muttered as Pavel jumped back from a gold chess set, wiping his hand on his pants. His dark swoop of hair fell over one eye as he straightened his skinny tie.

He began to speak in Russian, but Volodya held up an imperious hand. "English only. Don't be impolite."

Pavel's cheeks darkened. "Apologies, sir," he said quickly.

"You are terrified, Pavel. Is it because you are scared I will cut off your hands as a punishment for touching my possessions, or could it be that you're afraid I'm going to punish you for failing to bring Mattie and my relic to me?"

Pavel's Adam's apple moved as he swallowed. "I will never forgive myself."

Volodya grunted. "That is less important than whether *I* will forgive you. This is the chance to redeem yourself."

Pavel nodded curtly, and then his gaze darted over to the fireplace, where I realized two people were standing with their arms around each other. Volodya impatiently beckoned them both forward. "Come along.

Come along." He turned to me, his gaunt face stretched into a smile as he pointed at one half of the couple, a pale man who looked to be in his twenties. He had short brown hair and dark circles under his eyes. "Like my son, I am telling you."

I squinted at the guy. "*Like* your son?"

"Oh, I do not have children of my own. But I would claim Daniil, if he'd let me."

The young man bowed his head. "You are too kind, Volodya. My father would be so grateful that you honor him in this way."

"Daniil will be accompanying you," Volodya said to me and Pavel. "He is Strikon. And he has brought something of his father's for our use."

"Who is his father?" I asked.

"Arkady Igorevich Kalagin," the young man said solemnly. He unsheathed a knife from his belt and handed it to Volodya, who examined the blade.

I took an involuntary step back, and Volodya laughed. "You see, Daniil? Your father's power is renowned."

Daniil gave him a sad smile. "It is no consolation, I'm afraid."

Volodya clapped him on the shoulder. "We'll get him back, my friend. You may rely on that." He held on to Daniil—something most people were probably unwilling to do to a known Strikon—as the other half of the couple came forward, a woman who looked a little older than Daniil, maybe thirty, with round cheeks and striking blue eyes. She tucked a lock of her pin-straight black hair behind her ear and gave Volodya a tense, anxious smile.

"Mattie, this is Kira, and she is our new Ekstazo. Exquisite."

Kira bowed her head. "Thank you, sir," she said, her accent thick.

"And Mattie is our reliquary. Undetectable to magic sensors just like Pavel is, able to smuggle in the magic you will need to escape the venue after you capture my panel."

"What kind of magic are we talking about?"

"Something my father created," said Daniil. "Before he was taken by the Headsmen."

Volodya held up the knife and smiled at me. "You will carry the magic from this blade through security at the museum and make the transfer into a new relic just before you are ready to use it. Your tickets to the gala will be waiting for you in New York. I will be eager to hear word of your success. Call me for instructions as soon as you reach the safe house in Manhattan after the event."

Pavel and Daniil nodded, while Kira merely scooted closer to Daniil. He slid his arm around her and gave her a gentle smile. It was hard to believe he was the son of Arkady and Lishka, two people who were, by all accounts, straight-up evil. I reminded myself to watch them all very closely—these people were not my friends.

And I was safe only as long as our interests were aligned. "Wait," I said as Volodya began to gesture us all from the room. "Can I talk to you for a minute?"

The others looked at me, seemingly shocked that I would address Volodya in this manner. But they didn't have as much on the line as I did. Volodya only gave me a detached smile and gestured for the others to leave. "What is it?"

"I need proof."

He arched an eyebrow. "Proof of . . . ?"

"Proof that Asa's really with Frank Brindle. I need to know you're telling me the truth before I go on this hunt you've cooked up."

"You believe you have a choice?"

Anger lashed through my chest. "You know what? Yeah, I do. If you didn't need me, you could have just killed me by now. So if you want me to carry and release that magic at the right time and carry out your plan for you, then show me. Show me how you know."

He looked me over. "Are you sure you want to travel down this road? I told you it would hurt."

My heart pounded at the ominous tone in his voice—and the eager glint in his eye. "I'm sure."

He began tapping on his phone. "When Pavel told me that you believed I had taken Asa Ward, I began to make some calls. I will admit, I was curious about the man. So many stories. So much destruction. So sought after, and so hard to catch. Who had managed it?" He paused and looked down at his phone. "I consulted some of my agents in London and advised them to gather any information they could. One of them sent me this. It's from the VIP terminal at Stansted Airport."

He held it out for me to see. I cradled the phone in my palms as I stared down at the image. There were four men in the frame, their legs frozen midstride.

I didn't recognize two of them, but I bit my lip as I focused on the man between them.

Asa.

Their fingers circled around his biceps. His shoulders were high, like they were exerting upward pressure to keep him on his feet. He was wearing sweats and a T-shirt and flip-flops, despite the cold outside. And around his neck there was a thick black collar.

The light reflected the sheen off the planes of his face. I imagined it slick with sweat. His hair looked wet and disheveled. He was looking straight at the camera, so I could see that his expression was blank, his eyes dead.

"I have images from three other cameras in that terminal as they made their way out to their private flight," Volodya said quietly. I didn't look up, but I knew his eyes were on me, knew he was feeling—and probably savoring—every pulse of my anguish. "In all of them, he looks the same. It is the collar . . . they use it to control him."

I raised my head as a tear slipped down my cheek. Volodya was staring down at the image of Asa now, looking pensive. "I must say," he murmured. "He does look familiar."

I quickly shifted my attention to the fourth man before my brain settled on his statement. And immediately, a cold drop of fear slid right down my spine. Devilishly handsome, his dark eyes glittering, a smirking Reza Tavana walked behind Asa.

I glanced at the time stamp. "This was taken only a few hours after he was captured on the rooftop."

"Which means they could be anywhere, but my agent reported their flight was destined for New York City."

My eyes widened. "Not Las Vegas?"

"Frank Brindle is also in New York. He has been invited to the gala, in fact."

"Will Asa be there?" Would I really get that lucky?

Volodya shrugged. "It would depend on if he can be used. It's possible they will simply take as much magic from him as they can. Not as good as a sensor, who learns to interpret the signals he feels in his body, but still. If the magic is powerful, it can be a useful tool even to someone who does not wield it naturally."

I squeezed my eyes shut at the thought of Asa being drained. "Okay." I pushed the phone back toward Volodya. "Thank you."

"And now you believe?"

I opened my eyes and looked up at him, feeling rage and love tangle tight inside my chest. "Yes. Just tell me when we leave."

Volodya took a deep breath, nostrils trembling as he inhaled my suffering. "Tonight."

"Good. I'd like someone to get me a room and a change of clothes. I'm going to take a shower and rest. Then we can upload Arkady's magic for transport." My voice was steady. And hard. I couldn't get Asa's blank look out of my head—or the memory of Reza's smirk. He was enjoying seeing Asa submit.

He was enjoying Asa's pain.

I gritted my teeth as I headed toward the door.

"Mattie. One more thing."

I looked over my shoulder.

Volodya raised his gaze from the screen of his phone. "I will find out who he really is. You cannot hide it from me forever." Without giving me so much as a glance, he turned and walked deeper into his room, toward the darkened nook between the bookcases, once again just a lonely black silhouette set against the flames.

CHAPTER FOURTEEN

I perched on the edge of the leather office chair and looked around one more time. This terminal was part of the hotel's business center, just three computers and a printer in a tiled alcove with textured walls and a small fountain burbling in the corner.

Keeping an eye on the hallway leading to the lobby, I pulled up a browser and logged in to the e-mail that Theresa had given me. I could only hope it would still be active.

It was, but there were only junk e-mails in the inbox, advertising penis-enlargement drugs and dates with hot girls. I clicked on the "Drafts" folder.

> Hey. Wondering what you're doing for New Year's.

That was all it said. No address for the recipient.

I glanced over my shoulder for the billionth time and clicked "Edit," picking up the message where it left off.

I don't know if you want to join or not, but I'll be gathering with some fellow ancient art lovers and wearing something fancy to make that guy I have a crush on wish he'll be leaving with me.

I read it over a few times. Was that enough information to go on, or was it not specific enough? I peered at the clock on the wall. It was nearly noon, and in a few hours I was going to head to the Met with my little team of Russian mobsters to case the joint before the gala that evening. We were leaving nothing to chance—we had all arrived in the United States in separate cities and converged on New York from different directions. Pavel and I were both in this hotel, but Kira and Daniil were in another, closer to Central Park. They thought all of this was necessary to keep Brindle and anyone else who was paying attention from believing that Volodya was going to make a play for the panel—until it was too late.

Absently, I rubbed my chest. Thanks to my little vault, we'd easily smuggled Arkady's piece of Knedas magic into the city. I couldn't help but feel strange with it inside me. Arkady had been vicious. He had reveled in the thought of hurting people, or worse, making them hurt themselves—I remembered too well how he'd smiled as he influenced a bartender to blow up a crowded restaurant, just for fun.

"Spilling all our secrets?" I looked up to see Pavel striding down the hall.

I quickly logged out and closed the browser. "Yep. My mom is head of an international magical spy ring, so I made sure she knew exactly what I was up to."

He stopped behind me and glanced at the blank screen. "You understand there could be agents anywhere, yes? And that the Volodya will have us hunted down if we cannot follow through with the plan?" He looked terrified at the prospect.

I stood up. "You don't seem to understand that I want us to succeed as badly as he does."

"Then you should get ready. Daniil and Kira are going to meet us in an hour. You did not respond to your texts." He nudged my purse with his toe.

So he'd come looking for me. I'd been so absorbed in filling in Theresa that I'd almost gotten myself caught. "Must have had the ringer off." I stood, picked up my purse, and walked toward the lobby. After a few steps, I turned to see if Pavel was following.

He wasn't. He was staring at the log-in page I'd just closed.

By the time we hit the steps of the Met for the gala, I was wound tight. Also, my feet were hurting. However, I looked damn good. Though Keenan had said Volodya was strapped for cash, he had been generous with our expenses. My dress was sapphire blue, with a high neckline, but lace and mesh in the bodice more than hinted at my curves. I'd pulled my unruly hair into a sexy twist.

Pavel, Daniil, and Kira had all cleaned up well, too. Kira and Daniil seemed stunned by the grandeur as we entered under the center arch of the building and handed our invitations to the attendant. Pavel, on the other hand, looked slick as a snake. He had snubbed a tuxedo in favor of a blue suit, and when the jacket parted at his waist, I could see his silver belt buckle.

Nodding to it, I said, "It doesn't really match your outfit."

"I don't really care," he replied. Then he nodded at the little vial of sand that hung around my neck. "Neither does that. But I know exactly why you wear it. *Because* of this." He tapped the buckle.

I thought back to the first time we'd seen each other, on that street in Prague. *Something tells me you're the girl I'm looking for,* he'd said as he stared at my chest. I'd had no idea why at the moment, but now I knew my necklace contained Asa's magic.

"So the belt buckle is a magic-sensing relic. How powerful?"

"Enough to tell me who we're dealing with in there. At least who carries magic and who doesn't."

"Can you feel what's inside my vault?"

He slid his arm around my waist. "No. Not a trace. But that's why you're here."

I tensed but didn't push him away. We were supposed to be here together, one of two desperately rich and connected couples, here to mingle and be seen. "So," I said as we strode between giant pillars and into the entrance hall, full of glittering dresses and shiny black lapels, shimmering jewels and lips. Waiters were circulating with flutes of champagne and hors d'oeuvres. "Sense anything interesting?"

Daniil and Kira moved close—obviously they were wondering the same thing. Pavel shifted uncomfortably and grimaced. "This place is crawling with naturals."

I glanced around. No one seemed to be paying us much mind, but that didn't mean we weren't being watched. "We knew this thing was in high demand. Doesn't change the plan."

Kira touched Pavel's shoulder, and he relaxed. "Thank you," he said. "I don't know how magic sensors stand it."

At that I felt a pang in my heart. "If any of them are here tonight, they shouldn't be too hard to spot. Just look for the most miserable, sweaty person in the room."

Daniil took Kira's hand from Pavel and pulled it back to his own body. "Good to know. Are we all clear on the plan?"

I smiled and accepted a glass of champagne from a handsome waiter. "Lay eyes on the prize."

"Identify the players," said Pavel, eyeing a tray of passing salmon crostini.

"Download the glamour," whispered Kira as she leaned her head on Daniil's shoulder.

"Get in position." Seeing as Kira and Daniil had magic that could disable attackers, they were going to ensure we had a way to get out. Kira would head through the Great Hall toward the Medieval Art section, on the other side of which there lay an emergency exit on the Central Park side of the building. Daniil would make his way to the exit to our left, through the restaurant just on the other side of the Greek and Roman Art display. Our prize was in that gallery, and that's where Pavel and I were going.

"Then we get the party started." Pavel slid an entire crostino into his mouth.

"And I leave early," I said quietly. I was the one who would get the mosaic tablet out of the building while everyone else was occupied.

Pavel grinned, his cheeks bulging. "I'm looking forward to wielding Arkady's magic."

Daniil frowned. "Just control it, or we'll be caught up in it, too."

"I know what I'm doing."

"You have no idea how powerful my father is, do you?" Daniil asked.

Pavel rolled his eyes. "I know how to use relics."

My hand tightened around my champagne flute. "This isn't a game," I said from between clenched teeth. "Our lives are riding on this." And so was Asa's.

"Let's get to work," Daniil said, casting one more wary look at Pavel, who was touching his belt buckle and frowning.

I finished my drink and set the empty glass on a passing waiter's tray, then looped my arm into Pavel's. The crowd was slowly drifting in the direction of the Greek and Roman Art gallery to our left, and we followed. Our mosaic panel was in there somewhere. I'd spent the last few days memorizing every part of it, wondering what answers it could bring, wondering how men as dangerous as Volodya or Brindle might use it.

By the time we reached the gallery containing the collection, Pavel had guzzled three glasses of champagne. "I'll be right back," he said, looking around. "Got to drain the snake, as you Americans say."

"Only idiots say that."

"Don't go far." He pulled his arm from mine and headed off.

I turned my attention back to the art on display. Apparently most of the artifacts had been discovered in a tangled maze of tombs in the hills outside the city of Rome. I meandered past a selection of bronze gods, a few sturdy urns depicting javelin-throwing and running men, and a number of small portraits.

"You look a lot better than the last time I saw you," said a deep voice behind me.

I turned slowly, knowing who I'd find there. I gave him a smile. "So do you, Jack." No lie, either. His tuxedo was perfectly tailored to his muscular physique, and his dark-brown skin didn't have the greenish cast it had had when Asa and I had left him in a broom closet in that hotel in Atlanta, drugged out of his mind—but also clutching the original Strikon relic. "Did you redeem yourself?"

He gave me a sheepish smile. "Only halfway."

"You're lucky you ended up with anything."

"Only because Ward plays so dirty."

"Says the man who was trying to double-cross him. That you ended up with anything is a testament to Asa's sense of fair play." He could have done anything he wanted to Jack, but he'd left him with a priceless prize. "And his belief that the Headsmen are a shade better than the alternative."

Jack glanced around. "More than a shade. And the sooner you figure that out, the better off you'll be."

"I'll take that under advisement." I began to edge away, but he stayed close.

"I know why you're here."

Crap. "Do tell, Jack."

He slid even closer. "Choose the right side this time, Mattie. For all our sakes."

"Right and wrong feel like luxuries right now," I admitted. I looked away from him, focusing over his shoulder, where several mosaic panels hung on the wall. "Can we continue this conversation some other time?"

Like . . . after I'd done whatever was necessary to get Asa back. Because the panel I needed to steal was *right there*. No more than ten feet away.

Jack's broad hand closed around my upper arm. "Keenan said he would help you, and you screwed him."

I winced as he squeezed. "I am sorry about that. Is he all right?"

"Fine. Just wondering why you'd help a murdering, scheming psychopath instead of the good guys."

"I've seen the Headsmen in action, Jack."

"We do what we have to, Mattie."

"Then you should understand me perfectly." I lifted my chin. "There is one thing I care about, Jack. And I'll do what I have to do, too."

He let go of my arm. "I'm gonna hate to bust you, girl." He looked over his shoulder, right at the mosaic. It was masterful in its own way, thousands of chips of stone in dozens of different shades that somehow came together in the grisliest way possible. The original sorcerer, the blades entering his body, his face agonized yet full of fury and defiance, his eyes simple ebony shards. "But it can't fall into the wrong hands. The stakes are too high."

I crossed my arms over my chest. "The Headsmen have two of the four original relics," I said quietly. "It's not like anyone else could collect all of them."

Jack grunted. "Here's hoping." He glanced down at his waist, where his phone was vibrating. "Good seeing you, Mattie. Stay out of trouble, please. It won't be pretty if you don't."

I frowned as I watched him shoulder his way through the crowd, his phone pressed to his ear, just as Pavel sidled up next to me.

"Was that Jack Winchester?" Pavel asked, scowling. "What did he want?"

"You know him?"

It looked like Pavel had something very sour sitting on his tongue. "Volodya uses him for his transactions on this side of the ocean. He was going to engage him for this job as well."

No wonder he knew what I was up to. "But Jack turned him down?"

"Apparently he was already under contract."

My mouth went dry. "You think he's here for the same reason we are?"

"Why else would he be here?"

Jack had disappeared, of course. I'd assumed he was here as a Headsman, but that was stupid. He had told me he'd been undercover for years, and even Asa had heard of his Winchester alias. I leaned in close and pretended to kiss Pavel's neck. "Well, he had *his* eyes on *our* prize," I whispered. "So maybe it's time for us to download."

"Almost," said Pavel, putting his arm around my waist and turning me so I was facing the rest of the collection. "You need to know who else is here."

I gazed across the room. "Who am I looking at?"

"The blonde by the urns works for Donati. Local boss." Pavel studiously looked away from the woman as her sharp gaze slid over the room. "And the guy eyeing up the headless statues over there—that's one of Montri's."

I let out a breath and shot what I hoped was a casual glance toward the statues. Thankfully, the man standing there wasn't Ho-Jun or anyone else I recognized. "Okay. So two bosses represented."

"Three," said Pavel. "Look by the portraits."

I caught a glimpse of a dark-haired man in the midst of a crowd of guests, but it was enough. "Myron."

Pavel smirked. "The coward."

I didn't defend him. I was still mad at him for stopping me from even trying to help Asa on the Harrods roof. "So Botwright might make a play for it as well?"

"If *he's* her representative, she doesn't stand much chance."

"Still—shouldn't we get our glamour ready? What if one of these guys tries to get to the panel before we can?"

"Wait. There's someone else here," said Pavel. He looked pained as his fingers ran across his belt buckle. "In the entrance hall."

"You can feel him from here?"

"More than one," he said, beads of sweat breaking out on his forehead. "And they're strong." He grabbed my hand and tugged me toward the hallway, then both of us stepped behind a large pillar to peer at the crowd in the Great Hall. "See anyone you recognize?"

"Who exactly am I looking for?"

Pavel looked a little sick. "Strikon. And . . . something else. But it's hard to tell because—"

"The Strikon makes it hard to sense." I scanned the glittering wealth in the grand room but saw no one I recognized. "Where do you feel them?"

"I'll be back," Pavel said, covering his mouth. He made a retching sound as he bolted for the bathroom.

Concern rising, I turned back to the crowd. And that was when I saw them.

Hair slicked back from his perfect face, wearing a suave smile, the most powerful Strikon I'd ever met looked dapper and deadly next to an auburn-haired woman wearing a demure black dress.

There he was, behind them. Lean and tall, clad in a black tuxedo, his cheeks hollow and his face pale. I could just see the collar—he was wearing it in place of a bow tie. His expression was blank as his gaze raked the hall and homed in on me. But his eyes didn't meet mine. Instead, they focused on my chest.

He must have sensed his own magic.

"Asa," I whispered, breathless as need and love and hope fluttered mercilessly inside me. I was dying for him to look me in the eye, dying to know what his held for me.

There were only a hundred feet or so between us, closer than we'd been since that night on the roof. And my heart—it was beating so hard that it's a wonder my little vial of sand wasn't bouncing right off my chest.

I don't care what I have to do, I silently promised him. *I'm going to get you out of here. Tonight.*

CHAPTER FIFTEEN

I took a few quick steps back as Reza looked toward the Greek and Roman gallery, letting the enormous column hide me from sight. My thoughts were whirling, landing on possibilities and discarding them just as quickly. I was in a building full of naturals, nearly all of them agents of bosses from all over the world. They weren't here for me or Asa, though—they were here for the mosaic that could help decipher the secrets of the *Essentialis Magia* and the original relics.

Maybe this was the best possible place to get away, then. Maybe this was the *perfect* place.

What we needed, though, was the magic in my chest, the glamour that would occupy everyone nearby. I turned and walked quickly toward the sign for the bathrooms and met a pale, sweaty Pavel on the way. "I spotted the naturals you felt. It's Brindle's people. And one of them is Asa."

Pavel scowled. "Did they see you?"

"Asa did. I think. But he won't tell them."

My conduit companion let out an impatient sigh. "You don't know that."

"Yes, I do. Now let's download so we can get to work. It's getting crowded in here."

Pavel patted his pocket, where his phone lay. "Kira and Daniil are in position. They know we've got eyes on our prize."

"Good. Where do you want to do this?" I pulled a lipstick from my clutch. It was fake, just a casing filled with a steel slug made to carry strong magic.

Pavel steered me behind the headless naked statues. "Can you stay on your feet?"

I arched one eyebrow. "I'm not the one who was staggering after the upload."

He chuckled and held out his hand for the lipstick. "Ready when you are." He pressed me up against the wall and slid his hand up my bare arm to my neck.

I glanced around. People seemed to be deliberately looking away from our intimate moment. "Okay. Here we go."

I mentally opened the magic vault in my chest, and out rushed the Knedas magic like the slip of a knife across my skin. Sharp and potent and tasting like metal, blood, salt, sweat . . . power. Pavel flinched as it tore through him, and my fingers closed over his elbows, supporting him in case he stumbled. But he kept his grip on the relic, holding it clenched in his fist as the manipulation magic passed from his body and into the lipstick case.

We were both panting when it was done, but we were on our feet, still embracing behind the headless statues. Resisting the urge to shove Pavel away, I stayed with my back to the wall and let him slowly step backward. "Did Volodya tell you what it is, exactly?" I asked.

Pavel nodded. "It's a fire and the system that suppresses it." He pointed up at several knobs poking down from the ceiling, set at regular intervals throughout the gallery.

"Sprinklers?"

He shook his head. "In a museum? No. Gas. It goes off for ten seconds—and it's loud. That's all the time you have to get out of the room. The fire system will clear people out, and the alarm will blend with the one that goes off when we snatch the panel. All we have to do is get it down from the wall and get you out of here."

We straightened our clothes and stepped from our little hiding place. A man's genteel voice filtered through the intercom, announcing dinner in the restaurant in the next gallery. "Good timing," I said, watching people turn away from the mosaic panel and head toward food.

"I'll start it up when you get the thing from the wall," Pavel said quietly, positioning himself in front of me as I approached the panel. "Ready?"

Ready to roll, my thoughts whispered. But all my plans had changed in the last ten minutes. I looked around for Asa. Once the chaos began, could I get to him fast enough? If I had the panel, surely I could use it to pull Reza's attention from him long enough for us to get out, and it was so valuable that it had to be the Strikon's first priority. I knew Kira was waiting for me near the Central Park exit, but I was planning to leave the panel behind and head out the front, which was closest—with Asa. He might be weak and hurting, but I could get him into a taxi and be speeding away within a minute. After that we could figure it out together. Finally. "Okay."

Quick as I could, I reached up and grabbed the mosaic panel. It pulled off the wall easily but jerked loose from my grip. "Oh, crap. Pavel, there's a wire . . ."

Pavel turned around as someone shouted, "The panel!" He cursed and grabbed my hand as if trying to get me to let go of the artifact, and then used his other hand to steady the panel.

He let out a choked gasp, and my head snapped back as an unmistakable rush of magic, deep and rustling like a whisper from the grave, poured into me, filling my mouth with the taste of earth. For a moment,

I couldn't breathe as it filled my chest, but then it streaked into my vault and the door slammed shut. I opened my eyes to see a few people staring at us, and Pavel leaning on the wall. I stared down at the panel, still hanging from its wire. "Pavel, the glamour!" I kicked him gently in the calf to get him moving as guards barreled toward us.

Blinking and clearly still stunned, Pavel reached into his pocket and shoved a pair of wire cutters into my hand. He reached into his pocket again and withdrew the lipstick, tearing off the top and holding the small cylinder tightly in his palm. An alarm pierced the hum of conversation. Guards shouted and people screamed as one woman pointed at flames creeping across the ceiling above. The stench of smoke filled the air. The hissing of the gas began, and people stampeded, half rushing toward the restaurant and half back toward the Great Hall and the main exit. I clipped the wire and dropped the cutters. Another alarm screamed, but no one seemed to notice as smoke and billowing gas from the waterless fire-suppression system filled the air. I hefted the small but surprisingly heavy panel with both hands and tucked it under my arm. I left Pavel holding the lipstick and bolted for the Great Hall.

No one around me seemed the slightest bit aware or concerned that I was in the process of stealing a priceless artifact. In fact, I had trouble holding on to it as I was jostled by fellow gala attendees frantic for air. I began to cough from the smoke even though I knew it wasn't real. Arkady's magic was good.

As I reached the threshold of the Great Hall, I spotted Reza, Asa, and the auburn-haired lady I now recognized as Lila, a reliquary under the employ of Frank Brindle. While Asa stood impassive, Lila was gesturing toward the exit, and Reza was covering his mouth and nose with his suit jacket and scanning the room. I made for them, planning to hand over the panel and run with Asa. I was so close.

Until more than a dozen armed men poured through the main entrance, wearing black bandanas over their faces. They started shooting before they had even reached the Great Hall. The screams and wails redoubled in a deafening symphony of terror. I pitched forward as someone collided with my back, and the panel clattered to the floor next to me. A bullet hit the column behind me, raining stone dust on my head.

"Everybody down," shouted one of the men, but people were running and shrieking. As I got to my feet, I realized Asa, Reza, and Lila were gone.

Time for me to go, too. I grabbed the panel and, bent nearly double, ran toward the Medieval Art gallery. Sure a bullet would hit me in the back at any moment, my feet protesting every step, I sprinted past statues of saints and apostles and said a little prayer as I did. Almost everyone else must have been trying to flee out the front or through the Roman gallery, because this part of the museum had already cleared out. I reached a side gallery and turned for the final stretch before the exit where Kira was supposed to be waiting. But just as I turned a corner, an arm locked around my waist and swung me against the wall.

The moment I felt his body against mine, my brain exploded with frantic joy. "Asa!"

He reached down and ripped the panel from my grasp, then whirled for the exit. Stunned, I threw myself after him, wrapping my arms around his waist and wrenching him back. "Snap out of it," I cried. "Asa, it's me!"

He staggered as my weight stopped his forward momentum, and I reached up and touched his face, trying to turn his body toward mine. He froze for a split second as my fingers slid across his cheek. Then he tucked the panel under his arm and shoved me back, pressing a hand to my chest, right over my heart. I put my hand over his and held it there. "It's me. Let's get out of here right now. Together."

I looked at his face, taking in the dark circles under his eyes. He was breathing hard, the hair at his temples damp with sweat, his head tilted as if he couldn't quite place me, his eyes focused on my mouth. And then his lips were pressed to mine. I met his kiss with ferocity, relishing the slow, sensuous probe of his tongue, like he was savoring my taste. Finally, he pulled back. "Let's go." He took my hand and pulled me along, back toward the Great Hall.

"Asa, wait! All those men—"

"Glamour."

"Oh." I let out a strained laugh. "It was a good one."

"Come on."

My brow furrowed as I took in the flat, unemotional sound of his voice. "Are you really all right?"

He didn't answer.

I dug in my heels. "Wait."

He yanked on my hand. "No." He glanced at a watch strapped to his wrist. Beneath it seemed to be some sort of white wrap—a bandage? "We have forty seconds."

"What? Who has forty—"

He put his arm around my waist and forced me forward.

"No!" I jabbed him in the ribs and grabbed at the panel. "I'm not going that way!"

"Reza and Lila are waiting," he said in that cold, dead voice.

I began to fight him, slapping at his chest as he tried to wrestle me along. Horror and confusion had replaced my joy. "Asa, listen to me. You can get out. This is your chance. Come with me. We can leave this way!" I threw my body toward the Central Park exit, but Asa caught me and lifted me off my feet. I grabbed one of his forearms, right over the white wrap I'd seen, and he flinched, grunting in pain and dropping the mosaic to the floor. A piece of orange stone popped out and landed by Asa's boot.

"Freeze," bellowed a cop as he ran into the Medieval Art gallery. "Put her down and get your hands up, both of you!" He aimed his revolver at us.

Asa paused, eyeing the police officer. Slowly, he relaxed his iron grip and lowered me to my feet, taking just a half step behind me as he did. As I raised my arms I heard a soft smack, like a hard object hitting skin.

"Step to the side, sir. Hands up."

"You got it," said Asa. He took a large step to the side. But as he lifted his shaking hands, he flicked his wrist, sending a small object flying toward the cop. It landed at the officer's feet—and he screamed. His weapon spiraled halfway across the room as if he couldn't get rid of it fast enough.

Asa pocketed the piece of orange stone that had come loose from the panel. When he lunged for me, I scooped the mosaic from the floor and smacked him across the face with it, leaving him staggering. "Stop it," I shouted. "We're on the same side."

His steps unsteady, he advanced on me as I backed up into the side gallery again. The look on his face scared me—as did the realization that he hadn't once made eye contact with me. I wished Kira would appear and help me out. Maybe she could dose him with her magic and get him to come with us? I hated that I was considering doing that to him, but as more cops ran into the gallery and the room echoed with their shouts, I was desperate.

"Asa, please," I cried as he reached for me again. I stomped my heel down on his foot, and he cursed and shoved me away. My ankle buckled, and I fell to my knees.

"Mattie?" Kira ran into the room, her eyes wide.

"Goddammit," Asa said.

"Kira, get your hands on him," I shrieked.

But Asa was too fast. He ripped the panel from my grip and kneed me in the chest when I tried to follow him. Then, as Kira ran forward, he drew a water pistol from beneath his jacket and shot her in the face. She stumbled back, gasping, and Asa muttered something to her as he ran by. He was out of view in an instant. The Medieval Art gallery was filled with the shouts of police now, coming closer with every second.

I pushed myself up to my feet as Kira raced past me, shouting as she charged the cops.

"Kira, no!" I staggered after her.

She let out an animal scream and barreled into the Medieval Art gallery. I threw myself behind a pillar as the shots rang out. "Hold your fire," a man shouted, and the gunfire finally stopped.

I peeked out from behind my pillar to see Kira sprawled on the floor of the gallery, her eyes empty, blood trickling from her mouth.

"Hands up!" the cop nearest to me shouted.

Too stunned to do anything but obey, I raised my arms. The cop ran forward and grabbed my wrist, then jerked it down and behind my back. He did the same with my other arm and cuffed my hands tightly. Blinking in disbelief, my ears ringing with the alarms and the aftereffect of the bullets, I trudged past Kira, so obviously dead, and into the Great Hall. The burglar alarm was still shrieking, but there were no masked, armed men, no fire.

Only a lone body, lying next to one of the columns in the entryway. A man in a slick blue suit.

"We got one male victim here," called the cop who was escorting me out. "Someone get a paramedic."

As we walked past, I saw what lay next to the man's limp hand. A lipstick. My eyes darted to his face. Pavel's features were frozen in an expression of absolute agony. Frothy, blood-tinged saliva leaked from his parted lips. His face was covered in claw marks, and his fingernails were crusted with blood.

Magic wasn't supposed to affect him . . . but something certainly had.

Tucked in his collar was a note, scrawled in big letters, hastily written. As the cop marched me past the dead conduit, I was able to read it, the words carving themselves into my already broken heart.

Nice try.

CHAPTER SIXTEEN

My vision blurred with tears as I was marched down the steps of the Met to a waiting patrol car. They were parked up and down the block, police officers on foot everywhere, interviewing gala attendees, directing traffic. Two ambulances were up on the sidewalk, their rear doors open. There were a few paramedics providing first aid while others carried stretchers up the stairs.

It was too late for Kira and Pavel. I could only hope that Daniil had gotten away. He probably didn't even know that Kira was dead.

Or that Asa was responsible for her death. He'd told her to charge the cops after dousing her with manipulation magic, I was sure. I'd seen him do this kind of thing before, but only to someone who deserved it.

I couldn't figure out what had happened in those wild minutes. It felt like a giant hole had opened up inside me, like someone had torn him right out of my heart. The memory of his cold, flat voice . . . He'd barely seemed to recognize me, and yet he'd kissed me. He'd wanted me to go with him. He'd tried to *force* me to go with him. I shuddered.

"It's warmer in the car," said the cop. He opened the door and put his hand on my head as he guided me inside.

"Don't I have rights or something?" I asked. "I assume I'm under arrest."

"Lady, you are in serious trouble. Got at least one witness who saw you with that piece of art that went missing tonight. But right now we're just trying to figure out what the hell happened." He slammed the door and spent several minutes conferring with his colleagues while I pressed my face to the window, watching for Daniil. Things had gone wrong so quickly. Could he get word to Volodya?

And even if he could, with his empire crumbling and his money running out, could Volodya do a single thing to help us? And would he want to?

The cop came back with his partner, and the two of them got in the front. The cop who'd cuffed me read me my rights, his voice washing over me like white noise as I watched two news trucks pull up to the curb.

How was this going to be contained?

When we got to the station, I was taken to a small interrogation room, where a dour-looking cop asked me several questions I refused to answer, including my name. Finally, I just put my head down on the table. She let out an exasperated sigh and left.

Asa was gone. Whatever they had done to him, they were controlling him completely. He'd been planning to turn me over to Brindle, something he had been willing to die to prevent in the past. I didn't want to think about what they'd done to him to destroy his will. They'd taken him from himself. My fists clenched as hatred and fury trickled into the pit Asa had left behind.

The door to my interrogation room opened, but I didn't open my eyes. My forehead was pressed to the metal table. They could question me all night. They could toss me away. I didn't—

"What a mess, Mattie," said Keenan.

My eyes popped open. "Oh, great. Here to disappear me?"

He chuckled and sat down across from me, his blank badge held loosely in his fingers—probably a Knedas relic that had allowed him to fool the cops into letting him in. "That might be doing you a favor at this point."

"And I'll bet that's the last thing you want to do."

"It's not about what I want, Mattie."

I lifted my head. "What *is* it about?"

"Who has the panel?"

I sagged in my chair. "Asa took it to Brindle."

Keenan cursed under his breath. "Brindle is the last person who should have it."

"So you know about it? You know what it can do?"

"No one knows exactly what it can do. But if the exterior is any clue, the interior will reveal secrets that have been hidden for thousands of years."

I tensed. "The interior." Volodya had believed it was the underlying images that were valuable. He hadn't warned us that the stupid thing was full of magic—a kind I'd never felt before. A kind I now had stored inside my vault.

Keenan nodded. "X-rays will likely reveal layers beneath—"

I sagged in my seat. "Oh." Maybe none of them had known.

His eyes narrowed. "What did Volodya tell you?"

"He just said it was the key to translating the pages of the *Essentialis Magia*. Specifically the ones that say how to use the original relics."

"Exactly—can you imagine one of the bosses with that power?"

"I'm not even sure what that power is—only that it wasn't enough to protect that original sorcerer guy from execution, despite the fact that he also had all that magic and all those followers."

"My hope would be that the tome has answers to that as well. It was written by the survivors of those events. And we need to understand all of it, especially if any of the bosses is able to get hold of more than one relic."

"Well, you have two, don't you?"

"Right. But the Sensilo is still out there—"

"Might want to ask Zhong Lei about that." Assuming Tao made it back to Chicago to give it to him.

Keenan's eyebrows rose. "That's good to know. We still have no idea where the Knedas original is, though, and it's arguably the most dangerous of all of them."

"It's not in some boss's collection somewhere?"

"I've been searching for any hint of its existence for the last twenty years. If anyone does have it, they're not using it, and it's hard to see how any boss could resist that temptation."

"Would the *Essentialis Magia* offer any clues as to its location?"

A slow smile spread across Keenan's face. "The right pages, I would think."

"So this panel is basically the key to everything." I rubbed my hands over my face. I was pretty sure I had the actual key tucked inside my chest.

"And right now, our focus has to be on getting it back."

"Our?"

Keenan leaned forward. "You have some choices to make, Mattie. I want to make your options clear. I want you to think about your priorities."

My eyes burned. My priority had been to rescue Asa. But it didn't seem like he wanted to be rescued. I didn't know how to reach him, or what it would take. I couldn't reconcile the dead look in his eye with the passion of his kiss, with the way he'd laid his hand over my heart . . .

Wait. He'd laid his hand over my heart. Like he always did when he was trying to feel the magic in my vault. And then he'd kissed me, slow and deep—because being that close to me made it easier for him to detect what lay inside. Had he felt the ancient magic inside me? Is that why he'd wanted me to go with him?

"I'm listening," I said.

Keenan gave me a piercing look, one that reminded me he could sense everything I was feeling. "It wouldn't be hard for me to make a case that you're a danger to our world. I could imprison you indefinitely. I could take away the sun and the sky."

I stared at the one-way mirror, reflecting my exhausted face, my smeared mascara. "Or?"

"You help me. And this time you don't double-cross. You don't waver. You act as my eyes and ears, and you help me get the mosaic back from Brindle. When that's safe and sound, your debt will be paid."

"And Asa?" I whispered.

"Asa . . ." Keenan sighed. "Are you really holding on to him?"

"Someone has to," I snapped. "You of all people should know he'd never willingly work for a boss."

"Or anyone at all," Keenan said regretfully, rubbing his knuckles against his jaw.

I took in the sudden tension in his posture. "How long were you together?"

He sat back quickly, looking startled. But as our eyes met, he gave me a sad smile. "I saved him, you know. You're not the only one who's been determined to rescue him."

"From a boss?"

He shook his head. "From himself. The Headsmen have sweep programs in the prison system. We find imprisoned naturals, assess their threat level, and help nonmagical authorities manage them. Asa was discovered in the hole at the maximum security facility in Menard, Illinois, over fifteen years ago."

"Maximum? He was only serving a year for breaking and entering and assault!" Charges that were completely trumped up, pure betrayal by Asa's father, or the man he'd *thought* was his father.

"True, but he'd gotten into several brutal altercations with other prisoners. He had a penchant for fashioning improvised weapons and using them to pretty nasty effect."

"I guess some things never change," I murmured, thinking of what he'd done to Kira.

"So it wasn't actually the initial charges that had gotten him where he was. It was what he did afterward. How dangerous he was. How feral. But our sensing relic picked him up easily, and I was brought in to evaluate him." He chuckled. "Ever dealt with a wild animal that's cornered?"

My heart squeezed. *I've been in cages before. Every time, I thought I was going to lose my mind.* "How did you get through to him?"

"I had him set free. Immediately. And I made a deal with him. If he cooperated, I would have all pending charges cleared, and there would be no more prison in his future. He had no idea how valuable he was. He was lucky he hadn't been scooped up yet. But I made sure he knew, and I promised to protect him."

"I bet that meant a lot to him, once he realized you were serious," I said. At that point, Asa had been tossed out like trash. And here was this guy, taking him out of his cage and swearing to keep the wolves at bay.

"There was something about him," Keenan said quietly. "I wanted to protect him. He just seemed . . . wounded. But so, so gifted." He ran a hand through his graying blond hair. "It got personal for me quickly."

I folded my arms over my stomach. I knew exactly what he was talking about. Asa had this lethal combination of strength and vulnerability, charm and need, and all of it mixed together to make him utterly magnetic. For me, at least. And apparently for Keenan. "It got personal for him, too, I guess?"

Keenan shrugged. "You know, I'm not really sure. I thought so at the time. It was forbidden, of course. He was under my protection and authority. I should have left him alone. But he drew me in, and then . . ."

I squirmed. I hated the idea of Asa with someone else. It didn't matter if it was a man or a woman. "You fell in love."

His lips twisted. "It almost ended my career. I was playing a dangerous game, but he was addictive. I told myself it would *make* my career if I got him to join us. I could imagine it—as partners, we would have been unstoppable."

I bowed my head. "Yeah," I whispered. "I know exactly what you mean."

"Then you should know it could never last. He took off the day before he was going to be initiated. He left the Headsmen. He left me. And I didn't see him again until Bangkok, when he once again proved why I never should have trusted him in the first place, why I never should have forgotten how I found him, and why." Keenan touched my hand. "And I sense how much you feel for him, Mattie. It echoes inside me, bringing all those memories to the surface. We're more alike than you believe. And we could be on the same side."

"Is this about Asa, or the mosaic?"

"Maybe both, considering he's the one who took it. Considering both are priceless. And maybe we can get both of them back."

I let out a shaky breath. "He doesn't have all of the panel, though."

Keenan's brow crinkled. "It broke?"

I shook my head. "There was magic in it, Keenan."

"No, it couldn't be. Jack scanned it with a sensing relic before the gala."

"It was weirdly heavy. I think the magic might have been packaged inside the mosaic somehow. But it was there."

"Was?"

"I have it," I whispered. "When my conduit grabbed it, he was touching me, too. And the magic just . . ." I waved my hand at my chest. "It was like nothing I'd ever felt before."

"You—you have magic from that panel inside you." He let out a bemused laugh. "This is incredible. Who else knows?"

"The conduit I was with. But he's dead."

"Ah. Pavel Mizenov. Low-level Volodya associate. Not usually a first-stringer, but then again, most of Volodya's top agents have been killed or have defected from his service over the last fifteen years. Arkady was the last of his inner circle to fall. And as for conduits—Volodya usually contracts with Jack for stateside transactions."

"He decided to give Pavel a chance." I hadn't been crazy about Pavel, but I felt terrible about the way he'd ended up. "We uploaded the magic by accident. It was quick, and I doubt anyone else knew." I sighed. "But Asa might have figured it out."

"What?" Keenan's voice was like a whip crack.

"He was trying to sense what was inside me. And then he was trying to take me with him."

"Could he have just been trying to get you out of there?"

How I wanted to believe that. "I don't think so," I murmured.

Keenan's body was alive with tension. "So Brindle might know you have it." Our eyes met. "That makes you very valuable, Ms. Carver."

"Only as long as I'm carrying the magic, you mean. And I suppose you want to download it."

"No. For something this ancient, this fragile, it should only be transferred back into its original vessel. Doing otherwise would be a risk I won't take."

"Like the original relics."

"If it were to shatter or leak, or if part of it were to be lost, we might never know what it could have told us."

"How does this magic relate to the mosaic? Is the panel actually important, or is it just a shell—just a reliquary like me?"

"I don't know yet. We won't know until we have both."

"I have something you desperately want, in other words." I sat up a little straighter.

He arched one eyebrow. "Something tells me that your help now comes with strings attached."

"Yours did. But now you can't just disappear me. You need me."

"I can force the magic out of you if I need to. Jack will help."

"Sure—and risk damaging the magic? Because I'll hold on to it until the bitter end. And I'm stronger than I've ever been. Strong enough to take on Jack." I lifted my chin in defiance. "I also don't care about the magic nearly as much as you do. I'm not invested in keeping it whole."

He paled a little. "This is ancient, one-of-a-kind magic."

I leaned forward. "I *know*."

"And your conditions?"

"I'll help you get this panel. And you'll help me get Asa back from Brindle. No arresting either of us afterward, though. I'll download the magic into the panel once I'm satisfied we have our escape hatch."

"Mattie, even if you can get Asa back, you can't know what state he'll be in."

I gritted my teeth. "Asa will be fine." I sounded more confident than I was, because even as I said the words, I remembered the blank, heartless look in his honey-brown eyes. They'd done something terrible to him. They'd taken his will. "But you know he'll never survive being a slave for long. It'll kill him." I thought back to the bandage on his wrist, the way he'd flinched when I grabbed his forearm. "Or he might kill himself." Maybe he'd already tried.

Keenan winced. "If you're going back out there as one of my agents, however temporarily, you're going to have to conceal your emotions a little better than that."

I groaned. "What do you suggest? Forget I love him?" That had been Theresa's suggestion. "Use my motivation to save him to shield everything that lies underneath?" That wasn't working either. My shield had cracked, broken by the cold look in Asa's eyes, the way he'd kissed me just to get at what was inside.

He sat back, looking me over. "Neither. I suggest you learn some mental discipline. And I am prepared to offer you some training in that regard. Training only offered to our elite agents. Because if you're going back to Volodya, you need to be in control of yourself."

"I'm going back to Volodya?"

He smiled, but it was grim. "You have to convince him to be the wounded gazelle. He is anyway, really. Not that he'll admit it."

"Brindle will believe he's weak because of what happened tonight." I thought of the note in Pavel's collar. *Nice try.* There was blood in the water.

"Volodya is known for his collection. He needed the panel to make any use of it, though. He was once believed to be the biggest threat: He had original pages from the *Essentialis Magia.* He had the original Sensilo relic. He had his own magic sensor. Her name was Theresa Harrison, and she was known to be as ruthless as he was, and just as powerful. He had the most powerful known Knedas in the world in Arkady, and a lethal Strikon in Lishka Bondarev. But one by one, the pieces fell. Now the king is unprotected, his kingdom in ruins." He chuckled. "Brindle dealt him a terrible blow tonight. You have to convince Volodya to turn weakness into strength."

"Assuming he doesn't kill me for failing."

"He won't, if you tell him what he needs to hear."

"Which is?"

"I don't know yet, Mattie." Keenan's eyes met mine, and there was a knowing glint there, one that spoke of millions of revealed secrets. "But something tells me you're the person to figure it out."

CHAPTER SEVENTEEN

"The trick is to hide only things you need to."

"I knew that already," I snapped, closing my eyes. I had been encased in the tube of the MRI machine for what felt like hours, my legs sticking out of the bottom. Laid out on a table. Living imaginary scenarios and trying to control my stupid brain—and my stupid heart.

"And to focus on completely emotion-neutral tasks. You have to concentrate. It's like training a muscle."

"I *know*."

"You can do this, Mattie," Jack said patiently. He was in the scanning room, staring at pictures of the blood flow in my brain. His deep voice filtered to me through a little speaker in my tubular prison.

"But right now, from what I'm sensing, I'd love to play poker against you," Keenan said. He was standing next to the MRI machine, announcing my feelings as soon as they surfaced and triggering Jack to start a new scan. "Remember—focus on the details of the plan, on the words you're saying, on each step toward your goal, no matter how small. If you do that, the stray thoughts and feelings will subside or fall away because your mind is so efficient. You're a machine. Think like one. It's all about mental discipline."

I blew out a slow breath. "Let's try again."

"All right," said Jack. "Imagine facing Volodya again. Picture the room you described to us, every detail. And then think about presenting the plan. You have to believe in it, or he won't. So focus on each little piece of it and how each one is essential for building the whole."

"A mosaic, basically," I muttered.

"If that helps you hold it together, then yeah."

As the MRI machine began to clank and thump, I thought of Volodya's silhouette in his darkened nook, the glowing embers of his cigarette, the dusty side tables covered in artifacts, the crossed swords on the wall. Trying to ignore the annoying noise, I pictured his face, but as soon as I did, my heart skipped uncomfortably. Asa had looked more like him than ever the last time I'd seen him—now he had the same coldness in his eyes.

The machine fell silent.

"Longing," Keenan announced.

"Makes sense based on what I'm seeing," said Jack, at the same time I said, "No!"

"I call 'em as I sense 'em," said Keenan. "Something you're not telling us, Mattie? This isn't the first time I've picked up that emotion with Volodya."

"Ugh. Just . . . let's just keep going, okay?" It was Asa. I couldn't get him out of my head, couldn't stop the hurt as I thought about what he'd done, what it meant for him.

This time I didn't even notice the noise of the machine—until it went quiet again.

It took a few seconds for Jack to speak. "Her brain signature's reflecting fear."

"Perfectly natural way to feel if you're hiding something," Keenan said smoothly. "How do you think Volodya will respond to that, Mattie? I hear terror excites him. Your weakness might send him into a frenzy."

The MRI machine banged and chugged for at least a minute while I tried—and failed—to refocus on my task. But a wish to kick Keenan in the shins kept creeping into my consciousness.

"Ooh. Anger," Jack announced when the scan was complete.

Keenan laughed. "Mattie, you burn a little hot, which is not necessarily bad. But if you want to succeed, you have to control yourself. You must force your thoughts to lead, but you're letting your emotions rule you. It's an indulgence you can't afford."

A tear streaked from the corner of my eye, sliding down the side of my face and into my ear. This reminded me of all the times I'd been strapped to a table, how Asa would give me whatever I needed to endure whatever was coming. Sometimes he was fierce, sometimes tough, sometimes soft as a caress. But every time, he was there for me, focused on me as if I were the only thing that existed for him. Now all of that was gone. I was alone. The chasm inside me opened wide. In my whole life, I'd never really been on my own. I'd had my parents. I'd had Ben. I'd had Asa. Then Theresa. Some of them had faltered, but all of them had looked out for me.

Now I was in the den of the Headsmen, but they weren't here for me. I was just a means to an end. The sob escaped my mouth before I could stifle it.

"Okay, Mattie," said Jack. "It's break time."

"I need one, too," I heard Keenan say.

The table I was lying on began to slide out of the tube, and by the time my head emerged, Jack was standing there instead of Keenan. He offered his hand. I took it and sat up, then wiped my face with my sleeve. "I guess I drove him away."

"Even just looking at pictures of your brain, that was pretty intense. And Keenan feels every bit of it," Jack said slowly, helping me hop off the table. "Come into the prep room."

He led me into a small room with a few couches and chairs, a place to relax before being tested. All the elite Headsmen had to be able to conceal their intentions and feelings, and all had to make it past Keenan, to fool him while someone watched the brain scan to see the feelings that were actually occurring. Apparently science and magic didn't converge in this case—you could have the feeling but conceal it. I just hadn't figured out how to do it yet.

I sank down onto the couch, and Jack settled across from me in a chair. "I'm wasting your time," I said. "I suck at this."

"You have a lot on your mind," he replied. "Not the same thing as sucking. I'm sorry about what happened to Ward, by the way. I never got to say it."

"Are you really?"

He laughed quietly. "Yeah. Kind of wish I'd met him under different circumstances. The only time we worked together, we had competing agendas." His gaze found mine. "All *he* cared about was keeping you safe, Mattie."

"He talked to you?"

"Nope. But it was obvious. All of his priorities. All of his plans. Every move he was going to make. Every move he wanted *me* to make." He grunted. "Dude was focused. He didn't give a shit about the original magic, not really. Not if it came at your expense."

I set my elbows on my knees and bowed my head. "I feel like I've lost him, Jack. He was such a different person when I saw him last night."

"Kind of like you, when you had that splinter in you?"

"I was still—"

He waved his hand at me. "You were a shell, nothing like you are now. He said he wasn't sure you'd ever recover." He paused, then shook his head. "But he was determined to save whatever tiny piece of you was left—not for himself, but for you."

"All I needed was fifteen pounds' worth of french fries, though. Asa . . . I don't know how to get him back if he doesn't want to leave. It's like they've turned him into someone else."

"You spent five minutes with him last night, alarms screaming and bullets flying."

"Yeah, and he tried to kidnap me!" But only after I'd fallen for his trick. I hadn't even realized how different he was, but maybe that was because I hadn't wanted to see it. And it was probably my fault that Kira was dead.

Jack put up his hands. "I didn't say this was going to be easy, girl. I'm just telling you what I saw this past spring. And that was a man willing to go to hell to save the woman he loved, even if she didn't love him back. So my question for you—are you willing to do the same for him? Not just halfway, but the whole thing? How far will you go?" He stood up. "You haven't decided yet. But until you're willing to go to hell and lay yourself down, until you just don't give a fuck about your heart, your soul, your freedom, until it's not about what *you* get but about what *he* needs—we might as well stop trying." He strode to the door. "I'll be in the booth if you want to pick this up again. Give me the signal, and I'll slide you back into the tube. But stop wasting our time. Don't come back unless you're going to commit."

I flinched as the door clicked shut.

He was so right. Ever since Asa had been taken, my focus had been on how I missed him, on how I wanted him back, on how I needed him. Yes, I'd been worried and enraged over what might be happening to him. I'd wanted to protect him. But in the end, it was about what I got out of it. *Him.*

I'd fooled myself into thinking I was on a rescue mission, but what I was really trying to save was *us*. And all that had become pathetically obvious last night. My emotional shield had cracked as soon as I'd realized Asa was no longer who he'd been, when I understood that he wouldn't protect me.

But he shouldn't have to protect me. As many times as he'd said it, as many times as I'd believed it, it wasn't his job.

It was mine, dammit. And that was what Asa deserved—a woman who could take care of herself, who wasn't just there to fight a battle for him. He needed someone to go to war.

So many times, I'd worried that I wasn't enough for him. Now it was time to prove I was, in the only way that counted. I needed to let go of my fantasy of getting him back and focus on setting him free. Fists clenched in determination, I got to my feet and headed back to the testing room.

I approached the door of the hotel room carefully, waiting for the trap to spring. Already, there was a seed of pain at the base of my skull, and I knew it could very well get a lot worse.

I had to do this, though. If anyone could get me back in with Volodya—*without* me ending up being his chew toy—it was the guy Volodya had practically claimed as his adoptive son.

According to one of the hotel maids, whose tongue I'd loosened with a Knedas oil–infused handshake, Daniil had been holed up in his room for three days. The staff was scared to bother him and scared to leave him alone, because his sobs had been so loud at one point that the folks in the room next door had called the front desk to complain. But when a desk clerk had tried to check on him, he had promised to bring down unimaginable pain on anyone who tried to open his door. Volodya had paid through until Friday, so they were putting off disturbing him again until then.

I couldn't afford the same luxury. Bracing for agony, I knocked twice, quick and not too hard. "Daniil? It's Mattie."

No answer, but there was a muffled thump, maybe a footfall.

"Please let me in. I don't want to be out here in the hallway for long. I don't feel safe." I stared at the peephole as my headache intensified.

"Please." I touched the door and let out a shaky breath. "I've been so scared. It took all the courage I had to come find you."

"Where have you been?" A raspy, broken voice.

I winced as a shard of pain lanced through my brain. "I was arrested, but the police let me go for lack of evidence." Keenan had made sure of it. "I got on a subway and ended up in Brooklyn. I've been in some crappy hotel there, praying no one was after me. But I had to find you."

"Why?"

I glanced around. "Please, Daniil. Can we talk about this in your room?"

There was a long pause, but then the sound of the lock sliding. The door opened, and I stepped inside. The blackout shades were drawn and the lights were off, but I could see the chaos and disarray in the glow from the hallway. I turned to see Daniil, his hair disheveled and greasy, wearing just his tuxedo pants. No shirt. He hadn't shaved in days. His eyes were puffy and bloodshot as he regarded me. I gave him a sad smile. "I'm sorry."

"She's gone," he whispered, his face crumpling with grief.

Preparing myself, I opened my arms, and he collapsed onto me, a little boy in need of comfort. Except . . . the agony shot up my arms as soon as his hands touched my skin, intensifying as his forehead pressed to my shoulder. It was a heavy, hard kind of pain, like the worst hangover headache I'd ever had, but throughout my entire body. I groaned. "Daniil. You're hurting me."

"She's gone," he sobbed, his body heaving.

"I know," I said through gritted teeth as my stomach pitched. I pushed against him, needing space before I hurled all over him.

After I recovered, he allowed me to guide him to his bed, where he sank down and curled onto his side, pulling his knees to his chest. The pain faded just a bit, but I still ended up on my knees on the floor next to him, happy to have a shorter distance to fall if it came to that. "We have to get back to Russia," I said quietly. "We're not safe here."

"I don't care. Let them come find me. I'll make them hurt. Like she did."

Knowing I'd probably regret it, I touched Daniil's shoulder, but somehow he managed to control his power, and the pain didn't get any worse. "I was there when it happened," I said. "It was over so quickly that I don't think she had time to suffer." Although I wasn't exactly comforting Daniil for selfless reasons, my heart squeezed with sympathy as I remembered each awful second, and as I considered that Asa was the cause. "I know that doesn't help and won't bring her back, but I swear, it was fast."

"The news programs say she ran at the police. That she charged them."

I swallowed. "Yes."

"It makes no sense." He sounded calm, but through the point of connection, my fingertips on his shoulder, I felt the hurt coming, like melted steel running along my bones. Daniil might be young, but he clearly had some serious juice, perhaps like his mother. "Kira would never have done such a thing." His eyes opened and settled on me. "If she were in her right mind."

I pulled my hand from his body. I had a decision to make, one that might determine whether I made it back to Russia with Daniil or not. And I needed him. Needed his trust. "She wasn't. One of Brindle's agents dosed her with Knedas juice. I'm so sorry I couldn't keep it from happening."

Daniil sat up slowly, danger darkening his gaze. "Brindle's assassins. They killed Pavel, too. I was at the restaurant exit. I tried to find all of you, but the rush of people . . . and then the police would not let anyone in." He covered his face. "I saw Pavel and Kira brought out to the ambulances . . ." His voice broke again as he dropped his hand and his fingers clenched over his thighs.

My heart was beating hard. "Brindle's agents got the mosaic. But I have something just as important. Something we can use to get the panel back, if only we can make it to Volodya. I can't do it without you." Daniil had been primarily responsible for communications with Volodya, since he had more or less grown up at the boss's headquarters. "But we can turn this around. It's still possible."

His eyes glittered with tears as he raised his head. "There is no turning this around," he said in a harsh whisper. "They shot her eighteen times, the newspeople say to me." He let out a strangled moan. "They tore her to shreds."

My own eyes were burning, and not just because of the waves of searing pain he was giving off. Kira had been a gentle soul—and she'd been trying to help me right before she was killed. "I know. But we don't have to let her sacrifice be in vain."

He shuddered and pushed himself up, straightening his back. "If you mean what you say, this could be true." He eyed me with new suspicion.

I put my hand on my chest. "Daniil, there was something none of us knew about the panel. Something even Volodya didn't know. And it changes everything." I briefly told him about how the ancient magic inside the mosaic panel had ended up in my vault. "I'm carrying something important. But if Brindle gets it—"

"He won't," Daniil snapped. He stood up quickly, then swayed in place, clearly weak.

I got to my feet and put my arms out in case I needed to catch him. "When was the last time you ate?"

"I don't know."

"Okay. That's the first thing we'll remedy. You take a shower, and I'll get you something to eat, and then we'll make our plan to get out of here."

His brow furrowed and he looked away. "Kira cared for me in this way," he said faintly. "She always made me feel good."

As an Ekstazo, it had probably come naturally to her. "I know I'm a poor substitute. But we'll do this for her, right?"

He nodded and then trudged toward the bathroom, where he caught himself on the doorframe and turned toward me again. "Everything I do is for her now." His fingers curled tightly around the doorjamb. "We will get you to Volodya. And we will use what you have to lure Brindle. And I swear . . ." His jaw clenched. "Before this is over, I will find out who did this to my Kira. I will hurt him. I will make him scream. I will make him beg. And then I will kill him."

CHAPTER EIGHTEEN

With the excuse of getting Daniil a hot meal, I ventured out, but my first stop was a twenty-four-hour electronics shop. I spent some of the cash Volodya had given us on a burner phone, one I could use to access e-mail. Shivering as a sharp January wind blew along the vacant midnight sidewalk, lifting my hair and chapping my cheeks, I sent a text to the number Keenan had given me. *I got in with Daniil. Headed back to Moscow once we make arrangements.*

The response was immediate: *Go tonight. Police presence is heavy bc of incident but intel shows plenty of hunters loose in the city. Report when you're on the other side.*

Will do

Just stay focused. Do what I taught you and you'll be ok.

I stared at the message. It was like he could sense my tension and anxiety even from miles away. I had some work to do. *No prob.*

Next, I opened a browser and logged in to the new e-mail account using the instructions Theresa had given me.

She'd left a new message in the "Drafts" folder.

Happy New Year! That was quite a party foul. Where the fuck are you? Still hungover?

I rolled my eyes and typed, adding to the message.

I'm rehydrated and getting ready to do the walk of shame. Dad's gonna be mad when he finds out my ex-boyfriend stole his car. I was able to snag the registration from the glove compartment before it happened, though. Definitely counts for something.

It was pretty silly, but about as cloak-and-dagger as I could manage. Obviously, Theresa was trying to keep tabs, but I had no idea where she was or what she was up to. Would she try to help us get the panel back? I didn't know how to ask without outright asking. I also didn't know if I wanted her to show up and complicate things. Already I was basically a double agent, scheming with the Headsmen while I worked for the Russian boss. I wasn't sure how I could fit Theresa into that house of cards.

I logged out and called the emergency number Volodya had given us. After giving the password, I requested immediate transportation back to Moscow for two. While the person on the other end—a woman who didn't have even a trace of a Russian accent—made the arrangements, I bounced on my heels and wished I'd worn two pairs of socks. Finally, my lifeline clicked on again and assured me that our chartered flight out of Kennedy, direct to Moscow, would leave at four in the morning.

That gave us less than four hours. Fortunately, when I got back to the hotel with a meatball sub, Daniil was waiting. I gave him a reassuring nod as I entered the room agony-free. He ate with desperation but still seemed off as we set out again, this time for Penn Station, to catch the one o'clock Long Island Rail Road train that would take us to the AirTrain headed for Kennedy. I'd managed all the logistics, because Daniil looked like he could barely manage putting one foot in front of the other. He trudged zombielike at my side as we traversed the maze of the station and stood impassively as we waited for our train to arrive. I focused on our plan, on making each connection, on the tickets we needed. I tallied our remaining cash in my head. I counted the minutes. Keenan had said it was easier to control emotion if you kept your brain focused on minutiae. He and Jack had drilled that into me after I'd fully committed.

I did not think of Asa, because he wasn't part of the next six moves I needed to make. He was not a factor in this equation.

Once the train arrived, I helped Daniil board. I leaned my head back on my seat after settling Daniil in next to the window. He stared at his own reflection while I peered out at the frigid, clear night beyond the glass and let my guard down for a moment, knowing that as soon as I boarded Volodya's plane, I was going to be *on*. But right now, it was just me and the emotionally devastated Strikon by my side, who was lost in his own grief, who barely seemed aware of my presence.

It was a new year.

So many things had changed in the last twelve months.

I pictured my parents, taking down their Christmas tree while snow swirled outside. I pictured the lake, the ice built up jagged on the beach, the water littered with chunks of it, frothy and white. I wondered what I would have been doing if I had stayed, and whether I would have been content with what I had. Maybe I would have. But it would have been a life half lived.

I pulled my coat a little tighter around me and swallowed the lump in my throat. Right then, I would have given anything to be able to plop down next to Grandpa's bedside. He had been the one person who not only understood what it was like to carry secrets inside your rib cage, but who also actually cared about me as a person. I'd never gotten to really talk to him about what it was like to transport magic more valuable than your own life, to be so powerful and so vulnerable all at the same time. I'd never gotten to ask him if he ever felt lonely, even when he wasn't alone.

I'd never been truly alone before. But now I would have to be enough, because nobody else would help me figure this out. I had to find a way to get this ancient magic out of me before someone tried to take it by force and broke me in the process. For now, I had the benefit of possible secrecy. Even if Asa had sensed magic inside me, how could he have known it belonged inside the panel we'd stolen? It seemed like no one had known the ancient mosaic was a relic.

The conductor, a solidly built African American woman with braids neatly pulled back beneath her cap, entered the car. The cold air behind her swirled and warped as it hit the heat of the car. I squinted at the distortion as she punched the ticket of the one other person in the train car with us, a gray-haired man who hadn't looked up once from his phone.

Something wasn't right. Even though the door to the car had been closed for nearly a minute, even though the conductor was halfway down the aisle, the warp in the air was still following her.

I grabbed Daniil's hand. "Hurt me."

"What?" he whispered, pulling his bewildered gaze from the window.

"Hurt me. Now," I said, glancing back at the space behind the conductor.

"No!" Daniil whipped his hand from my grasp. "What's wrong with you?"

"Tickets," said the conductor in a bored voice.

My heart picking up in a frantic rhythm, I presented our tickets for her to punch. I tried not to stare at the space behind her but couldn't keep my eyes from flicking back and forth. The conductor punched a series of holes in each of our tickets and gave them back, then moved on, striding down the aisle until she reached the door to the next car. I twisted in my seat to see if the distortion in the air was still there, still trailing her.

But it was gone.

When I turned back around, Daniil was watching me with a frown. "Did you see something?"

I let out a shaky laugh and shook my head. "I'm just paranoid." Nobody could sense or track the magic inside me—it was too deeply hidden. They'd have to be on top of me to pick it up, and that's only if they were powerful. No sensing relic would do it. "Cannot wait to have some backup." I smiled at Daniil. "And I'll bet you can't wait to be home."

He grimaced and turned back to the window. "Kira's ghost will be waiting there for me," he mumbled. "She will stay until I've avenged her."

"Kira didn't seem like a vengeful person," I said. "She seemed gentle."

"She was," he whispered. "She was pure and good and should never have been with me. I brought her into Volodya's service. I brought her to this place."

He was on the verge of tears again, and as his control broke down, an uncomfortable ache rolled along my bones. I gave the seat across the aisle a longing look.

And as I turned my head, a shadow passed through my periphery. I spun in my seat to look behind me—and screamed. Asa loomed over my seat back, reaching for me. I threw myself into the aisle as Daniil shouted, "What's wrong?"

I turned to see Asa lean over and lift his open palm to his lips—and blow. Dust billowed off of his skin and right into Daniil's face. My Strikon ally blinked and coughed as Asa whispered, "Go get her. And bring her to me."

"Asa, no," I screamed as Daniil's jaw clenched with new purpose. He rose from his seat as I flipped over and scrambled along the aisle until I reached the gray-haired passenger. "Sir, help me. He's—"

Agony shot along my spine as Daniil's hand closed over my shoulder. I jabbed my elbow hard into his stomach and jumped back, bracing my hands on the seats on either side of the aisle. It was just like a gymnastics vault, and I made the most of it, swinging my legs up and slamming them into Daniil's chest. Pain crackled up my shins, making my bones feel like they were shattering, but Daniil staggered back and lost his balance. The gray-haired passenger continued staring at his phone, clearly under the influence of some Knedas magic as well.

I ran for the exit to the train car with Daniil and Asa behind me. Whimpering with panic, I ripped the door of the car open and edged through it before slamming it shut again. I lost precious seconds looking for a way to lock the darn thing and then had to abandon my search as Daniil grabbed the door. I let it slide open, but just as he put his hand on the edge to push it further, I yanked it shut with all my might. He howled as it smashed his fingers, and he fell to his knees, clutching his injured hand.

I didn't wait to see what Asa was doing. I ran. I was headed away from the conductor, but if I could reach the driver, maybe I could get him to stop the train. Maybe I could get off. Maybe I could run. This wasn't like last time, when I had tried to convince Asa to come with me. I knew that he couldn't hear me, that I couldn't reach him right now. It was pointless to try to loosen Brindle's control over him. Keenan had drilled that into my head, too.

"Mattie," Asa called as he stepped into the car. "You can't get away from me. Stop running."

I winced at the sound of my name, uttered in that dead voice I hated so much, and looked back. "I've always been stubborn," I snapped as I reached out to open the next door. Only one more until we reached the front car and the driver. I ripped it open as Asa started to jog unsteadily up the aisle. Both relief and fear flashed through me—he wasn't moving in the smooth, predatory way I'd grown so accustomed to. Now he moved in an ungainly manner that was slightly off kilter. As he came toward me he held on to the seats on either side of him as if for balance. His hollow cheeks were so pale that, added to the circles under his eyes, his angular face looked more like a skull. The collar was thick and ghastly around his throat. It looked like magic was eating him alive.

That didn't mean he wasn't dangerous, though. His hand slipped toward the pocket of his jacket, and I focused everything I had on reaching the driver's cab.

Not that it mattered when I did. I banged against the glass. "Help," I shouted.

But the driver was just like that passenger in our car, just like every other person I'd passed in my mad flight up the aisle. Completely oblivious to my presence. Asa had laid his trap while I stared out the window and thought about home and what lay ahead. Now I was on a moving train, the only person fully aware of the threat.

Desperate to escape, I darted to the side and grabbed the handle of the emergency exit window, but before I could pull it, Asa was on me, dragging me back into the cramped area between the front of the car and the driver's cab. He threw his weight against me, crushing me against the wall of the cab while he fished for something in his pockets. I grabbed his forearm and twisted, and he ripped his arm out of my grasp with a gasp of pain.

"Did you do that to yourself?" I asked, panting, struggling to keep him from pulling out whatever weapon he was about to use against me. "Did you try to hurt yourself?"

"We've got a flight to catch," he said flatly, pinning my wrist against the glass. I brought my knee up, but he pivoted to the side, taking the blow in his thigh. "Plane's waiting."

I was close enough now that I could see a bandage around his throat, just above the collar, sweat soaked and grimy and stained with dried blood. *Now* what had happened to him?

He wasn't meeting my gaze. Instead, he stared at my chest, his pupils dilated to the point that his eyes were almost completely black. He flattened his palm against my chest while I struggled. "You still have it," he said in a low voice. "And Brindle wants it."

"What exactly does Brindle want?"

"You have the key," he said, wrestling my other wrist up so he could hold both with one clammy hand.

"I have *the key*?" I asked. "To what?"

He paused, holding my wrists in a merciless grasp. "Nothing makes sense without it." His shirt collar gaped a little as he used his free hand to reach into his pocket, giving me a brutal view of the collar and the red swollen skin just beneath it. I tore my gaze away as he pulled out one of the little water pistols I'd learned to fear.

He aimed it at my face. "Now you're gonna do as I say."

With a roar and a crash, someone barreled into us. The liquid from the pistol—undoubtedly Knedas juice—splattered against the window of the driver's cab. As I fell to the floor beneath a tangle of limbs, I felt drops of it hit the back of my neck.

"Mattie, help," Asa shouted, then retched. "Get him off me."

Asa needed my help. I had to get the attacker off him. I reached up and punched at the pair of legs that were kicking at him, but they were moving too quickly.

"Are you the one?" shouted Daniil. I looked up to see his face contorted with fury, his teeth clenched as he landed a hard strike to Asa's ribs.

Asa doubled over, and his shoulder hit the door. Panting, gagging as Daniil's Strikon magic hit him, he banged on the glass, twice.

The train bucked as it slowed suddenly.

"You're Brindle's, aren't you?" Daniil's voice shook with rage.

I was supposed to be helping Asa. I shot to my feet and reached for him, but Daniil shifted his attention from Asa to me at the last second. As soon as his eyes met mine, it felt like someone had just ripped my pancreas out through my belly button. I let out a hoarse scream as the fog of Knedas magic cleared from my thoughts. "Don't let him off this train," I said raggedly as I doubled over, clutching my middle. I hadn't expected this chance, but if Daniil could subdue Asa, maybe we could get him to Russia right now. "Daniil, we need him. Alive."

"I'm going to end him," Daniil growled as Asa pounded again on the driver's door.

The train shook violently and lurched forward, throwing Daniil off-balance. He tripped over his own feet and went down hard. I clutched at Asa's leg as the train braked suddenly yet again, tossing me against the metal-and-glass door with a thump. Pain burst through my shoulder as the train shuddered to a halt. The doors slid open.

I swiped at Asa's pant leg as he lunged for fresh air. He barreled into the night, staggering across the tracks and then clambering up a hill toward a fence that separated the rails from the neighborhood beyond. As I limped out of the door and my feet hit gravel, I could see it was useless to chase him. He was gone again.

Daniil growled something in Russian, and I turned to him. "Are you okay?"

He glared at Asa's silhouette as it slid over the fence and jumped to the ground on the other side, where it staggered away. "Was he the one?"

I swallowed and looked away. "No."

"Liar," Daniil said softly. "At least now I know who to kill."

"You can't."

"Because he is who we are trying to save? He is the one, isn't he? Asa Ward. I know his face."

Probably because he resembled his father. "He's not in his right mind. He's under Brindle's control." I climbed back into the train and limped toward Daniil. "And we need to get to the airport and under Volodya's protection right the hell now."

Daniil chuckled. "I don't think he's coming back. Did you see how sensitive he was to my magic?"

I nodded. "It won't stop him, though."

"Why? What aren't you telling me?"

I put my hand over my heart. "Apparently that mosaic they took from us is useless without what I'm carrying. Asa said I have the key and Brindle wants it back."

I reached up and banged on the door of the driver's cab twice. The doors closed, and the train jerked into motion again. I leaned against the wall and watched Asa's silhouette become one with the darkness.

CHAPTER NINETEEN

Daniil and I touched down in Moscow late the next night, though it felt much earlier. I had caught a few hours of sleep on the flight, but was awakened a few times by jolts of agony as Daniil relived seeing Kira's body in his nightmares. I found myself wishing I was an Ekstazo, that I could ease his pain with a simple touch. But I knew it wasn't as simple as that. His heart had been shattered. It was obvious he had truly loved her, and his grief was black and bitter and deep. When he was awake, he stared straight ahead, his fists clenching and unclenching, and I just knew he was picturing making Asa scream.

I honestly couldn't blame him.

However they were controlling Asa, they'd done an amazing job. There had been no hesitation as he tried to capture me, no humanity in his voice, and no warmth in his gaze—no eye contact at all, actually. He was the perfect soldier. Except . . . he was slower. Unsteady. And I was willing to bet that before they'd gotten him caged, he'd done something desperate. There were those wounds on his arms. And now the bandage around his throat. What had he done? Had he tried to kill himself? The thought nearly took me out. But it only made me more determined.

I needed every ounce of that determination once we got back to Volodya's headquarters.

We were greeted at the entrance of Tower 2000 by a slender young woman with fine blond hair and heavy eyeliner, the same one who'd sensed my intentions the first time I'd entered Volodya's lair. She was wringing her hands as she approached us. She started to speak in Russian, but Daniil waved his hand, wearily. "English, Zoya. For the reliquary." He turned to me. "Mattie, this is my sister, Zoya."

She acknowledged me with a curt nod before turning back to my Strikon partner. "He wants to see you first, Daniil."

I relaxed a little, because this was what I wanted—Daniil to bring me back into the fold. But Daniil frowned at her. "What's wrong?"

"The Volodya is having one of his dark times."

Daniil paled. "How bad?"

"Oksana was screaming for nearly an hour before he let her go," she said in a choked voice. "I just took her back to her room. She's . . ."

My stomach clenched. "She's what? What did he do to her?"

Daniil said, "When our Volodya is in one of his dark moods, he does some rather dark things."

"Darker than *usual*?" My hand strayed to my throat. The bruises had faded, but my memory hadn't.

Daniil looked pained as he nodded. "He uses some of his relics to induce extreme emotional states, which he feeds off of."

Zoya looked vaguely sick. "It is not good, but no one can stop him. And after, he is soothed. For a short time, at least."

I thought back to Theresa's nightmares, how she screamed for Volodya and begged him to stop, all the while telling him she loved him. "How often does he have these dark moods?"

Daniil and Zoya gave each other a look. "It happened when our father was taken by the Headsmen," Daniil said. "Before that, not for a very long time. But it used to happen much more, after Aunt Ther—" He seemed to catch himself. "After the sensor disappeared."

I wondered if Volodya had forbidden his people to speak Theresa's name.

Zoya glanced toward the elevator. "When I was a little girl I learned to fear him."

"I don't blame you," I muttered. "He's kind of a sicko."

Zoya let out a nervous giggle completely absent of humor. "Daniil, please go before he chooses another of us to torture."

"Lead the way," Daniil said grimly. "He won't hurt me. Never has. But he can feed off my pain if it makes him happy. Perhaps that will be enough for him."

While Daniil had his audience with the boss, I paced the bunker and prayed he was putting in a good word for me, maybe mentioning how nice I'd been, how I'd helped pull him together and get him back home. The other agents had mostly cleared out, and the few who were present looked spooked and resentful, like maybe they'd drawn the short straws. They gave me a wide berth. I waited to hear Daniil screaming, but only silence emanated from Volodya's cave.

After what seemed like an eternity, Daniil emerged, looking like he'd been crying. His face was red and his hair damp with sweat. "I told him about everything that happened to us," he said. "Now he wants to hear it from you."

As I walked down the hall, I counted my steps and thought of all the places I'd been in the last week. I pinned the details in my mind. When I opened the door to Volodya's chamber, heavy warmth rolled outward. The artificial fire was turned on high, giving off a heat I easily felt as I walked toward the shadowed figure in the dark corner nook. The air reeked of sweat and suffering.

"You wanted to see me," I said, keeping my voice level.

"We had a deal," he replied, his voice dry and rustling. "You have failed me."

"I did the best I could. And I came back to keep trying. We can—"

"Daniil likes you. He trusts you. He wanted to protect you. But I felt his doubt, even when he could not. He admitted to me that after the theft of my mosaic, you were gone for three days." He slowly leaned out of the inky blackness, and the glow of the fire revealed the sheen of sweat on his face. His nostrils quivered.

He was probably sensing my fear.

"I laid low," I said. "Kira and Pavel were dead, and I was afraid Brindle's people might be after me, too."

"Truth." Volodya's eyes narrowed. "And *lie*."

"Okay, I *knew* they would be after me."

He rose to his feet. "Half truth. Which means it is also a half lie." He began to walk toward me. "But then again, you're a liar, aren't you?"

I took an involuntary step back. "In that I lie sometimes? Doesn't everybody?"

"Your fear is pungent. *Alive.*" As he said it, he bared his teeth, looking more than ever like a wolf.

"I don't know what you want me to say! I'm sorry the plan didn't work, but I know a way we can still get hold of the mosaic."

He let out a dry chuckle that made me shiver with its familiarity. I immediately focused on the fire, on counting the bricks in the mantelpiece, but Volodya was too sensitive. "More of that," he said in a low, shaky voice. "Do that again."

I blinked at him. "Do what?"

"You know very well what I mean," he snapped. "I want to feel that again. Do it or I'll make you regret your defiance."

The viciousness in his tone made my stomach turn. "Please. Let's make a new plan."

He grimaced and shook his head. "No, not that. It's boring."

"Planning?"

"No, your feelings. I want the longing of a moment ago," he said, raising his voice. "Give it to me." He rubbed his chest. "I want to feel it here." He bowed his head.

I stared at him, caught between terror and—

"Pity me and I will hurt you," he warned.

"I don't pity . . ." My voice trailed off as he drew near, as I spied his predatory walk, the grace of his movements. It was the way Asa had moved before Brindle.

Volodya groaned. "Yes, there it is again. What *is* that? It's exquisite."

I staggered back, my panic rising.

He opened his eyes. "Give that feeling to me, or I will hurt you." His body was trembling with tension. "Now," he roared.

I had both hands up and was halfway to the door when he advanced on me. "Stop it! Please! Don't you want to talk about what happened in New York?"

"I know what happened in New York! You failed." His eyes were alight with rage and madness, and his voice echoed in the stifling chamber. "Frank Brindle has my panel, because the thief gave it to him. Brindle will use it to obtain the Knedas relic and unite as many of the originals as he can. Because of you there will be war, on me in particular, because I possess the most pages of the original tome." His fists clenched, and spittle flew from his mouth as he shouted, "It will be bloody and protracted and in the end, Brindle may win, but I will burn down the world to stop him!"

I shuddered at the carnivorous look on his face. "People will die. Not just the two of you."

"This is war, little girl. Death is its currency." He took a sudden, deep breath, and his hands relaxed. A shrill, unhinged laugh bubbled up from inside him. "But ah, who can say they have truly lived until they have been on the brink of death? Do you have any idea how exquisite that sensation is? The moment someone who is about to die realizes how very alive they are, the moment they resolve to fight to stay that way, no matter how futile. There is nothing so electric. Not love or loyalty, not hatred or rage." He lunged forward and grabbed my shoulders, then pressed me to the wall. "Have you felt it? Can you imagine?" He pressed his cheek to mine and inhaled deeply while I clamped my lips shut over a scream. "Would you like to experience it right now?" he murmured.

"I-I'm on your s-side," I stammered. "I came here to help you get back what you lost."

His hands were bruising me. "What your thief took, you mean," he snarled. "He murdered Pavel and Kira. He gave my panel to Brindle." He shook me a little, my head rapping against the concrete wall. "When I catch him, he will know what it is to struggle for life as it is drained from him drop by drop. And I will savor every moment, including the one when he finally realizes he has lost the battle."

"Asa's being controlled! This wasn't his fault—"

Volodya tensed. "There it is *again*," he whispered. "You are lying to protect him. You're trying to hide things from me. You will fail at this, too."

"I'm trying to help you get what you want!" I needed to convince him to do what *I* wanted, but he was so scattered and dangerous that I could barely keep my thoughts in line. "Look—there's something you missed. It changes everything."

"Something about Asa Ward."

Yes. "No. It's the mosaic. It's not what you think it is! Let me go and I'll tell you its secret."

He shoved away from me. "I'll know if you're lying."

I sucked in a deep breath. "The key you're looking for, the one that's going to help translate the pages. It's not written beneath the mosaic. It was magic."

He peered at me. "The panel was a relic?"

I pinned my hope on the glint of sanity and reason in his eyes. "I think that magic is somehow the actual key, though I'm not sure how. But Brindle wants it." I touched my chest. "And I have it."

His gaze fell to my chest, where my fingertip hovered over my heart. "It is inside you."

I nodded. "I don't even know what kind of magic it is. Usually I can tell, but when this entered me . . . it just felt old. And powerful." I shook off the uncomfortable memory, how it had felt like being buried alive, dirt filling my mouth.

Volodya's eyes glittered. "So Brindle only has half of what he wants."

"And he'll come after the rest. He knows I have the magic. Asa figured it out. We can use his greed to get you the mosaic." My hope soared as Volodya looked thoughtful.

So much better than crazy.

But then he said, very quietly, "You expect me to make a deal with you. Again. You think that I will be charmed by you. Or fooled." He pulled out his phone and sent a text while I watched. "You do not understand who I am."

A moment later, the door to his lair opened, and Daniil poked his head in. "Boss?"

"Daniil, have Zoya bring Jack Winchester to me. I have a job for him."

Daniil nodded and began to withdraw, but Volodya put up a hand. "I'm not finished. Take Mattie to our juicing room."

Daniil's eyebrows shot up. "What?"

"Yeah, *what*?" I asked.

Volodya's eyes narrowed. He glared at me while speaking to Daniil. "Once you have her there, strap her to one of the tables. And then I want you to hurt her. Hurt her until she is too weak to fight."

I took several steps back, but then realized I was moving closer to Daniil. "Wait—I'm carrying valuable magic!"

"You are," said Volodya. "And I'm going to take it from you."

"But it's old and fragile! You have to put it back in its original vessel."

"Ah, but I do not have the original vessel," Volodya roared, his face turning monstrous. "Because your thief stole it!"

"We can get it back!" I put my hands out. "Just listen to me! Hold an auction. Pretend you're cashing out of the original-relic race and sell your pages. Brindle and his people will come, not just to get the pages, but to get me."

Volodya shook his head. "Not you. The magic."

"The magic is safe inside me—and harder to steal!"

"You give yourself too much credit."

"Asa tried to get me twice already, and he didn't succeed. I can fight back. A relic can't. Besides, you don't even know if this magic will go into another relic."

"Right now I just want to feel your pain," he growled. "Daniil."

"But—" Daniil began.

"Now. Or you will take her place."

Fear flashed across Daniil's features. "Yes, boss," he murmured.

The pain was a hard throb, battering my bones and making the floor look like a tempting destination. "You're going to regret this," I said in a strangled voice. "If you'd just *think* for a minute—" I groaned and fell to one knee as Daniil drew closer.

"I am sorry," Daniil whispered as he bent down and dragged me up from the floor. His touch sharpened the pain, like a hundred scalpels sliding across my skin. I screamed.

Volodya sighed. "Yes. More of that." I could barely hear him through the buzz of panic and white noise in my ears, but his next words only worsened the pain. "Asa Ward will feel this agony as well. I know how sensitive he'll be. I know it very well. He'll scream, too, when I catch him. Take comfort in knowing you share the same end."

I began to struggle, unwilling to surrender as Daniil began to haul me out of the room. Volodya started to laugh. "And there it is! That exquisite struggle. That fight for life." He shuddered, seemingly in ecstasy as he watched me writhe.

"Don't do this," I begged. "You're only hurting yourself."

"That is all I've ever done," Volodya said, following us as he scraped his fingernails along the walls. He looked both sick and savagely happy. "You have no idea what it's like to have this gift. This curse. To sense every emotion, to breathe them in. You have no idea how it feels, when you can't tell your own anger and love from someone else's. You cannot possibly understand."

"You're insane," I said, panting through the agony as Daniil reached the door.

"Yes," Volodya replied. "I should think that is obvious. Daniil, let me know when you are truly ready to get to work."

So this was just a preview? My head was on fire with pain, and my body felt like it was being slowly torn apart. Daniil was nearly as bad as Reza, who had only had me in his grip for a few minutes. I kicked and flailed, trying desperately to get free.

"Please, stop," Daniil said, his tone full of desperation. "Don't make this harder."

He moved to open the door—but it burst inward, knocking him back. He lost his grip on me, and I hit the floor at Volodya's feet.

Theresa strode into the room, a gun leveled at Volodya's head and another pointed at Daniil. Her gaze was so intense, so focused, that I forgot Volodya until he whimpered. I turned to see him gaping at Theresa, all the blood drained from his face.

"Are you a ghost?" he said, his voice breaking.

"Most definitely." She took another step into the room, and before the door swung shut, I caught a glimpse of Zoya and a few others lying on the ground outside, twitching, probably in the grip of some magical mojo Theresa had thrown down. She'd picked the perfect time—nearly everyone else had fled Volodya's craziness. "I knew you would do this. As soon as Mattie let me know what had happened, I knew."

"You're working with the reliquary. I should have known."

"Maybe you should have, or maybe Mattie is stronger than either of us believed." Theresa gritted her teeth. "Call off your boy or I'll shoot him."

"Stop." One word from Volodya, and all the pain faded quickly.

"Get out," Theresa said to Daniil. "Go help your associates out there."

Daniil blinked at her and turned to Volodya, who nodded and said, "Tell no one. Do nothing. Wait for me."

"Do anything else and I'll put a bullet in your *Volodya's* brain," she snapped.

"Aunt Theresa?" Daniil asked as he inched toward the door. He suddenly sounded years younger.

For a moment, Theresa looked startled. Her eyes darted to Daniil's face. "Daniil?"

"Yes."

She swallowed hard. "I don't want to hurt you. Go."

Daniil slipped out the door, leaving me on the floor between Theresa and Volodya. She didn't lower her gun. "Mattie, get up."

I clung to the wall and slowly got to my feet in the tense silence. As soon as I was up, Theresa holstered one of her weapons and pushed her palm against my chest. I froze, my heart ticking against her hand. She let me go a second later. "You still have it. That's good."

"Yeah. Um . . ." I looked back and forth between them. Volodya hadn't breathed since she'd walked into the room. Her skin was glistening with sweat—but her eyes were shining with tears. Of fury, of love, of terror—I had no idea. "Not that I'm complaining," I managed to say, "but what the heck are you doing here?"

"I decided it was time Volodya and I had a little chat about Asa Ward."

Volodya's brow furrowed. "The thief?"

"Yes, lover," she said softly. "That thief is our son."

CHAPTER TWENTY

Volodya looked as if he'd been smacked in the head with a tire iron. "I . . . we . . ."

"Have a son, yes."

"Asa Ward."

"Yes," Theresa said. She still had the gun on him, but now that the secret was out, determination seemed to have dried her tears.

"Asa Ward is my son."

"Yes," I added. "That's why he looked so familiar to you. It must have been like looking in a mirror."

Volodya turned to me, the first time he'd taken his eyes off Theresa since she'd stormed into the room. "And that's what I feel from you, this longing. You see him in me."

"More often than I'd like."

He blinked quickly, perhaps trying to shuffle this new knowledge in with all his memories. "So when you left me all those years ago . . ."

"I knew he was like me," Theresa said. "And I knew you wouldn't let me go. I also knew you would hurt him. Because you hurt everyone you love."

A shadow passed across Volodya's face, an echo of decades-old rage and hurt. His jaw clenched and his voice rumbled. "You took my son from me."

Theresa's eyes flared. "I will not apologize."

"I don't want an apology," Volodya growled, pushing himself off the wall and drawing himself up to his full height. "I want you to pay for taking the last thirty years from me."

She raised the gun slightly, aiming it at his face, and calmly thumbed off the safety. "Only if you're willing to pay me for the same."

"Don't pretend. You feel *nothing*." His voice was shaking. He looked like he was about to leap at her. I took a step back in case bullets started to fly. "You've *always* felt nothing."

Theresa flinched. "Is that what you think?"

"All an act. It was always an act. And I was always your fool," he spat. "You deserve to die for what you've done to me."

"You think *you* are the victim?" Theresa laughed. "I had forgotten your ability to twist reality until it is unrecognizable."

Volodya took a quick step toward her, and I took another step back. I needed both of them to rescue Asa, but it seemed entirely possible that they were about to kill each other.

"I'm the one who twists?" he asked quietly. "Or is it just that I have been twisted?"

Theresa stood her ground but moved her finger to the trigger. "You certainly are that, lover."

"Don't call me that!" shouted Volodya. "You have no right to call me that."

"Does it hurt?" she whispered. "Good."

His face contorted. "Cold-hearted bitch. You come back only to laugh at my destruction. You will probably dance as I burn."

"Who could blame me if I did? But that is not why I'm here. I need your help in saving our son before Frank Brindle destroys him."

She lowered her gun, looking resigned. "For that gift I would pay any price you name."

"And if I refuse?" His lip curled. "You stole him from me. He means nothing to me."

"Now you're the one who's pretending."

"Then I will let him burn to hurt us both," he yelled. "Just to make you feel *something*." His fists trembled as he clenched them.

"You used to understand me," she said. "It seems you've forgotten." She took a deep breath and closed her eyes. A small, quiet action. But the effect was seismic.

Volodya made a choked noise. His fingers scrabbled at his chest. With a strangled cry, he staggered back and fell to one knee, bracing his palm on the floor. His back arched as he pressed his other hand over his heart. It looked like he was about to throw up. "Too much," he said with a groan.

Bewildered, I looked back and forth between them. Theresa was just standing there, gun hanging from her fist, her eyes closed, her nostrils slightly flared, breathing hard but steady. And Volodya looked like he was dying.

"Enough," he begged. "Enough."

"Not by half," she replied. "You have earned this, my love."

Volodya fell to his side. His eyes were streaming tears, and his body was convulsing with silent sobs. "Please. I-I can't . . ." He curled his long body into a ball, as if he was trying to protect himself from the onslaught.

She'd leveled him with her true feelings. Whether for Asa or for him or both, she wasn't denying or shielding them anymore.

"I thought he enjoyed sensing others' powerful feelings," I murmured. "Seemed like he was getting off on it a few minutes ago."

I was surprised when Theresa responded. "But these are feelings about *him*. And he feels them inside," she said haltingly. "He has no protection from them."

In fact, it looked like they were killing him.

Theresa looked at peace as she opened her eyes and spied him on the floor. "Say you'll help me."

His fingers clawed over the carpet, and he shook his head. Theresa moved closer, staring intently at him, and he cried out and began to rock. "I hide it for both of us," she said. "I always have. But if this is what you want . . ."

"Please," he whispered.

"Our son needs us. Whatever happened after, he was created by our love. And he was nearly destroyed by it. But somehow, and in spite of both of us, he became a man." She glanced at me. "He is able to love and be loved, perhaps in a way we never could."

My eyes stung with tears of my own. I looked down at Volodya and stopped trying to focus on everything except Asa. I let my love and fear for him rise like a tidal wave.

Volodya screamed. He held up a hand as if trying to ward me off. "All right," he gasped. "All right. Just stop. Make it stop."

"Mattie," Theresa said.

I let out an unsteady breath and concentrated on a little tear in the carpet next to the baseboard, forcing my feelings beneath the shroud of my logical thoughts once again. And maybe Theresa was doing the same, because Volodya shuddered as some of the tension left his body. His face was so pale that it almost glowed in the dimly lit hallway. He lay there, limp.

"Will you agree to auction the pages of the *Essentialis Magia*?" I asked.

"Anything." He opened his eyes and looked up at Theresa.

"We'll work together," she said. "Like we used to."

His eyes squeezed shut again as his face crumpled, maybe with grief, maybe with memory. "Promise."

"You have my word. As long as you do whatever you can to free Asa from Brindle's service, you have me." Sweat had created a dark circle on the collar of her shirt. It trickled down her temples. I had to wonder what this was going to cost her. "But if you betray me, I will find a way to take you down with me."

"You always have, darling," he said, still sounding weak. "You always have." He rolled onto his back.

Theresa holstered her weapon, then knelt at his side. "No other magic. Just yours and mine. That is all that will flow between us. I will kill you if you try to control me again."

"Anything," he whispered.

I was feeling like a third wheel, but a little worried things would escalate as soon as I left. "I'm going to go find Daniil and make sure Zoya and the others are okay." I leaned down until I caught Theresa's eye. "Are you going to be all right?"

She gave me a haunted look. "How does 'all right' feel?" she asked. "I wouldn't know." She shooed me toward the door. "It's fine. We will both be alive the next time you see us."

Volodya let out another broken sound as her fingernails curled into the fabric over his chest, but he didn't protest. I looked over my shoulder one last time as I reached the door. Theresa had bowed over Volodya, and was now cradling his head and whispering to him—but she had the gun in her other hand and was keeping it pressed to his side.

I sighed and left Asa's parents to their strange reunion.

I sat in my chair at the conference table, casting occasional glances toward the Moscow River just outside the window, mostly to avoid the suspicious gazes of the people in the chairs around me. Seemingly in control of himself again, Volodya was standing at the front of the room, looking us over. "In one week, I will auction off some of my treasures, including various relics and some valuable artifacts," he said to us. "Potential buyers will be traveling here from all over the world.

My staff is making preparations for this event. You all are here to make sure it goes as it should."

"And how exactly should it go?" asked a middle-aged man, his thinning hair slicked back. He was sitting next to a woman with short red hair and a pinched expression. She eyed him with dislike.

Volodya turned to him. "This will be simple, Sambor. I want you to stop any and all attempts to steal my possessions. In the end, I will sell certain relics and artifacts, but some, specifically some very ancient texts, must end up back in my vault. In addition, I want the mosaic panel Frank Brindle will be carrying. And I want Asa Ward."

"You want many things, Volodya," said the pinched redhead.

"I want what is mine, Masha," he replied, his voice hard.

Masha pressed her lips shut and bowed her head. "I am sorry for the disrespect," she whispered. Sambor reached over and patted her hand—which she yanked from his grasp almost instantly.

Volodya chuckled. "I see that you two are still at odds."

"Only because Sambor likes to put his hands where they don't belong," she said, her voice sour.

"Well, maybe if you'd let me put my hands on *you*—"

"Enough," said Volodya, no longer smiling. Masha and Sambor flinched. "Get divorced on your own time, but for the next week, focus on my interests, or the two of you will spend an evening entertaining me."

Both of them folded their arms over their middles, almost completely in sync.

Volodya gave the couple a charming smile. "I see you understand."

"Who exactly are the potential buyers?" asked a ragged-looking young man in a flannel and jeans, with a few days of thick stubble fuzzing his jaw.

"All the major players will attend, Ilya, or send representatives. Many will come in person to see for themselves what I possess. But make no mistake—each will bring their best agents. No more than three from each organization will be allowed into the venue, but that will be more than enough for some of them."

Ilya cracked his knuckles. "Need me to persuade them to follow the rules?"

Next to Ilya, an elderly woman in a headscarf let out a deep laugh and said something in Russian. Ilya scowled and shot something back before continuing in English. "Does she have to be here? I work better alone."

"Olga specializes in glamours," Volodya said to all of us. "That is why she is here." He followed up with something in Russian directed at the old woman, and she made a little kissing face at Ilya, then laughed. She was the only person in the room who appeared relaxed and unafraid in Volodya's presence.

"With Arkady gone, you two are my best Knedas," Volodya said to Ilya. "Now is the time for discipline." He sniffed, perhaps detecting the thick funk of body odor and cigarette smoke emanating from the scruffy Knedas. "And perhaps better hygiene and a change of clothes."

Zoya muttered something that sounded like "Yes, please," while Daniil sat stone-faced. I had to wonder if hearing his father described as "gone" had put him in a foul mood. Or maybe it was just his ongoing grief over Kira. It suddenly occurred to me that Asa was responsible for destroying not one but two people Daniil loved.

"Each of you will be juiced today so that we can create the proper tools to aid security," Volodya said casually. As a slight smile played at his lips, I had to wonder if he was enjoying the obvious anxiety his announcement produced. All the naturals in the room seemed to shrink back in their seats, with the exception of Olga. "Dr. Teplov will take your donations of blood or plasma—you may choose which—and will give you guidance as to how to replenish your strength after. You'll be fully restored before the event begins next week."

Ilya raised his hand, then waved it in my direction. "Who is this one?"

"This is Mattie," said Volodya.

"And is she a sensor? I heard rumors you had a sensor again." He glanced at Zoya, whose cheeks darkened.

"Mattie is not a sensor."

"But you do have one?" asked Sambor. "That would be extremely helpful. We'd know more about who is walking through your doors, and we'd know who to watch."

"I do have one," Volodya said slowly, looking down at the table, maybe to hide his bemused smile. On anyone else, it might have looked sweet, but it sent a prickle of anxiety through me as I remembered Theresa's nightmares.

"Then where is this sensor?" asked Masha. "Shouldn't he be part of these meetings?"

"*She* will not," Volodya replied. "I will inform her of our plans." Theresa had refused to stay in Tower 2000 and had retreated to one of her hideouts in the city.

"If I'm going to work with this person—" Masha began.

"You seem to be under the impression that you have the right to question me," Volodya said. "Rumors of my downfall are everywhere, Masha. Have you been listening to them?"

She sat back from the table. "N-no, boss. No."

Volodya's nose wrinkled. "Your fear is rank—but wise. And as for my sensor, she will convey her observations to Mattie, who will share them with each of you."

All eyes around the table focused on me. "Hi," I said, waving.

"American," growled Sambor. "This is why we were told to speak English? Forgive me, but why is she here?"

"She is my special guest." He gave me a smile that actually looked sincere. "And we share the same goals. You will treat her as your colleague and protect her as you would me. Unless you wish to make me deeply unhappy."

All of them shook their heads.

"Excellent. My auxiliary guard will also be in attendance."

Daniil leaned over to me. "Nonmagical. But they are all former *spetsnaz*."

"Former what?" I asked.

"Specially trained," said Volodya. "Like . . . commandos? Is that what you call them?"

"Oh. Sure." It sounded as though Volodya, like so many bosses, had his own little band of mercenaries to back up his agents who were naturals.

"We will meet each day before the auction to go over the venue, the players as we receive their responses to my invitation, and your preparations. I expect each of you to focus on what I am asking you to do. My displeasure would be unfortunate for you, but the reward will be great when we succeed." Volodya clapped his hands. "Now. Off to the juicing room. Dr. Teplov is waiting."

Cowed, the naturals filed out of the room. I couldn't help but feel a little disappointed—this was the best group he could pull together?

"I know they do not look like much," Volodya said, staring out the window at the river, metal gray under an oppressive sky. "I have lost many of my best in the last ten years." He looked over at me. "I have not been myself."

I thought back to my conversation with Arkady, how he'd said that Theresa's last disappearance had devastated Volodya, but I wondered if he'd ever actually been sane. "I'm sorry."

"No, you're not." He turned back to the window. "But now I fight for something more than my wealth, more than my empire." Despite my wariness about Volodya, appreciation and relief flowed through me, and he smiled. "You're welcome, dear. I think perhaps my son is lucky to have a woman like you."

The same woman he'd been planning to torture not twenty-four hours ago.

Before I could respond, the door to the conference room swung open. "Am I late?" asked Jack as he strode into the room.

"Jack," said Volodya, inclining his head in welcome. "Thank you for coming."

"Heard about Pavel," Jack said with a frown. "They couldn't use magic on him—so they went with poison instead. All over the news in New York."

"We will protect you here, my friend," said Volodya, "but you will also stay in the background until the very end." He held out his arm. "And this is Mattie. She is the reliquary you'll be working with."

I offered my hand for Jack to shake. "Nice to meet you."

He grinned. This had to be the fourth time we'd met. "It's a pleasure, Mattie. Nice to have a fellow Yankee here."

His relaxed manner made it easy to smile. "Maybe we could go find some french fries and a hamburger."

"Excellent idea," said Volodya, ushering us to the door. "I have a few hours of work to do, but I will meet you later to discuss the magic that will be transferred." As soon as we were out in the hallway, he turned and walked quickly away. I wondered how difficult it was for him to wear a mask of sanity and how long he could keep it up.

Rubbing a chill from my arms, I turned to Jack. "Everything's going according to plan," I said quietly.

"The boss'll be glad to hear it," said Jack, glancing around. We were alone. "We'll have heavy backup both around and inside the venue. This is huge for us. A chance to get the mosaic and its magic, as well as all those pages."

I frowned. "What?"

"Keenan wants us to get the *Essentialis Magia* pages, too. They might contain information about how to find the original Knedas relic."

"But Jack . . ." I looked in the direction Volodya had gone. "He's already struggling, but he's doing this for a bunch of good reasons."

"Do you want to get Asa back or not?"

"I do. But so does Volodya."

"Don't tell me you feel sorry for the guy. He might be helping you now, Mattie, but you can't forget what he is."

"I know," I murmured.

"Then you need to take full advantage of this situation. Volodya is weak. He knows it. So does everyone else. Keeping these pages won't save him."

But helping his son might. "That's not the only thing he cares about."

"So again I'll ask—do you want Asa back? Because our firepower is probably the only thing that's gonna ensure it happens. Volodya can't outwit or outplay Frank Brindle. When he brings his people to the game, serious shit is going to go down. I saw Volodya's crew as I walked in. They look like a bunch of strays. How are they gonna stop people like Brindle, Reza, Asa? Or anyone else Brindle brings in?"

"What if we just went to Volodya and told him what Keenan wants?"

Jack snorted. "Volodya's too proud. It would also blow my cover."

"But he might—"

"Mattie. Trust me. No boss is going to cooperate with the Headsmen. It's just part of their code." He took in the doubting look on my face. "Look—you need us. And if you want us, you're gonna play by our rules. Don't get all soft on the old man. He's already dead in the water. And trust me, he's earned all the pain he's got coming. Let him play his part."

My heart squeezed. *Now I fight for something more than my wealth, more than my empire.* The look on Volodya's face had been hopeful and proud. He was fighting for redemption. For his stolen family.

But I was fighting for Asa. First and foremost. "Okay," I murmured. "I'll play by your rules."

CHAPTER TWENTY-ONE

I shivered a little as I walked into the antiseptic space that served as Volodya's juicing operation. It was a white-tiled room with rows of hospital beds and reclining chairs, each with a metal stand next to it, upon which was positioned a rectangular panel strung with a tangle of tubing. Plasma machines. Theresa was sitting on a reclining chair, staring at the wall as a portly man removed a needle from her arm and bandaged her up. But when he reached for the clear bag of plasma now hanging from the machine, her hand closed over his forearm. "It's mine, Dr. Teplov."

"But—"

"It's mine," she said, showing her teeth. "Go whine to Volodya if you have a problem with me. He and I have an agreement. Trust me—he will not be happy if you break it."

Dr. Teplov put his hands up and waddled into a back room. I walked forward as Theresa winced and rolled down her sleeve over the bandage. "I'm surprised that you were willing to shed even a drop of your blood here," I said.

She looked over at me. “Sometimes it’s more useful on the outside.” She glanced over at the plasma and swung her legs to the floor. “Are you ready for tomorrow?”

“I’ve spent the last five days getting ready.” I knew every inch of the auction venue. Every side hallway and stairway and exit. I knew the schedule. I knew the players. “Asa’s on the guest list.”

“I know. Volodya showed me. Brindle is bringing Reza as well.”

I shook my head. “I can’t imagine how Asa can be close to him.”

She sighed. “Mattie, he probably has Ekstazo juice running through his veins twenty-four/seven. It’s likely he’s numb to all of it.” She met my eyes. “And to everything.”

I looked away. “I know.”

“But because of the rules allowing only three people for every potential buyer, at least you know that it’s only Asa, Reza, and Brindle. It’ll be the best chance any of us will have to get him back.”

“And there are plenty of other bosses there to keep them busy.”

“Plenty of bosses to try to get ahold of you, if they figure out what you’ve got on board.” Theresa stood up and walked over to the plasma machine, where she disconnected the bag of clear fluid from its tubing. “You have to protect yourself.”

“I have plenty of bodyguards,” I said, rolling my eyes. Sambor and Masha were both Ekstazos, capable of rendering nearly any attacker all loose and giddy in a matter of seconds. The only problem was that they were so wrapped up in their own relationship drama that they weren’t always at their most attentive. Ilya was a relatively powerful Knedas, but he was also irritable and distracted if he couldn’t smoke a cigarette every fifteen minutes. Olga couldn’t speak English and seemed in her own world half the time. Only Daniil and Zoya seemed on the ball, but both of them were jumpy about what they were about to face—so much so that Daniil seemed to have temporarily sidelined his plans for revenge in favor of making sure his boss’s empire survived the week.

"They do have serious juice," said Theresa. "They just don't always know what to do with it." She glanced at my chest. "You should take that off," she said quietly.

I looked down at the tiny vial of sand and magic. "Oh." I'd been wearing it nonstop, and now it just felt like a part of me. "I guess I should."

"It's probably how he tracked you in New York."

My hand closed around it. "I was stupid not to think about that." I couldn't make myself lift the thin chain over my head, though. "I'll put it away later."

She gave me a pitying look. "You might have been better off marrying my other son."

I blinked at her. "Wow."

She shrugged. "We are not easy to love. And it isn't easy for us *to* love. Not in this world. Maybe not in any world."

"Just because you sense magic?"

"It changes how you think, Mattie. It shapes who you are. Imagine living in a world that hurts you every day, that pries away your sanity. It's like . . . being allergic to air, in a way. There's no way you can avoid it. There's no way you can protect yourself from it completely."

"I can't know what it feels like, not really, but I do understand that, Theresa."

She nodded. "Life becomes about survival, though. Love is a luxury. And sometimes it hurts too much to endure."

"You're talking about yourself. But I'm not magical. It doesn't hurt Asa to be with me." I shook off memories of this past spring, when the Strikon splinter inside me had caused us both such agony. "Not when I'm whole, that is."

"Maybe you're right," she murmured. "But when you learn to be wary of all pain, all pleasure, it's difficult to trust yourself with either. You learn to avoid all of it."

Daeng, the twisted sensor who'd tried to kill me and Asa in Atlanta, had said something similar—that he and Asa could never really trust themselves when it came to pleasure. "Right now, all I care about is freeing him and then helping him get healthy again."

"That's good," she said. "And maybe it will be all right."

She sounded so doubtful that my fists clenched. "You survived for a lot longer than he has," I said, unable to contain the frustration in my tone. "You were with Volodya for years. Asa's been with Brindle for less than a month."

Her honey-brown eyes were full of some unreadable emotion. "Volodya showed me the surveillance photos. I saw the collar they put on Asa. It probably has probes embedded in his skin, Mattie. Providing a constant drip of Ekstazo magic. Maybe a constant infusion of Knedas as well. Whatever they need him to do and believe."

"So we'll need to get that off him."

"If we can. Some of them have kill switches. Fail-safes to prevent unauthorized removal."

"What the heck does that mean?"

"It might do more damage than good to simply pull it off, and that's kind of the point."

My stomach turned. "It's so cruel," I whispered.

"He's a commodity," she said sadly. "We all are."

"You survived it, though. And you managed to get away."

"For me it was different." She gave me a regretful smile. "Only my heart held me back. But even then, my need to survive won out."

"What will you do when this is over?"

She wrapped her arms around her middle. "Run."

"Is it hard, being back?"

"It's murder," she whispered. "And magic. Both at the same time."

"I don't get it."

"No one ever has. And in the end we will probably kill each other. But not before we rescue our son." She took the bag of plasma over to a table covered in vials and syringes, where she drew a small amount of liquid from the bag and injected it into a little test tube, which she sealed up. Next, she slipped the tube into a gray sleeve, closed the top, and brought it back to me. "This is for you. If you keep it in the sleeve, it's almost undetectable."

I let her lay the gift on my outstretched palm. "What am I supposed to do with it?"

"Just keep it on hand in case of emergencies," she said. "Hold the outside if you need to sense. Open it up if you need someone else to."

"Thanks."

"It's all I can give you. I'll be watching as the event happens, but you won't see me. Volodya has an earpiece for you so that you can hear my voice and relay my observations to the security team. I'll stay until everyone's in, and then I need to get away from here."

"Because it's too painful?"

She nodded. "And because I need to stay dead. I don't want to be scooped up. It will be hard enough to escape Volodya one more time. I don't want to be hunted by all the other bosses, too." She chuckled. "Volodya is actually paranoid about this. In his own twisted way, he wants to keep me safe."

"Are you worried he'll be so focused on protecting you that he'll forget everything else?"

"Sometimes his emotions get the best of him," she said. "And sometimes others' do as well. But he won't be visible much, either. He presents a fairly tempting target for Knedas ambush. A weak boss with a massive collection of valuable relics and artifacts . . . He needs to focus his resources on protecting you, not himself and not me."

I fought off the feeling of loneliness that had been eating at me for days, then straightened my shoulders. "Okay, that's fine. I'll relay your observations, and I'll deal with whatever happens."

"We'll know more about what Brindle might be planning after tonight. But we have some idea when he'll try to take the pages."

"Daniil said that was what we were meeting about this afternoon."

"Get going then," she said, turning away.

I put my hand out to stop her. "I'm grateful that you came back, Theresa. I saw how scared you were of Volodya discovering that Asa was his son and how terrified you were about seeing him again. I know it took a lot of courage to show up like you did."

She gave me a pained smile. "I never protected Asa like I should have," she said in a strained voice. "I didn't know how. And now . . . I couldn't live with myself if I didn't do everything I could to save him. No matter what it costs. And I know you will, too." She leaned forward, her eyes shining with sudden tears. "That means getting him away from his father, Mattie. And probably from me, too. Our love could destroy him. Promise me you'll take him away from this place. Promise me you will care for him."

"No matter what it costs," I said quietly. "No matter what."

"Brindle and his entourage are staying at the National," Zoya announced as we gathered outside the entrance of a skyscraper across the river from Tower 2000. "He'll be here tomorrow afternoon." She gestured up at the massive building looming above us. "And this is where we'll do our thing."

The financial center of Moscow was considered an utter business failure, apparently, but as I looked up at the reflective surface of the double helix–shaped building, it looked pretty nice to me. Through his connections with local politicians and businesspeople, Volodya had marked out his territory. He might have been fading on the international scene, but he was still extraordinarily powerful within Moscow, and the location of the auction was meant to show it.

Daniil swept his arm toward eight men who were casually dressed in jeans and leather jackets that barely concealed the weapons bulging at their hips and calves. "This group will manage security at the door. Each player must present the invitation, which will be coded to their retinas." One of the armed men pulled a handheld scanner from his coat and waved it at us. "We have other scanners in the auction room itself and at the entrance to the vault where the artifacts will be stored."

We followed Daniil through the entrance of the tower. Another two tough guys were inside near a table, with a long, flat case. Daniil opened it, revealing a few dozen silver cuffs. "Each of you will wear one of these." He started handing them out. "They won't protect you from everything, but most Knedas and Ekstazo magic will be disrupted. Not the most comfortable thing to wear, but better to have a clear head, yes?"

He raised his eyebrows as he handed me one, and I nodded. These were exactly what the Headsmen wore, and Jack looked smug as he watched Daniil passing them out. I wondered if these were a plant—and if they'd stop working as the Headsmen raided the facility. Jack himself didn't take one—no need. I turned the cuff over in my hand, eyeing the little nodes that studded the inside of it.

Daniil continued. "Apart from Mr. Winchester, the only ones who won't wear them are Sambor, Masha, Ilya, Olga, Zoya, and myself. We need to be ready to use our own magic, which is much harder when you're being zapped every thirty seconds." Daniil's shoulders were straight and his steps were crisp, almost military, as he marched toward a set of double doors. It was so clear that he was trying to fill his father's shoes as Volodya's right hand—and he probably badly needed the distraction from his grief. "Tomorrow night will be the cocktail party and viewing, just a preview to give all the potential buyers a look at the items that will be auctioned the next day. We want them all to have a chance to explore this space." He gave me a grim smile. "It's when they'll have a chance to plan and scheme. And we'll be watching." He led us through the doors and into a ballroom, where numerous glass cases were being arranged down the center of the room and around the perimeter of the space.

At the very back of the room was a raised dais, upon which another glass display case was being placed. "Is that where the pages will be?" I asked.

Daniil nodded. "And through there is the exit that leads to an excellent escape route." He pointed to a door just behind the display case. Through the window set into its surface, I could see a long hallway lined with doors.

"Bullshit," Jack muttered.

Daniil grinned. "You see something different, Mr. Winchester?"

"Unless there's another door in that room I'm looking at, I'm thinking what you've got there is a holding cell."

"It's a glamour?" I asked. When Daniil nodded, I shook my head. "You're counting on all these guests not seeing through it?"

Ilya muttered something to Olga, who clucked her tongue and chuckled before making a comment in Russian. "She says it would take a lot more than your little bracelet for you to see the truth," he translated.

"Yeah, but there are ways to see through glamours without these cuffs," I said, holding mine up. "People in pain wouldn't be fooled."

Sambor and Masha stepped forward. "We're here to make sure everyone is feeling very nice," Sambor said. "Especially anyone who approaches this door."

"I'll be able to sense their intentions," said Zoya. "We work together."

"And Mattie, if anyone tries to grab you, all you must do is make it back there, all right?" said Daniil. "The room is the safest in the building once its security measures are triggered, and we'll be watching it at all times."

"Why would they try to grab *her*?" asked Sambor.

"Mattie has . . . knowledge. And Brindle is always very curious."

I glanced at Jack. The plan sounded okay, but far from foolproof. "So tomorrow you'll get a sense of who wants to steal what, and you're showing them a false escape route. If they plan to get out that way, with me or with any of the artifacts, they end up running into a trap."

"Exactly," said Daniil. "Meanwhile, we have people at the National. They will determine where Frank Brindle is keeping this mosaic panel the boss wants."

"It's going to be guarded," said Jack.

"And tomorrow we'll figure out how," said Ilya, fluttering his nicotine-stained fingers. "While you all are having your cocktails, I'll be at the hotel with the housecleaning staff."

Daniil walked forward and handed me an earpiece. "The sensor will convey information to you using this, Mattie. All you have to do is let someone know what she's saying."

"Who is this sensor, exactly?" asked Masha. "Why is this American the only one who talks to her? Why haven't we met her?"

"Because that is the way Volodya wants it," Daniil said, his jaw hard.

Sambor and Masha gave each other a look, then turned their suspicious gazes on me.

Jack shifted and took half a step in front of me. "Are we done here?"

"Photographs of the known players are in the surveillance-camera room, out the door and to the left," said Daniil. "Memorize their faces. Focus particular attention on Frank Brindle and his two agents. The sensor—Asa Ward—they are likely to use him as the thief, and he is also the individual Volodya wants to apprehend. But from all the intelligence we have on him, it will not be easy." His jaw clenched, his eyes glittering with hatred.

I nodded, eager to keep the conversation going. "You have to be very careful of concealed weapons with him."

"He'll be searched at the door."

"Whatever he's carrying will not be that obvious."

"We'll take everything," Daniil promised. "That is our right as hosts." He gave the retina-scanner dude a look, and the guy stood up straighter.

"We'll make sure he's emptied out," the guy said, his deep voice and thick accent making him sound particularly menacing.

We began to shuffle in the direction of the surveillance room, but Jack poked my arm and inclined his head in the opposite direction. "What's up?" I asked quietly as the others headed for the room.

"Keenan's surveilling the National, along with the Savoy and two others where bosses and their entourages have reservations. If anyone tries to nab you, we need to know immediately," he said in a low voice. "Because this operation isn't giving me a lot of confidence."

"Well, hopefully it won't give Brindle confidence in us, either, right? We want him to think taking the pages will be easy."

He gave me an edgy look. "We're more concerned about what he thinks about taking you. Especially because he'll have both Reza Tavana and Asa with him."

"I promise not to go wandering off on my own—don't worry. But what's Keenan's plan here?"

Jack glanced at the display cases. "If Volodya corners Asa in that room, there will be a raid on your signal." He slipped a phone into my pocket. "Text to the one number programmed in. We'll get to him while he's contained, and we're expecting him to have the pages. So we take both."

"And if Volodya doesn't corner Asa?"

"It's gonna be up to you and me to track him. I don't think it'll be hard." His deep-brown eyes searched my face. "Because he's gonna come after you." He reached forward, quick and deft, and pressed something flat to my cuff. It was silver and blended in with the metal. "Just keep that on."

"Great. I love being shocked."

"Better than being controlled."

I winced as I thought of that awful collar around Asa's neck. "Okay," I said quietly. "Let's get this done."

CHAPTER TWENTY-TWO

I shifted my weight to try to ease some of the discomfort in my feet. Zoya and I had gone shopping for our outfits for the event, and I'd thought I'd chosen practical shoes. Once again, I'd misjudged. Still, I knew I looked good in my retro form-fitting dress and the flowy jacket that covered my silver cuff.

"Here comes Botwright's crew," Theresa said in my ear.

I turned for the door to see a tiny woman with white hair walk through. She couldn't have topped five feet in her heels, and she moved in a cautious, birdlike manner toward the retinal scanner. Myron Forester was at her side, towering over her, his dark hair slicked back, wearing a slim blue suit complete with a patterned tie and a sapphire tie tack. Another man, this one blond, stood at her other side.

"Botwright is Strikon," Theresa said. "The brunet and the blond are both Knedas." She cursed. "And the brunet is putting out some ridiculous vibes right now." She made a gagging noise.

I glanced at Volodya, who was standing amid his bodyguards, holding court with each potential buyer. Myron would be within six feet of him in less than a minute.

"I'm thinking about it, too," Theresa murmured in my ear. "Get Zoya to move closer. If he's trying to get people to lower their guard to enable an assassination attempt, she could sense it. But she has to touch him."

I quickly walked over to where Zoya was standing with her brother. "Can you get over there and shake the brown-haired guy's hand? Just be ready—he's Knedas and apparently strong."

Zoya's blue eyes traveled to Myron, and she arched an eyebrow. "Nice." She smiled and headed over, squeezing the lightning bolt pendant hanging from her necklace.

"It's Strikon," Daniil said. "Mine. It'll keep her head clear."

Myron remained one step behind his boss as the woman marched forward and offered Volodya her hand. Volodya took it carefully in his and then slowly bent and kissed it. Botwright looked somewhat shocked—she was a Strikon, and probably not too many people were willing to lay their lips on her skin. She gave him a faint smile as he raised his head. "So sorry about our misunderstanding around the holidays," she said in a posh English accent.

"All in the past," he said generously. "You made things more interesting for this old man."

She patted his arm. "Far from old."

"Well, I certainly don't feel that way when I'm in your presence."

"That motherfucking flirt," Theresa said in my ear.

Then Myron straightened his tie and pressed forward to shake Volodya's hand. Zoya smoothly intercepted, however, and slipped her palm over his. "I'm Volodya's niece," she said. Technically, this was untrue, but since she was the daughter of Arkady, it made sense. "You are?"

He gave her a polite smile and looked down at their joined hands like he knew exactly what she was up to. "Myron Forester."

She looked over at me and gave me a nod, then stepped aside and allowed him to shake Volodya's hand. I guessed he didn't have any bad intentions after all.

"Maybe he's just insecure," Theresa said. "Sometimes, when they get nervous, naturals just kind of . . . leak."

I was still watching Myron warily. He didn't look nervous. I hadn't forgiven him for what had happened the night Asa was taken, even if he'd only done what Asa had wanted. And when he looked my way, his sheepish smile told me he hadn't forgotten that night, either. I stood my ground as he accompanied his boss into the auction room.

"Mattie, you may want to get in here so you're out of sight," Theresa said quickly. "Brindle, Reza, and Asa just got out of their car. Here they come."

Theresa had stationed herself in the surveillance room just behind where Volodya was standing. She was separated from us only by the wall and the door. My heart hammering, I skirted past Volodya, and a muscle-bound bodyguard quickly opened the door to let me into the darkened room full of video screens.

Theresa stood in front of one, sweat running down her face like raindrops, her eyes fixed on one of the screens. "There he is," she murmured.

I turned toward the monitor. Asa walked next to Reza, a few steps behind Brindle. His face was impassive. He wore a suit like all the men, but as before, the collar of his shirt seemed too large for his neck. Like something lay just underneath the fabric. As they walked through the doors and into the frisking and scanning area, Frank said something to one of the guards, gesturing at Asa's neck.

"He's telling the guard it's medically necessary," Theresa grumbled as the guard waved his scanner around Asa's throat. Next Asa placidly raised his arms to let one of the commandos check him for weapons. He calmly turned out his pockets, and I held my breath, waiting for the improvised tools and toys he always had.

But there was nothing in there. He took off his jacket and turned around, not objecting to being the focus of security. By now, Reza was standing off to the side, smirking. He said something to Asa, but I couldn't read his lips.

"They were ready for you," Theresa translated.

Asa didn't respond. As he turned around, though, his brow furrowed and he stared off to the side.

"What's he looking at?" I asked.

Theresa grasped my arm. "This room," she whispered.

"Is it you or me that he's sensing?"

"Probably me."

I swallowed and nodded, taking in the puzzled expression on his face, the first emotion I'd seen from him since he'd been taken. "He recognizes your magic, but he doesn't know it's you."

"Are you sure?" She sounded almost frightened.

"I'm sure. He looks just as confused by it now as he did that night in Prague."

"Look at Volodya," she said, her voice breaking.

Frank Brindle was stepping up to shake Volodya's hand while the bodyguards closed in, but the Russian boss seemed as if he were in another world. He was staring at his son with a look I can describe only as longing. Zoya, still standing at his side, looked up at him in confusion, probably feeling some possessive intention.

"Snap out of it," Theresa hissed, glaring at the screen. "Wake up."

I lunged for the door, opened it a crack while making sure to stay out of sight, and beckoned Zoya over. "Get Volodya to focus," I said quickly, then pulled the door shut with a snap.

By the time I made it back over to the screens, Volodya was shaking hands, first with Brindle, then with Reza, then with Asa, who barely looked at him—he was staring at the wall of our surveillance room again. Theresa's bloodshot eyes were riveted on the two men, but when she saw me watching her, she turned away. "See? It's fine," she said, her voice trembling. "Asa does not realize who he is."

"Once they're inside, I'm going to go circulate," I said, eager to give her some time to pull herself together. "I can't hide forever."

Theresa nodded as she mopped her face with a towel. She'd brought a stack into the room with her, knowing it would be a tough afternoon.

"Are you going to be all right?" I asked.

"Par for the course," she said with a strained laugh. "I'm used to it."

I squeezed her arm. "I'll see you later."

She looked down at my fingers as they slid off her sleeve. "Be careful."

As soon as Brindle and his little entourage disappeared, I exited the surveillance room. Volodya was pale but appeared composed for the moment. I didn't try to catch his eye as I passed—I didn't want to see the pain I knew would be there. I had plenty of my own to manage at the moment.

I strode through one of the side doors into the ballroom. All the potential buyers were assembled—nearly twenty bosses from all over the world, with varying levels of power and influence, along with two agents for each boss. Over fifty people, plus all of Volodya's staff, both natural and normal. Although waiters were circulating with vodka, champagne, and caviar, most people were clustered around the display cases.

Volodya's collection was truly impressive—and it was Theresa who had helped him acquire it. All their years together were stretched out and under glass, memories for sale. Each object had a plaque explaining where it was acquired and what it was. Many were ancient pieces, either covered with runes or possessing old magic. At the back of the room on the dais were the pages, in their special carrying cases that kept them from being exposed to the air. I leaned over, squinting. The pages looked kind of blurry.

"It's to keep anyone who actually manages to smuggle in a camera from being able to get a clear image."

I turned to find Myron standing next to me. "Makes sense. I guess it would take a lot of the value out of the pages if pictures of them existed." I glanced at one of the surveillance cameras mounted over the glass case in front of me.

"He's not trying to influence you, Mattie," Theresa's voice said in my ear. "I'm not sure why he was so nervous before, but he's toned it way down." She paused for a moment. "Way, *way* down," she added, sounding puzzled.

I looked Myron over. He did seem a lot more relaxed now—he'd removed his tie, and the top button of his shirt was undone. I gestured at his open collar. "You're not a tie guy?"

He smiled and patted his pocket. "Can't stand them. Feels like a noose. Just don't tell Madam. She likes us to look like gentlemen." He inclined his head toward Botwright, who was engaged in an intense discussion with Elina Garza, the boss of Spain, an olive-skinned, ebony-haired woman wearing a black pantsuit that fit her voluptuous figure like a second skin. Her two agents, who appeared to be twins, both tall and lean with dark hair and chiseled features, hovered behind her, eyeing passersby with wary suspicion. Theresa had told me that one could sense intentions, like Zoya, and the other could sense magic. "She's trying to negotiate an alliance with Garza because Frank Brindle has been making inroads on the continent, in both the relic-trade and protection business."

I watched Botwright for a moment. She carried herself with easy confidence, but she was the tiniest person in the room, weighing maybe ninety pounds with all her jewelry on. "Doesn't she need you over there protecting *her*?"

He laughed. "She's just as poisonous as Reza Tavana. Few people are willing to cross her. Even Volodya is cautious when she's standing right in front of him, despite his agents' big words in London."

I smiled. I didn't know the woman, but I liked the idea of her power not coming from her size or her muscles.

"Have you seen him?" Myron asked, interrupting my thoughts. He nodded toward Asa, who was standing at Brindle's side as the boss talked with Reza over a display case holding a few mosaic panels that looked a little like the magical one they'd stolen.

"Yeah."

"He doesn't look bad off."

I gritted my teeth. "Seriously?"

"He hasn't tried to get away from Brindle, has he?"

"Are you just trying to keep yourself from feeling guilty about that night at Harrods?"

"Perhaps they're making it worth his while. Brindle *is* known for paying his employees well—"

"And now we're done." I put my hands up, unable to stomach another moment at his side. And when he didn't back off, I simply walked away, ending up in front of a case containing several shards of pottery, laid out like a puzzle. I noticed a few of the sensors in the room had raised their heads and looked in my direction. I tried to calm down by mentally reconstructing whatever the broken pieces had once been.

"I knew you were here," Asa said quietly.

I focused on the glass and saw his reflection. He was standing right behind me. "I wasn't hiding."

"You were before."

"You can't sense me."

He shook his head. "But I can smell you. When you opened the door to the surveillance room."

I let out a shaky breath as his voice came back to me from the past. *God, Mattie. Why do you always smell so fucking good?* I bowed my head. "So here we are. About to try to kidnap me?"

"Not the time."

I turned around and looked up at him, then instantly regretted it. He looked terrible and wonderful all at the same time. It seemed like he'd lost weight, which made me angry as heck, because he hadn't had much to lose in the first place. His cheeks had gone from hollow to gaunt, and the circles under his eyes were brutally dark. He had changed so much. But he was still Asa. Crooked nose and honey-brown eyes and short, dark hair that wanted to be curly if only he'd let it grow a bit. "So why'd you come over here?"

He blinked, looking a little startled, his focus always just a few inches to the left or right of my face. "No reason."

"You never do anything without a reason, Asa."

His nostrils flared. "You're wearing a shock cuff. And an earpiece. Who are you talking to—the sensor in the surveillance room?"

Now it was my turn to look startled. "You can draw your own conclusions."

He smirked. "How about I conclude that you and this entire operation are woefully underprepared for what's about to happen?"

"I'm sure you'd like to think that."

The cruel smile dropped away. "Don't fight me when I come for you, Mattie. I won't enjoy hurting you."

I ventured just a tad closer, longing eating me up. "Then don't hurt me at all."

"I'll do what I have to. I've learned that pain is the one thing that nobody can completely resist or withstand."

I glared up at him. "And *I've* learned that I can tolerate a hell of a lot of it without cracking."

"I know," he said quietly.

"A few weeks ago you would have stepped between me and anything that tried to hurt me."

His expression turned blank. "That's gone now, Mattie."

"I know it's in there. You love me."

"You're an idiot if you're clinging to that." His fingers rose toward his collar but dropped to his side again, and he sighed, his eyes falling shut.

I wondered if he'd just gotten an infusion of Ekstazo magic, and it sent a hot wave of anger rolling along my limbs. "You never wanted to be like this, Asa. I could help you get free."

"Too late for that. There's nothing left." He said it so matter-of-factly. "And no matter what you say or what you do, the magic in your vault is coming out. Fight and you might not survive. Cooperate and you will."

"Nice to know you care."

"I don't. Brindle wants to use you as his reliquary."

His words stung, but I was already hollow inside. "I don't know if you're trying to scare me just to make your job easier, but it's not going to work." I lifted my chin, defiance filling the pit of my grief. "And you might be coming after me, but I'm coming after you, too."

"Pointless."

"It will never be pointless."

"I don't feel anything for you," he said slowly. "Let me go, Mattie. I'm gone anyway."

"I. Don't. Care." I poked his chest, my fury and determination bursting forth. "I'm coming after you, Asa Ward," I whispered, "because you are *worth* it. Because you deserve freedom. And because you deserve my love even if you can't love me back anymore. You think being mean to me is going to stop me? You think you can bully me into backing down?" I narrowed my eyes. "You've forgotten who I really am, then. So go ahead. Do your worst. But I'll be ready. And I'm going to win."

Asa's gaze began to slowly travel up my body, almost reaching my eyes. But then a hand snaked over his shoulder and squeezed. "Everything all right here?" Reza asked.

Asa shrugged him off quickly. "Mattie just said something really funny."

Reza smiled at me, and my head began to throb. "Yes, she *is* amusing, isn't she?"

"I need to take a piss." Asa stalked away.

"Trying to get him back?" Reza asked, bringing a glass of champagne to his perfectly shaped lips.

"One guess."

He waggled his eyebrows as he drained his glass. "He's even more useful than we thought he'd be," he said breezily. "I'm afraid Mr. Brindle would never give him up. Especially because he knows so many of our secrets now." He set his glass on a passing waiter's tray. "We couldn't let him live if we thought he might leave our employ."

The threat slid cold down my spine, and suddenly it all crashed down on me at once: Asa's indifference, the dead look in his eye, his gaunt, crumbling body, the absolute cruelty of the man in front of me, so casual about destroying my love. Another minute and I was going to gouge his eyes out with my pink manicured nails.

"Enjoy the party, asshole," I said. His amused chuckle followed me as I left the room.

CHAPTER TWENTY-THREE

Holding in tears, I stormed back to the surveillance room. Theresa was inside, sitting next to one of the commandos as he scanned the various monitors.

She handed me a bottle of water and held up a little pill bottle, which she shook. "Need a few of these?"

I accepted her generosity without a word, popping two of the headache pills and guzzling down half the water. Then I sank into a chair.

"I couldn't hear what was being said, but I could see how much it hurt."

I let out a strained chuckle. "Yeah. Did Volodya pick up anything when they came in?"

She shook her head. "He said Asa was a complete blank, like a vast wall of static. It left him shaken. He retired to his office on the top floor." She stared blankly at the monitor, and I knew she wasn't really seeing it. "I think seeing his son like that for the first time cracked his heart."

"I always knew Asa was a heartbreaker," I murmured. "He's certainly living up to that tonight."

She sighed. "We'll get him, Mattie. We just have to wait for him to make his move. We're all watching him. He's prowling around the edge of the room, looking at all the exits." She nodded toward one of the monitors, where I could just make out Asa's lean form crossing through the corner of the screen. "He's learning where the cameras are and starting to avoid them."

"Some things never change."

"We don't have many blind spots, though. It won't be easy." She pointed as he reentered the picture. He was hovering behind a display case near one of the back corners of the room, and his gaze was riveted on the camera. It looked like he was staring right at us.

"I'm more concerned that he'll find a way to take down the entire system."

"With what? He was searched."

I crossed my arms over my chest and frowned as I watched him move slowly toward the dais holding the *Essentialis Magia* pages. "He's up to something."

He was always up to something. Always playing. Whatever else he'd lost, I was betting his cunning wasn't on the list. Reza had said Asa was more valuable than they'd anticipated. He'd said Asa knew their secrets now. He was dangerous.

He was also dying. I felt sick as I watched the harsh light play across the hollows of his face. I remembered the bandages. No one could possibly know what was going on inside of him. While Keenan was training me, he'd told me that once Asa had got the hang of hiding his true feelings, the emotion sensor had never picked up another clue again. Just another way for Asa to protect himself from being controlled.

He'd moved near Garza and was sliding behind her two agents. One of the twins was staring at him, looking perplexed, while the other was glaring, sweat shining on his face. I could see only the back of Asa's head, but he must have said something to Garza's magic sensor, because his eyes widened and his posture tensed. His lip curled as he said something to Asa, and then he grabbed Asa's arm.

"Uh-oh," Theresa said, half rising to her feet as Asa shoved the Spanish agent, knocking him against a display case. The guy grimaced and grabbed his back, and something small and glittering fell to the floor.

"Did you see that?" Theresa asked.

"Yeah—what was it?"

But our questions had to wait, because now Asa was standing off against both agents, with Botwright, Myron, and her other agent coming to help. Theresa turned to the commando next to us. "Get your people in there to quiet this down before someone gets hurt."

Too late for that, though. I don't know if Asa threw the first punch, but a moment later there were fists flying and glass shattering and people screaming. I squinted at the melee, trying to keep an eye on Asa, but . . .

"Theresa, he's gone." I scanned all the other monitors while she leaned close and did the same.

"He's in there somewhere," she said. "But—"

The lights flickered as the commando next to Theresa spoke in urgent Russian into his mouthpiece. His men poured into the ballroom.

Then our cameras went dark. Even through the barrier of the door, we could hear a massive thump and a cacophony of breaking glass. The alarm went off, piercing and certain.

Theresa cursed. "He's going for the pages."

I bolted for the door and swung it open in time to see eight of Volodya's guards pushing their way to the front of the ballroom. The emergency lighting system was on, filling the space with wavering green and yellow light. But the lights on the other side of the door at the back of the room were still shining bright.

The glamour wasn't connected to the main electrical system. Or any electrical system, for that matter. A few people were peering at it curiously as they hovered anxiously near the back of the room, but there was still a tangle of brawlers near the cases on the right side of the space, where Asa had picked a fight with Garza's men. I couldn't see who was still over there, but—

Four commandos burst through the doors of the fake escape route, dragging a lean dark-haired man by the arms. They shouted something in Russian as I felt fingers close tight around my arm. "They got him," Theresa said in my ear, her tone breaking with excitement.

I turned to her in shock—the lure of seeing her son captured had drawn her out of her hiding place, but I totally understood. If Asa was caught in the act, Volodya would have jurisdiction to keep him and question him.

It was our chance to get him away from Brindle.

Except . . . if I didn't want both Asa and myself to be under constant threat from the Headsmen for the rest of our lives, I was supposed to be texting Keenan right now to come rescue both Asa and those pages.

My fingers groped for the phone in my purse as I pushed forward. The emergency lights were brighter near the front of the room, where a spotlight focused on the shattered display case on the dais. The trap had actually worked.

The commandos dragged Asa forward and tossed him to the ground in front of the case. The brawl subsided as people crushed closer to see the man who had defied Volodya's generosity and security. I took a step away from Theresa, my sweaty fingers tight around the phone.

The thief braced his palms on the carpet glittering with shards of glass. He raised his head.

And I let go of the phone.

It wasn't Asa. It was Garza's magic sensor. He looked stunned and confused as he realized he was surrounded. One of the commandos strode forward and handed the case containing a sheaf of *Essentialis*

Magia pages to Daniil, who had rushed into the room and ended up next to me. They had a terse conversation in Russian before Daniil turned to me. "He was trying to escape with this."

The lights came on, blaring and bright, as I blinked down at the man who was not Asa.

"Oh God," Theresa whispered.

She was backtracking, her eyes fixed on a spot just to my left. I turned.

Asa was leaning against a display case next to Reza and Frank Brindle, both of whom seemed to have avoided the brawl altogether. Asa looked relaxed, but his long fingers were curled hard over the edge of the case. His gaze was on Theresa. For the first time since he'd been taken from me, true, raw emotion shined in his eyes.

But it wasn't love. Or sorrow.

It was pure, unadulterated rage. "Hi, *Mom*."

Frank Brindle broke the terrible silence that followed. He placed a fatherly hand on Asa's shoulder, and Asa's eyelids drooped. The boss of the West Coast was a powerful Ekstazo, and I had no doubt he was letting his magic flow into his captive sensor right now. "Now, is that right?" Frank asked, peering at Theresa. "Yes, I see it. I suppose he has your eyes, doesn't he?"

Asa was staring at the floor now, swaying unsteadily, and Theresa was staring at him, stricken. She didn't seem to have the voice to respond to Brindle. She looked like she wanted to run, but I knew she was held there by her heart.

Daniil raised his hands, which were shaking slightly, maybe with hatred for Brindle and Asa, maybe with the pressure of the moment. "My friends, I think it's time to end this party tonight. You've all had a chance to view the merchandise that will be auctioned tomorrow afternoon. Please call your bankers to discuss your bid ranges. Our financial-transfer documents have been encrypted and sent to each of you."

"How do we know the merchandise will actually *be* here tomorrow?" asked Botwright, who was now eyeing Garza and her agents with distinct suspicion. Garza herself was nearly white with shock as she stood surrounded by Volodya's guards.

"Well, it's here now," Daniil said, his tone hard. "Because we were ready for the thieves." He was holding his head just a tad too high, and I could see the strain there. "Now please, ladies and gentlemen. We bid you a good night, and we will welcome you tomorrow when we have cleaned up after this scum who has abused our hospitality." He spat the word as he gestured to the commandos, who wrenched Garza's magic sensor to his feet.

The man muttered something in Spanish, and Garza's eyes went wide. "He just said, 'He did something to me.'"

"Who?" asked Daniil.

The accused magic sensor raised his head and opened his mouth to speak, but couldn't seem to push any more words out. I turned and gave Asa a look, but he was still staring drunkenly at the ground. Frank Brindle pulled him a little closer. "I think we'll be heading back to our hotel now."

I could only hope Keenan's team had pinpointed the location of the mosaic panel. Or that Ilya and the cleaning staff had done the same. My thoughts spun. I wasn't sure who I truly wanted to win. Right now, I just didn't want it to be Brindle.

Theresa and I stepped back to allow Reza, Asa, and Frank to pass. Reza smirked at me as he sauntered by without a single hair out of place. As soon as they'd left the room, everyone else turned to Garza's crew. The commandos were ushering them away to a series of improvised interrogation rooms and holding cells that Volodya had demanded.

Potential buyers shuffled out to their waiting limos while servers came in to sweep up the mess.

Daniil stood near an intact display case, holding the glass box full of priceless pages. He looked around at the overturned chairs, the shattered cabinet on the dais, and the door to the secure room that was now hanging open, still looking deceptively like a long hallway. His shoulders slumped. "Sambor, Masha," he said, and the two Ekstazos trudged over from the exit, where they'd been trying to soothe anxiety as guests left. "Call Ilya immediately and tell him Brindle is on his way back to the hotel."

The couple walked out quickly, arms linked.

"Zoya," said Daniil as his sister approached him. "What did you feel?"

"Just before Garza's agent charged the dais, I felt his need to steal the pages."

I frowned. "Just before? But not earlier?"

She shook her head. "When I passed him earlier, all he wanted was to be elsewhere. He was going to try to convince his boss to leave early."

"And then he decided to steal the pages, just like that? Why?" Daniil asked.

"Asa did something to him," I said quietly. "He picked a fight, and while everyone was brawling, he put some kind of whammy on the guy." I glanced around. "I did see something fall off the case after Asa shoved him . . ."

"A Knedas relic? But why wouldn't I have felt him bringing it in?" Theresa said. "His pockets were empty!" She sounded bewildered as she looked around. "I don't know what we missed." She started to walk around the room, her gaze on the floor, stepping over broken champagne flutes, caviar-splattered display cases, a few lost gloves, one broken pair of glasses, and a stained, wrinkled tie. She bent over and picked it up.

"That's Myron's," I said, recognizing the sapphire tie tack.

"It's soaked with champagne." Her eyes narrowed. "But there's a trace of Knedas on it."

"But Myron *is* a Knedas. Could it be from his sweat or something?"

She sighed. "Yes." She turned back to me, Daniil, and Zoya. "I need to go tell Volodya everything that happened. I think he will take it better if he hears it from me."

I gave her a surprised look. "Are you sure?"

"He's our son," she murmured. "I'm the only one who can understand what Volodya will feel." She trudged out of the room.

"This is bad," said Daniil.

"I really don't get it, either," I said, staring after her.

"Not them, Mattie. *This.*" With an expression of disgust, he gestured at the shattered display case.

"We still have the pages," said Zoya.

"The pages were never in danger," I said. "This was a scout mission." I kicked at a discarded tray. "Asa was looking to find out what security we had in place. Somehow, he used Garza's sensor as his probe, and he got the guy to trip the alarm, to use the escape hatch."

"And now they know it's not really a way out," said Daniil, slamming his hand onto one of the big display cases. "We're not even to the auction tomorrow, and already they know our tricks. Any changes to the layout or exits and they'll know we've rigged a different false escape system." He snarled something in Russian.

"What do we do now?" Zoya asked her brother.

"Call Olga. We'll talk to her about what she can do. Maybe little things," said Daniil. "The locks on the doors. The electrical panel. Perhaps we can slow potential thieves down."

"We could use Father's magic," she whispered.

Daniil nodded. "I think we'll have to."

"You have more of Arkady's magic?"

"Volodya has been saving it. And I think Olga might need the extra boost. With the two combined, we can probably work something up.

Something that won't be revealed by one big attack." He let out a deep breath and gave his sister a smile. "This could still be all right."

She touched his arm. "Of course it will be. We haven't actually lost anything yet. We still have our treasures." She gestured around the room. "And we still have Mattie."

I gave them a weak smile. "Thanks." I stretched and yawned. "I'm actually going to head back to my room to get some rest before tomorrow."

I had barely made it back to my room when the phone Jack had given me buzzed with a text.

Panel located. We acquire tomorrow. Report on your situation.

I sighed and texted back. *Asa figured out V's security. Probably will go for the pages tomorrow at auction.*

And you?

Probably tomorrow as well.

We're tracking you. You're safe. We'll take him down.

I glanced down at my shock bracelet where Jack had put the tiny tracker and laughed. "Yeah, right."

Now that Asa had probed the security system, there was little holding him back. Tomorrow we would face off, and yet I had no idea exactly when he would strike or how. I only knew that Volodya's commandos and naturals weren't enough. Possibly a whole crew of Headsmen wasn't, either.

I walked over to a shelf and gazed at the sleeve containing a vial of Theresa's magic and the pendant Asa had given me.

Everyone wanted to stop Asa. Almost nobody could, though. And I could only hope his habit of underestimating me would be the fatal flaw that made all the difference.

Assuming, of course, he hadn't been right about me all along.

CHAPTER TWENTY-FOUR

I couldn't sleep at all. I sat up all night, wondering how it would feel when he stood over me, prepared to do whatever was necessary to extract the magic from inside my chest. It wasn't the physical pain I was so worried about. No, it would be the hurt of knowing he truly didn't care. It would be the agony of betrayal.

Over and over, I told myself not to think about that. I had a lot of miles to cover before it came to that. A lot of moves to make.

A few hours before I was going to head over to the auction with the rest of our beleaguered second-string crew, Jack came to my door. I glanced up and down the hallway before letting him in. "Which Jack am I talking to right now?"

"Depends. Which Mattie am I talking to?"

I let out a shaky breath and sat down on the edge of my bed. "Did Keenan send you? Is he worried that I'll screw him over again?"

Jack shrugged. "Just wanted to see how you were doing. I talked to Daniil."

"And is he hell-bent on killing Asa today?"

"He wouldn't mind seeing him suffer. He won't defy Volodya, though." He took a seat near the window.

"He actually seems like a decent guy for having two evil parents."

Jack leaned back and hooked an ankle over his knee. "Speaking of parents . . ."

Our eyes met. "I knew that story would spread quickly."

"Not sure which surprised us more—that Theresa Harrison is still alive or that Asa Ward is her son."

I sighed. "How about that Volodya is his father?"

Jack laughed. "Doesn't that just figure? Makes a lot of damn sense, if you think about it."

I didn't share his amusement as I considered how freaking twisted Asa's parents could be. "Not sure I follow."

"People can come out of nowhere, Mattie. It does happen. But sometimes, heredity explains a lot."

"Let's hope not," I muttered. "But the good news is, Volodya wants Asa safe. He'll do what he can to make it happen."

Jack gave me a long, questioning look. "And then what? Keenan's not going to give you another chance. You go back on your word this time, and he's never going to let up on you. Might as well kiss the daylight good-bye."

"Awesome. Because more threats are all I needed today."

He put his hands up. "Good news is, there's really no better friend to have. Trust me—you want Keenan on your side. Once he decides you're on board, he'll stick by you. And no one's better than him at pulling people out of jams."

That friendship would come at the expense of betraying Asa's father, who, despite his insanity, was willing to risk his most valuable possessions to save the son he hadn't even known about before a week ago. "I wish things were simpler."

"Boring."

I let out a begrudging chuckle. "So, again I ask—which Jack are you? Winchester or Okafor?"

He leaned forward and set his elbows on his knees. "I'm whichever one you need. If we do this under controlled circumstances at the Headsmen's safe house, I'm Okafor, and it's all clean and neat. If things stay messy, then Winchester's got it covered. Volodya's already booked me."

"And if things go to hell?"

"Brindle's got my number."

"Yeah, and so does Asa." I shook my head. "You can't go anywhere near that, Jack. It's way too dangerous."

"You worried about me?"

"Yes!" I had already been partly responsible for his grandfather's death. There was no way I could have his on my conscience, too. "Besides, if it gets that far, I don't want you there. I have to stop Brindle from getting to the magic inside me." I reached out and patted his hand. "And I don't really want to arm-wrestle you for it."

His nostrils flared as he took a deep breath. "Nah, I don't really want that, either. But I don't like the idea of you in the lion's den all alone. So maybe Okafor's your man in that case. Because Keenan and I will find a way to shut that shit down."

"I'm counting on it, for my sake and for Asa's. You'll be able to track me if you need to."

"Not sure we actually will need to—Brindle might come to us. We're raiding his hotel this afternoon while he's here at the auction, so we'll have the panel. He needs both."

I let my head hang back. "God. There are so many moving parts to this. Volodya's people are trying to steal the panel this afternoon, too."

"I know. I talked to Ilya. We'll be in and out before they realize someone else was there. Good thing, too. Brindle's security is tight, and Ilya's little team isn't up for it. They go in there, they're not coming out."

I cringed. "But Keenan's team?"

"They can handle themselves."

I thought of Reza and Asa and Brindle—they were like an unholy trio. "I hope so."

Jack stood up. "You don't worry about that. Just worry about yourself. Asa will make a play for the pages, and either Volodya will take him down or we will. Depends on how quickly you can let us know. Just push that sensor on your cuff—it's pressure sensitive, and it'll let us know you need the cavalry. Once you do, we'll take over and get you out without Volodya knowing you had anything to do with it."

I looked over at the cuff, which I'd set on the shelf next to the vial of Theresa's magic. I was so relieved I hadn't set everything in motion the night before—it would have been yet another thing unraveled by Asa's trickery. "Okay."

Jack gave me a warning look. "We're the ones to get Asa up and running again. Remember that. It's nothing Keenan hasn't done before. You're gonna want professional help for him once we get him free. It's clear he's pretty far gone. You want to give him every chance you can of recovering."

I turned to the window. He was right—I wanted to give Asa every chance. But what would Keenan want in return, and would Asa really want that kind of help? I couldn't help but wonder if what was really on offer was just another cage. "It won't matter if we don't get him away from Brindle," I murmured.

"That's for damn sure. And I'll do everything I can to help, Mattie. I'm on your side in this."

I looked over my shoulder at him. "Really?"

He nodded, and in his broad, handsome face, all I saw was honesty.

"I'm glad, Jack." I took a steadying breath as I faced him once again. "Because I need to ask for a favor."

Having never been to an auction, I had no idea an event that included so many people could be so quiet—or so tense. Volodya's staff had cleaned up the ballroom, sweeping up the glass, replacing the shattered and overturned display case, rearranging everything so that now there were rows of chairs arrayed around the auction items at the front. Some, the most valuable, had been placed in the vault, to be brought out only at their special moment, but others were on display.

Those were auctioned off first. The auctioneer appeared to be British, or his accent was, at least. He stood at a podium on the dais, the bald spot on top of his head shining under the bright lights above. All the bosses and their tiny entourages were positioned throughout the room—Botwright near the front on the right, and Garza, now without her magic sensor, near the center of the room on the left. All the other bosses filled in the gaps—they'd come from at least a dozen countries, from six different continents. Volodya was not present. Theresa said he was nearby but could not stand to witness the dismantling of his collection.

Theresa warned me through the earpiece that Brindle's crew had arrived. In a strained voice, she told me how Asa was glaring at the locked surveillance room as he entered. Once again, he had nothing in the few pockets he actually had in his suit. Today, his black collar was on display—it took the place of his tie, only just inside his shirt instead of over it. It was almost as if Frank wanted everyone to see it.

When the deadly trio entered the room, they had everyone's attention. Daniil glared at them from his position next to the auctioneer, and Zoya watched them anxiously from her spot on my left. Sambor hovered near the entrance to the room, and Masha was standing at the door that led to the vault. Olga was nowhere in sight, but I knew that she'd been at work all night. The "escape" route was the same as it had been the day before, even though everyone who had been present now knew it was a glamour. I guessed we wanted people to think that nothing at all had been changed or modified. I could only hope that wasn't true.

The first item was the set of broken pottery shards I'd been staring at the day before, with the now-familiar runes etched all over each surface. Initially, things moved quickly, with the auctioneer calling out each new bid and the price sliding higher with staggering speed. But each time, there would be a point when things slowed down and the hard decisions got made—how badly did the bidder want it?

Judging from the nervous glances in the room, there was more at stake than money. I wondered if each item collected was a potential liability, in that the winner might have acquired something that someone else . . . like Asa . . . would want to steal.

"Stop looking back at him, Mattie," came Theresa's voice in my ear. "You look weak."

I stared stonily at the front of the room. Theresa's voice was hoarse. I was betting there were some tears shed the previous night, and I wondered whether she had been alone or had escaped her sorrows in Volodya's arms. Had she wept because of Asa's obvious rage—or Volodya's love, which sounded as painful as his hatred, if not more so? I couldn't help my fascination with Theresa and Volodya. I couldn't help hoping observing them would teach me something about the son they created.

"He just looked at you for the first time," Theresa said. "Just stay aware, all right? No! Don't look back there!"

I jerked my head around again, and my cheeks burned as I heard Asa's quiet chuckle from behind me. With the back of my neck pricking with sweat, I sat through the bidding for dozens of items, which increased in size and value as an hour went by. Hopefully, across town, Keenan's Headsmen had already nabbed the mosaic panel from Brindle's suite at the National—and hopefully Ilya's crew would survive their too-late attempt to do the same.

Meanwhile, the auction dragged on. How something could be simultaneously so boring and so nerve-racking still astounds me. The longer I sat there, the more fidgety I was. But with each minute came the knowledge that we were closer to the moment when Asa would make his move, when he would go for the pages or for me, when Reza would unleash his painful magic—which Masha and Sambor would counteract as best they could—or when Frank would unleash pleasure to sedate us all, something Daniil would be responsible for fighting.

I glanced over at Zoya, hoping she had some insight. She only shrugged helplessly. Whatever Brindle's intentions, whatever Asa was planning, they were concealing it well.

Or maybe she was getting overwhelmed, because all the people in the room had their own games to play, their own hidden agendas. Donati, the boss from New York, bid aggressively on several of the smaller items but went silent as the bids rose. Garza had a habit of opening the bidding but then losing her nerve, and other bosses outbid her every single time. She'd always exit the bidding with a dramatic roll of her eyes and wave of her hand, as if the item hadn't been something she wanted after all. Botwright bid on only a few items, and it probably wasn't a coincidence that Frank Brindle tended to want those artifacts, too.

He outbid her in every case, with a smug smile on his pitted face. Botwright aimed a venomous glare in his direction every single time, while Myron and his blond counterpart sat on either side of her, looking uncomfortable as they eyed Reza and Asa.

And then, finally, we reached the final item. An image appeared on the screen behind the auctioneer, a worn page of the runic writing. "Here we have a selection of pages believed to be from the original *Essentialis Magia*," intoned the auctioneer, "inscribed in the years following the execution of Akakios, in a language now extinct. There are approximately three dozen of these pages, believed to be consecutive. They were discovered initially in an excavated cave system outside of Rome and for many years were kept in a vault at the Vatican. However, within the last ten years, these pages have been in this private collection. The cases are specially sealed to preserve the vellum pages within, which must be protected from exposure to oxygen. These samples are considered to be in excellent condition, considering they are estimated to be over two thousand years old." The auctioneer smiled. "The reserve on this lot, which is being offered as one collection, is fifty. Shall we open the bidding?"

Fifty *million*, he meant. It was the highest price by far, but all of a sudden the room came alive. The auctioneer smiled and pointed, and I whipped around to see Reza holding up his bid paddle.

"Ah, we have fifty—oh, fifty-one, fifty-two, fifty-five!" The auctioneer's voice rose as Botwright lifted her paddle and increased the bid to fifty-five. Then he waved at the back of the room again, toward Brindle, who merely flicked his fingers at Reza. "Fifty-five going once, and fifty-six, fifty-seven!" The auctioneer smiled at Tang, the boss from China, Volodya's rival for control of the East. Then his head swiveled. "And sixty!"

Again, it was Botwright who had raised the bid. Flanked by her two agents, she looked like a sparrow sitting between eagles, but her hand was steady as she bobbed her paddle up and down, keeping up with the bidding. As she did, I glanced around at others in the room. Frank Brindle, Tang, and Botwright appeared to be the only ones in contention as the price soared over eighty million. Brindle's smug look had gone serious, but he was still poking at Reza to get him to raise the paddle every few seconds. Garza, whose magic sensor had ostensibly made a play for the pages the night before, had not made a single bid for the collection, but she appeared to be watching the process with avid attention.

Asa, on the other hand, seemed detached. Despite Theresa's admonishments, I used every Frank Brindle bid as an opportunity to peek at him, to see if he was about to make his move. But he was staring at the back of the seat in front of him. And instead of his usual hypervigilant fidgeting, he looked utterly bored. I frowned. He was running out of time to get this heist under way.

Finally, bidding slowed as each rise in price came with more contemplation. We were approaching a hundred million—at this point, about three million dollars a page. For something no one actually knew how to translate yet. To me, it seemed like a massive gamble, but here were the bosses, locked in a three-way war to claim the prize.

The auctioneer inclined his head toward Brindle. "And now we have one hundred million dollars, ladies and gentlemen," he said, grinning. "One *hundred* million." There was silence in the room, and the auctioneer looked at Tang, who shook his head, scowling. "No? Going once. Going twice . . ."

Brindle and Reza grinned triumphantly. They'd outbid Botwright yet again. Beside them Asa had his elbows on his knees, and his head was hanging. My palms were clammy with frustration.

"He looks like he's asleep," Theresa said. "He's faking."

That had to be it. I stared at Asa with new focus. What had he planned? How would he strike?

The auctioneer picked up his wooden gavel. As he raised it, I watched in disbelief. Did Frank think he was going to get to walk out of here with those pages, fair and square? Were we going to let him?

"Aha!" shouted the auctioneer. "One hundred one!" He pointed his gavel at Botwright, then swung it toward Frank. "One hundred one going once—do I see one hundred two? Yes, one hundred two, one hundred three, one hundred f— One hundred ten!" He sounded rapturous as Botwright signaled her new high bid with ten fingers. "Now we have one hundred ten, ladies and gentlemen, one hundred ten for this collection of pages! Shall I sell it, then? Hmm?" He leaned forward, staring at the back of the room.

I turned in my seat. We were all staring at Frank Brindle. He looked grim as he eyed Botwright. "You don't have the capital for this," he said.

Elizabeth Botwright turned, one eyebrow arched. "My finances have been vetted, my friend. But I think everyone will agree that this is a most indecorous time to discuss it." She tossed an amused glance at Garza, who smiled.

In my ear, I heard Theresa make a bemused noise. "I'll bet you everything I own that Garza threw all her capital behind Botwright. They made an alliance to keep Frank from getting what he wanted."

And I was betting that Botwright hadn't really wanted any of the earlier items she'd bidden for—she'd let Frank win every time, using up his cash. "Botwright's kind of a badass," I whispered, forgetting Theresa couldn't hear me. "She totally set a trap for him."

"One hundred ten million, ladies and gentlemen," the auctioneer yelled. "Going once . . . going twice . . ." Brindle sat back with a deep huff. And then he shook his head.

The gavel slammed onto the podium. "Sold!"

Whereas there was usually clapping at this point, everyone in the room was silent. We were probably all thinking the same thing—everything was about to explode. Reza patted Asa on the back, and he sat up with a jerk, like he really had nodded off. The trio stood up. Several guests did the same, stretching stiff muscles, and waiters filed in with more champagne for the after-auction reception. All of them were armed, of course.

"Get ready, Mattie," Theresa said. "Now's the time."

I got to my feet and edged over to the wall as I watched Frank, Reza, and Asa move into the aisle between the chairs. Daniil and Zoya inched closer to me while Sambor and Masha waited by the door, their focus on Reza. I kept my eyes on Asa's hands, my heart pounding.

Brindle looked around, taking in the tense Russian agents in a single amused glance. Then he clapped his two men on the shoulders. "I'm ready for some dinner," he said to Asa.

"Yes, sir," Asa said in a dead voice.

Maybe that was the signal. I tensed, waiting for the lights to go off or my body to flare with pain. My fingers flexed over my skirt and the vial of Theresa's sensing magic I had hidden in my stocking—covered in Jack's sweat, to prevent anyone from knowing I had it. If I nailed Asa with this stuff, he was going down.

I edged along the wall, ready to deploy my secret weapon—and then to summon the Headsmen. Just before the three men reached the doorway to the lobby, Reza turned his head, and our eyes met. I braced for agony. But instead, he merely smiled and shrugged, then followed his boss, who was moving toward the door. Asa didn't even look in my direction as he trudged behind Brindle.

And then they were outside, walking toward the street.

I blinked. Zoya shook her head, as if telling me she sensed nothing. Theresa cursed in my ear. "They've already got their car waiting," she said. "Shit! They're gone."

Brindle had lost the auction. Lost the pages he supposedly cared so much about. And he'd left them—and *me*—behind. "I don't get it," I whispered to Daniil. "Why probe the security if they weren't going to steal the pages? Why go to all that trouble?"

"To make us look like fools," Daniil muttered. He cursed. "I will go tell the Volodya."

"Will he really let Botwright walk out of here with the pages? Will we?"

Daniil was looking very pale. "I don't know how we'll stop her now. We didn't expect it to go this far." He ran a hand through his hair. "This is going to lead Volodya to a very dark place." He gave Zoya an anxious glance.

"He's right, and he and his sister are probably planning to defect to another boss as soon as they can, just to save themselves," said Theresa, whispering now. "I need to slip out as soon as I can before he tracks me down, too. I just can't believe . . ."

I couldn't, either. All of this—the whole elaborate scheme, the cost, the planning—and they hadn't taken the bait. After that spectacular reveal of Volodya's security, after Asa's promise to come after me . . . they were headed back to their hotel. I looked down at the silver cuff around my wrist, meant to protect me from Knedas magic, but also the key to calling the Headsmen when I needed them.

But I didn't need them.

Keenan had wanted those pages, though. And he'd promised to help me get Asa if I delivered. I was his eyes inside this room. I should push the sensor Jack had placed on my cuff and call them in. There was no better time, really. People were starting to relax now that the menace of Frank Brindle had departed. The pages were just in the other room. Botwright hadn't left with them yet. My fingers crept toward the cuff, then froze.

If I called down the Headsmen now, Keenan might get his pages. And if he'd gotten hold of Brindle's mosaic panel, he and Jack could get the magic from my vault back into the ancient relic.

But I still wouldn't have Asa.

My hands fell to my sides.

"If they hadn't already left, this would be the time for an ambush," Theresa's voice muttered in my ear as Botwright accepted the pages from the auctioneer. "But I watched them drive away. What are we missing?"

She was speaking all my thoughts aloud. Dizzy with our failure, I looked up and realized Myron was beckoning to me. I drifted a little closer, still in a daze, just in time to hear Botwright say she had called an armored vehicle to transport the case to the airport. Myron held his arms out as Botwright handed off the pages. "Let's get out of here," she said in a clipped voice.

"Madam, I'd like you to meet someone," said Myron. "This is Mattie Carver, the reliquary."

Botwright's snowy brows rose. "Is it now?" She smiled. "I've heard impressive things about your ability, Ms. Carver."

"Thanks, I think," I said. "I'm sorry we didn't deliver your magic in London."

Botwright swatted Myron playfully on the shoulder, and he winced as if she'd stabbed him, which is what it probably felt like. "That was hardly your fault. Poor planning, I say. But perhaps you can make it up to me." She gave me a speculative look. "Walk us out to our vehicle. We can talk on the way."

Myron grinned at me as Botwright strode past in her tiny heels, followed by her other agent.

"Thought you might like an in," Myron whispered as I trailed after them.

That wasn't why I was following her, though—I was following the pages, unable to believe Asa wasn't going to pop up out of a manhole and try to snatch them.

I held up one finger as we walked past the surveillance room.

"What are you doing, Mattie?" Theresa said in my ear. "Get in here. We have to figure out what to do before Frank takes Asa back to the States."

I ignored her, unable to shake the suspicion that Asa was still playing. Scanning the sidewalk, I picked up my pace and caught up with Botwright and her agents. "So, can I ask—what are you going to do with these pages? I've heard that no one knows how to translate them."

Botwright looked over her shoulder at me and smiled. "It's a long game, Ms. Carver. A very long game."

As she spoke, an armored vehicle pulled to the curb, and the driver got out and opened the heavy rear door, then stood at the ready, his hand on the gun holstered at his belt. I squinted at him as my bracelet gave me a buzzing shock, and realized he wasn't Asa disguised with Knedas magic.

"You all right, Mattie?" Myron asked, looking back and forth between me and the driver.

"Yeah," I muttered. "Just really confused."

"Myron," Botwright said, her voice taking on an edge. "If you please." She was looking around anxiously, too, as if she also suspected an attack.

Myron jogged ahead of us and carefully laid the case with the pages in a reinforced metal trunk in the back of the truck. He leaned forward and spoke quietly to the driver, then stepped back onto the curb to allow the guy to shut the goods inside.

"You told him to meet us at the airport?" Botwright asked Myron.

Myron nodded and leaned against the truck as the driver moved onto the sidewalk to get back into the cab. Botwright turned to me and held out her hand, a card between her slender fingers. "I'm going to be growing my collection over the next year," she said. "So I will be in need of a dependable reliquary. Please call on me when you next come to London. I—"

I flinched at the two sharp cracks that cut her off. Botwright's eyes went wide, and her mouth fell open as she crumpled. I stared down at the card as it fluttered to the ground, splattered with her blood. The blond agent shouted, "Myron!"

Another crack and the blond, too, fell to the ground, a bullet hole through his chest.

I turned toward the oncoming threat, already knowing there was nothing I could do to protect myself.

The driver of the armored vehicle strode toward me, his gun aimed at my head, his expression calm, as shouts and clatter filled my earpiece. There was chaos in the surveillance room. I heard my name, but I couldn't make sense of the rest. And it didn't matter.

Myron Forester pushed himself off the side of the armored vehicle and offered me his hand. "Come with me, Mattie. Quickly now, or else I'm going to have this poor fellow shoot you in the legs."

I tore my gaze from the driver. "What . . . why . . ."

He took my hand and yanked me toward the passenger seat of the armored truck, forcing me to step over Botwright's body, as the armed commandos burst through the door of the high-rise. But they were too far away to stop him unless they were willing to shoot me, too. Myron shoved me into the vehicle and slammed the door, then clambered up into the driver's seat as the actual driver ran forward, firing his weapon at the oncoming commandos, obviously doomed.

Myron threw the vehicle into gear. "Why? An easy question." He gave me a cocky smile. "Because Frank Brindle pays better."

CHAPTER TWENTY-FIVE

I held on tight as the armored vehicle lurched onto the road. The commandos had felled the driver, and a few were running up the sidewalk after us, but it was a futile effort. "You've been helping him all along, haven't you?"

"Of course. It's dangerous, being a double agent, so I'm well compensated."

I gritted my teeth. "You laid the trap at Harrods. You helped them catch Asa. You're the reason he's a slave right now."

"Oh, come on. If I hadn't helped, Brindle would have found another way to collar Asa. He spared no expense."

"You're scum."

"Rich scum, so there's that."

I crossed my arms, feeling the cold slide of metal against my skin. The cuff. It would protect me from Myron's influence, but it was also my lifeline. I threw my captor a sidelong glance—his eyes were focused on the road as he wove his way through city traffic, occasionally jumping a curb to keep moving. "You helped Brindle yesterday, too," I said bitterly. "Somehow, you influenced Garza's magic sensor—"

"I didn't. Not directly, at least," he said, smirking.

I thought back to what Theresa had said about him. When he'd first arrived at Volodya's stronghold, she'd said he was giving off ridiculously strong vibes, but later, she told me it had faded. "You brought in a relic filled with your own magic . . ." I rolled my eyes. "It was your tie."

"Tie *tack*, more precisely. All I had to do was leave it where Asa could pick it up. Small enough that he could jab it into Garza's man without anyone really noticing. And then it was just a matter of suggestion. It was Asa's idea. Not exactly what you'd expect from a slave, eh?"

I stared out the window, slowly inching one of my hands toward the cuff. "And now you've killed your boss and—"

"Technically, I didn't. We were attacked by the driver, and I just got both you and the valuables away from there."

"No one's going to fall for that, dude."

He reached over and encircled my forearm with his fingers. "Botwright was a vicious woman who deserved to be put down."

"You're full of crap."

He drew his hand away quickly and swerved as he looked me over. "Lift your sleeves."

I shrank against the seat. "Why?"

He pulled abruptly off the road and threw the truck into park. "Lift. Your. Sleeves."

For a moment, we simply stared at each other. And then I lunged for the door handle. My hands closed around it, and I wrenched it up just as Myron threw his arms around me. He grabbed my wrists before I could press the button on the cuff that would summon the Headsmen and dragged me across the seat toward the driver's side. "What is it?" he said with a grunt. "What are you using to resist my magic? Ah, there it is." He had pulled back my sleeve to reveal the cuff.

As he reached forward to remove it, I slammed my head back and felt my skull collide with his nose. With a strangled growl, he loosened his grip, and my fingers shot forward and found the tiny sensor. I had just begun to press down when Myron tore the cuff from my wrist. Breathing wetly as blood dripped from his nose, he rolled down his window and tossed my cuff onto the road, where it was promptly obliterated by a passing bus. "Should have checked for that before we left." He wiped his sleeve across his upper lip and winced, then chuckled. "Now we can have an honest conversation."

I pinched the inside of my forearm, my fingernails digging in. Had the Headsmen gotten my signal, or was I on my own? All I had left to defend myself was the vial of Theresa's magic tucked into my stocking. And I could already feel Myron's magic caressing the edges of my consciousness. I pressed my back against the window as he leaned forward and took my hands, holding them in a firm but gentle grip. "Mattie. I did you a favor by getting you away from Volodya. You know that."

Volodya *was* pretty terrifying.

He smiled. "No one wants to hurt you. Asa specified that you weren't to be harmed."

My heart squeezed. "He did?"

Myron nodded, even as a little rivulet of blood snaked along the corner of his mouth. "You're precious, Mattie." His deep voice massaged away the knots of fear in my chest. "You are rare and valuable. Damaging you would be like burning the priceless pages of the *Essentialis Magia*. You need to be with people who recognize your skill. Who reward it. What was Volodya using you for—some kind of lookout?" He scoffed as he reached up and plucked out my earpiece. That, too, he threw out the window, though we'd long since gone out of range. "What a waste."

It *was* kind of a waste. "But where are we going?"

Myron nodded at the road. "A safe place. It's not far."

God, being safe would be so nice. Even as I had the thought, the tiniest sliver of doubt poked at my mind. *Was* I safe? I glanced at the door that I'd managed to open just a crack. "Um. I—"

A black sedan swerved suddenly out of traffic and beached itself on the curb just a few feet from our truck's front bumper. Myron cursed and threw the vehicle into gear, then roared forward. I barely had time to brace myself before we crashed into the car, the impact knocking it out of our way. My head bonked against the window of the passenger door as it slammed shut, a result of another collision, this one on the driver's side. I scrambled to put on my seat belt.

"Headsmen," Myron shouted, stomping on the gas even as he sideswiped yet another dark sedan trying to pull in front of us.

Headsmen . . . wait. That was what I wanted to happen. As the pain in my head cleared the fog of Myron's influence, I glanced around to see that we were racing through a dark neighborhood, shadows on every corner. To my left I could see the soaring edifices of Moscow City, where Volodya had fought to keep his dying empire together—where he'd just lost everything. Racing along next to us were two of those black sedans. They kept trying to box us in, but Myron repeatedly swerved toward them in the armored truck, forcing them to cross lanes and brake to stay out of his way. I eyed his tense, hunched form and decided that trying to clobber him or douse him in Sensilo magic would probably result in my death. We were going too fast.

Then a line of shimmering lights appeared in the distance in front of us. Myron shouted a curse, jammed his foot onto the brake, and cranked the wheel. I screamed as the rear of the truck swung around, as I felt us tilting and falling. We slammed into the ground, sparks flying up as we skidded along the pavement, losing speed as we rammed one sedan after the other. My ears filled with the sounds of shrieking metal. My hands were clamped over my face as my body hung from the seat belt, the straps digging into me as we bounced along and finally hit something that didn't yield to our momentum. One side of the truck tipped up and then crashed to the ground.

And for a few seconds, everything was quiet. Or maybe that was the shock.

Myron moaned. I forced my eyes open and looked down at him, bleeding from cuts on his face, his head resting on the shattered window beneath him. I turned my head on my aching neck and looked up to see the night sky . . . and a face, dark eyes peering down at me.

"Jack," I whispered.

He turned his head and shouted something I couldn't understand, then turned his efforts to opening the heavy door of the armored truck. With a loud metallic complaint, it swung open, and I felt a rush of cold night wind across my cheeks.

"Mattie," Jack said in a rough voice. "Hang on."

He pulled on the seat belt strap, and I whimpered as he slid his arm around my body, as his grip tightened while he unbuckled me. With a grunt, he heaved me upward and out of the truck.

"How bad are you hurt?"

"No idea." I moaned as he pivoted with me in his arms.

"Got her," he barked. "But she needs transport."

"To where?" I whispered.

"Anywhere but here," he said curtly. I closed my eyes against the footsteps and shouts and sirens and flashing lights. "We got the panel from Brindle, but just when the crew was headed out, Volodya's players showed up and triggered his alarms."

I sighed and opened my eyes. "Poor Ilya."

"Screw Ilya," Jack said as he motioned to someone behind me. I was pressed against his chest, grateful for the warmth and steadiness. "It turned into a shit show."

I couldn't help but feel a pang. "But at least you got the mosaic."

"And now we have the pages, thanks to you," said a new voice—Keenan. He sounded out of breath but happy.

"Happy to deliver," I said as Jack gently maneuvered me down into Keenan's arms.

"Anything broken?" Keenan asked Jack.

"Doesn't seem like it. But she's at risk for shock. She should really be looked over by a doc. That was quite a crash."

"Someone needs to get in there and see if the intrepid Mr. Forester made it."

"I'd leave him for the authorities to find, but he's too dangerous."

Keenan called out to someone, telling them to get over to the truck and get Myron to something charmingly called "containment." I wondered whether it was anything like the way they'd held Arkady in Virginia, with a thick collar around his neck to keep him in enough pain to prevent him from wreaking havoc. Or whether it was more like Asa's collar, doping him up and twisting his mind.

I shuddered. Both made my stomach turn.

"We need to get the treasure off the streets," Keenan said. "And you and Mattie have to get to the safe house. I'll have a medical team meet you there. You can do the transaction tonight." He was talking fast, the cloud of his frozen breath swirling over my head.

Jack's eyes met mine. "Only if she's strong enough."

Keenan looked down at me and gave me a slight squeeze. "Of course. Do you want to take her while I manage the scene?"

"Yeah."

Jack moved close and started to take me, but I wriggled in Keenan's arms. "I think I can walk."

Keenan chuckled. "Something tells me it's almost impossible to keep you down." He carefully lowered my feet to the pavement and steadied me as I tested my strength and balance. It felt a little like I'd taken a spin in a cement mixer.

"And yet it can be done," I said weakly, clutching at his arm and breathing deeply. My whole body was tingling. Nothing hurt, but I couldn't stop shaking. My hand grazed my thigh, and I sighed. At least Theresa's magic was still secure.

"We need a blanket over here," Jack shouted.

Someone threw a blanket over my shoulders, and Jack pulled it tight around me and turned me around. Beyond the overturned truck lay a scene of chaos and destruction: crushed cars, twisted metal, and shattered glass, Headsmen helping their wounded colleagues out from behind deflated air bags, some shouting for medical assistance. "We got the cooperation of the authorities," Jack said as he helped me limp toward the line of headlights, a barricade of vehicles that had positioned themselves across Myron's intended escape route.

"The citizens of Moscow are grateful, I'm sure."

We were approaching an undamaged dark sedan at the end of the row of parked cars, and a young woman with a ponytail and earmuffs smiled and opened one of the back doors as we neared. "I'll be driving you, Agent Okafor," she said with a slight Russian accent.

"Sounds good, Agent Urasov," he replied amiably. "And could you—"

A wretched scream from behind us caused Jack to whirl around, his brown eyes wide as the noise multiplied in volume and intensity. Agents who had been standing next to cars near the truck were crumpling to the ground, clutching at their guts and writhing. I blinked, trying to process what was happening.

Jack cursed and dragged me toward the open car door just as I caught sight of two men standing on either side of the road, not close enough to see their faces . . . but I didn't need to. I recognized their silhouettes.

"Oh God," I whispered.

Jack tossed me onto the backseat, his gentleness gone as Agent Urasov shrieked and pitched over the hood of the car, her face twisted in agony. Through the windshield, I watched her body start to shake uncontrollably as Jack reached for her.

The night was filled with screaming as a bone-jarring pain swirled across my skin and terror jolted my heart. I yanked up the edge of my skirt and pulled out the vial, clutching it with an unsteady hand.

Asa walked toward us slowly and stepped into the glare of the headlights. His stride was unsteady and stilted but relentless as he approached us. "You have something of ours," he said to Jack as Agent Urasov made a choking noise and blood trickled down her chin. "Give me Mattie and this will stop."

Unaffected by the Strikon magic, Jack squared his shoulders and held Urasov with one arm as he began to reach for his waist. But before he had a chance to pull his weapon, Asa had raised a gun of his own. "Reza's magic might not hurt you, but this will."

"You won't kill me."

Asa's lip curled. "You don't have to be conscious to serve your purpose."

Jack's broad shoulders rippled with tension. "You're twisted up, man. You know you don't want to be doing this."

Asa glanced from Jack toward the car, and though I was nestled in the back, it was like he knew exactly where I was, like he was looking right at me. "And you know it doesn't matter," he said in a flat voice. He glanced over his shoulder. "I've got this, Reza."

"I'm just enjoying the show," Reza said mildly, coming up to stand on Asa's right.

Jack's hand twitched toward his holstered gun again. A sharp crack split the air, and Jack stumbled backward with a grunt. He dropped Urasov and staggered against the door. I quickly hid the vial again and scooted forward. Determination strengthened my shaking hands as I threw myself out of the car and landed in a clumsy crouch next to Jack, who was clutching at his shoulder. As Reza grinned at us, Asa started forward. I reached down and yanked Jack's gun from its holster, half expecting to hear another shot, to feel the flash of pain that told me I was going down, too.

I jerked the weapon up and aimed it at Asa's chest. The pain of being face-to-face with him, each of us aiming a deadly weapon at the other, was so profound that it stole my breath.

"Hands off," Asa said, his lips barely moving.

"I wouldn't dream of interfering." Reza chuckled. "I love this too much," he said quietly. "It's so poignant."

Asa simply stood there, his gun on me.

My finger curled around the trigger. "Don't think I won't shoot you," I said in a strained voice, tears starting in my eyes.

Asa gave me a sly smile that was strangely at odds with the rest of him, which seemed to radiate agony. "That's exactly what I think, baby."

"Don't call me that," I whispered.

He tilted his head, as if listening to the chorus of screams that still echoed up and down the surrounding blocks. "Stop it," he said quietly.

Reza shrugged. "Just finishing up."

Crumpled next to Jack, Urasov made another choked noise. Her fingers twitched.

Jack moaned. "Mattie, don't let them take you."

I moved to the side, placing myself between him and Asa. "I won't."

Asa let out a quiet laugh. "I told you that you wouldn't be able to stop me."

"I'm not helpless."

His mouth twitched, but it didn't look like amusement. It looked like it hurt. "You can make this easy, or you can make it very hard, Mattie. But you can't stop it."

I tensed my muscles to steady the gun as tears streaked down my face. "I can try, though."

I pulled the trigger.

Asa smiled. "Safety's on," he murmured.

When I pulled the weapon back to look at it, he stepped forward and kicked it from my hands. I cried out as he grabbed me and wrenched me to my feet.

"Such drama," Reza said breezily.

"The conduit needs a pressure bandage," Asa replied.

"Ah." Reza smoothly kicked the gun farther away from Jack, who had been trying to reach it. "No wonder he isn't affected by my magic."

Jack groaned as Reza planted an elegant patent leather shoe on his chest. Reza smiled. "There are other ways to hurt him, though." He raised his head and looked at me. "You understand that, don't you, Mattie?" He pointed down at Agent Urasov's body. Her eyes were wide and blank now. A ghastly reflection of the pain that had stopped her heart. "And if you don't play nicely, this will be how you end your night."

Jack let out a strangled moan as Reza pressed his weight into the Headsman's shoulder, grinding his heel against Jack's wound as Asa moved closer, keeping his weapon aimed at Jack. "We're taking him with us," Asa said. "He'll be useful."

"That was not our plan," said Reza.

"But it is *my* plan," said Asa. "Let me know if you want to argue with my track record."

Reza let out an exaggerated sigh, though he wore an amused smile. "I think it is time for us to make our exit. We need to complete our transaction and move on."

Asa glanced over his shoulder. "Keenan?"

Reza rolled his eyes. "Gone. Saved his own skin."

"You think you've won," Jack said, pain splintering his voice.

"Because we have," said Reza. He turned and motioned to a few burly-looking guys who came forward with eyes only for Jack. "Turns out we have an extra passenger. Get him into the van."

Asa pulled me against his back, and I felt the damp warmth of his sweaty body. "Let's go, Mattie. We'll get this over with."

"The Headsmen have the mosaic," I blurted as Brindle's henchmen lifted Jack roughly from the ground. "If you want it back, you'd better be careful with him."

"Got it from Brindle's suite tonight," Jack said. "Sorry to put a dent in your plans, but there's not gonna be any transaction tonight. Your boss is still out of luck."

"Speaking of your track record." Reza looked at Asa. "This went exactly as you said it would. Frank will be so pleased."

My stomach dropped as Asa gave him a tight smile. "Oh God, what did you do?"

Asa turned his hollow-cheeked grimace on me. Sweat trickled into the grimy bandage around his neck, just above the dark shadow of the collar that kept him prisoner. He looked like a monster.

"The Headsmen didn't steal the panel," he said. "They stole a replica, something to keep them busy while Myron stole the pages and got you clear of Volodya. And when they try to unpack it, they're gonna get a little surprise."

Reza grinned at me and Jack and flared his fingers. "A little present from us to them. Agent Keenan will feel the kiss of my magic one way or the other. And then he will know the power of original magic when Frank unleashes it on him. We have the real panel, and tonight, Mattie, you will give us its secrets."

CHAPTER TWENTY-SIX

After a long ride out of the city, we ended up at an abandoned airport miles from any other sign of civilization. It looked like it might once have been a military facility. Most of the runways appeared cracked and weedy, but as we zipped by, I saw one that looked smooth and well maintained. One hangar was lit up bright, too, and the massive door slid open as we approached, revealing a sleek little private plane, a few shiny black cars, and a small herd of Frank Brindle's agents and staff.

Our van pulled to a stop, and Asa and Reza hustled me and Jack, who was weak with loss of blood, onto the blacktop. Brindle himself, so fat and smug looking, was seated at a massive steel table in front of us. His people had set up an office of sorts for him, complete with an oriental rug and an electric fireplace to keep the boss warm.

"Ah, hello again," Brindle said to Jack as several henchmen rushed forward to grab the conduit. Brindle looked delighted, as if an old friend had dropped by for tea. "I never expected to see you like this, Jack." He nodded at Asa. "Excellent acquisition."

"Take him to the back room and secure him," Reza instructed. "And have Dr. Julian take a look at that shoulder."

"Don't bother," Jack said, sounding exhausted and pained. "I'm not gonna help you."

"Commendably brave," called Frank, still sitting at the table. He took a sip of wine and smiled as a plate of chicken was placed in front of him. "But I always get what I want. Right, Asa?"

All that followed was silence as Asa stared at the man. I looked up at my former partner, trying to read his blank expression. But then Frank leaned forward, his eyes intent on Asa. "Right?"

Asa let out a stifled moan, and his eyes fell half-shut. "Yes, Mr. Brindle," he said quietly.

"More of that later—you did well for us tonight."

"Yes, Mr. Brindle," Asa said again, and the look on his face tore at my heart. His eyes were suddenly shiny—I swear, I could see the war inside him. The need for more of Brindle's addictive Ekstazo magic, probably the very magic that ran through his collar and directly into his body, versus his need to be free.

I put my hand on his arm, and he yanked it away with a snarl. Brindle laughed. "He's mine now, Ms. Carver. You hold very limited charms for him. He only wants one thing from you, and that is the precious magic you've kept safe for us. We're very grateful for that, and we'll be grateful when you and Mr. *Okafor* here deliver it into our hands."

A chill zipped down my back, and they dragged Jack away. He seemed too thrashed to have noticed his cover had been blown. I glanced at Asa. "You told him who Jack really was," I whispered, my throat tightening. "It wasn't an accident you got both of us tonight."

"I knew he'd probably given you a way to call for backup, so it was just a matter of tracking Myron," Asa said, staring at a point just over Frank's left shoulder.

"Asa can't lie to me, Mattie," Frank said. "It's part of the Knedas magic we feed into his system every day. No lies, no escape, complete obedience. He'll give me a truthful answer for any question I ask." He grinned. "And I have asked him a lot of questions. I know him better than you do."

"You're the most evil man I've ever met," I said, my voice breaking as Asa turned his face away from me, keeping me from seeing his eyes.

Brindle feigned a look of sorrow. "I'm simply a businessman, Mattie. I don't hurt anyone unnecessarily."

I grimaced. "Right. That's what this asshole is for." I jerked my thumb at Reza and was awarded with a jolt of bone-rattling agony that nearly took my feet out from under me. I leaned forward for a moment and braced my palms against my thighs, once again feeling the little vial of Theresa's magic beneath the fabric of my dress.

"Reza," Brindle said, his voice gently chiding. "Don't be petty."

I straightened back up. Reza put his hands up and gave his boss a charming smile. "A momentary lapse of control."

"Asshole," I hissed again from between clenched teeth.

"Please take our Mattie to the back room. Asa, prepare her for the transaction."

"I don't need him," I snapped.

"Asa, I need you to protect my asset," said Frank. "Do whatever you have to."

"Yes, Mr. Brindle," Asa replied, his hand slipping into his pocket. "I know how to take care of her." He took my arm and led me away, and I let him, because throwing a fit was a waste of energy, and trying to use his mother's magic on him was, too. It was me against Frank, Reza, and Asa, plus a whole horde of agents.

My mind whirled with things I might say to him to try to convince him to help me, to save Jack, but as he pulled me through the hangar, ignoring the narrow-eyed stares of Brindle's other agents, I felt so far away from him. I couldn't help but think back to that moment on the road, when I aimed a gun at his chest and pulled the trigger. He'd known it wouldn't go off, but I hadn't. I'd been willing to kill him, even though I'd known it would kill me, too. He felt that *gone* to me. Gone to himself.

Reza followed us, looking relaxed and confident. When he saw me glaring, he said, "I'm really going to enjoy watching this, Mattie. You two have such a fraught dynamic."

Asa's fingers were digging into my arm, but I wasn't going to give Reza the satisfaction of whimpering. At the back of the hangar we reached a door, which opened to a large room stacked with boxes and metal shelves housing what looked like spare parts and tools. Several of these shelves had been pushed against the walls, leaving a space in the center of the room large enough to accommodate a large safe with a digital keypad and a long steel table.

There were ropes tied to the four table legs, spread across the table's surface. My feet stuttered to a halt. I couldn't get them to keep moving forward. Asa tugged on me, then turned to me. "I don't want to hurt you, Mattie."

"I do," Reza murmured.

"But you won't," Asa snapped. "Until I tell you to."

"Fair enough."

He pulled me toward the table. "You know what to do."

He wasn't looking at me. I wanted to believe the tremble in his hands was emotional, but it was probably the shakiness brought on by all the magic swamping his system. I climbed onto the table. I needed to save my strength for when I really needed it.

I raised my arms over my head. A flash of surprise showed on his face before it slid beneath his blank, dead-eyed expression yet again. "Did you think I was going to kick and scream?" I asked.

"Yes."

"You can control my body, Asa. But you can't control me. I'm not going to give Frank this magic."

His eyes closed briefly. "If that's how you want to do it." Without looking at me, he tied the ropes to my wrists. I half expected him to tell Reza to work his pain magic on me, but instead, he reached into his pocket, pulled out what looked like a little G.I. Joe action figure, and placed it on top of the metal safe.

"What's that?"

"You're gonna find out if you don't cooperate."

I tore my eyes from the toy, not wanting to ponder the kind of torture he planned to inflict. Whatever it was, I had to weather it and hold on to what was important. Instead of looking at him again, I stared at the high ceiling and listened to my heart drumming in my ears as he secured my ankles. Feeling his skin brush mine was the most poignant kind of torture, but with Reza watching, I stayed still as a corpse and used all I had learned from Keenan to conceal the chaos inside my heart. I needed to accept that the Asa I had known was dead, even though I still wanted to save whatever was left, for his sake. It didn't make it any easier, though. It didn't stop the waves of want and wish from breaking on my shore.

When Asa was finished tying me down, he pulled out his phone and sent a text. Looking pleased with himself, Reza leaned against the safe with his arms gracefully folded. I shivered in the cold, still air of the room and waited in silence until I heard a door open and the sound of someone being dragged across the floor. Two guys held Jack by the arms. His shoulder had been bandaged, but his brown skin was ashy and shined with sweat despite the cold. He was trembling and seemed unable to get his feet beneath him.

The two goons came to a stop at the edge of the table. "Where do you want him?"

"He can sit next to the table. Bring over a chair and tie him to it," Asa said, walking over to the safe and punching in a code.

Jack let out a low chuckle. "Hey. Asshole. You aren't gonna get anything out of me."

"Pain is a great motivator."

"And I'm trained to deal with it." He looked right at Reza and spat on the ground.

Asa opened the safe and pulled out the mosaic panel. "Everyone has a limit."

Jack raised his head and gave him a weary smile. "This is more important than my life."

Asa turned to me. "We'll see." He beckoned to the goons. "Get it done."

One of them struggled to hold up Jack's weight as the other dragged over a chair, along with more rope, which they wound around Jack's chest and tied so tight it made him groan. Then Asa yanked Jack's wounded arm onto the table. I gritted my teeth as Jack screamed.

Reza stood by the safe, his smile widening with Jack's agony.

"Hey," Jack said softly. "Look at me. Don't look at that asshole." When I obeyed, he murmured, "It's gonna be okay."

I let out a tear-stained laugh. "Wouldn't that be nice?"

His expression turned serious. There were lines of strain around his mouth and along his broad forehead. "You know what I have to do, don't you?"

"Yeah. And I'm not going to—"

My words cut off as Asa pressed a gun to Jack's temple.

Jack went very still, his jaw clenched. "What are you going to do, Asa? Kill the conduit? How's that going to work out for you?"

Asa smiled and looked at me. "If you let the magic go, Mattie, it'll flow through him. He can refuse to pull it out of you, but he can't deny the magic. His body will conduct it into the panel."

"Mattie, no," Jack said, his voice steady despite the cold steel leaving an indentation in his skin. "Don't fall for this. If I'm dead, he loses."

I looked up at Asa. "I won't do it."

Asa's finger snaked over the trigger as he glanced at Reza. "I don't play, Mattie. You know that. One way or the other, the magic comes out of you tonight."

"Without a conduit?" Jack asked.

Asa leaned down slowly. A drop of sweat fell from his chin and hit the table between Jack and me. The circles under his eyes were dark bruises in his chalky face, and he was trembling, too, almost as badly as Jack. He spoke softly, almost lovingly. "You don't think I have a backup? Come on now. I thought you knew who I was."

"I know who you are," I said, needing him to look into my eyes. "I know who you are, Asa. And I know you don't want to do this."

He let out an agonized chuckle. "Oh, Mattie." He straightened and glared at the bead of sweat on the table. "How about this?" He stepped back, aimed, and shot Jack in his other shoulder.

I screamed, and so did Jack, his head thrown back, his mouth wide and tears streaming down his face. But Asa just stood there, his eyes intent on Jack's wound. He lowered his weapon and walked over to the captive Headsman—and pressed his thumb into the hole he'd left. Jack cried out again, writhing. Reza moaned with pleasure.

"How about now?" Asa said to me. "Up for it?"

I looked back and forth between Jack and Asa. Jack turned his head to me. "Don't you dare, girl," he said between wheezy breaths. "Don't you dare."

"Jack . . ."

"No!" he shouted, his voice breaking.

"Mattie," said Asa. "Don't waste my time."

"I can't," I said, sniffling. "I'm not going to give it up."

Asa lowered his weapon and shot Jack in the thigh. My wail drowned out the rest of the noise, the squeak of metal as Jack's chair fell back, the shuffle of the goons' shoes as they rushed forward and yanked him back up, the patter of blood droplets on my table as he was jerked back into place. I didn't know which was more horrifying—that Jack was in so much pain or that Asa was causing it without even blinking.

"Asa, please," I begged. "Don't do this."

"Your choice, Mattie."

"Mattie, you give up this magic, you destroy us all. Only a matter of time," Jack said, cursing and groaning. "I'd rather die."

"I can't, Jack," I said, stifling a sob. "I can't watch this anymore."

"This is delicious," whispered Reza.

A shudder ran through Asa's body, but he remained silent.

Jack's deep-brown eyes met mine. "If you respect me, you will. Be strong for me, Mattie. And if you can't be strong, close your eyes."

I let out a shuddery breath and stared at him as my own tears fell. Asa moved forward and once again pressed his gun to Jack's forehead. "One more chance, Mattie. One more chance."

Jack gave me a sidelong glance without moving his head. His full lips curved into a gentle smile. And then he closed his eyes.

The shot echoed sharply. This time I didn't scream. I merely sagged back onto my table and closed my eyes.

I was all alone again. It was up to me.

CHAPTER TWENTY-SEVEN

When I opened my eyes, the henchmen were gone, and so was Jack's body. Asa stood over me, sweating and dead eyed, and Reza hovered next to him, looking refreshed and eager for the next act.

"I'll go get our conduit," Reza said quietly, his mouth twitching—it looked like he was trying to conceal a grin.

He disappeared from Asa's side, and I stared up at the man I had once loved. He looked down at me, focusing his gaze on my shoulder instead of my eyes. "I told you I was gone," he said. "Now you know it's true."

I let my tears speak for me, keeping my true thoughts to myself. Hope wasn't something I relinquished easily. It never had been.

With a scrape of metal against concrete, Reza pushed the door to the storage room open. By his side was a little boy, maybe six or seven, skinny and scared looking. "Here he is. Mattie, this is Peyta. We picked him especially for you."

Horror twisted inside me. "You can't be serious. He's a child."

"Exactly," said Asa. "And I have three more just like him at the ready. So don't think I won't do to him what I just did to Jack."

"Asa, he's a baby!" I shouted, my voice breaking.

"Bring him over," Asa said.

Peyta whimpered as Reza wrapped his fingers around the back of the boy's neck and pushed him toward me. "This won't hurt if the nice lady cooperates," he said, then laughed as he turned his gaze to Asa. "I don't think he understands a word I'm saying."

Asa held up his weapon. "He doesn't have to. It's all up to Mattie, and how many lives she wants on her conscience tonight."

Reza brought the pale boy over to the table. The kid looked sick, terror making him pliant. My eyes met Peyta's, and his filled with sudden tears. Asa grabbed his arm and began to tie it to mine. The boy's skin was clammy and cool. At the feel of it, a low sob escaped me.

Reza's cruel fingers caressed my cheek, sending a current of heavy agony along the length of my body. "Do you remember the day we met? Our conversation about wine?" His dark eyes glittered. "You didn't have much appreciation for it then, but perhaps now . . ." He reached forward and grabbed Peyta's hair, wrenching his head up so that the child's face was only a foot from mine. "Pain is much like wine, Mattie. Full of nuance. I've been a student of it all my life."

"And you enjoyed every minute of it, I'm sure," I said through gritted teeth.

"I didn't choose to be born with this gift. Why would I apologize for embracing what I am? Too few people do it, in my opinion. Eh, Asa?"

Asa was staring at the back of Peyta's head. "We have a transaction to complete."

"Then I will make sure Mattie knows what is at stake." Reza looked down at me, his expression almost loving. "You think you know pain now, Mattie. You think, because you can endure bodily suffering, that you understand what it means to hurt."

I tore my gaze from Peyta's to glare mutinously at Reza. He had no idea.

"Physical pain has a delightful bouquet, to be sure. One in which I revel. There's the acidic tang that comes with a sudden, sharp cut, the earthy note of bone-deep agony, the sweetness that accompanies muscles torn fiber by fiber. But none, my lovely, none is as satisfying as the full flavor of a completely broken heart, one so shattered that it can never be repaired. It coats the tongue and fills the belly. It leaves me wanting nothing but the next taste of it. And tonight, you're going to give me that."

Hatred made it hard to breathe. "Someday, dude, you are going to get a taste of your own medicine."

"Oh, but you've already given me that. Remember?"

"My only regret is that I didn't finish the job," I spat out.

"Hold on to that, Mattie," he said. "Know that you might have been able to stop me, if only you'd been strong enough to hold on. Instead, here I am, with Asa at my side, and together we're going to take you apart."

Asa let out an exasperated sigh. "Your supervillain monologuing won't work on her. Let's just get this done."

Reza looked up slowly. "Is she like you, then? Only action matters?" Asa flinched as Reza focused on him, and I knew that the Strikon had just temporarily broken through whatever haze of Ekstazo and Knedas magic was running through Asa's veins. "Do you remember the night I broke *you*, my friend? Do you treasure those memories like I do? I've never experienced anything quite so pure. So perhaps you're right. No talk, just action. After all, you did beg, in the end."

My stomach turned as I remembered Asa telling me that pain was the one thing that no one could resist forever. The idea of him falling apart as Reza tortured him, the idea of his surrender, hurt more than everything else. My entire body trembled with grief as Asa stifled a groan.

"Remember that?" Reza asked, his voice as gentle as a lover's. "And how about this?"

Asa convulsed, looking like he was about to puke.

"Should I offer her some of that, Asa? Would it help?"

Asa's fingers gripped the table and his lip curled, but he looked like he was about to sink to the floor. "Yeah," he whispered. "It *definitely* would."

"Have it your way," Reza said, his tone sliding toward boredom as he lowered his head over mine. As he did, a terrible burning sensation exploded in my chest, and I cried out. It felt like he'd clawed his fingernails along my lungs and poured acid into the cuts. Peyta began to cry, his little body shuddering, his fear passing through our joined arms. The little boy was a stranger to me, but he was a child, an innocent. And these evil men were branding his mind with memories he'd never be able to shake—assuming he lived through the night.

Because they were going to kill him if I didn't cooperate. They would hurt me and force him to watch, and if I didn't surrender, they would shoot him and force *me* to watch. I knew Asa would do it. He'd shown no compassion, no hesitation. He'd shot Jack just to hurt him, and then he'd killed him in front of me. He'd just said he had a line of little conduits in addition to Peyta. Children. He'd chosen children just to get to me. And he'd just told Reza to torture me. Maybe he craved my pain as much as Reza did.

And it was wearing me down. "It's okay," I tried to say to Peyta, even as agony wrung the words from me in gasps.

"He can't understand you, Mattie," crooned Reza. "He can only see your pain. He knows that he's next. And if you thought Asa made Jack suffer, you haven't seen anything yet."

Despair filled me up. I could endure physical pain. I knew I could. But I couldn't watch as they hurt this child. Reza's magic blazed through me, the pain making it hard to sort my thoughts, but one truth rose through the red sea of hurt—it was time for my final gamble. And if this didn't work, I would know I had done all I could do while still holding on to my soul.

"Okay," I sobbed. "Okay. I'll give up the magic. Just don't hurt him."

The pain evaporated, and my eyes blinked open. Asa put his hand on the little boy's back. "I knew you'd make the right choice."

"I have one condition."

"No," Asa said.

"Hear her out," Reza said amiably.

"Look at me," I whispered. "I'll tell you when you look at me."

Asa's jaw clenched. "You're wasting time."

"If you want me to do this, I need you. One last time."

Asa's mouth opened, probably to refuse, but Reza leaned forward. "Do what it takes to get this magic," Reza said. "That's why you're here. That's your mission."

Asa glared at him. "If that's how you want to do it." His lips were barely moving.

"Look at me," I murmured. "Look at me, *sir*."

Asa's gaze snapped to mine, our eyes meeting for the first time since the night he was taken. It felt like an earthquake inside me, shaking me to my core. For a moment, I felt myself recoil, the bars slamming down over my heart, trying to protect it from this final surrender. But then I reminded myself what was at stake, and I gave myself up to the feeling. "I'm yours, sir. You're in charge."

Something shifted behind Asa's honey-brown eyes, subtle but unmistakable. As if there were a thread connecting us, Asa drew closer, leaning down between me and Peyta.

"You know what I need," I said, not even trying to control the tremulous sound of my voice. "You always do. And you've got me. Don't you?"

He swallowed and blinked sweat out of his eyes. "'Don't you' *what*?"

Hope surged inside me. "Don't you, sir? You're the only one who can help me. You've always been the only one." A tear slid from my eye. "And you always will be."

His fingers slid along my skin before closing around my throat. Unlike his father's, though, Asa's hands were gentle. "You're mine." He was so close that the tip of his crooked nose skimmed along my cheek. "Say it."

Reza cleared his throat. "Asa, I didn't mean—"

"Shut the fuck up," Asa snapped. "Do you want this done or not?" His tone softened as he returned all his attention to me. "You're gonna let this go for me, baby. It's time to let it go."

The caress of his voice was rapidly undoing me. More powerful than any drug. But I forced myself to stay focused. "I'm scared."

Asa moved so that he was the only thing I could see. "I've got you, and I won't ever let go."

I stared up at him. This . . . this was what Reza had been talking about, even though he hadn't known it. The agony was waiting to embrace me—giving myself to Asa like this would break me forever. But I had no other choice, because it was the final card I had to play before I folded. "I love you, sir. I'm yours."

I don't know what I'd hoped for. A kiss. A tremor. A smile. Something. Anything. But instead, Asa simply stared so deep into my eyes that I felt naked before him, unable to hide a single thing.

There. I had done it. Laid my best weapon down. There was no more fight left in me. "I'm ready," I whispered, squeezing my eyes shut.

I heard the squeak and clatter of the mosaic being set on the table, of Asa pressing Peyta's trembling hand on top of it.

"Give it up to me, baby," Asa said, his lips brushing my temple as he spoke into my ear. His scent filled my nose, and my body reacted on pure instinct. My vault opened, and the ancient magic rushed out of me, paralyzing me, crushing me beneath its earthy weight, enclosing me in a grave of millennia. I didn't fight it. Unlike the first time, when the magic rushed into me unexpected and frantic, this time, I felt each strand of it, each brush of its power against my consciousness. Runes appeared, then melted into letters I recognized. Words I recognized. I strained to commit them to memory, but they fluttered past like a flock of birds taking flight, all fleeing in different directions. I tried to catch them—*death of the great . . . never again . . . if ever the four . . . goodness and all humanity . . .*

The phrases spun in my consciousness so fast that they blurred and overlapped, multiplying and splintering the more I fought to close my hands around them. And then it all disappeared in strobing flashes, and I sank into irresistible darkness.

Peyta's frail arm twitched against mine, and my eyes snapped open in time to allow me to witness the last of the ancient magic pouring from him into the panel. I knew the moment it had, because he sank down, exhausted and limp, no longer in its relentless grip. I wondered if he'd seen the same things I had, if instead of English, the runes had translated themselves into Russian for him. If he'd understood any of it.

"It's done," Asa said sharply, making me flinch. He untied the boy's arm, took him by the shoulders, and turned him around, briefly grasping Peyta's hands as he stared into his eyes. Slowly, he spoke in Russian to the kid, carefully enunciating every word. The boy shivered and nodded. Asa spun the boy to face the door. "Get him out of here."

"What did you tell him?" Reza asked.

"That he'd see his mom soon. Isn't that what every little boy wants to hear?" The bitterness in Asa's voice was impossible to miss.

Reza chuckled and then guided the kid to the door. At the last moment, Peyta turned around and found Asa's gaze. Asa pressed his lips together and nodded.

I froze, wondering if I had imagined the familiar look on his face. Asa leaned over me as Reza pushed the kid through the door. "You let me in."

"I told you I couldn't give up," I said weakly.

"Did you think it would help?"

"I had to try."

His expression was dead as ever as he raised his head. He drew one hand out of a bulging pocket, perhaps where he had a hit of Ekstazo magic hidden away, and gripped the panel as Reza returned. The Strikon held out his arms. "Excellent work, my friend. I'll take that to Frank."

"Nah. I'd like to do the honors," said Asa.

Reza chuckled and stepped back. "I suppose you've earned it. What about Mattie?"

"She can watch. She needs to understand who's in charge."

"I love it," said Reza, who untied the ropes around my ankles and wrists with a deft hand as Asa stood by, holding the ancient panel slightly away from his lean, sweat-soaked body. He swayed in place, looking sick and weak even though I knew he was still incredibly dangerous. His pockets had used to hold improvised weapons, but now I wondered if they just contained the Ekstazo relics that held him together. The collar was obviously powerful, but maybe it wasn't enough. Asa had once told me that he'd needed more and more to stay afloat.

And I guessed, when compared to the power of that addiction, my love hadn't stood a chance.

I sat up and rubbed my wrists, then swiped at my face with my sleeve, not wanting to give them the satisfaction of seeing me defeated. "Now what?" I asked. "Frank gets to do his victory dance, and then . . . ?"

Reza leaned in, a wicked smile pulling at his mouth. "Then, Mattie, he gives you to me. And I break you."

My hand pressed to my thigh, and I felt the reassuring lump of the vial. Maybe I *hadn't* played my last card yet. "Jeez. You guys are nothing if not predictable."

Asa mumbled something under his breath. "What?" Reza asked.

"Nothing." Asa headed for the door to the main hangar, the panel clutched in his grip.

We emerged to find things as we had left them, Frank at one end of the cavernous space, now hard at work on a cherry cheesecake. In the center of the hangar was the private plane. And on the other side of it were about a dozen henchmen. They were using wooden crates as both card tables and chairs, sneaking sips of vodka from bottles hidden within them. Crouched in a corner, his eyes wide and wary, was Peyta. He held something cradled against his chest, maybe a small stuffed animal.

Frank saw us coming, Asa leading the way with the panel in hand. Frank's pitted face glowed with triumph. "Ah, my boy. We knew you could convince Mattie to give up the goods. Women's hearts are such tender, fragile things."

Asa glanced around, looking jittery and unsteady. "Are they getting the plane ready?"

Frank nodded. "It has just been refueled. We'll leave within the hour."

Asa's jaw clenched, and his fingers spasmed around the panel as he shuffled toward Frank, whose smile wavered. "Are you feeling all right, my friend?"

Asa stopped where he was and swayed again. "Stop it. I'm fine."

Frank must have been turning his pleasure vibes on Asa. I could almost feel them from here, a seductive brush against my skin, draining some of the fear and defeat. Enough, in fact, to make me more aware of Asa. One of his pockets was unbuttoned, and the little action figure he'd set on the safe earlier was hanging out, like he'd jammed it in there hastily. Could I get hold of it? Maybe between it and Theresa's magic, I had a chance. I upped my pace, trying to get closer even as Reza put a hand on my arm.

I tore it out of his grip. "I'm not trying to get away." Except that was exactly my plan. I knew I probably wasn't going to get far, but if my alternative was spending quality one-on-one time with Reza until he'd cracked my mind and spilled my thoughts out for all to see, until he'd stolen my dignity and spirit, well then. It didn't seem like a hard choice. At that point I couldn't blame Asa for trying to hurt himself. I understood it completely.

But sometimes, fate is on my side. As we reached the table where Frank sat, the little action figure fell from Asa's pocket. Before Reza could stop me, I lunged down and picked it up, expecting to end up on my feet with the power to hurt or influence anyone who came near.

Instead, as soon as my fingers touched it, my head filled with flashes of bloody images: Asa with his gun to Jack's head, Jack bleeding and dying in agony. Confusion gripped me in the split second before it was knocked from my hand. I sank onto all fours, blinking the real world back into my vision as realization hit me hard and fast and stranger than any dream. My heart knocked against my ribs as Asa's hand appeared, and I took it. "I . . . you dropped it," I said weakly, afraid to look at him.

He pocketed the action figure again.

I raised my head to see Frank watching me with his eyebrows halfway up his shiny forehead. "You weren't hoping for a weapon, were you, Mattie?"

"No. I'm just in the habit of cleaning up his messes," I said. I couldn't believe it. Had I really seen what I thought I'd seen?

"Here it is," Asa said to Frank, holding up the panel, his hands shaking slightly. And while the three men were focused on the panel, I slipped the vial of sensing magic out of my stocking and surreptitiously began to unscrew the cap.

"Magic's all in it," Asa said, looking down at the mosaic. "If you can figure out how to use it, it should tell you what you want to know."

Frank beamed. "It's beautiful, isn't it? More beautiful with the magic inside." He leaned forward to get a good look at the ghastly mosaic of the man being slaughtered.

Asa shuffled toward Frank, and I glanced down at his boots in time to see his toe catch on the floor. As he pitched forward, his muscles tensed, and in the split second before it all happened, I saw the future and knew my part in it. In those seconds, all the time we'd spent apart evaporated.

The vial in my hand, I spun toward Reza and saw the unfolding craziness reflected in his eyes—Asa regaining his grip on the panel and the steadiness in his steps. Frank yelped as Asa charged, but the high-pitched sound was suddenly cut off when Asa slammed the edge of the mosaic into Frank's throat. As soon as the boss was silenced, searing pain tore along my bones—Reza joining the fight. Asa had it worse. He retched and collapsed over the table, convulsing just like Urasov had.

I managed to veer toward Reza and smacked into him with all my weight, my arms wrapping around his narrow waist and my knee slamming into his thigh, my other hand reaching up and dousing his face with Theresa's magic. He screamed and flailed at the agony of his own magic. As soon as I broke his laser focus, the pain dimmed a little, and I hoped that it would give Asa enough time to recover. I turned away from the still-screaming Reza, but his hands closed around my throat, the pain turning my brain into an erupting volcano of molten hurt. Both of us were shrieking as he tightened his grip.

But then a chair slammed into him, knocking Reza and me to the ground. I rolled to my hands and knees to see Asa on top of the Strikon assassin, pistol-whipping him so viciously that I knew it was personal. The smack of metal on flesh and bone turned my stomach, as did the waves of pain that rolled through me, weaker and weaker the harder Asa punched. Fueled by rage, perhaps protected by the Ekstazo magic in his collar, Asa brought the weapon down again and again, destroying a face that had once been the most handsome I'd ever seen.

Just as Reza went limp, Asa's body did, too, and he groaned and slid off the Strikon. "Stop," he whispered, then moaned. "Stop."

Frank rose from his chair, his gaze intent on Asa. "Very naughty, Asa. Guards!"

No. I raked my fingernails down my forearm, hard enough to draw blood, and then I ran at Frank. I picked up a chair of my own and swung it at him. He might have been a big man, but he was ponderous and slow, and I managed to land a blow to his head that left him staggering backward. He crashed heavily to the floor, his skull colliding with the edge of the electric fireplace as he went down. I braced for the heady pleasure of his magic to loosen my resolve, but he lay limp on the floor, unconscious.

I grabbed the priceless panel and whirled around, thinking to use it as a shield against bullets. But all I saw across the hangar were the henchmen calmly playing cards. I set the panel down and sank to my knees next to Asa, who was sprawled half-conscious next to Reza's bleeding body. "You didn't kill Jack. You just needed me to think you had. I felt the glamour as soon as I touched the action figure."

"Just because I did . . ." Asa let out a shaky breath. "Don't think I'm—"

"Where is he?"

Asa made a pained face and nodded toward the other side of the hangar, where all the henchmen sat. "There's a room. A closet, more like."

"Why aren't they attacking us?"

"The kid. He's holding a glamour to keep those guys seeing nothing over here but Frank eating his dessert."

I stared at him. "This took planning."

"Don't read too much into it." His fingers rose to his collar and fell away again. It was obviously still pumping him full of magic, but somehow, he was fighting it. And apparently he'd been fighting it all along.

I touched his cheek, and he winced and drew back. "Go get Jack," he said. "They won't hurt you as long as the kid stays where he is. You can just walk out."

"I'm not going anywhere without you."

"You're gonna have to," he said as the floor began to hum in earnest. When he saw the puzzled expression on my face, Asa pointed toward the closed hangar doors. "That'll be the Headsmen. It sounds like they've brought half the Russian army with them." Our eyes met. "And if you and Jack don't make yourselves seen, my guess is they're going to come in with guns blazing."

CHAPTER TWENTY-EIGHT

Asa pushed himself up from the floor on trembling arms. "Go, Mattie. Get Jack out of here. The kid, too."

I hesitated, not wanting to leave him when he was so weak. His jaw clenched. "Go. They need you."

So do you. But now wasn't the time to argue. "What about the other children?"

He shook his head as his eyes met mine. "No others. I knew you'd cave on the first one."

"I'll be back." I got up and jogged past the plane, slowing as I neared the henchmen, but they took no notice of me. Peyta gave me a frightened look as I approached, but I offered him a reassuring nod and smile. He clutched the blue teddy bear he was holding a little closer to his chest, focusing once more on the deadly men surrounding us.

I headed straight for the only door on this side of the hangar. It was open just a crack, and when I swung it wide, there was Jack, lying on the floor, gagged, bound, and only half-conscious. "Jack," I whispered as I turned him over.

No gunshots except the one he'd taken in the shoulder. He'd never even been in that storage room with me. His eyelids opened just slightly. "Mattie," he whispered.

"I think your colleagues are about to bust in here."

"I'm wearing a tracker," he mumbled. "Knew it was only a matter of time."

"I think Asa knew it, too," I said as I worked at the tight knots at his wrists. "He just took out Frank and Reza."

"Huh?"

I couldn't suppress my smile. "We haven't lost him. Whatever he's up to, he wasn't going to let Frank get the magic. It's back in the panel, but Asa has it."

"Where is he?" He rubbed at his wrists, then hissed when the movement pulled at his shoulder. He lay still as I yanked at the ropes around his ankles, feeling the vibrations of heavy machinery through the floor.

"He's still in the hangar. He's weak and hurt. We have to get him out of here."

Jack was frowning as I pulled him up to a sitting position. "You sure he's on our side?"

"He won't admit it yet, but I know he is."

Jack didn't look convinced. With my help, he got to his feet, and I pulled his good arm over my shoulder and supported him as we walked out of the storage closet. He tensed when he saw the men arrayed in front of us, smoking and relaxing, but then I pointed to Peyta. "He's the conduit who did the transaction with me."

"I wonder why they didn't use me."

I closed my eyes, pushing away memories of what I'd thought were Jack's final moments. "Because they needed me to be desperate enough to cooperate. Asa used a glamour. He killed you in front of me."

Jack's eyes were wide. "No shit?"

I swallowed back nausea. "I don't know how he got hold of that magic, but it was really realistic."

"Could have made it himself with the right juice and proper know-how."

"His imagination is pretty vivid."

Jack snorted. "He probably enjoyed it a little bit. Where is he?"

I looked over but all I saw was Frank, calmly eating his cheesecake.

Jack squinted. "I still don't see him. Only Reza." He whistled low, but the sound was drowned out by the roar of engines.

My heart began to race as I looked over at Peyta, who was still crouched in his corner, clutching the small blue teddy bear that was keeping us alive. He was staring at the hangar door, looking ready to bolt. "This could get really bad," I choked out. "Will the Headsmen attack?"

Jack's tense expression wasn't reassuring. "Given the slaughter back in the city, they might. But they have my tracker signature, so that might keep them from leveling this place. Still, we'd better get out of here. They might assume I'm dead if I'm not moving. And I've been *not moving* for quite a while now."

"Peyta," I said in a loud whisper, gesturing him over to us. If he stopped focusing on controlling that glamour, the henchmen would see exactly what was happening around them, but I wasn't going to risk a child's life just to cover my own ass.

The little boy rose to his feet, still holding the bear, and he seemed to understand instinctively that his life depended on keeping that glamour in place, because the henchmen continued to ignore us.

"Almost there," whispered Jack, pointing to a side door. "We can—"

The huge hangar door started to slide open, and above the roof of the plane I saw a sliver of clear night sky. Jack, Peyta, and I limped along the side of the plane, our pace increasing. Were the Headsmen coming in? Where had Asa gone? I couldn't fight the gnawing fear that had taken form in my gut.

And as soon as we reached the plane's tail, I saw that the fear was very justified.

Arrayed in front of the open hangar door were eight armored military vehicles, like SUVs on steroids, with huge, heavy guns mounted on their roofs. Behind each was a gunner. Peyta whimpered and hugged the bear, and I pulled him close—just as I caught sight of Asa.

He trudged toward the semicircle of death machines in front of us, carrying the panel. The gunners adjusted their aim to put him in the crosshairs. My heart stopped.

"I want to talk to Keenan," Asa called, holding up the treasure.

From somewhere inside the cluster of vehicles came the scratchy, amplified sound of Keenan's voice. "You've got my attention, Asa. Is the magic inside it?"

"You bet." Asa stopped when he was about fifty feet away from the vehicles. "Which means that if you want it, you can't kill me."

"Sadly," said Keenan, the rage evident in his voice, "that's true."

The gunners lowered their weapons, aiming them away from Asa and the priceless relic in his hands.

"Good," said Asa, the black collar stark against his chalky skin, sweat glistening in the harsh headlights of the SUVs. "Then we understand each other."

Jack, Peyta, and I had reached the threshold to the outside, and Jack raised his uninjured arm, receiving a wave of acknowledgment from two of the gunners and nods from several others. Asa, holding the panel in front of his chest, looked over at us, and all my hope and joy vanished as I read his expression.

It wasn't relieved. Or happy.

It was defiant. Asa raised the panel over his head.

As Keenan began to shout and Jack cursed, I put out my arms, as if I could stop him.

But no one could. None of us were close enough. He slammed the mosaic into the blacktop with all his strength. Shards of wood and clay and bits of stone exploded up from the ground as the thing shattered into hundreds of useless, broken bits. Smiling, Asa straightened and spread his arms. "Now do your thing."

For a moment, stunned silence filled the air. "You bastard," Keenan rasped. "Do you have any idea what you've done?"

Asa grinned, his smile a razor as the gunners zeroed in on him once more. "Found my escape clause."

"No," I screamed, tearing myself from Jack's side. I barreled into Asa like a miniature linebacker, and he was too weak to hold me back. With my arms wrapped around his torso, we crumpled to the ground even as a sharp crack echoed all around. A slice of searing pain cut across my upper arm, like someone had lashed me with a whip, but I ignored it. Shouts and Peyta's cries reached me as Asa's head smacked against blacktop and his muscles went slack.

I glanced over at the boy in time to see the teddy bear—the one piece of magic that had been holding the bad guys back—fall from his hands as he clamped them over his ears. Knowing what would come next, fully aware that Asa and I were sandwiched between two deadly opposing forces, I found a strength I'd never known I had. Fisting my hands in Asa's shirt just above the shoulders, I dragged him to the side as the bullets started to fly. A moment later, Jack joined me, along with Peyta, and the three of us raced with Asa toward the shelter of the Headsmen's SUVs, with Jack shouting orders not to fire.

Asa stirred, his long arms flexing without a clear mission, while the Headsmen sent thousands of bullets into the hangar. The henchmen went down like puppets with their strings cut. I knew Frank and Reza were still in there somewhere, probably full of holes at this point. "Plane," Asa mumbled.

I looked up at Jack. "Brindle said the plane had just been fueled!"

He cast a single horrified look into the hangar, where the plane, along with everything else, was being shredded by the Headsmen's artillery. "Fall back," Jack roared, helping me drag Asa farther behind the line of SUVs. "Fall b—"

We were thrown across the tarmac as a massive boom and wave of heat plowed over us, sending some of the SUVs onto their back wheels as the gunners dove off the rear to safety. I landed on top of Asa, cradling his head against my chest and letting Jack cover us both with his muscular body. Peyta was curled in a tight ball against Asa's side. The night was filled with flames and heat, but the staccato horror of the bullets was slowly falling silent, interrupted only by a few stuttering bursts. But Frank and his henchmen presented no threat now.

Asa's pulse ticked frantically against my fingertips when I pressed them to the slick skin just below his collar. He was alive, even though he didn't want to be, and I was going to make sure he kept breathing until he changed his mind.

I kissed his forehead and held him tight, finally allowing the tears to fall.

We were taken to a Headsmen facility in Warsaw. Asa was kept heavily sedated and restrained during the journey, both for his safety and everyone else's. Once we arrived, he was wheeled into an operating room, where a bomb technician and a surgeon worked together to defuse and remove the collar from his throat.

I watched with my nose pressed to the reinforced glass of the operating room, my eyes burning.

"Coffee? You look like you could use some."

I turned to find Keenan next to me, two cardboard cups in his hands, contents steaming. "Sure. Thanks."

His blue eyes zeroed in on Asa, breathing mask over his mouth and nose, long limbs still and limp. "They've gotten through the most dangerous part." He pointed to the technician, who was packing a section of the collar into a reinforced steel box. "That's the piece that could have killed him if anyone had tried to take it off."

"It looks like he tried to do it himself." I couldn't take my eyes off the piece of his throat I could see, where a few short, deep wounds had been stitched up. "Did he know it could kill him?"

"Probably." Keenan sighed. "My guess is that he tried—and that Brindle then controlled for that with the Knedas magic being pumped into him."

"But he *did* try to kill himself," I whispered.

"No, he tried to get *us* to kill him. Every single thing he's been doing has managed to skirt the orders he was probably given. Brindle ordered him to acquire the panel and to give it to him, but most likely didn't specify that Asa had to let him keep it. Brindle ordered him to capture you, but didn't add that he couldn't capture anyone else, so he grabbed Jack. Brindle underestimated Asa, pure and simple."

"He thought he'd broken him."

"Asa probably made a calculated decision. He wanted them to think they had him."

"Why, though? Why would he willingly submit? It doesn't sound like him. He always said he'd rather die than be in a cage."

Keenan chuckled. "But think about it. If Asa had refused to surrender, they would have killed him weeks ago."

I stared at Asa's long fingers, those dangerous hands. "He decided he wanted to live long enough to kill them." And he had. They were still sifting through the bodies in that hangar, but word had already gotten out that Brindle was dead. "He found a way around all their orders and influence, and he destroyed them." My fists clenched. "But then he tried to destroy himself."

"It took its toll, Mattie. God only knows what they did to him. What they made him do. He's got to be one of the hardest men I've ever known, but he's not invincible. I don't know who exactly is going to rise from that table. Or if anyone will rise at all."

I sniffled and wiped my face with my sleeve. "Don't say that."

"I know you love him, Mattie. You've more than proven it. You've also more than proven that you're a woman of character—Jack told me you were willing to kill Asa rather than let him and Reza have their way."

"And I'm unbelievably thankful I failed!"

"I know, but that kind of strength and determination is rare. You chose principles over emotion, even though I can feel how strong those emotions are. You did everything you could."

"I gave up the magic," I said quietly.

Keenan put his hand on the glass. "No one blames you for that. Jack told me what Asa did."

"But I didn't choose principles, like you said."

"Yes, you did. You chose to protect the life of a child. You were under unbelievable pressure, and you kept your head. You helped Asa take down Reza and Brindle, and you rescued Peyta and Jack. Without you, they wouldn't be here. Without you, Asa would be dead." He touched my upper arm, where the graze wound I'd sustained had been stitched and bandaged. "I've disciplined that agent, by the way. But he was engaged to Agent Urasov. I should have taken him off duty immediately, but we needed the manpower."

"I get it," I said. In addition to the lives lost, so many hearts had been broken. "And I'm sorry the magic is gone. I'm sorry I couldn't bring it to you."

Keenan's hand slid down the glass. "There's got to be another way to figure it out. Understanding the magic is the only way to keep people safe. Two of the four relics are still out there." He looked down at me. "I could use a few more good agents to help me hunt them down and transport them to a place where they can be kept secure for all time."

I blinked up at him. "Are you offering me a job?"

He gave me a gentle smile. "I'd love to have you on my team. So would Jack."

I turned back to the glass just as the surgeon laid what was left of the thick black collar on the cloth-covered metal tray. Leads dangled from it, Asa's blood glistening on their steely tendrils. "I can't leave Asa."

"Mattie . . ."

"I have to do whatever I can to bring him back."

"Assuming there's something in there left to rescue. Removing the collar won't erase his memories of what happened. It will, however, send him into withdrawal from the Ekstazo. We're going to taper it, but it's going to be brutal. After that . . ."

"Asa's never left me behind. And I'm not going to leave him. If you get him through the withdrawal, I'll do the rest."

Sometimes I can be really naive.

I thought I had it all worked out. But after a few days of watching Asa struggle against his restraints, avoiding eye contact and refusing to speak to anyone, including me, I realized it wasn't going to be that simple. He had repeatedly torn IV lines from his arm with his teeth, shouting at us to leave him alone, to quit pumping magic into his body. Finally, I begged Keenan to do as he asked.

So Asa went cold turkey. I've never seen anyone so sick.

And after a few days of that, he went quiet and slack, no longer raging and writhing but instead staring at the walls and refusing to eat or drink. "He can't lose any more weight," I said.

"Unless we're willing to tie him down and put another IV in him, there's not much we can do," Keenan said as we peered at Asa through the tiny window in his metal door. His knees were drawn to his chest, and his head was bowed. He hadn't moved in hours.

"I need some air," I said, my voice cracking.

He nodded sympathetically as I headed out the door and into the city of Warsaw.

It didn't take me long to find what I needed. I scurried into the Internet café, grateful when the dude at the front nodded as I held up a handful of euros. I stuffed them into his hands and lunged for an open terminal, where I held my breath as I logged in to what I guessed would be the latest iteration of Theresa's e-mail account.

There was a draft message waiting for me.

> Another party fail, but one that helped me make a graceful exit. Ex went underground as his guests looted the place, and nephew is trying to clean up the mess. Seems like everyone had a wild night. I heard you had some issues with cops. I'd like to know where our mutual friend is.

So Volodya was alive, but in hiding, and Daniil was trying to take over. Theresa had gotten away and was wondering about her son.

I checked the message, wondering if she was still on the loose, and my eyes went wide—the draft had been modified only a half hour earlier! Could she still be online?

I had no presence of mind for cloak-and-dagger, but I did the best I could as my fingers danced across the keys. I left out the part of the story where Asa tried to get himself killed, because I couldn't bear to tell her. In fact, I skipped everything until:

> We're with the cops. A is in trouble, though. No more collar, tough withdrawal. He won't accept drugs, won't respond to me. Help.

I hugged myself and stared as the minutes passed. The attendant gave me a worried look. I smiled and waved. And when I turned back to the screen, the draft had been updated.

He needs pleasure. Joy, comfort, the full range. But it has to be natural, not magic. It has to be real. Take care of him for me. Please don't let him go. You're the only one who can help him.

I stared at the message, a new determination steeling my spine. I erased her latest draft and replaced it with one of my own, just two words. But they would have to be enough for now.

Message received.

CHAPTER TWENTY-NINE

I shouldered the duffel bag of Asa's possessions—the contents of his pockets the night he brought Brindle down—and unlocked the cabin door as a crisp breeze blew my hair around my face. I looked over my shoulder. "As soon as we get settled, I'll get a fire going."

Asa stood on the porch step, looking like death's cousin. He hadn't shaved in a week and had a patchy dark-brown beard tinged with red. His cheeks were hollowed out. But he wasn't sweating—I had been very clear that there was to be no magic on or near the premises.

Asa didn't say a word in response to my offer of a fire, but then again, he hadn't said a word when I'd told him we were coming here. He hadn't argued or fought or made threats. Keenan had made all the arrangements, down to the last detail—and I had been very specific. There were Headsmen posted at the bottom of the mountain, on the road that marked the only way out, but they'd been given instructions not to bother us unless I called them.

I looked at my phone and frowned in the silence. She should have been here by now.

And as soon as I slipped the key into the lock, a bark echoed from inside, and doggy toenails clicked on the hardwood floor. I pushed the door open and stepped back as Gracie emerged from behind the overstuffed couch, sniffing the air.

"Gracie?" Asa murmured. He made a wrenching, helpless noise. "Girl?"

She ran forward as he sank to his knees, and I choked back tears as she wriggled into his arms, as his fingers curled into her silky, short fur.

"I called Daria, and she drove her most of the way," I said. "Jack picked her up in Asheville and brought her over here this morning. Daria says hi, by the way."

Asa's eyes were closed as Gracie frantically licked his face. "Thank you," he whispered.

"I'm going to give you guys some time." With a lump in my throat, I set about completing the tasks on my mental to-do list. I grabbed some firewood and got a fire going. And as Asa settled himself on the floor just inside the front door, never taking his hands or eyes off his dog, I headed into the kitchen.

Keenan had stayed true to his word. The fridge was stocked. I spent the next few hours making vegan pesto with zucchini and carrot "noodles," marinated kale salad, granola with almond butter and agave, and a raw strawberry pie with nut-and-date crust. Asa's favorites.

And by the time I was finished, I heard a sound that brought a huge smile to my face—the whisper of water in the master bathroom upstairs. He was taking a shower on his own.

He came down as I was putting food on the table. He'd shaved and put on a clean pair of cargo pants and a T-shirt that I'd asked Keenan to leave here for us. For a moment, I wondered what he would expect in return for all these accommodations—so determined to pull Asa back from the brink, I had been unabashed in my requests. Surely Keenan would want something as payment for all he'd done for a man who had caused him nothing but trouble for years. Right now, though, I was concerned only with Asa.

"How did it feel?" I asked, gesturing at his wet hair.

Asa ran his hand through it and sank into a chair at the table. Gracie trotted over and settled herself next to his chair, laying her head in his lap. "Strange," he said quietly.

I put a plate in front of him. "It's going to get better."

He glanced up at me and looked away quickly. "I can't believe you're doing this for me. After what I put you through . . ."

I swallowed the lump in my throat and dished up the food. I avoided the temptation to heap it onto his plate. I was afraid he would get sick after having nearly starved himself over the past week. "You weren't yourself."

"Why does that matter? I still did all those things." His gaze strayed out the window. "People died because of me. I can't take any of it back."

"Then you'll find a way to make amends and move forward. But first you have to take time to heal and recover. You've been through a lot, Asa."

He looked down quickly like he didn't want me to see his expression. As he started to eat, I felt an ache in my chest. He had always been so strong, and it was painful to see him so unsteady. But he was here and alive and finally speaking again, so I knew I was getting somewhere.

"I don't know everything that happened while I was with Brindle," he said after a few minutes of silence. "I want to." His fingers flexed over his fork, bending it slightly. "You didn't tell me how you found my mother."

My stomach went tight. "She found me. She sensed the magic in the sand vial."

"I never meant for it to put you in danger," he muttered.

"I know what you meant by it," I said in a husky voice.

He nodded, keeping his gaze on his plate. "She was following us. She was in Prague."

"She was checking in on you." I steeled myself. "Asa, she loves y—"

"No, Mattie." He put his fork down with a clatter. "Not tonight."

"Okay," I whispered.

"Just tell me one thing."

"Anything."

"Volodya," he said slowly. He seemed to be holding his breath.

I sighed. "He's your father. But he didn't know that until after you were captured by Brindle."

His shoulders sagged. "It makes so much sense," he murmured. "I was created by two monsters and raised by a monster." He put his hands on the table. "And now I'm the biggest monster of all."

"You're not a monster, Asa." I said it louder than I intended to, and he flinched. "You've been through hell. For pretty much your whole life. And somehow, despite all of that, you kept your heart and soul."

"Until they were destroyed."

He sounded so defeated that it brought tears to my eyes. I wanted to reach across the table, grab him by the shoulders, and scream in his face. *I will not give up on you. I will fight for you until my last breath.* But instead, all I said was "Well. You can't put them back together on an empty stomach."

Asa bowed his head. "Dammit, Mattie," he whispered. A moment later he picked up his fork again.

When he had eaten his fill, he went to sit in front of the fire with Gracie while I cleaned up. My hands shook as I did the dishes and thought about what I was going to do next. I had no idea how he would react. But I had to take the risk.

I dried my hands on a kitchen towel as I watched him stare into the fire, lost in the twist of the flames. Gracie was sleeping on the rug near the fireplace. My heart beating a thousand miles per hour, I slowly walked over to him and sank onto my knees in front of him.

He blinked and looked down at me, wariness and surprise in his eyes. I offered a nervous smile. "The night you were taken," I began, but then the memories and emotions rose up so quickly that they nearly choked me. "Sorry," I whispered, clearing my throat. "But the night you were taken, we had plans. We were going to talk."

Asa sat up straighter and opened his mouth to speak, but I held up my hand to stop him. "Just hear me out," I said, slowly and carefully laying my hands on his thighs. Asa sucked in a sharp breath, but his mouth closed again. "Is this okay?" I asked.

He looked down at my hands on his body. After a few moments of terrifying silence, he nodded.

"For months, I had been trying to keep my feelings for you contained, Asa. I was so afraid you would hurt me." I chuckled. "But that night, I decided that it would hurt a lot more not to risk it, because I would know I'd let you go without even trying. I couldn't live with that." I stroked my thumbs along the seam of the pockets beneath my hands. "So I was going to tell you how I felt. I was going to admit it. And I never got to do that."

I closed my eyes. *It's worth it. He's worth it.* "I don't know when exactly I fell in love with you."

His thighs tensed, and I squeezed my eyes more tightly shut, not wanting to see his face.

"It was long before London, though. A part of me knew it when I sent you away that night in Nevada. And it made no sense, but eventually I couldn't push it away. It was too big, claiming more territory every day." I forced my eyes open, forced myself to meet his honey-brown gaze. "And it hasn't changed, Asa. Not for me. I know you might not feel the same anymore. I know you might not even be able to feel that way. You said all your feelings were gone, and if that's the way it is, I'll accept it."

I rose up so that we were closer to being eye to eye. I could feel the warmth of the fire at my back as I stared at the shadows that played across Asa's angular face. The face I loved, the one I dreamed of. "But what I said that night when you had me tied to the table—"

"You said you were mine," he said, his voice strained.

"It's true." My lips trembled as I tried to smile. "It always will be. No matter how much it hurts."

There was a storm brewing in Asa's eyes, a tension growing in his body. I could feel the vibrations as I slid my hands off his legs to find his hands. I squeezed them, but he didn't squeeze back. "I know you're afraid of feeling good, Asa. I know you probably don't trust it. Or maybe you don't trust yourself. But you need it. And"—I leaned forward and kissed his hand—"that's what I'm offering. However you need it. However you can find it. Take it from me tonight."

"Mattie . . ."

"You can say no. You can always say no. But only say it if you don't want me. Don't deny yourself because you're scared. You know I'm strong, and you know I love you. Say you know that."

Our eyes met. "I know," he whispered. "I feel it. But—"

"Show me that you know," I said. "Take what you need from me. Whatever you need. No apologies. No explanations. We're past that."

My heart was pounding, but I was dead serious. I'd made my choice. It didn't mean I wasn't nervous. I watched indecision flit across his face just before he said, "You have to be able to stop it."

"Does that mean . . ."

He blew a long breath through pursed lips. "If you need to stop, you're gonna say 'red,' okay? Promise."

Excitement curled low in my belly. "I promise."

Asa didn't move. He'd gone completely still. But every muscle in his body had tensed.

"Tell me what to do," I murmured. "I'm yours, sir."

He let out an unsteady moan and closed his eyes. "Stand up."

A zing of excitement pulled me tight. "Yes, sir." I got to my feet and took a step back.

His eyes opened, and his gaze traced from my ankles to my face. "Strip."

My hands closed over the hem of my sweater.

"Slowly," he said.

"Yes, sir." I let my fingertips skim up my ribs as I pulled the sweater up inch by inch. The fabric caressed my skin as I lifted it over my head and then let it fall to the floor.

"Pants. Off."

I breathed steadily. Though I wanted to shove my pants down my legs, though it actually would have been easier and less suspenseful, I knew the tension was exactly what he wanted. So I took my time undoing the button and zipper, in peeling the skinny jeans off my hips and down my thighs and calves.

It probably didn't look too sexy as I battled with my socks to get the whole mess off my feet, but Asa didn't say a word. He just watched. And when I straightened up and stood before him in just my lacy panties and bra, which I had specifically picked out in the hope that this would happen, I could see the bulge in his pants. The satisfaction was intense. I started to take off my panties.

"No," he snapped.

I froze with my fingers hooked under the elastic.

"You wait for me to tell you." He stood up suddenly, and for the first time since he'd been taken, he didn't sway in place. "And you don't deny me what's mine."

I shivered as he moved closer. "Yours, sir?"

His fingers closed gently around my throat. "All of you. All of you is mine. Say it."

"All of me is yours. Every part."

"Your body."

"Yes, sir," I whispered.

"Your *heart*."

"*Yes.*" My eyes stung with the truth of it.

"Your pleasure. Your pain. Tonight it's mine."

Always. "Yours, sir."

His lips curled into a smile and he smacked me on the ass. "So don't make a move unless I tell you to."

My skin was hot, and my body was taut and trembling. Seeing him find his strength again was the biggest turn-on ever. Knowing that I'd done it was going to push me over the edge. "Yes, sir."

His fingers were tighter around my throat as he guided me over to a large window facing the driveway. I knew there was no one out there, but it still felt strange to be standing inside, mostly naked, exposed to the darkness of the night. "Hands on either side of the window."

I obeyed, realizing that it was like standing in front of a mirror. I could see my own reflection clearly. And I could see Asa looming behind me. I watched as his hand slid from my throat to my breast. My fingernails dug into the wood of the window frame as he peeled back the fabric to expose my skin to the cool air wafting in from the frigid outside. I bit my lip as he rolled my nipple between his fingers. There was a current of fear that ran just beneath my skin. I wasn't so much afraid that he would hurt me—first, because I could take pain, and second, because he'd insisted on a safe word—I was more afraid of making a wrong move and knocking him from whatever world he'd stepped into, the one where he was totally in control.

Because control was what Asa needed to feel safe, what he needed to feel himself again. It had been stripped from him completely. He'd been forced to make terrible choices about which parts of him to surrender and which parts to hold on to until the end. He bore scars both visible and invisible because of the damage they'd done as they'd tried to take his will from him. To regain his sense of self, he needed his control back. And tonight I would give it to him.

So I stayed perfectly still as his hands slid over me, claiming what was his. He touched every part of my body, unhurried, his eyes riveted on my skin, on his hands running over it. The sensation was overwhelming, and I fought to stay quiet to keep from distracting him.

"Mattie." He was on his knees behind me, and his hot breath was on my thigh. "You're not a fucking blow-up doll."

"What . . . sir?" My voice was quiet from disuse and strained because his fingers were stroking along my inner thighs, closer and closer to where I wanted them but not quite there.

"I want to hear you, baby. I want to feel you. If it hurts, I want to hear you cry out. If it feels good, I want you to moan. When I make you come, I want you to scream. And we're both going to know I did it to you."

Even the words, even the thought, got me halfway there. I pushed my ass back a little, closer to his face. His fingers squeezed my thighs hard enough to bruise. "Yes, sir."

I cried out as he smacked me again, hard. "Good girl." Then he pulled my panties aside and his tongue was inside me, and my thoughts blanked out, leaving me aware only of him, only of his hands and his mouth and his heat. I held on to that window frame like it could save me as he flicked his tongue over my clit and made me gasp.

"Open your eyes, Mattie. Watch yourself. Watch what I'm doing to you."

"Yes, sir," I said in a choked voice. He had pushed me so close to the brink that I was already skating along its edge. My lips and hands tingled. My reflection showed my flushed cheeks and the unfocused look in my eyes. And the shadow of Asa rising behind me and pressing in close. I listened, shivering, to the clinking of metal as he undid his belt, the whisper of his zipper as he lowered it. I was dying to turn around, to peel off his shirt and see his body, to pull off his pants and explore him. But there would be time for that later. Tonight was his, and he could hide or bare himself when he wanted.

Asa looked me over, his head tilted. He reached forward and wrenched my bra down so that my breasts were free, then shoved my panties halfway down my thighs. His fingers slid between my legs, slipping along my most sensitive parts while I moaned. "Keep those eyes open," he said, giving me another smack. "Do it or I'm going to use the belt."

Startled by the threat, I tensed, but then Asa began to stroke me, and I felt the hot length of him against me and melted again. I watched his fingers curl into the flesh of my hips, felt him pull me back so that I was bent over, holding myself up against the window frame, staring at the wild sight of him, fully clothed, pants hanging open around his narrow hips. Hunger and need quickened my breath.

"How much have you wanted this?" he asked quietly as he caressed me with his shaft, as he slid it along my folds, all the time rubbing my clit until I squirmed to keep from coming too soon.

"So much that I dreamed of it, sir," I replied, panting. And still those dreams had nothing on this, the visceral terror and tension of it, the craving. "So much that sometimes I couldn't think of anything else."

Our eyes met in the window glass as I felt the tip of him enter me. "That's nothing compared to how much I wanted *you*."

And then Asa Ward slid himself inside me, slow and relentless, and by the time his hips were pressed to my back, I came apart, constricting around him. As if my body didn't want to let his go, as if it already understood. "Dammit, Mattie," he growled as he ground against me.

After that, I just held on tight. I moved however he told me to. I kept my eyes open and watched him fuck me, because there is no other word to describe it. He was rough and merciless, and I loved every minute of it, because I could translate the craving in his hard hands, in every thrust. His gaze never strayed from my face in the window glass. I knew he wanted to see his effect on me, and I didn't try to disguise it, either the pain or the pleasure. I let him have all of it, and it drove him wild. For the first time, I reveled in the tremors under his skin, because I knew he was starting to lose himself in me, that he felt safe enough to let go. I knew he couldn't have done it with anyone else, not now, not tonight. I was the only one in the whole world who could offer this gift, and my heart ached with joy as he wrapped his arms around my waist and bit my shoulder, as I felt him come inside me.

He was completely quiet as he came, but it was seismic all the same. I shook with his weight and the pain of his teeth, with the ecstasy of his pulsing heat, until I wasn't sure I could stay upright much longer. "Sir . . . ?" I whispered.

Asa pressed his sweaty forehead to my shoulder blade, then drew back and laid a gentle kiss on the red teeth marks he'd left on my skin. I peered into the window, trying to see his expression, but he turned his face away. He slipped out of my body, but even as he did, he scooped me up into his arms. "Put your head on my shoulder," he instructed.

I did.

"Arms around my neck."

I obeyed.

"Gracie, stay."

Gracie whined, but she stayed put as Asa carried me up the stairs to the loft bedroom. Despite the release, the tension was already building again, because I had no idea what he was going to do, what he wanted. Fortunately, he did.

Keeping his face turned away, always just in shadow, he laid me on the bed, took off his T-shirt, and then ripped it until he had a strip of fabric in his hands, which he tied over my eyes. His hands were gentle as he finished undressing me, and I listened as he took off the rest of his clothes. The desire to push the blindfold off my eyes was almost overpowering. Did he have any idea how badly I wanted to see him, how much I wanted to look at his face and his body?

Maybe he did. Maybe denying me those things was turning him on. Maybe he was hiding. Maybe it was both.

Then he was close, winding me impossibly tight as his mouth closed over one of my breasts and I felt the exquisite pull. Not being able to see heightened every other sensation and emotion. He had all the control, but my surrender had its own quiet power. Absolute trust has a sway all to itself. And as he held my wrists to the bed, as he sank into me yet again, I knew he felt it.

What we were doing now was just another version of the dance we did during magical transactions. I gave myself to him, and I knew he would take care of me. That no matter how much it hurt, no matter how rough it got, in the end, Asa would make sure I was okay. He would carry me through. And in that bed, he took me apart and put me back together. It crossed every divide. It erased the past. It blew the future wide open.

He owned my pleasure. He owned my pain. He owned my heart and my body and my soul, and he knew it. He claimed every cell and every thought. He kissed me hard and fucked me hard and then traversed the same territory with absolute gentleness. He kept me off-balance and wanting, but somehow completely satisfied. He kept me scared and uncertain, but somehow completely safe.

"I love you." I said it over and over. I screamed it. I sobbed and whimpered and moaned it. I meant it every single time.

And finally, long after I'd lost track of time and of myself, long after I was spent and sweating and sore and so full of love and hope that I wanted to cry, Asa pulled me close, my back to his front. His fingers caressed my face as he untied the blindfold and let me stare into the darkness. He pressed his sweaty cheek to mine and held me tight, his fingers spread over my ribs. "I love you, too, Mattie," he whispered as I relaxed into his arms. "I always will. Don't ever forget it."

I smiled, even as a tear slipped from my eye. "Yes, sir."

He kissed my temple. "Good girl."

CHAPTER THIRTY

I slept like a sack of cement. At one point, though, I woke up to find Asa sitting next to the bed, dressed. "It's still dark," I muttered.

"Gracie needs to go out. Go back to sleep."

"'Kay." I plopped my head back onto the pillow.

The bed dipped as he leaned over to kiss my forehead. "I love you so fucking much," he said, his voice strained.

I frowned. "You okay?"

"I will be," he whispered. "Thanks to you." He kissed me again. "Now go back to sleep. Dream of me."

I smiled sleepily. "No worries."

I listened to his footsteps descending the stairs and to the jingle of Gracie's collar as she rose to her feet. As the door clicked shut, I sank back into my exhausted, happy slumber.

And when I woke up, sunlight piercing through the windows, the day bright and clear, I was alone. I sat up abruptly and looked toward the bathroom, but it was dark, the door open to show me Asa wasn't there. "Asa?"

Silence.

Memories of Ben's kidnapping came over me all at once. My stomach clenching, I threw back the covers and walked to the edge of the loft, looking down toward the kitchen, the living room. He wasn't there. "Gracie?"

More silence.

"Oh my God," I whispered. Pulling a quilt around me, I clumsily descended the stairs, walking past my discarded jeans and sweater next to the couch. I looked toward the front door.

Asa's duffel was gone, too.

"Please tell me you didn't," I whimpered, my heart pounding. "Please."

I walked into the kitchen. On the counter there was a scrap of paper with Asa's cramped handwriting.

Can't stay. I'm sorry.

The blood drained from my brain as I sank to the floor. "No no no no no," I muttered, starting to rock as everything inside me melted down and my tears started to fall. "No."

I don't know how long I sat there, sobbing, but eventually I became aware of a phone ringing. As I looked around wildly, I spotted my purse near the door and crawled over to it.

"He's gone," I whimpered in lieu of "hello."

"I know," Keenan said. "He stole an agent's car when the guy went into the woods to take a piss. When did he leave?"

"I honestly don't know. At least a few hours ago."

"Do you think he's going to hurt himself?"

I thought about that, and a tiny measure of relief soothed the raw wound that had opened up in my heart. "I don't think so. He took his bag. He has Gracie with him. I . . ." I pressed my lips together, remembering what Asa had said about his relationship with Keenan, the one phrase that had haunted me as I'd thought about getting involved with him. *Just another cage.* "I think he's just gone."

Then I started to cry, and I didn't stop until Jack and Keenan arrived at the door.

"Hey, Mattie," Jack said, his voice gentle. "How you holding up?"

"How do I look?" I asked, certain my face was tearstained and pale.

"Fucked," Jack said.

"Perceptive," I whispered.

Keenan cleared his throat. "We're going to keep trying to track him down, Mattie, but . . ."

I waved away his words. "If he doesn't want to be found, you're not going to find him."

"Did he give any hint that he was planning something like this? You guys weren't here very long," said Jack. "Did anything happen?"

Something had happened, all right. "I . . ." I sniffled. "I-I think . . . I think maybe he just . . ." My face crumpled as I uttered the devastating words. "I think he just didn't want to be with me."

And he'd left in the cruelest way, telling me he loved me only minutes before he walked out the door. I hadn't even questioned whether he was going to come back. I'd trusted he wouldn't leave me behind.

"He left me behind," I said to Keenan, and then I began to cry again, deep sobs that came up from the heart of me. Jack sat down next to me and hesitantly offered his embrace, and I accepted it, needing something to hold me together. I was done. I had nothing left.

"Maybe he'll change his mind," said Jack. "Maybe he'll come back."

"No, he won't," Keenan and I said at the same time, and I pressed my face to Jack's shoulder to keep from screaming.

Asa was gone. He'd left me behind. He'd taken what he needed from me and walked away, even as I was dreaming about a future with him.

"I don't know what to do," I said. "I don't know what to do now."

"You have family in Wisconsin," Jack said slowly.

"I can't go back there." I didn't belong there anymore. Nothing fit.

"I've got an idea, if you're open to it," Keenan said. "Join my team."

I lifted my head from Jack's shoulder. "You really want me to become an agent? A Headsman?"

He nodded. "You could be a key part of the team I'm building to hunt down the Knedas and Sensilo relics. If you need some distraction, Mattie, this would be a good one. Because it would require all your attention and time." He gave me a rueful smile. "And trust me. Nothing's better for heartbreak than plunging yourself into an all-encompassing mission."

Our eyes met, and I saw the compassion there. He could feel every ounce of my sorrow and pain, and probably remembered feeling the same. "Pay's not bad, either," he said quietly. "Full benefits."

I let out a sniffly laugh. "Company car?"

"When the mission calls for it," he said. "Come on. You need this. And we need you."

I looked up at Jack, and he smiled. "Would be kinda nice to have you around, I guess," he said, giving me a friendly squeeze.

"You don't have to decide right away," said Keenan. "We can give you some time."

I swiped tears from my cheeks and looked around. Unless I wanted to go back to Sheboygan, I had no home to return to. My life had become so entwined with Asa's that I had no vision of the future without him. Now it stretched in front of me like a cloudy, dusty chalkboard. There had once been writing there, but Asa had erased it all, leaving only the residue. I already knew that if I went out on my own, I'd spend every day wondering where he was, wondering if he'd change his mind, if he'd find me. And I already knew it would slowly eat at me until there was nothing left.

"I don't need to think about it." I stood up and faced Keenan. "I'll take the job."

Keenan grinned and held out his hand for me to shake. His palm was warm and his grip was strong. "You will not regret this, Mattie."

Jack patted me on the back. "Guess we'd better get your stuff, then. We've got a plane to catch."

"What?" I blinked at him. "Don't I . . . don't you guys have some place like Quantico where I go and train for a while?"

Keenan laughed. "Usually there's a training process that takes two years. But in your case, we're going to hit the ground running. We have to get to the Knedas relic before anyone else does. And trust me, now that Brindle's gone, there isn't anyone to scare everyone else into staying home. The outfit that ends up with the original Knedas is going to have every advantage, and we're going to make sure it doesn't fall into the wrong hands."

"So . . . where are we going, exactly?"

Jack grinned. "Patagonia."

"What?" I yelped.

"A backpacker traveling near Ushuaia took shelter in a remote cave and discovered pottery containing some very familiar-looking runes. It's the first anyone has seen of that writing system on the continent."

"So we're gonna go sniff around and see what we can find," said Jack.

"Might be dangerous," said Keenan. "Definitely could use a good reliquary on the team, both to carry some powerful magic in undetected but also to carry anything we find out. Up for it?"

I hugged myself. My body was covered with reminders of Asa, little bruises, a few bite marks, the residual soreness of our intense collision. But it would fade. As would the magic inside the vial of sand I was wearing around my neck. And until then, I would keep moving. Maybe, just maybe, if I went on long enough, this would stop hurting.

I had to try. It was that or let this kill me. Asa had made his choice, and he hadn't chosen me. Now I needed to find my way without him.

"Cool," I said, drawing in a deep breath, and with it, summoning the energy for my next adventure. "I'll get my stuff."

ACKNOWLEDGMENTS

Special thanks to my team at 47North for all the behind-the-scenes savvy and dedication, without which this series could never have succeeded. To Jason Kirk, thank you for your patience, enthusiasm, and masterminding. To Courtney Miller, thank you for bringing everything together across imprints and projects. To Britt Rogers, thank you for quick responses and awesome support. To Leslie "Lam" Miller, you went over and above on this one and left me in awe—thank you for staying ringside as I wrestled this book into shape. To Jill Taplin, thank you for ushering these stories through the process as they transformed from raw manuscripts to actual novels. To Kimberley Cowser, many thanks for getting the word out and managing all things PR. To my copyeditor, Janice Lee, and my proofreader, Phyllis DeBlanche, thank you for your relentless attention to detail and for leaving the occasional funny and sweet comments in the margins. To Jason Blackburn, thank you for a cover that fits so seamlessly with both the book itself and the overall series. To Paul Morrissey at Jet City Comics, as well as Alex de Campi, Dennis Calero, and Andrew Dalhouse, thank you for bringing Asa to life and introducing him to new fans.

As always, my heroic agent, Kathleen Ortiz, deserves my intense gratitude for handling all things logistical and business, as well as the more squishy interpersonal stuff. Thanks for doing both so well, lady. Additional thanks goes to Danielle Barthel for hopping aboard and steering the ship when called upon.

Thanks to all my friends—Brigid, Lydia, Sue, Claudine, Jackie, Paul, and Jim—for caring about me and refusing to let me sink below the waves whenever things got stormy. Thanks to my family for being my joy. And thanks to all my readers for coming back, book after book, to root for Asa and Mattie. I will do my level best to keep earning your loyalty.

ABOUT THE AUTHOR

Photo © 2012 Rebecca Skinner

Sarah Fine is a clinical psychologist and the author of the Servants of Fate and Guards of the Shadowlands series. She was born on the West Coast, raised in the Midwest, and is now firmly entrenched on the East Coast.